You have been revealed to us as the Dream Warrior, long awaited. If you do not help us, we are lost. This is your geas—your quest, Corri Farblood—to take up the battle for the Peoples or turn aside, knowing you betray us into a terrible fate. What has placed this responsibility upon you, I cannot say. But the Goddess bade me tell you to remember Her words and your promise."

OTHER BOOKS BY THE AUTHOR

Celtic Magic
Norse Magic
The Ancient & Shining Ones
Maiden, Mother, Crone
Dancing With Dragons
By Oak, Ash, & Thorn
Animal Magick
Flying Without a Broom
Moon Magick
Falcon Feather & Valkyrie Sword
Astral Love

FORTHCOMING

Magickal, Mythical, Mystical Beasts
Soothslayer (fiction)

THE
Dream
WARRIOR

A NOVEL BY

D. J. Conway

1996
Llewellyn Publications
St. Paul, Minnesota 55164-0383 U.S.A.

FIRST EDITION
First Printing, 1996

Cover art: Kris Waldherr
Cover design: Anne Marie Garrison
Book design, layout, and editing: Jessica Thoreson

Cataloging-in-Publication Data
Conway, D. J. (Deanna J.).
      The dream warrior: a novel / by D.J. Conway. --
      1st ed.
         p.   cm.
      ISBN 1-56718-169-4 (pbk.)
      1. Title.
PS3553.05455D74   1996
813'.54--dc20   95-47961
                                               CIP

Llewellyn Publications
A Division of Llewellyn Worldwide, Ltd.
P.O. Box 64383-K169 St. Paul, MN 55164-0383

To Sharon,
who truly is a Dream Warrior now

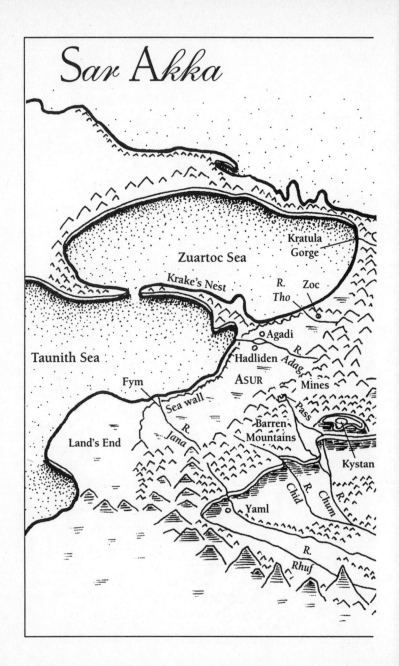

Sar Akka

Zuartoc Sea

Kratula Gorge

Krake's Nest

R. Tho

Zoc

Taunith Sea

Agadi

Hadliden

R. Adag

ASUR

Mines

Fym

Sea wall

Pass

Barren Mountains

R. Jana

Land's End

Kystan

Chid

R. Chum

R.

Yaml

R. Rhuf

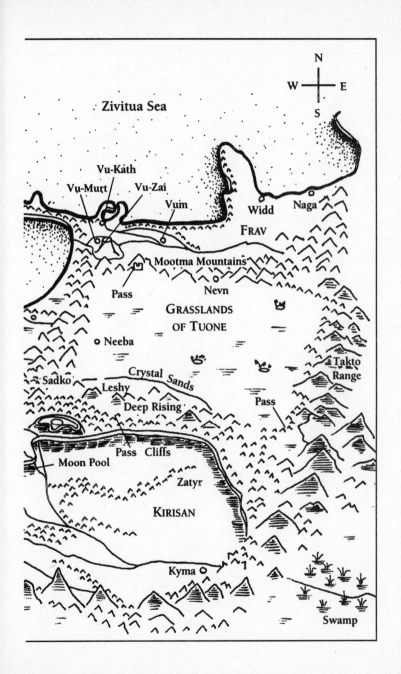

Chapter 1

Corri Farblood did not have permission to be at the Red Horse Inn. If the master thief Grimmel found out where she was, she would be punished severely. She shivered when she thought of Grimmel. He was repulsive, a toad of a man who ruled her every action, her very life in its entirety, even more strictly than he did the others he used in his vast illegal enterprises. The girl chewed her lower lip as she thought of the many legal businesses which the master thief ran to cover his more profitable and shady ventures.

The air held the chill of late summer. A night breeze wafted across the walled compound, bringing with it the scent of stale river water, the ripe odor of fishing docks and floating garbage from Agadi on the far bank of the wide docking bay formed by the River Adag. The sea tide was turning, bringing with it a salty seaweed smell. Off-key notes of sailors deep in their cups at the tavern on the far street corner drifted through the crisp autumn air.

1

She was determined to free herself of Grimmel and leave Hadliden. But that would take careful planning and money. The only way Corri knew to get money was to steal something valuable, something besides the mysterious owl stone she had in her belt pouch. She was reluctant to part with that.

Why does he treat me differently? Corri thought. *The things he said tonight, the way he looked at me, and now Grego's warning.* She shivered at her thoughts. *The other thieves can eventually buy out of Grimmel's employ, especially if they become too well known or lose their touch,* she admitted grudgingly. *But Grimmel told me I can never be free. Why?*

Her thoughts jerked back to the scene with Grimmel as she prepared to leave that evening. In innocence, she had asked the fee to buy out of his service.

"No, Corri," the master thief had said, his wide, thin-lipped mouth stretched in a humorless smile. "You have a value to me far beyond your abilities as a thief. You cannot buy your way out, now or ever." His blunt fingers stroked her cheek as she forced herself not to flinch. "Do not discuss this with me or anyone again."

Corri stiffened at the touch of those repulsive fingers. *Why does he touch me in such a manner? That is how men touch their pleasure women!* Her stomach tightened in disgust.

"Tonight you will scout the house of the gem merchant Jimma Karuskin," Grimmel had continued, turning back to his desk. "See if he is installing extra guards, stronger locks, the usual things. I have heard that he is expecting an extremely valuable shipment of stones, one of which is a perfect Qishua Tear. I want it."

"That is all?" Corri had asked, still fighting to not wipe her cheek.

"No. After you scout out Karuskin's house, rendezvous with Korud in front of the baker's shop on Dockers Street. He will have papers for me." Grimmel turned and raked her tense body with his eyes. "Then go to the Golden Woman. Wait outside and do not go in. The dancers should be back from their journey into Kirisan. They will have news for me, I am certain."

Corri left as quickly as she could, breathing easier once she was free of Grimmel's presence. The dark streets held little fear for her, as long as no one discovered she was female. Asuran females were not allowed to go out alone. Her senses alert, the girl slipped through the maze of streets and alleys as easily as she could find her way through the master thief's house. It was not long before she stood unnoticed in the shadows, watching the merchant's house.

Not much different from a dozen others I have entered, she thought. *The usual guards and locks. At least Karuskin does not keep dogs. I dislike dogs!*

Breaching the security of Karuskin's house, one of several heavily guarded buildings in the merchants' section of Hadliden, was a challenge Corri enjoyed. She watched the two armed guards from the deep shadows, then grinned and retraced her steps to the next street. There she openly walked into a smoke-filled tavern and wove her way through the crowd to exit by the tavern's narrow rear door. Wrinkling her nose at the ripe smells of the alley privy, she quickly and silently climbed to the roof, using the cracked, weathered stones of the tavern itself. She frowned at the moaning sounds of pleasure inside one of the upper rooms as she passed. The tavern had its own pleasure women, available to its patrons at a small fee.

From atop the tavern, Corri easily reached the higher roof of an adjoining building. She made her way, silent as a ghost, from rooftop to rooftop until she found what she sought: a thin plank lying behind the decorated edging of an observation walkway.

Right where Druk said he left it when he killed that Kirisani trader last half-year. She grinned at the laxness of Hadliden merchants who never thought to check their roofs unless, like Grimmel, they were paranoid or had a roof-garden.

Gently she eased the plank out over the narrow space between the buildings until it formed a dangerous bridge stretching high over the malodorous alley. She pushed down her fear of heights as she stepped out on the plank, keeping her eyes carefully on the placement of each booted foot.

The girl crept like a wind-blown shadow over the tops of two more buildings until she faced a spiked fence which enclosed the roof of Karuskin's home. Her eyes noted the narrowness between the iron bars, the razor-sharp tips at the top, the metal flowers used as cross-pieces. With a grin, Corri grasped two of the bars, easing her foot onto a rusted rose. She quickly made her way to the top of the fence, then paused to stare at the sharpened spikes.

You fortified your house well, merchant, she thought, *but not good enough to keep me out.* Her slender fingers locked tight around the base of the spikes until she could ease herself upright, balanced on the metal flower-rim of the fence. The moonlight winked on the spear-like bars as she bent her body over the spikes, grasped the bars by her feet, and lifted herself in a controlled, graceful arch over the fence. Without a sound, she swung over and walked down the bars and flowers.

Within minutes, she was crouched in the black shadows of the roof-garden on top of Karuskin's house. It took only seconds to pick the lock on the stairway door leading inside. She relocked the door after briefly peering down the black stairway. With a grin of triumph, she retraced her route to the tavern where a few coins to a drunk by the door gave her the other information she sought: Karuskin had hired no new guards. Corri then sped to the baker's shop where she found Korud waiting. The man said nothing, only handed her a folded paper sealed with red wax before disappearing into the dark alley which led to the harbor. The girl scowled at Korud's back; she disliked both him and his brother Druk, who worked as an assassin for Grimmel.

The forecourt of the Golden Woman was well-lit as usual. Since this was one of Grimmel's legitimate businesses, Corri knew the eunuchs who guarded the women there. Still, out of long habit, she loitered at the edges of the torch light, watching the richly garbed eunuch at the door until he noticed her. She liked Grego; over the years they had developed a friendship of sorts, something they both knew Grimmel would not like. The man walked with one of the patrons to the waiting carriage, then beckoned to the girl with a plump hand.

"The dancers have not yet returned, Corri," Grego said softly. "I have word that the caravan came too late and has had to camp outside the city. I will send the Master what the dancers bring as soon as they arrive in the morning." He shook his head as he gently patted her arm. "Poor child. A young girl such as you should not be a thief. Nor should you have to face the future the Master has planned for you. Run away, Corri. Run far away."

"What plans?" Corri felt the hair on her arms rise. Grego was putting himself at risk warning her, her instincts told her. He sighed and shook his head as she stared at him.

Whatever else the eunuch might have said was lost, for a patron slipped on the steps and dropped his money pouch. The merchant cried out, and the eunuch rushed to help him recover the coins and valuables which spilled from the leather bag as it hit the cobbled street.

Corri jerked her head up like a startled horse as a tendril of strange energy struck her mind. The girl fought against the summoning, keeping her place in the shadows with difficulty.

What is this? she thought. *What calls to me?* She took a step forward, then froze as the merchant and the eunuch turned in her direction.

"You there, boy." The merchant held up a silver coin. "Find the stone I dropped and this is yours."

The girl held her tall, boy-slim body perfectly still. Wearing her scuffed brown tunic and trousers and dark gray supple half-boots, Corri knew she could blend into the background anywhere she chose, as long as her fluff of sun-streaked red hair was covered by her hood. She did not fear being recognized as a female since Grimmel had made certain that she walked and moved like a boy.

Corri shuffled into the torch light, keeping her face toward the cobbled street as she half-heartedly searched the ground. The mental summoning struck again, stronger than before, as she spied two stones, half-hidden in the shadows of the curb. She picked them up with trembling fingers. Although she often felt the power within stones, particularly the ones which had been worn by people for years, she was not prepared for the strength of one of these. Her sensitive fingers flicked over the dark gem, noting its strange shape. The energy emanating from the carved stone cried out to her in a distinct voice, so powerful and clear that her slender fingers tightened around it possessively.

"Give it to me, Corri." Grego's soft voice was close to her ear. Out of habit, she palmed the other gem, sliding it up her narrow sleeve so quickly that the eunuch never noticed. She reluctantly dropped the carved stone into his outstretched hand. "Take the coin, child, and go have a glass of ale at the Red Horse Inn. Enjoy your freedom while you may."

The merchant bustled up with a cry of happiness, grabbed the dark stone, and dropped the coin into her numbed fingers. "You have done a great deed, boy," he called back as he climbed into a carriage. "There is only one stone like this in all Sar Akka."

Corri slipped back into the shadows, her thoughts on the strange stone. *Shaped like an owl,* she thought. *And old, so very old, with a powerful voice. I must have it!*

As the carriage rumbled past in the darkened street, Corri caught a dangling baggage strap and pulled herself onto the rear step, neither driver nor passenger any the wiser. As the driver slowed the horses to enter the courtyard of the Red Horse Inn, the girl dropped silently to the street and faded into the darkness.

So he stays here, she thought, smiling to herself. *I have lifted a dozen purses for Grimmel here. There is no way in or out that I do not know.*

After several minutes, Corri boldly walked through the gates and into the inn itself. She chose a seat near the back door of the common room, where she watched the merchant through half-closed eyes. The room was crowded, a smoky haze from the lanterns obscuring the far corners. Twice the merchant was jostled by customers, but he jovially ate and drank, his pouch lying beside him on the table. He was familiar enough with the inn to feel safe.

No way to steal the stone here, she told herself. *I have to get closer and there is no logical reason for me to do that.*

The girl could still feel the pull of the owl stone. Its call to her was making her nervous; it was all she could do to not leap forward and grab the pouch. But the merchant kept casting glances at her. Finally, she rose and headed past the man's table toward the outer door, her thoughts busy with the various methods she might use to get the stone.

"Sit beside me, boy." The merchant suddenly jerked her onto the bench beside him. He tipped her face into the light and smiled. "Do I know you? Ah, I think not or I would remember. What a fair lad you are. Almost too pretty to be a boy. I have been watching you since you came in." The fumes of wine and garlic made Corri swallow hard. "Have a glass of ale, and then perhaps we can go to my room." The man pursed his mouth as he leaned closer.

Insatiable bastard! "I think not." Corri smiled as she stood up.

The merchant held her by one wrist as he fumbled for the leather pouch. "But I can pay, boy. Do you want gold? Perhaps a gemstone?" With his free hand, the man loosened the ties of the bag and dumped its contents onto the table.

Corri felt more than saw the owl stone tumble behind the merchant's glass of ale. She jerked out of the man's hold and stood up, then pretended to lose her balance. As she fell against the table, her hand closed about the stone.

"No!" she said as she stood again, fists clenched. "Keep your gold. I am not that kind." The room had grown quiet except for noise from the kitchens. She bent and picked up two fallen krynap stones from the dirty floor and laid them on the ale-marked table. "These fell," she said, holding the merchant's eyes with hers as she kept the stolen gem tight between her fingers. "Just so you do not call me a thief because I refused you."

Corri turned and stalked out of the inn into the shadowed courtyard. *Did you think you were safe from the best thief in Hadliden, old man? In front of a room full of people all watching me, I took what you valued most!*

In the half-shadows of the courtyard, Corri stealthily held the stolen gem so she could see it cupped in her hand. The oval stone was worked into the rough shape of a bird with two brilliant yellow eyes. But the body and eyes were all of the same piece, a natural phenomena of the strange gem.

It looks like an owl. She gently rubbed its surface with her sensitive fingers. *So old, and so powerful! What are you?*

The sound of hasty footsteps drew her attention. She tucked the owl stone into her belt pouch as she stepped aside for a runner who had come ahead of a carriage.

"A merchant comes who needs a room for himself," a boy panted to the innkeeper. "And he says to tell you that there is a sorcerer, he thinks, right behind us."

"Afraid of sorcerers, are you, boy?" Rympa laughed. "Those kind are safe enough unless you cross them."

Curiosity held Corri to the deepest shadows. She could not believe her luck. A sorcerer had to have something of great value, even if it was only a spellbook. Perhaps something so valuable that she could bargain with Grimmel, this time gaining more than a few silver pieces. *How could Grimmel refuse me my freedom if I bring him something beyond price, something from a sorcerer?*

Chapter 2

*T*he girl stood motionless in the shadows of the inn's courtyard. It was late for travelers to be about in Hadliden; the gates had closed two hours after sunset. She dismissed the arriving merchant; obviously he had reached the city by ship. But the sorcerer, how and when had he entered Hadliden? *This one must have great power to cloak himself,* she thought, *or Grimmel would have had news of him.*

Her dark blue-green eyes were intent as a tall, slender man moved into the lamplight that poured through the open door. Her glance flicked once to Rympa, the innkeeper, wiping his hands on the apron across his thick stomach, before she again stared at the traveler.

"We seldom have such a powerful sorcerer lodge with us." The innkeeper's voice carried on the still night air. "A thousand welcomes to Hadliden, sir."

Strange that old Rympa should treat that one with respect, she thought. *He chases off the dog-wizards that hang about the inn gate seeking clients. Well, whatever you have, old man, I intend to steal it. You do not have a chance against this thief. I am the best in Hadliden.*

The sorcerer turned slightly in the light streaming from the inn's door, so that his features were clearly illuminated. The well-honed muscles of his forearms flexed in the blaze of light as he lifted his saddlebags. A strand of silver-flecked dark hair slipped across his tanned cheek.

Corri's breath caught in her throat. *I have seen him before. When I was dream-flying, I am certain I saw him on the road to Hadliden.* She wondered at the strands of fate that had brought them together and what the final outcome would be.

Her mind went back to her dream, at least she thought of it as a dream. Dream-flying, she called it, that sense of rushing through the air in a body but yet not a body, of going somewhere important. Throughout her life she had these experiences, her very private method of gaining important information. At first the experiences came unannounced and unbidden during sleep, often following intense pressure from Grimmel to locate a certain valuable article. Later she learned a little how to control this ability.

Some of her first memories as a child of three, newly come into Grimmel's control, were of such flying during her dreams, seeing places and people she later learned existed. She thought back to the first time she had told the master thief of such a dream. Grimmel had sought the location of a cache of old maps and books hidden by a rival. Corri told him precisely where they were and how to get them. But how she knew all this, she kept a secret. Even as a small child she was uncomfortable with Grimmel, knowing in some uncanny way that the master thief would exploit her talents.

He could not have known how I obtained the information, could he? Corri chewed her lower lip in thought. *But it was after that dream that he began training my memory and had me taught all the skills of a thief. By the Goddess, the master thief did not gain his position by being stupid. He must have guessed! And I thought I was safe, never telling him about the dream-flying or that I can remember everything I see, even for an instant.*

True kindness had never entered into the relationship between Corri and Grimmel. Discipline followed by material rewards for a job well done or punishment when she failed, this was the foundation of the strange life Corri lived within the walls of Grimmel's fortress-house in Hadliden. She had never been beyond the city's walls, was not allowed to learn the history or legends of the land, was kept apart as much as possible from Grimmel's other workers, from normal life itself. Until she was five, this isolation and lack of love did not matter, for she had an old nurse who comforted her and dried her tears.

I do not even remember her name, Corri thought. *She just disappeared one day and never came back. I remember I called her Mother once, and she looked sad.*

"Poor little one," the nurse said. "I do not know where your mother is. And your father, pah! If you put your trust in the Goddess Friama as I have taught you, She will be your mother and father."

Right after that, the nurse had left and never returned. When Corri asked, Grimmel had told her she was old enough to do without a nurse. She had persisted in asking for the nurse and was punished.

"Learn to rely only upon yourself," the master thief said. "Love will bring nothing but hurt. Friendship is a distraction, something a thief cannot afford."

When her overtures to others in the household were firmly rebuffed, Corri learned to keep her thoughts and feelings to herself, to trust or rely upon no one. In her life she had learned to leave no room for friendships, which could prove treacherous, just as she had learned to be inconspicuous wherever she was.

"If you are unseen, if no one knows your name," Grimmel had said, "then no one will call out to you, thus drawing the attention of the authorities." He leaned down until his toad-like face was close to hers. "If the authorities catch you, my punishment will be as nothing." He had then proceeded to give her vivid details of the atrocious punishments handed out to thieves. "Only I can protect you. I am the only one you can trust."

However, Corri had instinctively known, child as she was, that there was something about Grimmel that could not be trusted. Her only contact with the city's people was when she was sent on an assignment, not the best circumstances for learning about normal life. Sometimes she managed to talk with Grimmel's other thieves or the assassins, but they were evasive and uncomfortable around her. She had overheard some of the other thieves talking. Word had come down from the master thief: do not be friends, or even think of being anything closer, with Corri.

Corri's thoughts darted on to her latest dream, uninitiated by any demand upon her from Grimmel. She had soared beyond the walled Asuran city of Hadliden and seen a tall man riding along the dusty road toward the coastal center. The image of his face was clear to her, lit as it was by the full light of the afternoon sun before it dropped beyond the horizon. Then she was jerked back to Hadliden, swooping down to a grimy room near the great market center. An old man, darkened by the weather and wrinkled with age, sat bent over a strange parchment.

"Imandoff Silverhair will want this," she heard him mutter. "It must be a map, perhaps to a lost temple. And just perhaps it is a clue to the Valley of Whispers he's always talking about." Somehow she knew the traveler and the map were connected.

With a jerk she had been drawn back to her body lying in her curtained bedchamber in Grimmel's fortress. Restless, Corri lay staring into the dimness of the shuttered room, knowing that the map was valuable, possibly another link in her plans to escape. Her whole mind was tuned to escaping the suffocating relationship between her and the grotesque Grimmel.

Escape! How she longed to be free of Grimmel's control, his harsh protection, his somehow possessive treatment, so different from the way he handled other thieves of his organization. Somehow, he always seemed to know where she was.

Her mind called up a vague, blurred picture of a red-haired man leaving her with the master thief, her terrified baby cries as her father disappeared into the night.

Someday I will find my father. Someday I will hear from his own lips why he left me, and where he left my mother. She clenched her fists, keeping the anger deep inside. *But escape takes plans and resources. And as a thief, I will find the resources.*

Her thoughts wandered to the leather bag tied at her belt. The strangely carved black stone, now nestling there, had drawn her; she could not have avoided its call.

She had strolled out of the inn and disappeared into the dark shadows of the courtyard as if she had not a care in the world. It was while hiding there that the sorcerer had come in through the gate and caught her attention. Now she was as attracted to his presence as she had been by the owl stone.

The owl stone is mine! I will find another way to get free from Grimmel. She thought of the places she could run. Other thieves had told her that Tuone had few cities and was a land of roving Clans and wide grasslands, while Kirisan was fertile and full of towns and villages. *Once in Kirisan I may sell the stone. I will steal something else for the old toad. Maybe a spellbook. The sorcerer should have one in his saddlebags. Surely to be a sorcerer, one must have a spellbook. With such a prize, Grimmel will be less interested in me and my comings and goings.* Corri eyed the worn leather satchels hung over the man's arm. *I think there is enough in my hidden place, along with the other stone I stole tonight, to get me far away.*

Corri turned her mind back to the business at hand. The sorcerer seemed in no hurry to leave the courtyard and enter the frowsty inn. Instead, he lingered in conversation with Rympa.

Corri caught her breath as the tall sorcerer turned suddenly and stared straight into the shadows at her. She felt a strange prickling and pushing against her mind. The thought of retreat, of abandoning her plans, floated through her consciousness, but she quickly banished it.

No! What am I thinking? Nothing will turn me aside from what I will do, she told herself firmly. *I will leave Grimmel and Hadliden. I will find my father. I will be free.*

The sorcerer and the innkeeper stepped inside the Red Horse, closing the stout door behind them. Corri watched the dark upper windows intently. Presently, a lamp's warm glow outlined a square on the third floor. Light spilling past the open shutters fell on a narrow ledge beneath the window and illuminated a section of the stable roof below and to the left.

The sorcerer thrust up the window and casually ran his hands along the edges of the frame before stepping back and easing it closed.

Perfect, Corri thought. *Put two steps between here and the moon and a good thief will be able to get there.*

Chewing her lower lip, the girl gauged the distance between the slanting roof and the high ledge, mentally calculating each placement of foot and hand to reach the perch high above. Satisfied with her plan, she moved quietly across the cobbled courtyard, avoiding the gatekeeper's cubbyhole. She crept past the line of wagons along the outer wall. A chorus of rumbling, whistling snores told her they were occupied. Flitting from shadow to shadow, she gained the dark warmth of the stables, fragrant with the earthy smells of pack animals.

Corri caught her thin, slender hands on the open window of the stable and levered herself up until she crouched on the narrow sill. Twisting like a tumbler, she caught the edge of the roof, swinging her lithe body out and upward, until she could hook one leg over a drain spout to gain the tiles above.

For a moment she paused to check the knife concealed inside her soft boots. The booter slid easily, its plain wire-wound hilt winking for an instant in the light from the window above. Corri slid the weapon silently back into hiding before she crept on, testing each tile before she placed her full weight on it. Cautiously, she went up the lower roof of the inn and out onto the narrow ledge.

So far, so good. No one ever looks up, unless there is a sudden noise. Corri listened intently for any outcry from below, but there was only the dulled sound of voices from inside the inn.

The great city of Hadliden lay nearly silent around her, its stone buildings and massive central shrine to the Asuran god bathed in cold white from Sar Akka's single moon. The smell of the sea was stronger here, although it lay almost three miles away behind the massive wall that stretched along the beaches, the ancient wall that kept the drifting sand from encroaching on the farm lands surrounding Hadliden and Agadi, main cities of Asur.

For an instant Corri froze as she looked down at the courtyard, then up at the cold face of the moon. Her slender fingers gripped the rough-set stones behind her as she fought the fear rising in her throat. The moonlight glowed against the milky stone of the small earring in her left ear.

I hate heights, but this is just another tricky gambit, she told herself fiercely. *Like the errand to Kuraskin's home. Heights are nothing. I will manage this like I always have. Only this time Grim-mel will pay what it is worth if he wants what I steal. No more holding back.*

She inched along the ledge, the sensitive fingers of her left hand seeking the shutter of the sorcerer's room. Her soft boots made no sound as she stepped to the window and furtively peered in.

The lamp was well back in the room, set on a worn table. Near it the sorcerer sat in a stiff chair, his booted feet to the stone hearth where a low fire crackled. His heavy, dark gray cloak lay across another chair, his packsack on the bare floor beside it. The girl carefully scrutinized the features of the sorcerer's face. He was definitely the man from her dream, the one on the road to Hadliden, the one the old merchant with the map awaited!

Corri watched as the man pulled out a pipe and a bag of smoke-leaf. She noted the patches and worn spots on his dingy, travel-stained white robe, the faded blue of his trousers where the robe opened down the front. The garment's long, full sleeves were splotched with dirt, as were his calf-high boots.

The sorcerer crumbled a leaf into the clay pipe and lit it with fire called up by snapping fingers. He leaned back and sent a puff of smoke swirling toward the low ceiling. His black beard was short, his shoulder-length black hair heavily frosted around the front with white.

He is younger than I thought, perhaps not much older than Rympa. I wonder how soon he will contact the old merchant of my vision? She pulled back into the shadows as the gatekeeper emerged from his cubbyhole for his hourly walk around the inner walls of the compound. *Does he already know of the map, or is he here to sell something, perhaps to set up in business as a dog-wizard?*

She thought of the few who called themselves sorcerers in Hadliden, old dog-wizards dealing in love potions and questionable spells. Her memories darted on to Grimmel, the master thief whose tentacles of power reached far beyond Asur.

I will do this one last job, Grimmel, you old toad. Then I am out of Hadliden to someplace where the air is clean and smells of trees, not dead fish. She remembered Grego's cryptic words. *You have something planned for me that even the eunuch of the Golden Woman thinks is evil. I think I will not stay around to see what it is.*

As soon as the gatekeeper was out of sight, she again peered cautiously inside. The sorcerer stretched his arms, laid aside his pipe, and walked toward the window. Corri pulled back out of sight, scarcely breathing, as the man again touched each side of the open window frame with a long fin-ger. The words he spoke were so faint that Corri barely heard them. There was a brief flare of blue light at each point the sorcerer touched, but it was quickly gone.

The girl felt a tightening, swirling sensation between her eyes when she dared to touch the frame with a questing finger. She jerked back her hand.

By the blessed Goddess! A warding spell! She inched back from the window. She had come across these before; the wealthy paid stacks of gold for such protection. But there was always some way to steal if the will was strong enough. It was just a matter of time and thought. *Well, sorcerer, I will find a way. I will be free of Grimmel and this city.*

She heard the door of the room close. Easing herself back to the window and avoiding the spelled frame, Corri looked in. The man was gone. His cloak and packsacks lay where he had dropped them. Her anger rose; so near, yet so inaccessi-ble. Corri climbed back down to the stable. She knew she risked a beating from Grimmel if she stayed out all night, but her stubbornness at being thwarted overrode her fear. Choos-ing a place in the hay pile farthest from the animals, she bur-rowed into the insulating fodder, dropping off to sleep as she planned her next move.

Chapter 3

At dawn Corri slipped out with the first wagons and waited in the shadows of an alley for the sorcerer. She watched the caravans heading out of Hadliden and the early-bird merchants going to set up their stalls. The morning air was crisp, but promised to warm fast as the stone and stucco buildings heated with the rays of the sun.

Patience, Corri told herself. *Soon or late he must contact the old man with the map. The importance of reaching this sorcerer was strong in the merchant. And the dream-visions never lie.*

Imandoff waited until Hadliden was fully awake and bustling before he left the Red Horse Inn. She followed the tall figure as he made his way to the central market where he purchased a horse and riding saddle.

How strange. He rode in on a horse last night. Why does he need another? Her curiosity about and attraction to this strange man drew Corri like no other person ever had. *There is something familiar about him, beyond the dream-vision, yet I do not remember meeting him.*

She delved through her memories until she came to the blank places. This gate within her mind had always been there, walling off whatever memories existed before Grimmel had taken her. Many times she had tried to open that gate, only to fail. This time Corri pushed harder, her instincts telling her that something of importance was just on the other side. The gate seemed to open a crack. For an instant, a picture of the sorcerer as a much younger man flashed into her mind's eye, then vanished as the memory-gate slammed shut once more.

So I have seen you! Corri jumped as someone jostled her in the crowds. *Before I came to Grimmel I saw you. But where? Were you friend or foe of my parents?*

Loitering at a pastry stall, she watched him hire a boy to take the mount back to the Red Horse Inn. He then walked directly to the cart of a bent-backed old merchant. The sorcerer idly scanned the cluttered display of used weapons, picking through the merchandise until he held up a tiny lady's knife no longer than his finger.

"Imandoff, you old donkey!" The aged merchant of her vision clapped the sorcerer on the shoulder. "Imagine running into you in Hadliden. Get lost, did you?" The sorcerer's reply was drowned in the man's laughter. The merchant leaned close, speaking in a voice too low to hear.

I knew following you would pay off, you sly old demon, Corri said to herself as she saw a small scroll change hands as Imandoff paid for the knife. *What you have there must be the map. But why must it be passed in secret, unless it is very valuable?*

The sorcerer deftly stowed the scroll and knife in his belt under his robe and continued on his idle, browsing walk of the market place. Corri wove her way through the crowd in pursuit, carefully narrowing the distance between her and her victim. The air of the market grew dusty with the growing crowd, thick with the smell of horses and cooking stalls offering fried breads, roast meats, and pies. Soon she was within touching distance of the man she followed.

Loud cries sounded over the babble of voices as a petty thief grabbed a meat pastry and ran straight through the milling people toward the sorcerer. As the boy shoved past, Corri fell against the sorcerer. One quick hand had the scroll in an instant, tucking it under her tunic.

"Forgive me, sir," she murmured in apology. "It was unavoidable. Pardon." The girl tried to avoid the probing eyes, then turned and walked away.

You never guessed it was more than an accident, did you? The girl grinned as she walked on, but she could feel the sorcerer's gaze on her back.

Once around the corner in a garbage-lined alley, Corri sprinted through the smelly muck. As she gained the next street, she ran straight into the waiting arms of two men.

"Well, Farblood, fancy meeting you here," smirked the taller of the men. A puckered scar scored his cheek and drew up one corner of his mouth. His pale eyes glittered with malice. He bent his slim form down until his mouth was close to her ear, his coarse black hair brushing against her skin. "Grimmel sent us to fetch you. You are not allowed to stay out all night. You know that."

"Why send assassins after me?" Corri's arms were pinned effectively against her back. "Not your usual job, is it, Druk?" She winced as the man twisted her arms tighter. "How did you know where to find me?"

"Grimmel knew exactly where you were. Though why he takes a chance someone will discover he uses a female thief is beyond understanding." Druk's voice was edged in contempt. "Asuran females are not allowed the freedom you enjoy, Farblood. And well you know none of us dare expose you, or the master thief would have our lives for it."

"Grimmel said not to harm her." The short assassin frowned at his companion. "I want no trouble with that one. You know how he thinks of her."

Druk kept his tight hold on Corri's arms even after they had her safely between them in a waiting carriage. Corri nervously looked around her as the driver whipped the horses through the streets toward Grimmel's villa, but both men were alert to her every movement.

"You like gold neck-chains, Farblood?" Druk sneered at her. "The ones with bells? Grimmel has a real surprise for you." He laughed.

Chains? Bells? Corri's mind shrank from the thought of the delicate, but strong, chains worn by Grimmel's pleasure-women; always announcing their movements, the tiny bells were locked on for life. *Is Grimmel going to make me one of his pleasure-women? Surely not. I am the best thief he has.*

"Quiet. You want trouble with the old toad? You are crazy, Druk." The second man twisted to glare across her at his companion. "It is not for you to say anything."

"I do not like being second to some thief and a woman at that." Druk's washed-out blue eyes flared with anger. "Just because the old toad wants her—"

"Shut up!" The short assassin's voice was a hiss of fear. "I do not want a taste of that lead-studded whip. Do you?"

It was not long before the carriage stopped before the forbidding door of Grimmel's three-story villa. The villa crouched at the front of vast grounds, which reached down to the river, the house itself and the surrounding walls well beyond the throw of grappling hooks from its neighbors. Corri stared at the villa's seemingly unprotected front wall which nearly touched the cobbled street, as if she saw it for the first time. Her eyes trailed along the high stone walls topped with very narrowly-set spikes, seeing within her mind their enclosure of the rest of the grounds. The grounds and the house itself were heavily guarded from within, Grimmel's second line of defense.

A thief-proof house for the master thief, she thought. *I have lived here since I can remember, yet until today I never really saw it as it truly is—a flaunting of Asuran laws against thieves, a daily reminder to the Keffin and the temple Magni of the bribes their leaders take from Grimmel.*

She tilted her head to look up at the wall facing the fashionable street—no ledges, no ornamentation of any kind that would allow anyone to gain entrance. There were no windows facing the street on the ground floor, and the ones on the floors above were narrow and barred. The tips of shrubs jutted above the iron-spiked fence on the very top of the house—a secluded roof-garden, similar to the one between the villa and the river.

Druk yanked Corri down, her arms still held at a painful angle behind her back. A small panel slid back in the thick door as the short captor rapped the brass knocker. The guard grunted in recognition, then the door opened and she was dragged into the dim hallway of Grimmel's fortress-house.

The floor of the entrance hall was paved in an exotic mosaic of blues and greens and shades of red, water flowers swaying among rare fish. Red limna wood on the walls reflected the light streaming in from the expensive glass fan-window high over the door.

I used to sit here as a child, Corri thought, *imagining that I was one of the fishes, dreaming even then of getting far away.* She remembered herself as a small child, watching the artisans painstakingly set the fan-window into place.

"Save your daydreams for another time." Druk gave her arms a painful twist as she paused. "The master thief does not take kindly to waiting."

The assassin kept Corri's arms pinned behind her back as he marched her down the hall to the carved double-doors of Grimmel's private chambers. The master thief's office was dim, with thick curtains blanketing the windows, black carpet eating the glow of the widely spaced lamps. Fragrant smoke from an incense burner drifted through the room, the billowing, twisting coils of smoke hanging in ripples near the ceiling.

In an enormous chair behind a table inlaid with shell and precious woods sat Grimmel, a grotesque fleshy figure of a man. His face was almost flat on his wide bald head, the eyes round, the nose only two slanted nostril slits. The extremely wide mouth was cruel, merely a red slash against the white skin, exposing abnormally sharp teeth when he smiled.

"We found her in the market, Master Grimmel, just where you said she would be," Druk said.

"You caught me in an alley by chance." Corri tried to pull free but the assassin held her in a cruel grip. "I just stole something from a sorcerer and was coming here."

Why is this happening? Surely not just because I was gone for the night. Grimmel always lets his thieves explain their actions before he passes judgment.

"Really?" Grimmel pulled his fat body out of the chair and came to stand before her. "Where is your prize?"

"In my tunic." Corri grimaced with disgust as Grimmel fumbled against her breasts, withdrawing the parchment scroll.

The master thief dropped the scroll on the table and picked up a thin cane. He stared past her at the assassins, no emotion on his bland face.

Corri stood motionless before Grimmel, her arms still pinioned behind her back by Druk. Her blue-green eyes flicked from Grimmel's toad face to the whip-thin cane in his hand and back again to the cold eyes—eyes so washed out they were almost colorless. Fear gripped her, tightening her chest and making her mouth dry. She had felt the nerve-screaming slash of that cane before.

"I did not send you to the inn. And I did not give you permission to stay out all night." Grimmel tapped the cane against his fat palm. "I hope you are not thinking of going into business for yourself, Corri. Or of escaping." The soft voice held an undercurrent of curbed violence.

"There was a traveler, one old Rympa at the Red Horse treated with much respect." Corri licked her dry lips. *I must not let him know that I followed the sorcerer because of my dream,* she thought. "I thought it likely he had something of value.

You taught me to follow my instincts. I found out later he was a sorcerer, but I decided it was worth the risk."

"Ah, I see." Grimmel laid the cane on the table and held up the square of yellowed parchment. "Release her."

Corri rubbed her aching arms as she stepped closer to the table, away from the assassins. She watched as Grimmel carefully spread out the old map, one fat finger tapping it impatiently.

Goddess, help me, she thought. *They must not search me and find the owl stone. If I can make Grimmel think I desired only to steal the map, then perhaps he will not question me further.*

"You always were a precocious child." Grimmel stared at her, then looked back at the map. "Come, show me what made you think this was of value." He anchored the corners of the map with objects from the desk.

Corri bent over the map, fear drying her mouth. She gazed at the parchment in fear. *I will have to make up something,* she thought. *Goddess, I wish I had taken the time to look at the map.* She delicately touched the strange lettering and symbols with one long finger as she frowned down at the parchment. She blinked in surprise, for most of the drawing made sense.

"These signs might be mountains, that a river. And this in the center, beside that strange mask-thing, this might be the halls of a temple."

Grimmel paused to drop a few incense pellets onto the coals in the squat open burner, then bent his head next to hers. "Possible. I have no knowledge of the writing, but it is apparent that this is very old, Corri. However, if I cannot translate the lettering, it is of no use to me as a treasure guide. The only possibility then would be to sell it to a collector."

"They were so secretive, it has to be valuable," Corri insisted. "Even if it cannot be read, collectors will pay you much gold for a map this ancient."

"And who are they, besides the sorcerer?" Grimmel's pale eyes bored into hers.

"An old merchant in the market place." Corri felt a bead of perspiration trickle down her cheek. "He gave the map to the sorcerer. I took advantage of a disturbance and snatched the parchment. The sorcerer probably does not know it is missing." In desperation, she tried to change the subject. "But why send assassins after me? And what is this Druk tells me about bells and chains?"

"I told you to keep silent!" The short assassin turned to Druk, his cheeks pale.

I should never have brought him the map! Corri watched the master thief from the corners of her eyes. *Somehow he knows stealing the map was not all of my plan. I must do something to turn his attention away from those thoughts.*

As Grimmel turned his attention to the two assassins, she grabbed the parchment and threw it onto the coals of the incense burner. With a yell, the shorter captor leaped forward and raked out the map, tossing it onto the polished desk and beating out the flames with his hands.

"So." Grimmel grunted as he bent to pick up the charred map, a third of one side burned into nothingness. "You surprise me, little thief. Is this rebellion? Why?" He held up the parchment.

"You never pay me as you do the others." Corri quivered with fear, yet could not stop the bitterness that entered her voice. "You keep me under strict rules and surveillance while the others are allowed the freedom of Hadliden. Am I not worthy of the same privileges? I have long proved my worth."

"I buy whatever you need. Your room here is decorated with fine things. Although you are female, you are not subjected to the Asuran laws pertaining to women while you are in my care. You have more freedom than any Asuran woman is ever allowed to have. You are the only female thief in Hadliden, indeed in all of Asur." Grimmel's thin mouth stretched into wide grin. "I think you thought I would pay you extra for your memory of this map? Yes, I have not forgotten you can remember everything you see, Corri. I have known since you were a baby. Do you recall the remembering exercises I had you practice when you were small?"

Corri nodded, a clear picture surfacing in her mind. A tray of items covered by a cloth in Grimmel's fat hand. The tray was uncovered, then quickly covered again, and she had to name everything that was on the tray, or receive a controlled smack with the cane.

"To answer you, yes, you are worthy, but I groom you for something of greater value than stealing. Druk was not far wrong when he mentioned bells. But, I assure you, you are not destined for the pleasure rooms." His cold eyes raked her body slowly. "I have told you that a child would take my place someday. You thought I meant you. No, Corri, not you. Our child, yours and mine. It is time now for you to repay me for the years I have invested in your training and care."

He pulled off her hood, dropping it to the floor and exposing her brilliant red hair. He drew one thick finger gently across Corri's cheek and stopped at her earring. "I shall always know where you are, Corri, always. An exotic and talented creature you are. With me as the father, you should produce a most unusual, gifted child."

Corri stiffened as Druk gave a low snicker. All the seemingly innocent words and gestures out of the past, Druk's mention of slave chains, her special position in the house, came into focus. Her guts went cold at the thought, her mind whirling with revulsion.

What talents do you have? the girl thought. *I have seen you do nothing out of the ordinary. The only thing different from others are your repulsive looks.* Her skin went cold at the thought of becoming Grimmel's wife. *I should have known the Asuran laws concerning women would affect me one day, especially if it suited your purposes.*

"At last you understand how special you are." Grimmel pressed closer, lifting her chin with one thick, ringed finger. "I feel I can no longer let you run free to practice your profession, Corri. You must stay here with me, within the villa. You must learn all there is to know about running this business. And you must resign yourself to having a child." Grimmel sighed and turned away. "You must also learn that to try to deceive me brings punishment. Lock her in her room until I have decided what punishment will be appropriate."

Corri shook off the reaching hands of her guards and walked out into the hall. *Never will Grimmel touch me in that way,* she determined. *I will die first.* She moved automatically up the wide stairs, her thoughts reluctantly on a scene out of the past—a very young pleasure-woman who had tried to escape. *If I try to run, they will only beat me and still lock me in.* Hope dying within her, the slim girl continued down the long hall to the door of her room.

"Inside." Druk opened the ornate door and pushed her through. "And be certain that one of us will be out here in the hall watching. So forget about picking the lock." The heavy door slammed shut behind her. The lock clicked into place.

Her mind still numb from Grimmel's revelations, Corri crossed the carpeted floor to the window that looked down upon the street below. Out of long-used thief's habit, she half-hid herself behind the rich draperies before peering out.

Why did I never guess the truth? How could I be so stupid, so blind? There must be a way to escape, she tried to reassure herself, all the while knowing that there were no possible paths of ledges or handholds by which she could lower herself down the masonry wall, even if she managed somehow to get through the stout grille. As the master of the haven-swill, Grimmel had made his villa absolutely thief-proof. No one could get in or out without using the heavily guarded doors.

Chapter 4

The day passed slowly. Corri alternately paced the floor like a caged animal or lay in a state of depression on the rich coverings of the curtained bed. An occasional muffled voice outside her door warned her that the guards were still there. As the shadows lengthened in the room, she left the lamps unlit, preferring the solitude of the darkness. Finally she pulled her thoughts together and began to make what plans she could.

I must be ready at all times, aware of any and every possible method of escape. She pushed open the window, running her hands over the stout bars. *Solid! No way out through here. The rest of the house, the gardens?* She frowned. *No, Grimmel will see that I am never left alone.*

Corri thought back to the secret childhood teachings of her nurse, ones she knew even then were forbidden by Grimmel. "If you are ever in trouble, call upon the Goddess Friama," the nurse had said as she held Corri in her lap. "The Goddess will always answer."

Goddess, if You help me escape, I will take whatever opportunity You give without question or hesitation. She waited, but nothing happened. "So much for help from that source," she murmured, turning back to the room.

Her boot-dagger and the leather pouch containing the owl stone she secreted high up in folds of the bed curtains. An extra change of clothing and boots were hidden in the floor panel she had long ago worked loose under the far corner of the carpet, a cache for her few treasures and coins.

The door-lock clicked as she again stood staring through the barred window down into the darkening street two floors below. She whirled at the sound of a belled collar to see one of Grimmel's pleasure-slaves slip into the shadowed room. Druk followed, a lighted lamp in one hand, the other on his dagger hilt. He set the lamp on a table, then stood near the open door.

"I am Minna. The Master has sent me to help you dress." The willowy girl smiled and held out the pile of clothing she carried. "I am to be your personal servant. You must learn how to apply the face paints that make a woman attractive, dress to please the Master. Perhaps you even have a talent for dancing." The girl smiled again, her black eyes pleading that Corri make no outbursts.

"Her?" Druk threw back his head and laughed. "She moves like a man, not a woman. Can you imagine what she would look like trying to dance?"

"Silence!" The girl whirled, her collar bells clashing wildly, her long black hair whipping about her slender body. "I have only to tell the Master that you question his choice of women and he will give you a taste of his whip."

"No need for that." Druk held up his hands and backed through the open door, closing it behind him.

"Please, you must dress now." Minna again held out the clothing. "It will soon be time for the evening meal, and the Master wishes you to dine with him."

"And if I do not?" Corri folded her arms across her chest in defiance as her eyes took in the girl's brief, brocaded vest and semi-transparent skirt that swirled about the slender muscled legs.

"The Master will punish us, both of us." The girl shivered, the little golden bells ringing faintly. "Please, Corri, it is such a small thing to do." The iridescent paint on the lids above the dark eyes sparkled in the lamplight. "You are a woman, no matter how you have lived your life. And in Asur women have no rights under the law."

Corri sighed. She knew well that Grimmel would punish the girl and make her watch. The old toad had learned long ago that it hurt Corri more to see someone else punished in her place than if he had laid a hand to her. And she had always known of the plight of the pleasure-women within Grimmel's house. But until this moment, she had never felt the Asuran laws concerning females applied to her.

"I have chosen a dress according to the Master's orders." The girl's long fingers arched gracefully as she smoothed out the dress's bodice, revealing a delicate neckline of lace that would conceal, yet hint at bosom cleavage. "You are not used to the ways of women, the Master says, so he will allow you to wear more conservative gowns for a time. This is made of the finest leaf-worm silk. Is it not beautiful?"

Corri started to retort sharply, then saw the girl's kohl-rimmed eyes, wide with anxiety. *It is not her fault,* the thief thought. *She has never known anything but being a pleasure-slave, and she has always known the pressure of Asuran tradition and law.* A core of hard rebellion against the treatment of the women of Asur formed deep in Corri's heart.

Corri unlaced her tunic and pulled it over her head while the slave shook out the folds of the cream-colored dress. She kicked aside her boots and slid out of the trousers. The cloth of the long dress was soft against her skin as the raven-haired girl helped her into the unfamiliar garment.

"The seamstress needs to make adjustments, but it will have to do for now." Minna fastened the back-hooks and stood aside as Corri reluctantly viewed herself in the mirror. "Tomorrow I shall bring the face paints. And the Master has called for the seamstress to come. You are most fortunate."

Corri stared at the unfamiliar form in her mirror and frowned. "This is not me," she said to her reflection. "I am a thief, the best Grimmel has. I hate this."

"Patience," Minna replied in a soft voice. "It will take time, but you will adjust. One does because one has to. You always adjust to the things that happen because you have no choice. To continue fighting against the unplanned happenings of life will only make you miserable, and sometimes drive you mad." Corri looked at the girl closely for the first time. Although Minna's ripe body made the thief feel self-conscious of her own small curves, it was obvious upon closer scrutiny that Minna was no older than Corri.

"Please, we must hurry!" Minna's voice took on an edge of urgency as the dinner gong sounded up the stairs. She knelt to slide soft slippers onto the girl's feet.

Minna rapped on the door for Druk. Uncomfortable and nervous, Corri followed the pleasure-slave down the broad stairs with the assassin walking close behind.

The dining room was lit with hanging lamps, their vari-colored glass globes sparkling tints of color around the room. Three guards stood at Grimmel's back at the end of the table.

"Well done, Minna." Grimmel smiled, his wide mouth stretching in a tight line to reveal his teeth. "You may leave now. Sit beside me, Corri." The master thief indicated a chair with his ringed hand.

Corri moved down the room slowly, the unaccustomed skirts dragging against her legs. Grimmel's pale eyes never left her. She sat down, tugging at the dress until she was comfortable.

"Such grace as a thief, but alas none yet as a woman." Grimmel frowned slightly as Corri pulled her hand out of his grasp. "Your training will begin tomorrow. Minna is most

accomplished. You can learn much from her." He gestured
over his shoulder to the guards at his back.

Before Corri realized what was happening, the men surrounded her chair, pinning her arms against the gilded wood.
One held her head against the high back. She twisted and
turned, using every trick she knew, but she was no match for
the guards.

No! This cannot be happening! she thought. But she finally
faced the fact that Grimmel planned to do just as he said. *Goddess, help me!*

Corri turned her eyes as the door opened. Another
guard entered the room, a delicate gold collar hung with tinkling bells in his rough hands. The guard laid the collar
before Grimmel, then stood waiting while the master thief
examined the workmanship.

"Beautiful, beautiful." Grimmel held the collar before
Corri's eyes. "See, it is not an ordinary collar, Corri. Look at
the pearly sheen of the krynap's eye on each bell, the moss
stones on the collar itself. Truly a beautiful piece of jewelry."

Corri's shocked mind estimated the value of the stones
at the same time another part of her consciousness was frantically seeking a way out of what she knew would come
next. Grimmel reached toward her with the collar. Corri gritted her teeth and struggled against her captors, but she was
held fast as a fly in thick honey. She felt the smooth metal fit-
ted around her throat, heard the snap as the locking ends
slid into place. The imprisoning hands dropped away.

"That will do you no good," Grimmel said as he sat back
in his chair, watching Corri tug at the locked collar. He dismissed the guards with a wave of his hand. "You will only hurt
yourself. There are ways to treat the abrasions without removing the collar, you know. I will be patient, Corri, but you will
accept the inevitable. You are mine. We will have a child, you
and I. There is nothing you can do but eventually submit."

Never will I let you touch me in that way! Corri thought as
she stared at her hands, now clutched together in her lap. *I*

will die first. The hated bells tinkled softly with the slightest movement.

"All your daggers have been removed from your room by now," Grimmel said as a procession of servants carried in the meal. "Your thief's clothing also. You are now a high lady of Asur, and on this night will become my wife by Asuran law."

"I will not marry you," Corri said through clenched teeth.

"As your guardian I can marry you to whom I please." Grimmel filled her plate with delicate pieces of crab tucked in a salad, tender vegetables and boned breast of jakin covered with a rich sauce. "You have nothing to say about it. That is the law where Asuran women are concerned."

"My father—"

"Your father?" Grimmel laughed as he heaped his own plate. "Your father sold you to me. Sold you, do you understand? You were nothing more to him than the few pieces of gold I laid in his greedy hand. Never once has he returned to ask after you. That is how much your father thought of your worth."

Corri's throat tightened. She felt the sting of tears against her eyelids and willed herself back into control. *Patience,* whispered the rational part of her mind. *Eat now, then make your plans. An opportunity will come.*

The meal passed as if in a nightmare. Occasionally, Grimmel would attempt conversation, then smile smugly at Corri's brief, clipped answers. The servants cleared away the dishes, but still the two sat at the long polished table.

"At last." Grimmel stood up as the door opened and a small man, robed in a somber black cape over equally dark clothing, stepped into the room. "Magni, you are welcome in my home."

The little man looked nervously around the room, pulling at the neck-fringe of his temple robe. "The papers you sent are in order. Nothing in the law says a guardian cannot marry his female ward. But this is most irregular, the hour being late, and I see no witnesses for the ceremony."

"Not to worry." Grimmel rang a small bell. "I provide my own witnesses. And the gold will make it worth your time."

The Magni gave a sigh of relief as three guards entered the room. He pulled a rolled paper out of the large pouch slung over one shoulder. "Which ceremony do you prefer?" he asked.

"The briefest allowed by law." Grimmel's pale eyes glittered as the man set the official seal on the table beside the paper.

"Do you, Grimmel of Hadliden, accept the hand of this woman?" The Magni's voice took on its ceremonial tone.

"I do," Grimmel answered, his right hand held out palm forward. "I accept all that she is and has, until death separates the bonds."

"No!" Corri's hands tightened about the chair arms. "I will not marry him!"

"You have nothing to say about it." The Magni looked down his thin nose at her, disdain in his eyes. "You are a woman."

Corri sank back in the chair, a feeling of helplessness dropping over her. *I never realized what being a woman means. I hate it,* she thought. *How can they stand to live with no voice in what happens to them?*

She watched as the Magni dropped a glob of wax on the bottom of the paper and stamped it with his seal.

I will escape. And when I do, I will spend my days planning a way to kill you, Grimmel. Corri's thoughts churned with hatred, but she kept her expression blank.

The guards all placed their marks below Grimmel's signature, signing away her freedom and her life.

The dining room was silent except for the click of boot heels as the Magni and the guards left. Grimmel poured wine into two etched goblets, handing one to Corri.

"To your new life … as my wife." Grimmel drank deeply but Corri barely touched her lips to the wine.

There was a knock on the door and Druk entered. In a hesitant voice, the assassin said, "Master Grimmel, the guards say there is a strange man loitering about in the street. A very tall man in a dark gray cloak. It sounds like the stranger she stole the map from, but I swear no one followed us here."

"Did you see for yourself?" Grimmel set down the goblet with a sharp click against the polished table.

"I looked, but I saw no one."

"There are many shadows in which to hide." Grimmel rubbed his chins with one fat finger. "Keep a strict watch on all the doors. There is no other way to enter this house; therefore, we need not worry much." His pale eyes turned to Corri. "Did you speak to this sorcerer?"

"No." Corri sat up straight, indignation in every line of her body as she lied. "I am a thief, the best you have. You know I would not do such a stupid thing, Grimmel."

"No, of course not. But why should he come here, skulking in the shadows?" The master thief tapped his fingers against the wine goblet.

"The map; it has to be the map." Druk's hard eyes glared at Corri. "It seems probable that your thief here brought you a hornet's nest instead of a treasure."

"If that is so," Grimmel answered, "then its value is much greater than I thought. It seems, Corri, that your instincts are correct again. I congratulate you. Nevertheless, you must return to your room. Druk will accompany you. And tomorrow you will begin the lessons necessary for your new life."

Corri rose without a word and left the room, her back held straight. Druk's quiet footsteps followed close behind.

If I try now, will Druk kill me, or will he simply beat me into submission? She weighed the value of a porcelain vase on a side-table as a weapon, debating on whether the skirts would hamper any sudden move she made.

"Do it." Druk's cold voice broke the silence of the hall. "I would welcome an opportunity to kill you, Farblood. All I need tell the master thief is that you fell on my dagger while trying to escape."

Corri pretended she had neither thought of escape nor heard the assassin's threat. Up the stairs she went without a backward glance, her long skirts gathered in her hands, and let herself into her room. The lock clicked into place as she looked about the lamplit chamber.

Nothing seems out of place, she thought as she walked to the dresser. Her reflection stared back at her from the mirror. *But I am willing to bet that everything is gone, just as the old toad said.*

Full of apprehension, she inspected each drawer, then the clothes cupboard. All her carefully tailored thief's clothing, the extra pairs of supple half-boots, were gone. A pale green nightrobe lay across the bed, its gauzy hem rich with silver embroidery.

Quietly, she hitched up her skirts and climbed on the bed to reach high in the folds of the curtains. To her relief, her slender fingers closed about the boot-dagger and the leather pouch.

At least they did not take everything. Corri sat down on the bed, then slid the knife and pouch under her pillow. *If that old toad comes creeping in here during the night, he will not leave this room alive.*

She crept to the edge of the thick rug, knelt down to lift up its corner. Her sensitive fingers grasped the tiny edge she had notched in the floor plank and levered the board off her hiding place. She released her breath with a hiss as she saw her clothing and boots still in the shadowy hole. But on the top of the clothing lay a tiny statue of the Mother Goddess Friama, the consoler of Asuran women. A scrap of parchment lay half-curled around it.

Minna! Corri sat down on the floor as she took up the little statue, no longer than her forefinger. The pure white of its moonstone form glowed in the semi-dark. *It must have been Minna's task to remove my things. But why did she leave these? The statue, I can understand. The Mother is the only consolation the women of Asur have. Well, if she had found the dagger, she would have taken it. Use of that on one's husband would be against Asuran tradition and law, quickly bringing the death penalty no matter the cause, but the clothing?* Corri reflected on her conversation with the pleasure-slave. *She probably thought to console me by leaving these, knowing full well that there is no way out of this fortress.*

She smoothed out the scrap of parchment and slowly read the hurried scrawl: I wish for you the freedom I cannot have. This statue of Friama I brought with me to this house. May the Lady bring you your heart's wishes.

For the first time Corri had an insight into the feelings and lives of the pleasure-slaves. Minna's compassion toward her was the only expression of sympathy Grimmel would allow. Then, after some time, even the remaining clothing would disappear, a sign that Corri must fully accept her new life. Her days would be spent going no farther than the high-walled garden between the house and the river, guards constantly at her back.

A thought tugged at her. Druk had said the sorcerer was seen in the street below.

Now what does the sorcerer want here? If he searches for his map, he just might provide me with a distraction, a means of escape. I must be ready, she thought. *How did he discover I took the map, and how did he come to know it is here?*

Corri pulled herself to her feet, silently cursing at the encumbering skirts of the dress. She instinctively half-hid again behind the rich draperies bracketing the barred window as she peered down at the street three floors below.

Be ready! A mental message gently slipped into her thoughts. *Escape is near.*

Corri was jolted by the flow of words into her mind. She jerked back her head in surprise.

I asked the Goddess to provide a means of escape, and She has sent the sorcerer. I cannot ignore this chance, for it may be the only one I have.

Chapter 5

Corri pressed closer to the barred opening of the window, bringing into view the broad step before the main door. The empty step was lit by bright torchlight. Her sharp eyes surveyed the vacant street until she spotted the almost invisible form of the sorcerer in the deep shadows of the alley on the far side. He stood motionless, enveloped in his cloak, hood up to cover his frosted hair. Only the pale outline of his face was visible in the near-darkness, a faint reflection of torchlight touching the ridge of nose, the prominent cheekbones, a curve of lips.

Corri stepped out into full view in the window, glaring at him as if he could see her expression. *At first I thought it an unlucky day that our paths crossed, sorcerer,* she thought. *But perhaps not. Grimmel must have laid his plans to marry me long ago.* She raised one hand in acknowledgement.

Imandoff's head came up at her movement; a long-fingered hand briefly waved at her. The flickering light of the torches near the door spread across the cobbled street to reveal a coiled rope attached to an anchor hook lying at the sorcerer's feet.

Corri whirled from the window, ripping at the dress-hooks. She threw the garment on the bed and pulled out her hidden clothing. Hurriedly, she shrugged into the tunic and trousers, tugged on the boots. She ripped a strip of fabric from the hem of the dress and wound it around the neck-collar to silence the bells.

Whatever your motives, sorcerer, right now you offer the only way to escape from this place. I will go with you, at least until you win us free from Hadliden and Grimmel's domain.

Dropping the little statue into one of the leather pouches, she added her cache of the owl stone and the few coins and semi-precious stones she had managed to withhold from Grimmel. As she listened intently for any sound from the corridor, she slipped the dagger into her boot and tiptoed back to the barred opening.

Stand well back from the window! Corri shook her head as the sorcerer's words again sounded clearly in her mind. *First I must create a diversion.*

Imandoff took half a step into the light and turned slightly to the left, scanning the roof of the villa. Then he brought his hands together in a cupping motion, his head bent forward as if praying.

What is he doing? Corri held her breath in anticipation. *How can he help me escape when the windows are barred and the door guarded? Well, Friama, I said I would take any opportunity to get free of Grimmel, and this sorcerer seems to be the way.*

Imandoff's hands were suddenly filled with a fiery ball of scintillating blue light. With a swing of his powerful arm, he pitched the ball at the villa.

Corri tensed, waiting for the sound of running feet, the shout of guards. *Did no one see?* she thought.

Still silence from Grimmel's fortress. Another ball appeared in the sorcerer's hands. Another pitch, still silence. A third ball of fire snapped into existence. Another pitch, this time followed by frantic female screaming.

The pleasure-slaves, thought Corri. *He's hit the window of the pleasure rooms.*

"Fire!" Voices edged with fright filled the villa. "Fire on the roof and inside!" Feet pounded down the hall. She half-turned toward the door, then heard Druk's voice where he still stood guard outside her room.

Corri turned back to the barred window, staring down at the sorcerer. In his hands was another fire ball.

Stand clear! The mental shout came as he drew back his arm.

She barely had time to jump aside as the energy ball hit the bars, tearing them apart and setting fire to the carpet. The anchor hook flew through the opening, digging into the frame, sliding, then catching. Coughing in the rising smoke, Corri squirmed over the broken bars and down the rope to the street below.

"This way." Imandoff grabbed her arm and pulled her across the vacant street and into the dingy alley. "Now, run!"

The two of them pelted through the dark alley, slipping in garbage, stumbling over discarded trash, darting around startled cats. They darted across another street and into a darker alley, ever deeper into Hadliden. At last they paused, gasping for breath, by the back door of a tavern.

"Now we walk as if nothing has happened." Imandoff straightened his cloak and stepped out into the torchlit street, busy with evening traffic. He completely ignored the people clustering around the tavern door. Corri followed, every nerve alert to sounds of possible pursuit. The muffled clink of the collar set her teeth on edge.

"Why did you help me escape?" Corri asked in a hushed voice. "And how did you know what happened with me?" *And do you know I stole your map?* she thought.

"You are part of an old debt," he answered, never pausing in his fast stride. "Did you want to stay there?"

"No!" Corri glared up at him to see a smile tug at his mouth. "How do I know I can trust you?"

"I suppose you do not know." Imandoff turned into another alley, glancing briefly behind for anyone following. "But those within the villa know I waited. By now they also know I caused the fires and escaped with you. So we are both fugitives. I have friends who will help us. Do you?"

Corri shook her head. *I was a thief. Good thieves do not make friends.*

"How far does Grimmel's reach extend?" Imandoff asked in a low voice. "Would we be safe leaving by ship?"

"The waterfront is the worst. Too many there know me."

"Then it will have to be on horseback. But not tonight. They will be expecting us to flee the city at once. I think we still have time to reach a hiding place before they discover where we have gone."

Corri's muscles were tense, her palms sweating, as they crossed two more streets before disappearing into another garbage-filled alley. It took all the discipline she knew not to constantly turn around, searching for Grimmel's men.

Imandoff reached back to take her arm as he tapped three times on a wooden door set in the rough stones of an alley wall. A faint glint of lamplight shone briefly as the door opened a crack and the two slid inside. The old merchant of Corri's dream shut and barred the door behind them.

"That was a dangerous venture," the old man whispered as he led the way up a rickety flight of stairs. His graying hair hung below a little black cap. "Is she so important that you risked your life against the master thief of Hadliden?"

"Yes," came Imandoff's low answer. "As you well know, there was an old debt to be repaid."

The little merchant, back curved with age, his faded robe dull in the muted lamplight, led them across his cluttered workroom to a narrow cell with a high window. Corri leaned against the cold wall and shivered as he shut the door.

"Who are you?" she finally asked. "And what is your connection with me?"

"My name is Imandoff Silverhair," he answered. There was a quiet swish of robes as he sat on the floor. Imandoff's voice came from beside her in the dark room. She had not even heard him move in the stuffy silence. "I am an initiate of the Temple of the Great Mountain at Kystan. The rest I will answer in time."

"I thought initiates all wore fine clothes and did not have to worry about being hunted by such as Grimmel, whatever they did."

Imandoff chuckled. "I am not high on the Temple's list of respectable initiates." His voice turned serious. "Besides, we are a long way from the Temple and its power, and this Grimmel, I am certain, is not impressed by the traditional respect given to initiates." The sorcerer reached out to gently pat her hand. "Try to sleep. Tomorrow will be tricky, getting out of the city, especially since he resents my making off with one of his people."

"I am legally his wife now, against my wishes," Corri whispered, fingering the collar. "He will hunt me relentlessly, to the very borders of Kirisan. I would rather be dead than submit to Grimmel." Bitterness hung in every word.

"Yes, the nothingness of women here. I had forgotten." There was a snap, then a brief flame as Imandoff lit his pipe. The sweet, spicy scent of smoke-leaf filled the darkened room. "I think we shall wait until late in the day before we leave," he said. "If they do not find us in their search, they will expect us to make for the gates at dawn."

Corri sat down with her back against the wall. "Do not underestimate Grimmel. He knows every trick."

"I well understand the thinking of minds such as his. He will expect two things." The pipe glowed softly. "Either we will try for the gates at dawn. Or, if he does not find us there, then he will expect me to try to retrieve my map tomorrow night. No thief could imagine anyone leaving behind such a treasure. You did an excellent job of stealing it, you know. I had a demon's time finding you."

Corri felt a smile in the words. "I am the best thief Grimmel has, the best in Hadliden."

"Then why force you to marry him?"

"I do not know. He is determined to force me to have his child." Corri's voice was sharp with distaste. "He said something about such a child having special abilities."

"Very possible, knowing the family background." Imandoff settled down beside her. The tiny glow of pipe coals was all that was visible. "And what I suspect to be the truth behind this Grimmel," he added.

"What do you know of my family?" Corri turned toward the sorcerer, wishing for light to see his face.

"I will tell you of that later. Now, sleep. Tomorrow will be a busy day."

"I want to know now," Corri demanded.

"Later. Sleep now."

Corri sensed movement of the sorcerer's hands in the blackness. A drowsiness slid over her, a deep desire for sleep that she could not resist.

The day dragged on for Corri. The only time she left the tiny cell was to use the chamber pot in the old merchant's nearby private rooms. The wizened man shoved a tray of food inside the closed room before he opened his shop and again when he closed for the noon hour. Imandoff seemed to spend most of the day in sleep, although Corri could not be certain of that. For long periods of time he sat motionless, his head against the wall, never moving or making a sound. She sensed, however, that he was alert, listening to voices well beyond the little room, although she could not put into words why she felt this. Several times she attempted to question him about her background, her parents, but he only smiled and shook his head.

Finally she gave up and sat, her knees hunched up, her chin braced on them. *I know I dare not go into the streets now. Grimmel will have all his men out searching for me. But do not think I trust you totally, old man. The first time I suspect you are up to something, this thief will be gone.*

As the sunlight began to slant sharply in the window from the west, the sorcerer rose and stretched. He stood listening, his head cocked to one side, while Corri sat watching.

"It is time," he said in a low voice. "If we can get into Kirisan, and I am certain we can, you should be safe enough."

The door to the cell slid open, and the old man peered in. "The gates will close soon." His bird-like eyes stared at Corri. "The master thief's men are no longer combing the streets for her. They are now searching the docks and all the ships in the harbor. I have placed a petition before the statue of Iodan for your safety. And your horses have been sent from the Red Horse. Rympa found a way to deflect suspicion."

"One can ask no more than that." Imandoff gripped the old merchant's hand, then motioned for Corri to follow him.

Outside in the dusky alley, Corri looked about her in the half-light. The ripe smells of Hadliden filled her lungs. Imandoff took her arm just as she spied a man with two horses, a roan gelding and a mousy-brown mare, standing at the lighted end of the passageway.

"Say nothing," he murmured. "He expects me." Corri hung back in dismay. "Have you never ridden? Then just hang on and try to remember to sit up straight. We will go slowly until we are out of the city gates."

Imandoff greeted the man in a soft voice. There was the sharp clink of coins as their hands briefly touched; the man vanished down the alley behind them.

Rummaging in one of the bulging saddlebags of his own mount, Imandoff pulled out a dirt-stained cloak similar in color to his own and thrust it into her hands. Corri swirled the covering into place, adjusting the buckles at the throat. Instinct made her pull up the hood, covering her brilliant hair. Without another word, the sorcerer boosted Corri into the mare's saddle, then quickly swung himself onto the roan.

"Hold the reins gently. Your horse will follow me."

Corri's sweaty left hand gripped the pommel of the saddle while her right held the leather reins. *Well, I am now committed,* she thought. *I am not going back to Grimmel. What lies ahead with this sorcerer cannot be worse than what is behind.*

Imandoff guided his horse at a leisurely pace out into the street and toward the massive gates of Hadliden, Corri's mount following as if on a lead. No one gave them more than a passing glance as the two fugitives continued toward the great opening leading out into the countryside.

Goddess, smile on me. I want to be free of Hadliden and Grimmel forever. I asked for aid and You send me this man. Now help us win free of Asur.

Corri felt sweat trickling down between her shoulder blades. From the shelter of her hooded cloak her eyes swept the passing faces in the crowd, seeking for one of Grimmel's men, one who would betray her. But they were all nameless faces, intent only on their personal errands, disinterested in the two riders.

Slowly the open gates drew nearer. Every sound grated on Corri's frayed nerves. Each vendor's cry became a possible sound of pursuit, every shriek of a childish voice a potential danger.

The horses passed between the lounging guards and into the tunnel through the city walls. The air was still, oppressive even in the semi-darkness.

We are going to make it. Corri breathed a deep sigh as they emerged into the sunlight and openness of the surrounding country. She looked around her at the wide stretch of coastal farmland, a sight she had never seen. A blurred line of blue-tinged mountains rose in the east along the border with Kirisan.

Suddenly, a barking dog darted in front of them, snapping at the horses' legs and loudly voicing its dislike. Corri fought to stay in the saddle, dropping the reins and grabbing the saddle pommel with both hands. As the mare skittered and danced away from the dog, the girl's hood slipped. Her distinctive short sun-streaked hair made a glowing red halo about her head in the bright sunshine.

Imandoff leaned over to take the freed reins while shouting "Begone!" at the menacing dog. Tail between its legs, the animal slunk off.

"Now we must be doubly clever," Imandoff said as Corri whipped her hood back into place. "Hold on. We dare not run, but we must hurry."

Urging his mount into a trot with his heels, the sorcerer led Corri's horse down the dusty road, weaving a passage through late travelers to the city.

The girl clung to the saddle, grimacing as she bounced. Before long she felt as if she had been pounded and buffeted by Grimmel's heavy hand. Her legs and lower back sent sharp streaks of protest up her spine; her head ached. She watched the sorcerer's roan prance in a mincing step along the thoroughfare, glad that her own mount showed no inclination for such fancy footwork.

"No one yet follows." Imandoff turned in the saddle to glance at her. "Our luck may hold, but we cannot count on that. The gate-guards saw your hair. Red is a rare color among the Peoples, except for those of Frav. Up ahead is a little used trail that leads through a back way into the mountains. We will take that and avoid travelers."

"When can we stop?" Corri asked through clenched teeth.

"Not yet. It is not safe here." Her companion smiled at her. "I think we will have to do something about your hair. Much too noticeable."

The sun was a red ball, low in the west and glinting off the Taunith Sea in the distance behind them, when the two left the main road and plunged down an embankment into a rush-filled swale. The towering reeds, well over their heads, rustled and rattled softly at their passage, but effectively screened them from view on the road behind. The lingering heat of the day clung in the swale; not even a breath of a breeze cooled the air. Clouds of swarming, biting insects buzzed around the riders. For hours they rode in the sweltering torment, in and out of the marshy, reed-filled lowlands.

"Not much farther," Imandoff softly called as he swatted and waved at the annoying insects. "Just beyond we begin to climb out of this swamp. We will have to pass through farm land, but it is dusk now. Few will be out to observe us."

Corri smashed a driller actively working on the back of her hand. Her buttocks were numb and her legs ached more than ever from tensing herself against the rocking motion of the horse.

This is freedom? she asked herself. *Just as well I did not know what to expect.* She clenched her teeth as the horse stumbled over the uneven ground.

They pushed on in silence, through patches of swamp filled with reeds and insects, and across the edges of farm lands. Imandoff's choice of hidden paths lay parallel to the River Adag; the Barren Mountains drew ever closer.

I used to stand in the roof-garden at Grimmel's, looking at these mountains so faint in the distance, and wish I could go there. Corri called up the memory with its feelings of temporary peacefulness, the sun warm on her bare head. *The only time I did not have to hide my hair,* she thought, and remembered how Grimmel had frowned at the golden tints made by the sun in her red locks and asked what she had done to it.

It was dark before the horses worked their way into the first mowed fields of a farmstead on the foothills of the Barren Mountains. The bright moonlight made it possible for them to avoid the house and the ever-present dogs. Once safely past the danger, Imandoff helped Corri dismount and rub down her horse with handfuls of dry hay. Then they proceeded on foot, leading the mounts, until they came to a barn at the far edge of the holding.

"We will sleep here tonight," the sorcerer said as he showed her how to remove the saddle. "They will search for us first on the roads. At dawn we will move on to the mountains. Then, I think we must do something about your hair."

Corri was too tired to question or protest. After tying the horses near a pile of hay, the two rolled themselves in their cloaks and dropped into a dreamless sleep.

*W*hat are you going to do?" Corri tried to work the aches out of her protesting muscles as she watched Imandoff hunched over a bowl of mashed roots beside the little stream.

"Bend over." Imandoff motioned her to him. "We have no hope of avoiding notice unless we change your appearance."

Corri choked at the smell as the sorcerer worked the black mixture into her short hair. The pungent odor clogged her nose and left a bitter taste on her tongue.

"Now the eyebrows." He pulled her upright and carefully ran a finger above her eyes. "Do the same with the white streaks in my hair." He handed her the bowl.

"Will it keep smelling like this?" she asked as she applied the dye to Imandoff's hair.

"The odor leaves as it dries. Quickly, wash your hands. No one will recognize you now." He grinned at her. "You are free of Grimmel, at least for now. And with a little luck, forever." Imandoff reached out a long-fingered hand to touch the silk-wrapped collar at her neck. "Time to remove that. Slavery, even disguised in this form, is disgusting. It is so easy for some men to see only the outer softness of women and miss the inner core of mountain steel. To treat them as lesser creatures, that I cannot understand."

The sorcerer pulled away the wrapping and laid his hand against the jeweled neck-piece. Corri watched his lips move in a silent spell that heated the collar against her neck. Just when she thought the heat would burn into her skin, the collar parted with a snap. Imandoff gently removed it. He fingered the pearly krynap's eyes and the dull green of the moss stones.

"Do you want to carry this?" He held out the collar, but Corri shrank back and shook her head.

"If I keep it among my things, perhaps Grimmel can find a way to trace me. You carry it."

Corri rubbed her throat as she watched the sorcerer tuck the wealth of gems and gold into his saddlebag. *From the looks of your sword, I think I shall be safer riding with you for now. Grimmel's men would be very stupid indeed to face you, old man.* "The stones in that should take us anywhere we wish to go," she said. "It seems only fair that Grimmel should pay for my travels."

"Indeed. From what I have learned, you earned him many thousand times over the price of that collar."

Imandoff took his horse's reins and started up the rocky slope. "We are not far from a trail. Then we can ride again."

Corri groaned at the thought as she led her mare to follow. "Why did you come to Hadliden, sorcerer? Surely not to find me."

"I came in search of old scrolls and maps, information about the Forgotten Ones. It was by chance that I saw you in Hadliden." He paused for a moment. "But there is no such thing as chance, so the initiates are told."

"What do you want of me now, Imandoff Silverhair? In my world, no one aids another without a price in mind."

"Not much, Corri Farblood," came the soft answer. "Only to see you free in Kirisan."

"How did you know my name?" She stumbled as they crested the hill and came out on a thin trail. "I did not tell you."

"You looked familiar, so I asked certain friends who would know. I knew your mother. I was there when she named you. You look like her, you know, except for your father's hair. When I saw you in the market place, I knew the wheel of fate had turned and I must pay back my debt." Imandoff boosted her into the saddle. "You are very good as a thief, but yes, I saw you. What kind of a sorcerer would I be if I had not?"

But you did not see me at your window, Corri thought smugly. "What debt?" she asked. "And my parents, where are they?" The trail was too narrow to ride side by side. Corri was uneasy about sound carrying, but was determined to find out whatever the sorcerer knew of her family and her past.

"As to the debt, your father saved my life once, long ago. But your mother, a beautiful, gentle woman, she loved too well and not wisely," came the reply. "When she died, your father disappeared with you. I was never able to find out where he went. I am not certain where your father is even now. Rest easy, Corri. I lay no burden on you. First we must win free of Grimmel's pursuit, then we will seek adventure and your father."

Everyone wants something, Corri thought. *No one does a deed of kindness without wanting something in return.*

"Did you manage to keep the map?" Imandoff's voice floated back to her.

So that is the way of it, she thought. "No, Grimmel took it. But I remember how it looked. Every line, sorcerer. Is that not enough to buy me safe passage with you?"

"More than enough, though you need not pay for journeying with me. We will seek that place on the map, Corri Farblood. A place of the Forgotten Ones."

She plodded along behind Imandoff, wondering if she had exchanged one form of captivity for another, but unwilling just yet to strike out on her own.

I know nothing of the world or the people outside of Hadliden. Until I learn more, how to blend in without drawing attention, I will ride with you, sorcerer.

After seeing her reflection in the still backwaters of a mountain pool, Corri relaxed. Surely no one would recognize the thin-faced girl with black hair. If they kept to the back trails, the searchers Grimmel was certain to send out would never find them or hear of their passage.

She watched her mare grazing beside the pool, the skittish roan's attention divided between the grass and the mountain calls of birds.

"Mouse," Corri said, turning to Imandoff. "The mare reminds me of a mouse. Her coloring, the quiet way she moves. Can I call her that?"

"Why not?" The sorcerer leaned back against a tree, its shade now curling with the smoke from his pipe. "Everything has a name. One of the great secrets of working magic is to learn the names of creatures, the names which they call themselves. It takes special training and skill to be able to know this." He gazed briefly at Corri, the pipe smoke making a thin veil between them. "The roan, now, his name is Sun-Dancer. We have ridden long miles together. Whenever the sun is out, he dances his way along the road, but when it is overcast or rainy, he plods along without a spark of enthusiasm." The roan pricked his ears toward the sorcerer and snorted. "You know you do," Imandoff said to the horse.

"Does he understand you?"

"Of course, just as Mouse understands you, as you will find out if you take the time to make her your friend." Imandoff tapped out his pipe on a bare spot of earth, crushing the used smoke-leaf firmly with his heel. "Time to ride on."

The farm country lay far below them, fingers of cultivated land reaching up into the lower brushy slopes of the Barren Mountains. The trail wound higher, into the vast stands and groves of the mighty limna trees, losing sight of the isolated pockets of civilization, then headed east toward Kirisan.

As they crossed the summit, the scenery changed. Thick forests of firs, pines, and the purple-leafed meppe filled the mountain slopes. To Corri, everything was new and strange. The purple-leafed meppe she had seen in Grimmel's garden, but Imandoff had to name the other trees to her. His low voice kept up a constant drone of information about the country-side, the flora and fauna, the people, until Corri's head felt over-stuffed with facts. Although she occasionally felt a pang of fear at being out in the open country for the first time, she reveled in the strange sights.

The two riders stayed on the tree-brushed paths, avoiding the barren area of the metal mines.

"The Wella who live here did not look kindly upon tres-passers," Imandoff explained. "But if we should get separated up here, go to them and they will protect you. They trade their rare and mystical items, forged from the unusual metals of their mines, only with a select few of the initiates at Sadko. The Wella are a mysterious race. They were mining and work-ing the mystic mountain metals before the Peoples came."

Then, for the first time in her life, Corri looked upon the white stone buildings of the Mystery School of Sadko crouch-ing in silence against the red bark and dark green needles of limna trees. She could see the great gates standing open in the sunlight, a few of the white-robed initiates tending the small plots of cultivated ground.

"Few come this high on the back trails of the Barren Mountains," Imandoff told her, "except the occasional hunter and the Green Men, Kirisani rangers who patrol the moun-tains. The only others are those seeking healing or contempla-tion at the Mystery School. Most travelers take the broad road through the main pass into Kirisan. If we are fortunate, Grim-mel's men will search for us there."

My bottom is getting tougher, she thought as Mouse trotted along a smooth stretch of the trail. *But I still wish we could find an inn for the night.* She thought longingly of hot water and a tub, a soft bed to sleep on instead of the hard ground.

They traveled for another week through the rugged Bar-ren Mountains, meeting nothing more than a few deer on the

high trails. Corri kept alert for any telltale signs that Imandoff
planned treachery against her, but the sorcerer was his usual
self—full of information, talkative at times, at others riding in
silence for miles.

   *We have to come to the road into Kirisan and other people
soon*, she thought. *Then we shall see what you do, old man. Then
we shall see how you act toward me. One slip of word or emotion,
and I will be gone before you know I plan to leave.*

Chapter 6

It was late in the afternoon when Corri and Imandoff rode down into a remote village set up against the border between Asur and Kirisan near a branch of the main road. The village was little more than a cluster of low mud-daubed log huts huddled about a larger building, which turned out to be the Doe and Stag Inn.

"This is nothing like the Red Horse," Corri murmured as she followed Imandoff inside the dim common room. "It looks like a winter wind would collapse it."

While the sorcerer haggled for lodging, her eyes noted all the possible exits, the areas where she could be trapped with no way to escape. She said nothing when Imandoff chose to pay for sleeping arrangements in the barn, but frowned at him as they walked out the back door of the inn toward another rickety structure.

Imandoff laughed at her expression. "I thought you would be overjoyed at sleeping in a civilized area tonight."

"Do we not have enough to bargain for a better room inside?" she finally asked. "Sleeping in a barn is not what I call luxury."

"Fewer vermin to get rid of later," he said, laughing as Corri shuddered. "You have had an easy life, girl. No encounters with fleas or bedbugs? Surely you were in some disreputable places as a thief, or your friends were."

"I had no friends," Corri answered as she peered inside the open barn door. "Grimmel had his methods of discouraging friendships with me. All his thieves and assassins lived by the master thief's law: friendships make you vulnerable, open to betrayal."

"You really believe that?" Imandoff dropped his saddlebags beside Corri's on the clean hay. "Was there no one to talk to, no one who liked you for yourself, not what you could do?"

"When I was small, I had an old nurse. But Grimmel sent her away." Her thoughts went back to the pleasure-slave Minna. "Just before you helped me escape, one of the pleasure-slaves tried to comfort me in her own way by leaving a gift in my room. But, a friend? No, I could not call her that."

"The gift puzzles you." Imandoff's eyes held hers. "Friends often give each other gifts for no particular reason."

"This is different." Corri stuck her thumbs in her belt and scuffed one foot on the dirt floor. "This gift is a very old thing, a statue Minna said she brought with her when she became one of Grimmel's pleasure-slaves. I know gems, sorcerer. I can place the value of one easily if I see it in good light." She paused. "And this, I think, has great value."

"May I see it?" Imandoff raised his hand to forestall her protests. "I have no wish to take it from you, Corri. The Goddess knows you have no way of knowing I will keep my word, but I pledge to you I will not touch it without your consent."

Slowly, she pulled the tiny goddess statue out of her belt pouch and held it up for Imandoff to see.

"The Asuran goddess Friama, the comforting Mother of Asuran women. Known to the Kirisani and Tuonela as Frayma.

Quite an excellent carving." Imandoff stroked the delicate curves with one rough finger, but made no move to take it from her white-knuckled fingers. "Made from a single moonstone, and one of high quality at that. Very valuable, Corri, and I would say very old. To make a gift of this, the girl must have cared deeply about your distress."

"Perhaps we could sell it." Corri turned the statue over and over in her hand.

"I think it would be best not to. That gift probably cost the girl a whipping after you were gone. Keep it to remind yourself that there are those worthy of friendship." Imandoff's smoke-colored eyes held hers for a moment. "Between us, and with Grimmel's contribution, we have more than enough to pay for our lodging and supplies for some time."

Corri sighed and nodded as she returned the statue to her pouch. *I wonder what happened to Minna. Grimmel always vented his wrath on the nearest person. He had a cruel streak, wide as the sea, and cold-blooded as a snake.* She shivered as she again thought of the young pleasure-slave who had tried to escape, and the beatings that finally killed her. *To him we were all just things he owned, not people.*

The sorcerer watched the emotions play across the girl's face and his mouth tightened in a grim line. When she added nothing further, he said, "There is another reason for sleeping in the barn. It will be an easy escape from here if we should need to depart in haste."

"We are followed?" Corri's hand dropped to the knife at her belt.

"Not that I have seen. But if Grimmel is as determined as you say, then I prefer not to take chances. Although we have stayed away from the main roads, one of his men just might decide to seek traces of us up here." Imandoff counted the coins in his belt pouch. "There is not much in this village, but I think I can find enough supplies to get us over-mountain."

"I will brush down the horses and see that they are secured for the night." Corri pulled the saddle off Mouse, patting Sun-Dancer on the shoulder when the big horse edged closer.

"When you are finished, the innkeeper tells me there is a tub in that little shack just behind the inn. Perhaps you would like to wash off the travel dust." He grinned as her eyes brightened at the thought.

"And you? You do not smell so fresh yourself, sorcerer." Corri smiled back.

"When I return, I will take my turn. Then we will eat. This inn has no food as fancy as you find in Hadliden, but it is good country cooking."

As soon as the horses were cared for, Corri hurried to the bath-house. She inspected the tiny shack with its large wooden-slatted tub, a thin pipe perched over one end. Rough, worn towels lay on a shelf, a jar of soft soap beside them. Following the pipe to the far wall, she discovered a turn-valve; the pipe was warm behind the valve. With a grin of satisfaction, Corri opened the valve and filled the tub with water. Blocking the door with a crate she found inside, she stripped out of her dusty clothes and into the warm water.

After relaxing a few minutes, she reached over the tub and grabbed her body linen. *I have no fresh clothing,* she thought as she vigorously soaped and rinsed the linen, *but I can at least have clean linen next to my skin.*

When Imandoff finally returned from the tiny village, Corri was scrubbed clean and her hair washed. Although her body linen was still damp, she sat in a patch of sunlight just inside the barn door, refreshed and hungry.

Imandoff dumped a bundle of supplies near the saddle-bags. "So far I have seen no sign of anyone following us," he said. "I think we should rest here for a while, a day or two at the most."

"Why?" Suspicion moved through Corri's mind.

"The mountains ahead are rugged," Imandoff answered as he headed through the barn door toward the bath-house.

"That way will be hard on the horses and us, but safer than the main roads."

There is something else you are not telling me, Corri thought as she watched the tall figure duck to enter the low door of the bath. *I will give you two days, old man, no more. Then you will either tell me what goes on in your mind, or we part company.*

When the sorcerer and Corri sat down to supper, she let her suspicions slide to the back of her mind. The innkeeper's wife quickly brought the meal Imandoff ordered. The ale had a nutty flavor, one Corri found more satisfying than the ales of Hadliden or the wines served at Grimmel's table. Without asking, the sorcerer filled her plate with thick, juicy slices of roast beef, boiled potatoes, and a mixture of buttered vegetables.

"No one here I recognize," Corri said as she buttered a slice of warm bread. Her eyes flicked around the room, checking two men just entering the inn. "Those men I saw when we entered the village."

Imandoff turned on his bench to eye the men, then returned to his plate with a look of slight disappointment on his face.

You are seeking someone, Corri thought, narrowing her eyes. *But who, and why? Be careful, old man. I am beginning to like you. I would rather stay in your company, listening to your talk, than venture in these mountains alone. But if you play me false, I will not hesitate to do what I must.*

By the afternoon of the second day at the inn, Imandoff began to show signs of restlessness. But still he delayed their journey, as if waiting for someone. That night, Imandoff lingered in the inn's common room over a tankard of ale while Corri fidgeted beside him. She could not put her finger on anything, but she felt exposed and vulnerable, a danger sign in the past she had learned to heed.

The evening was growing late when a traveling tinker slid onto the bench beside them, a sloshing mug in one gnarled hand. He began a rambling conversation with the sorcerer about his journeys and the distant city of Kystan in particular. Before long, Imandoff had directed the conversation into the retelling of old legends, ancient misty tales of the Forgotten Ones, the strange race who had inhabited the land long ago and disappeared before the Four Peoples came from their original home beyond the seas.

Corri could not shake off the prickly feeling at the nape of her neck. She nervously surveyed the other customers in the dimly-lit, low-roofed room, the tinker's stories only a drone in her ears. Nervous with apprehension, she mentally cataloged the inn's clientele as to their degree of danger.

To one side sat a farmer and his friends, their rough clothes still covered with hay chaff. Two blacksmiths were arm-wrestling near the door. Four soldiers of the border-guard, Imandoff had identified them as Kirisani, were quietly drinking ale by the hearth and rolling dice. No one seemed to be the least interested in the sorcerer or her.

I wager those soldiers are not supposed to be on this side of the border, Corri thought. She absently fingered her earring. *This is probably the only place to get a drink for miles. There seems to be no danger here, yet ...*

She tried to sort out her increasingly uneasy feelings, make them clearer. Nothing unusual was happening in the inn; there were no suspicious glances her way, no quickly-turned heads when she scanned the room.

Corri glanced up as the door opened, and a man entered. In the light of the tallow sconces hung on the door frame she could see the deep scar down the man's cheek.

Druk! She ducked her head and watched him with upturned eyes. *How did he come to be up here? Imandoff said we should be safe on the mountain trails.* She aimed a kick under the table at the sorcerer, but he had moved just out of her reach. *If I move now, he will see me,* she thought, her mind frantically going over escape routes.

The assassin looked over the crowd in the common room, then called for an ale and food. Clutching the tankard between his strong fingers, he settled himself against the wall where he could watch the door. His narrowed eyes passed over her briefly as he surveyed the people in the room, but there was no sign of recognition. Corri saw his glance flick over Imandoff, then dart back again. A slight frown creased Druk's brow. He stared for a few moments before turning back to watch the door.

Corri slid carefully to the end of the bench, but the sorcerer was too involved in his conversation to notice. She waited until the innkeeper's rotund wife bustled up to Druk with a plate of gravy-covered roast and bread. The plump form momentarily shielded Druk's view of the corner where Corri and Imandoff sat. With two quick steps, the thief was through the kitchen door and out the back way.

I should have tried to warn Imandoff, Corri determined as she ducked into the deep shadows of the wood shed. She hefted a stick of firewood in one hand and waited quietly in the darkness. *Druk recognized him, I feel it. I could leave the old man behind and escape into the mountains alone.* Corri's conscience, tempered by new emotions, rebelled. She sighed. *Well, nothing for it but to wait and guard the sorcerer's back when he leaves. It is not Druk's way to attack openly in a crowd. He will follow Imandoff out here and then strike him down.*

It was not long before Imandoff ambled through the back door into the moonlit yard. He moved across the grassy slope and stopped directly before the shadowed door of the shed. Taking out his pipe, he casually tamped it with smoke-leaf and snapped a light. In the brief flare he looked straight at Corri but said nothing, then moved on toward the barn. Before he had gone six steps, Druk emerged from the inn and ghosted after him.

As the assassin passed her, Corri stepped out and brought the stick of wood hard against the side of Druk's head. The man dropped in a heap. Corri jumped over him in a flash, running toward the barn. Imandoff met her at the door, sword in hand.

"Trouble?" He looked past her at the man lying in the faint patch of moonlight. "I have never seen him before."

"Druk, one of Grimmel's men, an assassin and no friend to me. The old toad must have sent his best after us. How did he find me? We saw no one as we traveled, and there has not been enough time for anyone at the inn to send back a message." Corri scooped up her belongings. "We stayed too long, sorcerer."

"By the hell fires of Frav!" Imandoff swore as he grabbed up saddlebags. "I should have kept my inner senses alert instead of listening so intently to that tinker."

Something that tinker told you was important, Corri thought as she helped Imandoff. *What is your true quest, sorcerer?*

They saddled the horses and led them into the night. Imandoff guided them onto a little trail that ran straight away from the border road up into the hills. Even with moonlight it was too dangerous to ride, so they trudged on, the restless horses pulling at the reins as they snatched a tuft of grass. In a manner of moments, the pair was hidden in the forest.

I thought once I escaped, things would be easier. Corri fought to keep her eyes from closing in weariness. *This constant living on the edge of danger is draining.*

The trail wound around, up and down, over the sharp edges of the folded mountains. Thick needled trees carpeted the slopes, filling the air with their sharp perfume, their black shapes edge-touched with moonlight. The broad leaves of the meppe showed a dull silver in the faint light.

"Been in trouble many times, I see." Corri pushed closer so that her soft voice did not carry on the night air. "You seem to know all the back ways."

"For years I have traveled most of this land, searching for traces of the Forgotten Ones." The scent of smoke-leaf reached Corri's sensitive nose. "There are always those who follow, thinking I seek treasure. Besides, it is only common sense to know all the escape routes, just in case." The sorcerer chuckled. "That man we left behind in the inn's yard will have too much of a headache to pursue us soon. But if he is one of the master thief's best, and an assassin as you say, then we must expect pursuit."

"Where there is one of Grimmel's men, there are bound to be more. When Grimmel sends out searchers, they are seldom alone. The master thief is a sly old toad. He makes certain that the odds are in his favor. But all this trouble because of me, that I find difficult to understand."

"It does seem strange," Imandoff answered. "But for an Asuran woman to run away, that is unheard of. Male pride is a touchy thing, Corri, especially among the men of Asur. You did say that this Grimmel had some plan for a child, believing it would be powerful in some fashion. However, my instincts tell me this affair is more than the loss of a thief and the failure of plans. I feel this goes far beyond what Grimmel knows and wants. I suspect we shall find out in time." There was a pause. "We can mount now. The trail is wider and smoother."

The fugitives rode on through the night, stopping several times to rest Mouse and Sun-Dancer. Just before daybreak, Imandoff led them off the trail to a tiny mountain spring hidden among boulders. They watered the horses and hobbled them. While the animals grazed, Imandoff and Corri dozed on beds of ferns, then chewed on journey bread from their packs when they awoke.

When the first warm rays of the sun dipped over the knife-edged mountain ridges, they forged ahead on horseback, turning aside to follow a narrow track that led higher into the mountains. For two more days, they moved along hidden trails, camping for the night wherever they found a suitable place. Frosted peaks edged the sky, their snowy tops heralding the coming chill of winter. The nights were cold, even in the high meadows and tiny hollows.

Morning of the second day found them cresting a chilly, wind-swept pass and dropping down the other side toward a series of valleys connected by narrow clefts in the walls.

"Where are we going?" Corri tried not to look at the sheer drop by her side as they negotiated a difficult part of the trail. Mouse picked her way carefully along the pebble-strewn path.

"This is Deep Rising, the mountains that lead to the plains of Tuone. Hidden somewhere within these peaks is the Valley of Whispers."

"What is that?" Corri gave a sigh of relief. The trail ahead no longer twisted along the edge of the cliff, but turned to meander downward among tall trees.

"A very old place of power of the Forgotten Ones, guarded by the Whisperers, spirit voices that mislead and create illusions. I have faced the Whisperers before in other ruins." The sorcerer shuddered. "The few old manuscripts I have found hint at its importance. I suspect that the map you stole was a key to its hidden knowledge. I hope you spoke true when you said you could remember what it looked like."

"I remember," Corri answered. *But whether I tell you will depend upon what you do and say now.*

"I seek an ancient temple that is said to be there. In his rambling way, the tinker brought the last clue I needed to find an underground burial chamber. Perhaps it will hold the knowledge I seek. Part of an old legend that meant nothing to the tinker, but to me it was sent by the gods. And with your memory of the map, I hope to discover another piece of the puzzle of the Forgotten Ones."

"Why are those old legends important? Who cares what the Forgotten Ones did? And with these Whisperers guarding the ruins, why take the risk? You sound as if the Whisperers are terrible things, something to be avoided."

"The Whisperers are not physical beings, Corri. They are mental guardians left by the Forgotten Ones. As to the legends, I listen and gather them, as you would gather gems: for treasure of the mind, for knowledge, Corri. My instincts tell me there will come a time, and that not far off, when Frav, led by its evil priests, will again threaten the freedom of the Peoples.

Perhaps the Forgotten Ones left behind some knowledge, some clue, that will help us defend ourselves."

They rode on in silence, branches of the resin-scented trees brushing against the horses. By mid-morning a mist of rain began to fall. Several times they entered mountain meadows rich with flowers where the wild bees hummed and buzzed in a final gathering of nectar before the winter snows.

"We will camp there." Imandoff pointed below them to another small opening in the stands of trees. The misty rain rolled in beads down his cloak and fell in shining drops to the ground. "We will have to walk the horses the last part, as it will be dark before we can reach the meadow." He looked up at the sun sinking behind the knife-edged mountains, then sniffed the air. "Strange. It has been years since I came across that scent. Is it possible that the priests of Frav have turned bold and found some way to get past the old spells at the border?"

Corri looked at him, a question on her lips, but he turned away and started down the rain-splattered trail under the trees, musing on his own thoughts. Far below, Corri thought she saw movement, like a faint glint of sunlight on metal, but when she looked closer, she saw nothing. The mist of rain continued to drift down, working its way through her cloak and hood.

Chapter 7

Takra Wind-Rider guided her gray-speckled black horse carefully along the winding mountain trail. Although anger and the need for revenge ate at her heart, her amber eyes were alert, constantly surveying the thick trees around her. She was uneasy in these tree-crowded mountains. The rolling grasslands, open to the blue sky, the wind whistling through the waving grass, that was the place for a Tuonela warrior.

Once again she checked her sword, sliding it quickly out of and back in the sheath that slapped against her leather trousers. The sword hilt occasionally rubbed the smooth spear shaft tucked in its holder by her left leg.

He cannot be far ahead now, Takra thought. *By the hell-fires of Frav, that priest could be anywhere in these trees! How did he manage to pass the spells at the border?*

She wiped a thin mist of rain from her face with a tanned hand as she watched the brushy trail ahead. Out of habit, Takra fingered the silver amulet that hung over her chain mail shirt, then shrugged to shift the leather and padding underneath to a more comfortable position. The rain lay in silver beads on the fur tips of her barsark jacket.

He is traveling fast, she thought. *But where is he going?* With a light touch of the reins, she signaled Lightfoot to stop, then slid down. The narrow path was damp with the light autumn rain, but the dense layer of needles and leaves under the trees was dry to the touch. She knelt on one knee to examine the trail dirt, tracing the outline of a footprint with one sword-calloused finger.

From under her thick leather helmet her pale hair streamed down her back. She brushed aside the front-braids that hung below the cheekpieces, her nostrils flaring as she tested the faint breeze.

"He is not close." Lightfoot pricked up her ears to catch the soft words. "But how did he get across the spell-guarded border between Tuone and Frav?" She shook her head in puzzlement. "That Volikvi priest will pay, sword-sister. I will return your hand to your grave. He will pay for your death and desecration."

Takra set her jaw as she swung up onto the low saddle. She pulled her barsark fur jacket closer as the wind strengthened, its force divided into cutting breezes that swept in among the heavy branches. With a nudge of her knees, she sent the dappled horse on up the trail.

The thick forested hills of Deep Rising grew steeper, more rugged, as Takra moved farther to the west. Far below, long out of sight, lay the Mystery School of Leshy and the vast grasslands of Tuone. Farther still, across vast miles of grasslands, where the foothills of the Mootma Mountains reared up from the rolling plain, was the guardpost manned by Frayma's Mare—a group of Tuonela warrior women. There, beneath an unmarked mound, lay Dalorra's ashes—Dalorra, sword-sister who had been killed by Fravashi priests from the Fire Temple, one of whom Takra now hunted.

Somehow crossing the spell-protected border between Tuone and Frav, the disguised Volikvis had not only struck down Takra's closest friend, but had desecrated her body by severing her sword hand. One Fravashi priest had quickly been hunted down and killed, but the other escaped, taking with him Dalorra's hand. Then, instead of trying to retreat back across the border, the priest had struck out across Tuone toward Deep Rising.

If I had not waited for the burial ceremony, if I had realized sooner that this filth had headed south, I could have caught and killed him long ago. Takra set her jaw in anger.

Once she realized that a second Volikvi was loose in Tuone, Takra had followed relentlessly, narrowing the distance between her and the priest with each rising sun. When she discovered his exhausted mule near Leshy, the sword-woman knew the priest would soon be hers.

She had dipped the dagger at her belt in Dalorra's blood. Takra swore knife-oath that the sixteen-inch blade would never be cleansed until she washed it in the priest's own blood. Although the need for revenge burned hot within her, she was enough of a professional warrior to follow with caution.

The Volikvi's trail now led her on into the higher valleys of Deep Rising, along faint twisting trails, and finally into high meadows and sheltered hollows where frosted peaks cut off the dying sunlight. Lightfoot's breath puffed like a cloud of smoke in the cold air.

"We will never catch him this night," Takra said, stroking the horse's braided gray forelock. "We are both tired, as is that Fravashi priest. Even so, I would rather face him with my sword arm fresh than stumble into a trap. We will camp here." She urged the horse out of their cover of trees and into a small meadow, fragrant with flowers. Under the trees at the edge of the meadow she dug a firepit to hide the meager flames she coaxed with dry branches. Stripped of saddle and bridle, Lightfoot grazed freely at the edges of the open hollow.

Trained as Lightfoot was, she knew that no one but she dared
to approach the horse, and that her mount would give warning if anyone approached. Takra chewed on trail rations,
washing them down with cold water from a nearby spring.

*Tomorrow you will be mine, Volikvi filth. And you will not die
quickly under my sword.*

With a supply of firewood at hand, the sword-woman
leaned back against a tree, her fur jacket pulled tight against
the deepening chill of the mountain night. Her sword lay
sheathed by her side. She caressed the cold circle of her personal amulet, recalling the wrinkled face of the old woman-
shakka who had spelled it for her. Her fingers went over and
over the intricate design, the spiral of her Clan interlaced with
the moon-symbols of Frayma's Mare.

Imandoff and Corri saw the rider cross the edge of the
meadow below them just as the sun slid partly behind the
peaks, plunging the hillside into twilight. When Corri started
to question, the sorcerer touched a finger to his lips and continued down the slope. As soon as they saw the spark of fire,
they tied their horses to the low-swinging tree limbs and
crept forward.

Wait here for me. Imandoff spoke directly into her mind.
*Perhaps this is the camp of other travelers, but one must always be
on guard against the renegades who sometimes come up this high.*

This is madness, Corri thought as she watched Imandoff's
shadowed form move down the slope. *I do not want to stay
here by myself.* She shivered as an owl hooted above her, then,
her heart beating wildly, she followed the sorcerer.

She ran into the sorcerer's outstretched arm about ten feet
above the meadow. A warrior sat under a tree next to a glowing firepit. From somewhere in the meadow Corri heard the
breathy snort of a horse. The warrior, lost in her own

thoughts, pulled out a long dagger and held it up to the fire-light. The long, slender blade, the length of a forearm with its down-curved fingerguard, was a shimmer of brightness except for its blackened tip.

"I vow to avenge you, Dalorra." It was a woman's soft voice, but edged with determination and strength. "That priest will never again see Frav, never again stand at the altar of Jevotan in the Fire Temple. Never!"

Imandoff's long strides carried him to the very edge of the tree-lined clearing. "Knife-oath against you by a Tuonela warrior is to be avoided at all costs. Such a one will follow you into the Courts of Vayhall, Between Worlds, for revenge."

At the sound of the sorcerer's deep voice the warrior leapt to her feet, dagger ready. She glanced at her horse now slowly pushing toward her, ears pricked forward in curiosity, but showing none of the battle aggression toward an enemy.

"Who are you to hide in the darkness and give advice?" The face turned toward them was brown from the sun and wind, but an oval framed by the palest hair Corri had ever seen. On her left cheek, a delicate swirl of blue tattoo was clear in the firelight.

"Who am I?" Imandoff chuckled. "Why, I am the sorcerer Imandoff come from Hadliden. And this is my apprentice, Corri Farblood." He stepped into the faint firelight and motioned Corri to join him. "Who are you, beyond a rider of Frayma's Mare?"

"Takra Wind-Rider." The woman eyed the two suspiciously as they came to the fire.

Corri stared back, noting the deadly lean spear next to the saddle and the sheathed sword at the woman's feet.

"Imandoff. Imandoff Silverhair?" The warrior stepped closer to the sorcerer. Her eyes dropped to the belt at his narrow waist where a blue-stone buckle winked. "Well met, sorcerer. It has been many seasons."

"Yes, many seasons," Imandoff answered. "When last I saw you, Wind-Rider, I stood with your shakka to see you raised to ride in Frayma's Mare."

Corri breathed a sigh of relief as the two clasped wrists. *What other surprises do you have, old man?* she thought. *Companying with you is never boring.*

"I have a flask of mountain water." Imandoff pointed back up the hill. "Corri, wait here while I fetch the horses." He was gone into the darkness, leaving the two women eyeing each other in distrust.

At last Corri sat down on the dry needles under the tree, one hand never far from her concealed boot-knife. "Tuone is far from here," she said to the warrior.

"I fulfill knife-oath." Takra slid the dagger back into her belt-sheath. "Time and distance have no meaning. Did you smell anything strange on the trail above?"

"Imandoff did, but he did not say what it was."

"Volikvi!" Takra spat at the fire. "How could you miss the corruption of such a one?"

"I have other talents." Corri bristled with indignation. "Being a warrior and sniffing the ground is not the only way of life."

What is a Volikvi? Imandoff talked of Frav and their fanatic religion while we traveled. Yes, I remember. A Volikvi is a priest of the dangerous country of Frav, a follower of the One God who condones and welcomes sacrifice of all who do not follow his ways.

"Peace. Let us not wrangle when an enemy is near." The sorcerer's deep, rich voice broke the uneasy silence and made both women jump.

Imandoff led the horses out of the trees and began stripping off the saddles and bridles. He hobbled the mounts before turning them loose to join Takra's dappled mare.

"What does a Volikvi do here, I wonder?" He dug out a leather flask and tossed it to the warrior.

"I do not know." Takra took a long swallow of the powerful mountain water and coughed. "I seek him for personal reasons."

"Are the ancient protection spells worn so thin that Frav now can raid across the border? For a Tuonela warrior to journey this far from the grasslands, you must be avenging the death of blood kin." Imandoff sat and pulled out his clay pipe and bag of smoke-leaf.

"Sword-sister." The words hissed through Takra's clenched teeth. "But not only for her death, sorcerer. That filth carries with him Dalorra's sword hand!"

"What?" Imandoff straightened, gray eyes intent, pipe hanging forgotten in one hand. "And he came this way instead of retreating back over the border. Very strange, indeed. That is her blood on your dagger?"

"Two priests crossed; one is dead. The other cut off Dalorra's sword hand and went toward these mountains as straight as an arrow flies. But before the sun sets tomorrow, I shall kill him."

"The priests of Frav are notoriously difficult to kill, warrior. Seldom is sword alone enough. But to take a sword hand! This Volikvi plans the very darkest of Dark Magic from the books of Jinniyah, I know it. Such magic has not been done since the Journeying of the Four Peoples to this land." Imandoff slammed a fist against his knee. "That priest has trapped her soul for use in a vile ritual. But why here? Why in Deep Rising?"

"What lies this way?" Takra asked, pointing up at the mountains. "And why should he flee all this way to practice his evil?"

"Why indeed." Imandoff puffed his pipe in thought. "There is only one place that comes to mind, the Valley of Whispers, a place legends say is neither good nor evil, only filled with power. Old stories tell that it is dangerous to the uninitiated, but of great importance to those able to wield magical powers. I believe the legends speak true. How the Volikvi knew of the valley's hiding place when I have just discovered the clues to find it, that is a mystery."

"Would he dare go there?" Corri turned questioningly to the sorcerer. "If he is adept at the Dark Magic, surely he would perform his rites within the Fire Temple."

"The Fravashi are a strange people, surrounding themselves with strict religious laws. They believe that only their God has power over them, that they are the Chosen People," Imandoff answered. "The priesthood condemns and punishes any magical talents among the common people, but condones it among themselves. Perhaps there is dissension among the higher priests. This Volikvi may be trying to overthrow the High Priest, Minepa. If so, it would make sense that he came here to an infinite source of power where his magic could not easily be detected and countered by the High Priest. A great risk for a greater prize."

He turned back to Takra. "By using the sword hand of your companion, he can offer her soul as a sacrifice to their blood-thirsty god, Jevotan. In exchange for such a strong soul, a daughter pledged to the Goddess Frayma, their bloody demon-god is likely to aid him."

Takra groaned in anguish and leaped up, sword and dagger in hand.

"No!" Imandoff threw himself in front of her. "To rush in unprepared is utter foolishness and sure disaster. Think!"

"Out of my way, sorcerer," Takra said. She glared at him.

"I will not let this priest send two of you to Jevotan." Imandoff's heavy brows drew down in anger.

"Takra Wind-Rider answers to no man!" she spat at him. "I cannot let him—"

Imandoff's muscled hands clamped on her wrists. There was a brief struggle, toe to toe, each glaring at the other. Then Takra's fingers loosened, and the sword and dagger slipped to the ground.

"Shall I take those?" Corri asked, pointing to the fallen weapons.

"No need." The sorcerer dropped Takra's hands. "The moment of madness is past."

Takra gathered her weapons, then retreated to her tree, rubbing her wrists. "You are right, Imandoff Silverhair. To rush out into the darkness now is to court certain defeat, no matter my need for revenge."

She slid down to sit against the rough trunk and watched the sorcerer pace a circle around the camp. Every five steps he bent down to touch the ground with his hand, calling up a faint blue, smoky light which quickly faded.

"We are protected now." Imandoff sank down by the dying fire and arranged his blankets and pack for sleeping. "The Volikvi cannot find our life signs within the circle. At dawn we will press on to the Valley of Whispers."

"And when we find the priest?" Corri's muffled voice came from her blanket-wrapped form nearby.

"We will do what we must." The sorcerer rolled into his coverings and turned his back to the fire.

Chapter 8

$\mathcal{E}$arly dawn was cold and gray within the mountain hollow. The drizzle of rain had stopped during the night, leaving bright gems of water edging the foliage. Only the sky high above was tinged with pink light. The three set off up the sloping track, Imandoff in the lead.

"Why do you travel alone?" Corri asked Takra as her mare scrambled over the rocky trail. "Imandoff said you were a long way from your people."

"It is my right and duty to avenge Dalorra. I need no help. When I was old enough to take up a sword, she became my sister-friend. We rode patrol together, practiced together, fought together. One does not leave the death of such friends unavenged."

Corri shrugged and clung to the saddle as Mouse half-slid down the rocky side of a ravine to where Imandoff waited by a trickle of stream at the bottom. Takra urged Lightfoot forward and reached the sorcerer in a clatter of pebbles.

"We are near." Imandoff pointed to a pair of carved monoliths a short way down the ravine. "These pillars are path-markers."

I have never seen anything like them, Corri thought as she stared at the huge stones. *What are all those strange markings? Writing, perhaps? I remember similar markings on the map I stole.*

"He has gone this way. Do you catch the Volikvi's magical scent?" The sorcerer looked questioningly at Corri.

She sniffed the still air, detecting a faint, irritating odor. "I am not certain. Something smells like a cross between a tavern full of people and a tomcat's spray markings. Very faint, but still in the air."

"A good enough description. You are learning. His robes are permeated with his stinking incense. There are many things you do not know about life outside of Hadliden, Corri, things which might cause you great harm." Imandoff looked around, a frown drawing down his brows. "I am not familiar with this trail. Close your eyes, Corri, and think of the map. Does anything around you look familiar?"

Corri closed her eyes briefly, then opened them to stare at the monoliths. She pointed at the tall stones. "Those strange swirls were drawn on the map, then a twisting line that seemed to lead in that direction." She pointed up the ravine.

He turned to Takra. "He is less than an hour ahead now. It would be better if we catch the Volikvi before he starts his ritual."

"If we do not?" Takra caressed the hilt of her sword.

"It will be dangerous. He must be stopped, whatever the cost."

"I will have my revenge." Takra's voice was metal-hard.

"Understand that there is more at stake here than your sword-sister's soul, warrior woman." The sorcerer's hand tightened on the sword at his own belt. "No Fravashi priest must be allowed to complete such an evil ritual within the Valley of Whispers. It will contaminate the power there and perhaps open a gateway for Frav's long-planned conquest of this land."

They went up the gently sloping ravine until they reached the top of the ridge. There they drank from a bubbling spring that fed the tiny stream they had crossed earlier. Their progress under the forest canopy was nearly silent. At intervals along the narrow path stood tall, thin monoliths engraved with the strange swirl of markings.

Several times Corri looked back along their trail. The sense of being followed was strong. The spot between her shoulder blades itched with apprehension. But each time she turned, she saw nothing but the ragged ranks of trees.

When they emerged into a small valley, the sun was still climbing toward its high-point. The rolling valley floor was littered with broken and eroded stone walls; in some places, nothing was left of their forms except the shadowy outlines of the foundations.

Arrow-straight avenues crisscrossed the valley floor, separating the ruins into neat squares. Trees and long grass had pushed their way up between the massive stones, creating copses and grazing spaces in the abandoned streets.

The air was overlaid with a shimmer of distortion over the sprawling ruins, the scenery wavering as if from heat waves. Every clattering pebble, each clink of bridle sounded overloud and echoing. A growing sense of oppression pressed upon the travelers as they worked their way further into the crumbling city.

Finally, the three dismounted and led their horses along the upturned cobbles of the long-deserted streets. Imandoff pointed to a row of monoliths that led toward a distant cliff-face. A blurred figure, black against the ocher cliffs, climbed the far incline.

"The Volikvi!" Takra's whisper was harsh in the still air. "We must hurry, sorcerer."

Imandoff turned to look at her. "Now, more than ever, we must take care. If he hides in any of those piles of rocks, we could pass by him without knowing." He peered back at the retreating figure, one hand shielding his gray eyes. "Either he does not know we are here, or he is certain we cannot follow. Have you noticed how sounds are distorted here?"

Corri nodded. "Sometimes the sounds we make come back to us from another direction, as if we were in two places at once."

Sun-Dancer snorted; the noise reached their ears from a different side in a muffled echo.

"The priest is at the base of that cliff. See, there he goes behind that copse of trees." Imandoff pointed again at the barrier ahead of them. "There must be a hidden entrance."

"There was a maze drawn on the map." Corri wrinkled her forehead in thought. "Like corridors. But the strangest thing, there appeared to be only one small room. I remember the form of mountains, and there was a picture of a sword hanging over what I think was a door. If my directions are right, the maze lies up there." She pointed at the cliff-face.

"Very good." Imandoff stared at the shimmering rocks.

A faint whispering sound buzzed at Corri's ear. She brushed it away, then shivered as her hand passed through a cold space. She looked back at Takra. The warrior's face was set in grim determination as she waved her hand about her face and neck. The buzzing came again. In her peripheral vision, Corri caught glimpses of wispy forms, staring faces, clutching hands.

"The Forgotten Ones left protection." Imandoff's soft voice carried little on the still air. "Mental guardians of some kind, but I detect no physical danger. Legend calls them the Whisperers. They are said to be spirit voices that talk in your head, tempt you to follow them, make you see and hear things, lead you off in the wrong direction. I have discovered them in other places, some much stronger than these. I have not found them to be evil, just protectors, creators of terror."

Corri was suddenly filled with an irrational fear, a desire to ride away and leave this strange place. Perspiration ran down her cheeks and dripped from her chin, even though the air was chill. Mouse walked along quietly, undisturbed by the feelings that plagued the girl's mind.

What is happening? she thought. *The horses do not seem to feel this terrible sense of danger, of wanting to flee.* She glanced quickly at Takra and Imandoff, noting their grim looks of concentration. *Hold on, I must hold on.*

Their winding path through the ancient city took them into a section where the walls were still stone upon stone, more than a body-length higher than the horses. The air in the closed-in streets was more chill and oppressive than in the open.

The atmosphere of the ruins changed from vague feelings of depression and the need to look over your shoulder to a more physical threat. The Whisperers seemed to gather physical force here, running their ghostly tentacles over face and arms, plucking at hair and attempting to directly invade and influence the mind.

"Hold fast." Imandoff said grimly. He slipped a slender silver wand from his belt pouch, and with it drew symbols in the air.

The feelings of fear subsided. They quickly pushed ahead, into a more open space, then on to the far edge of the ruins.

"Do we have to go back that way?" Corri hunched her shoulders, her voice barely loud enough for the others to hear. She still felt the presence of the Whisperers in the city behind.

"I do not know," Imandoff murmured. "Perhaps we can find another way out of this valley." He stared at the path ahead. "But that may do us no good. Sometimes the Whisperers are at every entrance to a place."

"More great stones like we saw on the mountain trail." Takra pointed at the monolith-guarded trail that led toward the rugged cliff to the west. "I suppose we go that way, sorcerer?"

"The Volikvi went that way," Imandoff answered. "We have no choice but to follow. We cannot let him roam free in Kirisan."

"Then let us go." Takra's brows were drawn down in determination.

I may not agree with your quest, sorcerer, or with this warrior woman's vendetta, Corri thought as she followed the two, *but, by the Goddess, I have no desire to go my own way in this place!*

As the travelers moved onto the trail leading between the long lines of monoliths, the power of the Whisperers faded completely. By the time the sun stood just past the mid-heaven, they were resting beside a spring at the foot of a slope below the cliff. On the rising slope ahead, were the faint marks of ancient steps leading toward the cliffs. The trail appeared to branch at the steps; a side-way led on across the open rocky ground and into scattered trees.

"I will go up ahead," Imandoff murmured. "You two search for signs of the Volikvi along the side-trail. Be careful," he admonished. "He is dangerous. He has nothing to lose by killing you."

"Only his life, if he tries." Takra's dark eyes were hard.

Corri watched Imandoff scrambled up the hill to explore, checking the dusty steps and hard ground for marks. Then she followed as quietly as she could behind the Tuonela warrior woman. The side-trail was more open, with fewer places for concealment, than the way to the cliffs.

"No place here for him to hide." Takra turned back toward the spring. "He must have gone in the direction the sorcerer seeks. If the old man thinks to cheat me of revenge ..." Her hand tightened on her sword hilt as she hurried on.

Imandoff was not at the spring when they returned. Corri grabbed Takra's arm as the Tuonela started up the path.

"There," she said softly and pointed.

Takra and Corri watched Imandoff cautiously make his way from the grove of brush and trees which grew right against the cliff face. He scrambled down the rock-strewn steps, a puzzled expression on his face.

"He is gone. I found not a sign of him on the ground or in the trees."

"How can he have vanished?" Takra's eyes raked the edges of the valley cliffs from one side to the other. "We saw that Volikvi come this way and disappear into those trees." She pointed at the thickest copse against the cliffs.

"We were some time among the walls," Imandoff answered. "When I walked up there, I found doors to a temple, cleverly hidden in the cliff." He pointed to the top of a flight of wide steps, beyond a smear of dark green where a copse of dense trees lay at the very foot of the cliff. A fall of rock, loosed by time and erosion from the cliff above, lay thick over the steps. "The Volikvi's scent lingers there. He may be within the temple halls."

"He could have gone inside without our seeing him." Takra nodded.

"Or he could have sneaked out and gone another way around the mountain. We saw a shallow pass to the north." Corri paced back and forth beside the spring. "We should leave the horses here where there is grass and water, with everything still packed. We might have to leave in a hurry."

Imandoff nodded absently, his gray eyes still on the cliff. "Mouse and Sun-Dancer seem to have accepted your horse."

"Lightfoot is no troublemaker," Takra replied. "She is well-trained."

"Somehow this does not have the feel of the temple I seek. Yes, I know." Imandoff raised his hand as Takra started to speak. "First, the Volikvi, then my quest."

"Just what is your quest, sorcerer?" Takra hooked her thumbs in her sword belt.

"Information," he answered, as he gathered up three dry branches. He smiling at his companions' inquiring glances. "Torches to light our way inside the temple. Why waste magic with these at hand?" The sorcerer beckoned them to follow. "We must take the time to go inside and see if the priest is there."

He looked back over the valley. "No, I do not think this is the true Valley of Whispers. But who knows what is still within their cliff temple?" He faced the cliff, curiosity plain on his face.

"I like to know where my enemy is," Takra said as she checked her sword and took up her spear. "Walking into the hands of a Volikvi is not an easy way to die."

"It is too rocky here to leave any sign." Imandoff sniffed the air. "His scent lingers in the area around the temple doors."

"That stench lingers long in the air, sorcerer. The breeze may have carried it from another direction." Takra followed the tall figure toward the flight of steps.

Corri started to follow, then turned back. "I will get a water bottle," she called softly. "We may be long within the cliffs."

Imandoff raised a hand in acknowledgement as he picked his way cautiously up the steps. Corri climbed diagonally across the rocky slope until she reached the horses, hidden in the green dip surrounding the spring. She glanced nervously up at the shallow cut in the cliffs that edged the valley.

I feel as if someone watches, yet I see nothing. She looked back at the ruins behind. The distorting shimmer of the air made everything indistinct. *Surely no one else would try to follow us through that!*

Slinging the strap of a water flask over her shoulder, she made her way back to the bottom of the stairs.

The broad stone steps were worn in the center from use and time, but mostly free of debris on the lower levels. Corri's progress was slow, as time and again, she stopped to look back the way she had come. She shrugged her shoulders to ease the prickling feeling of being watched. There was no sign of life within the strange valley, no echo of sound.

Imandoff and Takra were well up the steps. As the warrior woman and sorcerer climbed over the last rock fall toward the hidden doors, Corri stumbled and fell flat on the rock-strewn stairway, the leather pouch at her belt spilling open. She hunted around, gathering up her few coins and the goddess statue, but the owl stone was gone.

Where is the owl stone? She felt a pressing urgency to find the strangely shaped stone, an urgency she did not understand but could not refuse. Faint, indistinguishable echoes bounced through the ruins below. *I have to find it!* She stood, her hands cupped about her mouth to call Imandoff, but some inner warning dried the words in her throat.

The others were at the top of the climb now. Takra looked back and waved for the girl to hurry. Corri saw Imandoff snap fire to the torches with his fingers before the two disappeared into the copse of trees. Frantic at being left behind, yet unwilling to leave her strange treasure, Corri searched among the loose debris. Turning back toward the ancient city, she saw something glitter in the sunlight. There on the white steps lay the owl stone, its yellow eyes glowing in the sunlight.

The rocks on the slide were loose and treacherous, but Corri was drawn to the glistening object below.

There it is! She felt the debris turn under her boots as she recklessly started down the steps. *I must not hurry. A fall now would put me in danger.* She paused and shook her head in bewilderment. *Why did the thought of danger come into my mind?* Then her glance fell on the glistening eyes of the stone, and she forgot about the warning.

Cautiously, she worked her way downward, slipping and sliding, then reached out to cup her precious stone. As she turned back, tucking her find into her leather bag, her foot slipped again, as if someone had jerked her ankle. The cold aura of the Whisperers swirled around her. Their ominous buzzing beat against her ears.

Rocks began to rain down upon her. She tried to protect her head and face with her upflung arms, but one stone bounced hard against the side of her head. Her vision blurred; a swirling blackness engulfed her. Corri slipped into unconsciousness.

Chapter 9

Corri struggled to her knees, closing her eyes against the blinding sun. She raised a shaky hand and found a bleeding lump on the side of her head. The blood was sticky, not flowing freely.

What happened? she thought. *How long have I lain here? Goddess, but my head hurts!*

The sound of skittering gravel reached her ears, rang painfully inside her head.

"At last we have caught you." A gruff male voice sounded in her ear. "You caused us no end of trouble, Farblood. Grimmel is most unhappy with you."

Corri gritted her teeth in pain as she was yanked to her feet. She opened her eyes just a slit and saw a bearded, squint-eyed man leering in her face. She cried out as he painfully twisted her wrist.

"Too bad Grimmel wants you unharmed. We could have a little sport before returning you to the old toad." The man's foul breath made her gag. "Real helpful of you to knock yourself out like that. Looks like you laid there waiting for us to arrive. Come on, girl. The others should be through that accursed city by now."

Grimmel must not find the owl stone. Corri's confused mind struggled to remember where she was and why she was there. A flash of the master thief's face came before her. *No! I will never have his child! I will escape.*

Corri sagged her body as if in a faint, falling against her captor and jerking out her boot-knife. As the man caught her against him, she brought up the deadly knife, driving it under his ribs and up into his heart. The hot, coppery smell of blood filled her nostrils as the red flood poured over her hand and arm.

Gasping at the tearing pain in her head, the girl shoved him away and scrambled up the rock fall toward the thicket. She pushed her way inside, then turned to look back down the hill. The man lay where he had fallen.

I must hide, she thought frantically. *Grimmel and his men must not find me.* She slipped between the partially open stone doors.

A lighted torch, stuck in a stone socket several paces down the tunnel, had three images in her blurred vision. She grabbed it and fled farther into the ancient maze. The tunnel led into a larger corridor; radiating from it were other halls leading off into blackness.

What now? Corri walked out into the chamber, looking about in bewilderment. She wiped the blood from her knife and hand on her trousers and tucked the weapon back into hiding in her boot. *Where is this place? If I could only remember how I got here.* She brushed a blood-stained hand across her eyes. *Goddess, if I could just see right!*

Faint voices and a dim glow came from one of the side tunnels.

I was with someone. Oh, Goddess, it hurts to think. Who was I with? We were running from something, someone. Yes, from Grimmel, but who was I with?

The voices seemed to be getting closer. In panic, Corri darted to the far end of the chamber and dived down one of the passageways.

Why would I be with someone? I always went alone. But there was someone, was there not? Run now, think later, or you might be back in Grimmel's hands.

Head throbbing, heart pounding, the girl staggered along the torch-shadowed tunnel. She was barely aware of the rough walls hewn from the bones of the earth, the dust-covered floor with a sprinkling of small pebbles dropped by time from the ceiling. Her pain, the blurred vision, and dizziness were such that she marked her way with one hand on the wall until her fingers met an empty space. A half-open stone door beckoned.

Corri slipped through the opening and looked around the small room. Although her vision was still blurred, she saw that the walls were carved with figures, animals, and some kind of twining vine. Only faint traces of color still clung to the murals. She walked twenty paces to the rear wall, then measured the same from side to side. Her boots left smudged footprints on the dust coating the smooth block floor. The flame of her torch sputtered and flickered in the draft from the tunnel outside.

No place to go, she thought. *The tunnel just ends here in this room. Trapped. I cannot go back. Whoever follows will be waiting in the dark. Where is this place? I remember nothing like this in Hadliden. This has to be Hadliden, but where in Hadliden?*

Looking up, she saw two deep sockets, one on each side of a central mural on the rear wall. She slid her dying torch into one of the brackets and backed into the far corner.

Goddess, but my head hurts. She pulled the hood of her cloak around her face to shield her burning eyes from the light, then leaned back against the cold stones. *I will just have to wait here and hope they do not find me. I am so tired.* She closed her eyes, but the throbbing pain kept her from sleep.

A pebble rattling against the tunnel wall brought her to instant alert. Her hearing was supersensitive from the pain. She caught the sound of metal lightly tapped against rock, then silence.

I thought I lost Grimmel's men. Corri yanked down the torch and scrubbed it out against the floor. In the total darkness she bent to seek her boot-knife. The cold wire-wound hilt slipped easily into her hand. *I will not go back to Grimmel. I would rather die here than become mother of his child.* She gave a shiver of disgust. *I remember all that, why cannot I remember who was with me?*

A faint, cool light shone around the crack of the stone door. Whoever held it was coming closer to the opening. Corri crouched in the corner, determined to win freedom or die trying. The approaching light illuminated the dust-covered floor. Her footprints were clearly visible.

Not very smart for a thief, Farblood. A blind man could follow the trail you left.

The telltale prints mocked her. She was too good a thief to leave such evidence. She had let her fear and haste lead her into a trap.

A free-floating globe of pale light slid into the room and hung quivering near the ceiling, filling the room with bobbing rays of light.

Sorcerer's light! What is a sorcerer doing here?

A memory pricked at her confused mind. There was a sorcerer, one who rode with her. But his name, she could not remember. Corri pressed herself into the corner as Takra Wind-Rider slipped into the room.

"Corri, we heard you enter but could not find you." Takra started forward, then stopped as the girl swung the knife in a dangerous gesture.

"I do not know you." Corri struggled to focus her eyes.

The sight of the well-used sword scabbard and the long shaft of spear in the woman's calloused hand made Corri uneasy. From within the shelter of her hood, the young thief's eyes went over the warrior woman inch by inch, analyzing, categorizing. Something about the warrior was familiar, if she could just remember, just focus the wildly moving faces into one face.

Nothing of value there, she thought, *even if I was stupid enough to try to steal it. Goddess, but my head hurts! But I did steal something. I remember now. A stone to help me escape from Grimmel. Then I ran, and Grimmel's men followed.* She grimaced with pain.

Takra leaned against the side wall, facing the door. One weather-darkened hand rested lightly on the hilt of her sword. Her amber eyes flicked briefly over the slender figure across from her, then returned to their scrutiny of the room's single entrance.

An elusive memory skittered through Corri's mind, vanishing when she turned her attention its way. Thinking hurt. She gingerly touched the side of her head to explore the lump there. The wound had stopped bleeding, leaving a drying crust in her short hair. She glanced down at her trousers splattered with dark blotches. The right sleeve of her tunic was darkened to the elbow, coated with damp blood.

Why can I not remember what happened? she thought. *I need to remember. Yes, one of Grimmel's men tried to stop me, I remember now.* She groaned as she fought to bring up the memories. *I killed him! I must stay ahead of Grimmel's men. They will want revenge now. I was going somewhere with someone, but I cannot remember who. It must have been the sorcerer, yes, the tall sorcerer.*

The door to the tiny room opened further, sending up a whisper of dust. A tall man wrapped in a dark gray cloak stepped inside. His gray eyes quickly went from Corri to the sword-woman and back again. For an instant he hesitated, then strode purposefully to the Tuonela's side.

"Well, Takra?" Imandoff pushed back his hood.

"Nothing." Takra eyed Corri warily. "She does not remember. I thought it foolish to push." She nodded toward Corri's knife.

"There are men in the valley below. They have yet to discover the entrance, so we are safe for now." Imandoff focused on the thief crouching in the far corner. "Did you find any other way out?"

"All the halls deadend, except for this one. And it ends in this room." The warrior gestured at the ornately carved walls with one hand while the other nervously twisted at the hilt of her sword. "Walking about under tons of stone makes me uneasy. When can we leave?"

Under stone? Corri tried to focus her eyes on the warrior woman. *Outside Hadliden then. Mountains, we crossed mountains. Then Druk found us at the inn.* The rest of the memories slipped from her grasp like water.

"The men have set up camp just beyond the city-ruins," Imandoff answered. "We must find another way or wait here without food and water until they leave. They are posting guards on the trail. It will be impossible to go that way, even in the dark. I do not think they have found the horses."

"Sorcerer, I must be crazy to company with you." Takra shook her head, her pale braids swaying with the movement. "First we fight our way through a valley of spooks, and now we hole up in some ancient underground temple. The horses and all our supplies are outside, out of our reach. I have an unfinished task, killing that Volikvi. If we are delayed long, he will have completed his abomination and Dalorra's soul will be lost."

"How did those men get past the Whisperers?" Imandoff frowned in concentration. "My use of magic against the Whisperers must have weakened the power. Unless they have someone of power with them." He shook his head. "They looked like a mixed band to me, fighting men, thieves, perhaps assassins. At least there is nothing in this maze of tunnels except a few snakes and spiders."

"I hate snakes and spiders! Hiding underground is no place for a Tuonela warrior. Give me open skies and a clear space to swing my sword."

"We cannot leave without her." Imandoff sighed. "And if she does not remember us, I do not know if she will trust to go with us."

"There is blood on her face, perhaps from a head wound. And look at her eyes. She must have fallen." Takra stared at the girl still huddled in the corner. "But there is more blood on her than comes from a fall."

"I killed him." Corri's voice was harsh with pain. "One of Grimmel's men, I killed him." She squinted her eyes against the pain of the light. "I should remember you, but it is so difficult to think."

"Go beyond the pain. Think, Corri." The sorcerer stared at her intently. "We were seeking the Valley of Whispers, you, Takra, and I. We are searching for a renegade priest and an ancient temple. What happened?"

"Temple? This is not Hadliden then?" The girl's eyes scanned the strangely decorated walls, then flicked back to Imandoff and Takra. Disconnected memory-pictures flashed through her mind. "And who are you?"

"Mother of mares!" Takra swore. "What do we do now?"

"I fled Hadliden with you." Imandoff moved a step closer to the thief. "We met Takra Wind-Rider on the trail. We came to a city of the Forgotten Ones. Now we are hiding from armed men."

"Grimmel's men wait outside." Corri put her hand to the side of her head. "How did they find me? I will not let them have the owl stone." Her hand dropped to the leather bag tied to her belt. "And I will never let Grimmel get his child by me!" She slipped partway down the wall, then caught her balance.

"Holy Goddess, she must have injured her head on the rock slide. But what is this stone she speaks of?" Takra stepped forward, but stopped at Imandoff's upraised hand.

"You cannot have the stone!" Corri whipped the deadly slim knife outward. "The stone is mine, and I will not go back. I will die before I have Grimmel's child!"

"We will help you hide from Grimmel. We do not want your owl stone, Corri. Did you stay behind because you dropped the stone?" Imandoff inched closer, moving his long fingers in a series of complicated patterns before her eyes.

"The rock slide." Corri leaned back against the cold wall. All sound seemed to be coming from a great distance. "But I found it. Then I fell. A big rock hit me." She touched the wound on her head. "One of Grimmel's men came. He was going to take me back. I killed him."

She held up the knife, staring at it as if she still saw the blood spouting from the assassin's death wound.

"Corri," Imandoff's voice was very soft, "do you recognize this place? The map you stole from me, and Grimmel took from you, is this part of that map?" Imandoff inched another step closer, still tracing the figures in the air.

"The map." Corri closed her eyes, and the memory of a map played across her mind. "There was a mask in the center. Guardian of a treasure?" When she looked up, partial memory returning, Imandoff stood directly in front of her. "I am so tired, Imandoff."

The sorcerer reached out to draw her close, then pushed back her hood to look at her wound. "We need to clean this and get an herb plaster on it." He turned questioningly to Takra.

"Not possible." The warrior moved to stand beside them. "Everything is packed on the horses. At least Lightfoot will keep the mounts away from those men. She is well trained to avoid enemies."

"Now to find a way out of here." Imandoff looked around the room. Stepping to the rear wall, he bent closer to inspect the intertwining carvings. "A mask on the map you said, Corri. Like this one?" He touched the center of one mass of decoration.

"Yes. It looked like that." Corri stood beside him, struggling to focus on the carving. "Half white, half black."

"A sign of Natira, the Judge of souls Between Worlds." Takra edged closer to the sorcerer.

Imandoff's sensitive fingers moved over the deeply etched designs around the edge of the grimacing mask, pulling, twisting, until there was a loud grating sound. A narrow section of wall, barely wide enough to squeeze through, slid back. Imandoff shoved it further to reveal a black opening.

"Are you going in there?" There was a hissing as Takra drew her sword.

"Of course." Imandoff called the light globe to him and sent it whirling before them, scattering the dusty-smelling blackness.

The hidden room was no bigger than the room in which they stood. Against the rear wall was a low stone altar covered with a decaying cloth that hung in tattered strips. On the altar, propped against the wall, was a half-black, half-white skull-shaped mask, empty eye sockets aimed menacingly at the door. Ancient symbols, a hand's span high, were embroidered in fading gold thread across the remains of the altar cloth. Scattered across the altar were an incense burner, goblets, and other pieces of metal. The wall behind the altar was still hung with time-worn tapestries.

"What is this place?" Takra looked around with suspicion.

"An ancient shrine to Natira, the neutral judge of gods and men, the weigher of souls. It appears that one of the Peoples, some time after our arrival in this land, found this temple and used it. Though what god the Forgotten Ones worshipped here before then, I do not know."

Imandoff carefully picked through the items on the altar. He held up a headband of silver, an oval hole in the center above the eyes. The frame around the hole was twined at the edges with delicately engraved garlands of flowers and leaves. The metal showed little sign of tarnish, although it was encrusted with grime and must have been in the hidden room for many years.

"We know so little about the Forgotten Ones." He laid the headband back in its dust-marked place.

"Are these things dangerous?" Takra fingered a broad wrist-cuff set with dull green moss stones.

"I detect no evil influences. Besides, these things were not made by the Forgotten Ones." Imandoff bent to inspect a bronze staff-cap lying in the corner, the wood long rotted away into nothingness. "I think I shall make myself another walking staff." He tucked the cap into his belt pouch.

Takra slid the cuff on her arm without a word, then turned to guard the door. Corri stood staring at the silver band in silence. She pulled open her leather bag and withdrew the black owl stone.

"Look, it fits," she said as she slipped the owl stone into the central opening. "Do you think it belongs there, Imandoff?"

"By Natira, it does fit, as if it were made for the band." Imandoff tried to pull the stone free, but it stuck fast. "This looks like the circlet worn by the Oracle at Kystan. Perhaps it belonged to some long-dead priestess of this temple."

Takra dug into her belt pouch, withdrew a white water-tumbled stone marked with strange black veins. "In exchange," she said as she faced the altar. She bowed her head toward the mask of Natira.

Imandoff nodded, laying a silver coin beside her offering.

"Why are you doing this?" Corri asked. "There is no one here now. They are all long dead."

"I know," Imandoff answered gently. "This may be difficult for you to understand as a thief, Corri, but what we do is a gesture of respect."

Reluctantly, under Imandoff's steady gaze, the girl fished in her pouch, then laid the other stolen gemstone on the altar. *The merchant at the Red Horse Inn never missed it,* she thought. *I want to please this sorcerer, why, I do not know.*

"Enough of this," Takra said. "I need to be about my business. We need to find another way out, unless you want to die of hunger and thirst in this place." She looked up at the rock ceiling and shivered.

"I am not leaving my owl stone," Corri muttered and slipped the headband into the front of her tunic.

"Wait." Imandoff held up his hand for silence. "Hear that? And can you smell the moisture? There is water close by."

Imandoff ran one hand carefully along the tapestry to the left of the altar. Pieces of the wall hanging broke free, sifting down in shreds as he pulled it aside.

In the smooth wall was a short, narrow corridor, revealing at its end a dimly-lit natural cave with a thin stream of water dropping from a small crevice overhead. The water splashed into a deep basin. Its circular form was smooth on the inner side, the marks of tools still faintly seen. Water trickled over the fluted edge into another crack to disappear into the earth. Water-worn columns of rock stretched from floor to ceiling, sometimes in clusters, sometimes alone. The far sides of the cave were shrouded in darkness. Imandoff snapped his fingers and the light globe behind him winked out of existence.

"Someone is coming!" Takra's urgent tones brought Imandoff hurrying back into the chamber.

"We shall be trapped!" she whispered as the sorcerer heaved the altar room door shut. "How will we get out?"

"There has to be another way." Imandoff hurried them into the cave. "It has not been my experience that the Forgotten Ones made only one way in and out." He looked up at the gleaming, quartz-speckled rocky formations on the ceiling. "Amazing. They left this cave untouched except for the water basin. I wonder what significance it had for them."

Takra brushed by him, sheathed her sword, and took Corri by the arm. "Enough that you do not remember our adventures thus far, but that head wound needs to be washed."

She dragged the reluctant girl to the basin and made her sit. Tearing off a piece of Corri's tunic, Takra dipped it into the icy water and began washing the blood out of the girl's hair.

"I remember you, Takra Wind-Rider." Corri grimaced as the cold water cut into the wound. "Some things are still hazy, but I remember now. And my sight is better."

"Bruising, but no indentation." Imandoff bent closer. "The skull is not badly damaged. She will recover with rest and time." He wandered off to inspect more of the cave.

"My brains feel as if they have been scrambled." Corri winced as Takra continued to clean the wound. "And what does he do? Go exploring."

"Sorcerers are strange, little sister." Takra grinned at her. "Heat, cold, pain, what are these things to him when he has discovered something new, something out of the long forgotten past?"

"Takra, I still cannot remember everything clearly. It frightens me."

"Your memory will come back." Takra leaned down to drink from the basin. "Rest now. I will search for a way to escape. Imandoff will stay here until his curiosity is satisfied, which could be days, unless I find a way out. I have no intention of staying in this stone tomb any longer than necessary."

She scrambled off over the debris-covered floor to investigate the walls and dark side openings of the cave.

Chapter 10

Corri leaned back against the stone basin, her head throbbing. The coolness of the rock seemed to help. She fumbled the silver headband out of her tunic and stared at it. The yellow eyes of the black owl stone winked back at her in the dim bluish-light of the two balls Imandoff had cast to float around the cavern.

It feels so cold, she thought, touching the metal to her forehead. *Perhaps if I put it on it will ease the pain in my head.*

As soon as she slipped the circlet on her head, the pain did ease. She peered upward at the filtered light.

How strange. My body feels so light, like it could float away. How will we get out of here? I wish I knew the way.

Her eyes closed, her breathing slowed. She felt herself slipping into sleep.

Corri became aware that a part of herself was hanging near the rough cave ceiling, looking down at her sleeping form. She saw Takra carefully inspecting the perimeter of the underground cavern. Imandoff's faint outline stood near the corridor to the altar room, ear pressed to the stone.

I am dream-flying, she thought. *How can that be?*

She thought of joining the sorcerer, and instantly she hung in the air beside him. When she brushed one hand against his shoulder, the sorcerer whipped around. His eyes seemed to look right through her.

Corri tried to touch him, but her hand did not seem to occupy the same place as the sorcerer's physical body. Imandoff, however, shivered as if touched by a cold draft.

Who is there? he called with his mind. Corri felt a probe of his thoughts seeking her, but she easily pushed it away.

I must find a way out, she thought. *We must escape from Grimmel's men.*

She found herself speeding through the musty air, every sense alert to some inner prompting. A mental picture of the stolen map flashed through her mind's eye. There had been something like a stairway, yes, in that direction. She turned her attention to the shadowed cave wall farthest from the light. Her eyesight seemed unhampered by the blackness. Behind a series of rock columns on the far side of the cavern she spied steps going upward into the darkness. Massed spiderwebs covered the stairs from wall to wall, but she could sense fresh air coming down that black well.

"Corri! Come back at once!" Imandoff's imperative voice demanded her attention.

She tried to stop her headlong rush across the cave, but was helpless before Imandoff's voice. The sorcerer stood over her reclining form, one long finger pressed against the owl stone in the circlet. She dove toward the sleeping figure and with a sharp crack slid back into her body.

"Corri!" She opened her eyes and stared up at the sorcerer. "Do not wear the owl stone until I have time to study its powers." He gently removed the headband. "Have you done this mind-travel before?"

"What?" She sat up slowly, still disoriented from her experience. "Oh, the flying dream. I used to dream-fly often when I was very young. Sometimes I still can, like when I saw you coming to Hadliden."

"What you do has nothing to do with dreams, Corri. You should have told me you have this ability." Imandoff frowned. "This gift of spirit traveling, it is rare that someone uninitiated in the ancient ways can do it. You should know how to protect yourself when you dream-fly. Unfortunately, I am not the one to teach you."

"It is of no importance, just a dream," she insisted. She rubbed her eyes and found that most of the pain was gone. She felt the wound on her head; the edges were nearly healed. "I saw a way out, a stairway over there." She pointed across the cave. "But it is filled with spiderwebs, black jumpers." She took the headband and stowed it again in the front of her tunic.

"Jumpers? In here?" Takra's voice had a brittle edge as she scrambled around the rocks to stand beside Imandoff. "Their bite is poisonous, sorcerer." The warrior shivered.

"There is always fire." Imandoff smiled grimly and held out his hands.

Corri led them over the debris-strewn floor toward the blackness of the far wall. From ground level the way through the tall columns was different, almost impossible to see. After several attempts, Corri came suddenly upon the tunnel mouth, so suddenly that she jumped back into Imandoff when her hand met a sticky strand of web.

"Beware!"

A small fireball zoomed past her to scorch the rocks at her feet. Two black jumpers curled up in death. Corri scrambled behind the sorcerer.

"So many of them!" Corri felt the hair on her arms rise in fear. She stared at the remaining spiders crawling on the tunnel floor, some as wide as her hand. Their long bristly legs stiffened in rage, raising their bodies higher, the better to attack.

The large faceted eyes glinted evilly in the light of the fireball Imandoff held in his hands.

Imandoff threw the glowing fireball into the tunnel mouth. There was a backwash of flames as the webs caught fire, withering as the fire crawled along treacherous lines, popping from the collection of dust. Hundreds of jumpers scurried back up the tunnel into the darkness.

"This will take time. Pray to the gods that my power will last." He tossed another fiery ball up the stairway.

"You could not find a better way?" Takra asked, her long dagger held ready in one hand, the lean deadly spear in the other. "One without spiders?"

"This is the only way out," Corri answered. "With the jumpers burned we will be safe." In the flashes of light she saw Takra arch an eyebrow at her.

"If there is nothing worse at the end of this tunnel."

"The map did have a sword and a strange design drawn at the stairway end. Perhaps a guardian or something, I do not know."

Takra grunted and shook her head as they inched along behind Imandoff up the smoke-scented tunnel. Soon the odor of burning jumpers and webs filled the air with a choking, acrid smell that irritated the nose and throat. When Corri thought she could endure the stench no longer, Imandoff's next fire ball splattered against bare rock, sending sparks whipping back around them.

"Now what?" Takra stepped up beside Imandoff, carefully checking the tunnel for surviving spiders as the sorcerer created a cool globe of light in his hand.

"It appears to be another door in the rock. But where it leads, there is no clue." Imandoff felt along a crack in the scorched wall with his free hand. "Corri, can you remember what was on the map at this point?"

"Nothing that made any sense. A sword hanging over what I think is a door. I think there was another picture of the mask. But I can feel fresh air."

She moved closer and peered at the crack in the stone, just wide enough to get her fingers into. She glanced down at a row of shallow pits across the floor of the tunnel just in front of the door, then up at the ceiling.

"What are those?" She pointed upward. "Part of a trap?"

"It looks like a second gate which could be lowered to help protect the temple." The sorcerer, after a brief glance, continued his inspection of the door.

Imandoff tried again to peer around the stone. "Nothing but a crack. Beyond it could lie the outside world or another part of the tunnels."

"Look." Takra pointed to a metal plaque fastened to the stone of the side wall. "The mask, but with a figure wearing it this time. There must be a fortune in small moon and sun stones on it."

"Do not touch it!" The sorcerer yanked Takra's fingers away. "Many times the Forgotten Ones used such markers, often full of hidden signs, to guide the initiate and trap the unwary."

He turned back to the crack of a door and shouldered his weight against the slab. A sigh of fresh air tinged with a strong animal odor seeped into the musty tunnel as the stone door reluctantly opened a hand's span.

"Back!" Takra whispered as she pushed them away from the opening. There was a hiss-ching as she drew her sword. "Barsark! Douse the light, sorcerer."

Corri shivered as the tunnel blackness swept around them. *Barsark,* she thought, *what next?* She cringed against the stone wall. *Barsark will kill anything just to kill. Those demon-bears are almost impossible to defeat.* Horrid tales of their murderous rampages were told even in Hadliden.

"I hear nothing," Takra whispered, her ear close to the door crack. "It must be gone." She and Imandoff carefully shouldered the stone open. "An empty den, but still in use."

The rancid animal odor and stench of rotting meat was almost overpowering as the trio cautiously crept out of the tunnel. Bones cracked and slid underfoot as they moved about the cave; a faint light from the cave opening revealed a half-eaten deer carcass near the rear wall.

"Wait." Imandoff leaned back into the tunnel, dagger in hand. There was a scrape of metal against metal as he forced the point of the dagger under the plaque, quickly prying around the edges. He jumped back as several sharpened metal rods shot from the ceiling of the tunnel to embed themselves in the shallow pits in the floor. Imandoff turned, the plaque tucked into his belt, and shut the door. The soft hiss of his sword sounded over-loud in the narrow space.

"Go!" Imandoff's low order was urgent. "It is almost night-fall. The barsark may return at any time."

With Takra in the lead, they picked their way out of the barsark den and found themselves on a boulder-strewn hill-side. Below and beyond them lay a second valley. Like the ruins behind them, the view of the valley was twisted under a veil of distortion. Midway in the basin stood a row of black columns and tumbled walls among a grove of trees. From the valley edge, thick ranks of trees rose along the mountain slope to meet them. On a monolith at the edge of the trail below was incised a huge design, not like any Corri had ever seen before.

"The true Valley of Whispers. The other may have been a decoy to confuse intruders, or merely the dwelling places of the Forgotten Ones. This valley has the feel of deep power." Imandoff looked around. "The temple I seek is there." He stared down at the wavering scene.

"Look, there is the Volikvi." Takra pointed at the slot of a deer trail below them. "He just entered the trees. It seems he also seeks your ancient temple, sorcerer. He must have avoided the barsark and come over the open ridge."

"Quickly! I thought I saw movement on the hill above!" Imandoff pushed Corri ahead of him.

A growling roar pierced the air, echoed off the rocks and sent shivers through Corri's flesh.

Corri followed Takra in a wild scramble down the rocky hillside onto the worn trail. The three pelted along the dusty path and under cover of the resinous trees before they stopped to look back.

"What if it saw us?" Corri gasped for breath.

"They have poor eyesight." Takra continued to scan the slope above. "But their sense of smell is unequaled. Once a barsark gets on your scent, the only thing to do is kill it before it kills you."

"Perhaps I have enough energy left to mind-send it elsewhere." Imandoff stared at the barsark as it approached its den.

"Not possible for our shakkas," Takra answered. "They say its mind is too alien."

To Corri's whispered question, Imandoff answered, "The Tuonela shakkas are like priests and priestesses." His smoke-colored eyes never left the demon-bear while he spoke.

The barsark gave another howl and pressed its nose to the ground at the den entrance.

"By the Goddess, it has found our scent." Takra's words left Corri with a deep urge to run.

"Listen." Imandoff raised his hand. "Grimmel's men are coming. They walk into a trap better than any I could create." The harsh sound of men's voices echoed over the hill.

The barsark reared up on its hind legs, a great black and white bulk against the skyline, and turned to face the crest of the hill. It stretched out its enormous front legs, the curved claws flashing in the sunset, but remained silent.

Over the top of the ridge Corri heard, then saw, the first of Grimmel's men. Seemingly unaware of the danger, the armed men clambered over the rocks, directly into the path of the barsark.

With an ear-splitting roar, the animal raced into the pack of men, its fanged muzzle ripping and savaging. It towered over its prey, swinging its great arms, its razor-sharp claws caving in one man's head, the backsweep knocking two others

senseless. Then it leaped onto the injured men, tearing out
great chunks of flesh.

Corri gagged as the wind carried the scent of fresh blood
down the hill. She covered her ears to shut out the screams.

"Go!" Imandoff shoved Corri farther down the slope
under the trees. "Run!"

"The Volikvi, we might run upon him unawares." Takra
hesitated. "We do not want to find him waiting in ambush
for us."

"If he has any sense, he ran as soon as he heard the first
roar, just as we should have."

They dashed down the tree-sheltered hill, dodging rocks
and low-hanging branches. They followed the twisting trail
downward until they were breathless.

"No." Takra threw out her arm to stop Corri's headlong
flight. "The Volikvi. We must not come upon him unawares."

"The entrance to the valley is near. I can feel it." Imandoff
sheathed his sword. "The barsark will be occupied for a time.
We need not fear it following for now."

"You know little of barsarks then, old man." Takra slid her
sword into its scabbard but kept her spear ready. "True, the
barsark will stay to tear apart and devour some of its prey, but
it will eventually follow us. Once on a scent, they never give
up, unless we can find moly to rub on our boots." She
grinned at Imandoff's look of surprise. "That is a Tuonela
secret, but I doubt there is any moly growing around here."

"Then the valley is our only chance." Imandoff started off
down the trail. "It will not follow us there, I am certain."

"What is this valley?" Takra asked, edging closer to Corri.
"More spooks? The last was bad enough."

The thief shrugged. She was tired to the bone, and her
head was pounding again now that the adrenalin rush was
leaving. Corri staggered after Imandoff as the sun dropped
further behind the distant hills. Just as the sky turned dark,
they reached the edge of a rolling valley, its entire form covered by a fog of distortion.

"Over here." Imandoff created a feeble ball of light and directed them into a circle of monoliths, set so close together that only a hand could be passed between the stones. A narrow opening on one side led into their center. "We should be safe in here for the night. Pray that the barsark did not spook the horses, or worse, kill them."

"Lightfoot is smart enough to stay away from such a creature," Takra said. "And she will keep the others with her."

They squeezed through the narrow entrance into the grassy center. Corri and Takra fell to the ground in exhaustion. Imandoff slowly walked around the inside of their enclosure, touching the ground and the monoliths at every fifth step. A quickly fading blue light sprang up at his touch.

"A warding spell." Takra shook her head. "Pray that it holds, sorcerer. I am too tired to fight a barsark tonight. It took all my strength the last time I faced one in battle."

"You fought one of those things?" Corri asked in amazement, absently tugging at her earring.

"Only a small one. Not much taller than the sorcerer." Takra grinned as she leaned back against one of the stones. "He left me a love-mark."

Working up her chain mail shirt and its leather padding, the warrior exposed her left side. Five puckered lines scored her ribs.

"Just a tap," she said as she settled the shirt back into place. "A fair exchange since I now wear its skin." She brushed her tanned hand across her fur jacket. "An unusual earring," she said as she watched Corri fingering the piece of jewelry.

"The last tie with my old life," Corri answered. "It was a gift from my nurse when I was small. I am keeping it in case we run short of money."

"You should sell it and buy a good sword," Takra said as she lay back, her hands clasped behind her head.

I am companying with crazies, Corri thought as she stretched out on the grass. *A sorcerer who wants to explore ancient temples rather than escape assassins. A Tuonela warrior who thinks a battle with a raging barsark is a minor incident. Great Goddess, what have I gotten myself into? Barsark or no, this night I have to sleep.*

Her eyelids drooped as she watched Imandoff bent over the metal plaque he had taken from the tunnel, a weak globe of light hanging at his shoulder.

Chapter 11

"The ritual has begun." The sorcerer's face looked bleak as he watched tendrils of fog beginning to form across the valley floor in the morning light. "Hurry! See that?" He pointed to the rapidly gathering mist. "He must be stopped."

Imandoff plunged ahead with Corri and Takra hurrying to keep up. The Valley of Whispers spread a half mile across a rolling floor with sheer rugged cliffs on both sides. The center of the valley before them was blanketed with a swirling fog that was quickly expanding.

"Where is he?" Takra frowned in bewilderment.

"There. Straight ahead." Imandoff loosed his sword and pointed at the fog. "He must have found the old temple at the sacred grove and spring, the heart of the power. It is best if you do not come with me. It could be dangerous. The Guardians of this valley will be stronger than those we met before. If we could have challenged him before he began his magic, your sword, Wind-Rider, would have been of use.

Now, I think not. Besides, the Volikvi will run when he sees another sorcerer. I will send him into your arms, Takra."

Takra's face showed her inner war between fulfilling her oath and her fear of magical powers. "I am a Tuonela warrior. I have ridden with fear many times. I will not give up my quest for vengeance."

"You cannot fight magic with mountain steel, Wind-Rider." Imandoff placed a hand on her shoulder. "You know that. I will take up your quest, for Dalorra and for the Free Peoples."

The warrior woman fidgeted, but said nothing.

Imandoff crossed the clear space and disappeared into the thin fog that now lapped up against them. Within a few steps his gray cloak hid him from their view. Time dragged on as the two women waited impatiently.

"Give me the spear," Corri suddenly demanded. "We should never have listened to him. That priest will not run, and Imandoff knows it. I am going after him."

"Are you certain he will want our help?" Takra answered, straining to see into the thick fog bank. "He did not act as if he needed us. And the spooks, if they are worse than back there ..." She shivered.

"I think he lied. He strikes me as the kind of man who does that sometimes. The Volikvi will not run, I know it. I feel it. Give me the spear!" Corri held out her hand.

"What of the Whisperers?"

"Stay here if you wish, but lend me the spear. Imandoff is all that stands between me and Grimmel. And I would rather die than return to the master thief and what awaits me there."

Takra looked at the girl's determined face. With a grim nod, she handed over the weapon and unsheathed her sword.

"We will go together. You are right to remind me of a warrior's duty. If what you say is true, then Imandoff thinks to keep me from harm, and that is not the way of the Tuonela. Mine is the revenge for Dalorra's death. I will blood my sword on that Volikvi. I will not be cheated out of my revenge, Corri Farblood. Stay clear of my sword arm when battle begins."

The two women strode forward side by side and entered the thick, misty fog. Within a few paces they could see no more than five steps before them.

"By the Goddess," Corri whispered, "how are we to find Imandoff and the temple in this? I did not think it would be like this. I cannot tell one direction from another."

"He called you his apprentice. Use your magic. Dispel the mist."

"I cannot," Corri answered. "Imandoff has not taught me any spells. I am just a thief. A very good thief, but not one with magic."

Takra pulled out a tiny belt knife, scarcely as long as her little finger, and balanced it on the palm of her hand. "We came in from the east, and Imandoff headed straight west, that way, directly into the fog."

Corri sucked in her breath in surprise as the blade quivered, then jerked slightly to the right.

"You have a wand." She looked at Takra with suspicion.

"I am no sorcerer, and this is no wand." Takra glared at the concealing mist. "I am a warrior, not a magic-maker. I trust only in mountain steel." She held up her sword. "The shakkas spell all homing knives so they will point to the north. That keeps us from being lost during snowstorms on the grasslands."

Corri looked dubious, but shrugged. They hurried on, from time to time checking the tiny pointer for any change in direction.

Time seemed to be stopped in the clinging mist. Faint whispers of calling voices began to plague them, rising and falling like the sound of the sea. The protective guardians of this valley were much stronger than those they had experienced before. Corri found herself perspiring as she fought against the voices and visions of the Whisperers. She could only guess what Takra was enduring.

"Corri, why do you seek to help this sorcerer?" Grimmel's bloated image rose before her. "Come back to Hadliden, little thief. Think of the riches we can share." The round, almost lidless eyes on the flat face filled her vision.

"No!" Corri said under her breath. "Never! You are not here, Grimmel. Not here!"

"Dalorra! Sword-sister!" Takra groaned in anguish and reached out.

Corri grabbed her companion's arm. "There is nothing there, Takra. It is an illusion."

When the sword-woman tried to stagger off to one side, Corri wrapped one of Takra's long braids about her hand and yanked hard. The helmeted head jerked around to face her.

"Listen to me, Takra. Your friend is not out there. It is all an illusion. Fight it!" Corri gave the braid another painful jerk. "Count, and keep counting!"

"Count?" Takra's eyes focused on the girl. "Yes, count. Dalorra is dead. We must find Imandoff. Count."

They began to count each step forward. It was like walking through clinging mud. Each movement was an effort.

A black pillar loomed before them, dripping with moisture and moss. As Corri focused on it, the monolith shifted its form. In its place appeared a black robed Fravashi priest, arms raised in a magical gesture, the face contorted in hatred.

With a cry of alarm, Corri thrust forward with the spear. The iron blade rang against stone, sending a shower of sparks into the fog. The priest vanished back into the stone pillar.

"Illusion." Corri's eyes were wide with terror. "If we do not find Imandoff soon, I fear we will succumb to the Whisperers. If I only knew a spell!"

"Take my hand." Takra reached out to her. "If we stay together, we are stronger. It looks like more stones ahead, there among the trees."

"Yes, a double line of them. Perhaps they lead to the temple as they did in the other valley."

"Then we must be close. We follow the stones, and the Whisperers can go to the deep pits of Frav's hell-fires!" Takra squeezed Corri's trembling hand.

Step by step, the women passed through the ragged grove of trees and gained the scattered remains of an ancient stone building. Takra grabbed the rough edge of a massive fallen block and levered herself forward. Beside her, Corri groaned and thrust out her arm to ward off the ghostly form of her old nurse. The two women pushed forward another step.

Suddenly, the Whisperers were gone. The invisible resistance vanished. The clinging damp mist weakened enough to see deeper into the moss-dripping trees. Takra and Corri found themselves breathing hard as if they had run a long race.

"There! Just ahead. See it?" Corri grabbed Takra's arm in excitement.

A faint red glow seeped through the mist like the coals of a forge fire. But there was no sound. *Although the fog deadens the echo of our footsteps on the stones, there should be the sound of battle,* Corri thought.

"You go that way." Takra slipped the tiny knife back into her belt and pointed off to her left. "If we come at the Volikvi from two sides, we can create a distraction. But remember, that one is meat for my sword!"

Corri reached down to pull out her boot-knife before slipping off silently. Angling to the left and using the red glow as a guide, she worked her way in among the fallen blocks of stone, dagger in one hand, spear in the other. As she drew near, she halted in shock.

The air fairly crackled, the same sensation one felt during a great lightning storm coming in from the sea. Corri's hair lifted into a halo about her head. She saw that the intense red glow came from a small pottery bowl set on a stone altar. Beside it lay a severed hand, half concealed in a leather bag. Embedded in the side of the altar glittered strange blue stones, just beginning to show signs of an awakening light deep within. Corri blinked, then blinked again. Imandoff stood beside the altar, wand in one hand, sword at his feet, while two sword-lengths beyond him stood not one, but two Volikvi priests, black robes a blot against the swirling mists.

He is tired, his magic worn thin from yesterday, Corri thought. *There is no way he can win by himself.*

The voices of the Volikvis and Imandoff were intense whispers as each chanted spells. But the two magical chants counterbalanced each other. Imandoff and the priests stood locked in enchanted combat with none able to best the other.

Imandoff moved on his toes like a dancer as he fought to find an opening for his magical powers to penetrate the Volikvi's defenses. Their eyes locked on each other, the sorcerer and the Volikvi priests circled, inch by inch, in a battle of wills and power.

What happens to us if Imandoff loses? Corri thought, the spear griped tight in her hands. Her mind rebelled at the possibilities she imagined from Takra's earlier words. *Oh Goddess, he must not lose! I find myself liking this sorcerer and the warrior woman.* She felt deep bitterness at Grimmel for having poisoned her against friendship, for creating a distrust of everyone around her. *If this is friendship I feel, then I call them friends. I do not wish to ever be without such friends again! What can I do to aid him, tip the balance?*

No answers came. Corri stood watching, her teeth set tight, her head aching. She was unable to decide whether to stay where she was or leap forward into a magical battle in which she would have no protection if she came into the cross-fire of power.

Chapter 12

Corri inched her way into a crouch a stone's throw behind the altar. She saw a slow, careful movement from the corner of her eye. Takra Wind-Rider was creeping closer, using the moss-covered, mist-slicked ruins as cover. Neither Imandoff nor the priests seemed aware of their presence. She could see the sword-woman's helmeted head, clear now above a fallen stone.

What can I do? she thought as she watched Takra's slow, deliberate movements. *I have to do something, yet I know nothing of fighting and battles.*

The intensity of crackling magic stirred the hair on her head and arms and ran down the spear point in a thread of sparking light. She saw Takra's free-swinging hair lift into an aura around her helmet. A whisper of light flashed down the woman's uplifted sword blade. The mist curdled, broke apart, then drew closer again with each magical gesture from the magicians. Tiny sparkles of strange light winked from within the mist, making Corri's eyes ache if she stared at them.

Another black form suddenly appeared. Three Volikvi now stood facing Imandoff!

Only one of the priests can be real, Corri thought, *but which one? Does Imandoff even know?* She steeled herself for attack, knowing she had little, if any, chance of surviving. *Holy Goddess, help me! I am no sorcerer, only a thief.*

Corri rose from her hiding place with a quick fluid movement, spear in one hand, boot-knife in the other. Her clumsily thrown spear passed harmlessly through the nearest black form. One of the spectral priests gave a negligent wave of his fingers, and she sailed backward, knife falling from her hand, her slender body slamming into the damp ground. Imandoff's eyes never left his opponents.

Fumbling for her dagger, Corri crawled forward again, her left arm filled with pain. She could see the perspiration beading on Imandoff's face and trickling down his jaw.

The sorcerer's eyes flicked constantly from one black figure to another, as if he must keep guard against them all. The priests raised their daggers, spell-light gleaming on the deadly hooked blades.

So, she thought, *they all have power, although only one is real.*

The glow in the bowl began to pulsate, sending flashes of blood-red light whipping through the fog. The crackle of magic intensified, but with a deeper, deadlier feel.

Corri paused in her struggle to stare at the bowl. *What is happening? What is being loosed into our world?*

Fear like she had never experienced in her life rose in her mind. She felt as if she were falling into a bottomless pit of torture, a place full of deathless creatures who would cause her endless pain, yet never kill her, so that she would suffer agonies forever. She wanted to scream out her terror, but her jaws would not open. As if from a distance, she heard the strangled sounds in her own throat.

"Too late, sorcerer," one Volikvi laughed. "The ritual now feeds upon itself for completion. You should have brought another magician instead of a weak girl thief."

The priest's voice seemed to break whatever spell lay upon her. Corri saw Takra rise silently from her hiding place. Drawing back her long dagger, the sword-woman sent it hurtling, whistling across the open space to strike against the bowl. The vessel skidded over the mist-slicked altar to spill its contents onto the ground in a cloud of evil-looking red smoke.

In a split-second movement, the warrior woman sprang forward, sword hilt in both hands. With a lightning quick sweep, the shining blade cut through the necks of the black figures just as Imandoff lunged forward with his wand. The deadly sword blade and the silver wand touched the central figure at the same instant. The built-up magic exploded in a ball of black light, the noise of the explosion booming through the mist-covered ruins. The two outer priests winked out of existence.

The sudden release of force lifted Takra off her feet and threw her to the damp ground, sword flying from her grasp. She scrambled back up, hands pressed to her ears, eyes struggling to focus. Shaking her helmeted head, she staggered forward to stand over the body of the Volikvi priest.

The force of the explosion slammed Corri's body back against a block of tumbled stone, the pain in her injured arm sending cascades of shattering pain through her.

"Well done." Imandoff's hoarse voice finally reached through the noise in Corri's ears. "If you had not come to my aid, Wind-Rider, we could have stood locked together in battle for ages. And Corri?"

"Here." Corri walked forward, cradling her arm. "I feel as if Grimmel had beat me. I think my arm is broken. And you?"

"Very tired." Imandoff stepped to the altar and stamped the bowl into pieces. "Now, Takra Wind-Rider, you can take your sword-sister's hand back to Tuone. Her soul is free." The sorcerer gently put the severed hand back into the leather bag in which the Volikvi had carried it. "Neither of you follow orders well. You should have waited as I told you. This battle could have ended other than it did. But I am glad you came."

"I could not let Dalorra's soul go to Jevotan. I needed to be here in case you failed." The warrior woman grinned at him. "And it looked to me as if you might lose in spite of your mighty powers. Magic is not always the way to battle magic, sorcerer." Takra took the bag. "I am a warrior, Silverhair. I will trust in mountain steel in any fight."

"No, magic is not always the answer, sword-woman," Imandoff said. "But sword alone would have never defeated the Volikvi. He would have easily defeated you. It took both of us. In the heat of a magical duel such as this, the hand of a trained warrior or a thief," he turned to smile at Corri, "can swing the balance of power." He nodded grimly.

"What now, sorcerer?" Corri asked. "If any of those men back there survived to tell Grimmel where I am, he will still seek me. There is no guarantee that Druk was with them and died under the claws of the barsark, you know. And I want to find my father. I need to hear from his own lips why he left me with Grimmel. Will you help?"

"If I can. The journey may be long. Your father's trail is long years cold; he may even be dead. In fact, you may not ever get back to Hadliden."

"Small loss." Corri grimaced as Imandoff splinted her arm with sapling limbs and strips from his cloak. He fastened her arm into a sling with another cloth strip. "You are beginning to look like a disreputable old dog-wizard, ragged and dirty. Next you will start making love potions." She turned to Takra. "We could use your strength on our journeys, Takra. I think it will take both of us to see that this mighty sorcerer comes to no harm. She should come with us, Imandoff."

"Why not?" Imandoff moved first to the dead priest, detaching a strange metal brooch from the man's belt, then turning to carefully pry one of the strange blue stones out of its setting in the altar. "You never know when a warrior's arm will be needed."

"Company with a liar and a thief?" Takra grinned at Corri's frown and Imandoff's raised eyebrows. "At least she admits she is a thief. You pretend to be a sorcerer, yet I have seen you steal a belt-brooch from a dead man, a plaque from an old temple, and now some strange stone from an altar."

"Life would never be dull." Imandoff's gray eyes twinkled as he cupped the palm-sized stone in satisfaction, then slid it and Volikvi's brooch into his saddlebag. "Come, Takra Wind-Rider. Your soul longs for adventure, you know it. I have never seen a Tuonela warrior who did not yearn after the unknown and danger. It is born in the blood."

"First I have a promise to keep." Takra tied the leather bag to her belt. "I swore knife-oath to a sword-sister."

"After that is fulfilled, ride with us."

Takra nodded her assent as she turned to the body of the Fravashi priest. Neither Imandoff nor Corri watched as she plunged her dagger into the body of the Volikvi, then wiped the blade on the damp grass. As she cleaned the blood from her recovered sword, Lightfoot trotted out of the dissipating fog, nickering to her mistress. Mouse and Sun-Dancer followed.

"How did they get around the barsark?" Corri wondered aloud. "What if that thing followed them?"

"Lightfoot is very intelligent." Takra slipped her spear into its holder near her stirrup. "Probably waited until the demon-bear went after what men were left alive, then herded the other horses over the ridge to follow us."

"Still, I think it would be wise to seek another way out. There may well be men who survived, men who now will be out for our blood. Alas, my search for the underground burial chamber must wait for another time."

"Your quest brought you here in search of that old legend?" Takra shook her head in disbelief.

Imandoff shaded his eyes as he scanned the far valley walls. "There appears to be a small canyon leading to the north. Will you ride at least to Leshy with us, Wind-Rider?"

"Battle companions should be trusted friends, even as Lightfoot is," Takra said as she caressed the horse's braided forelock. "Will you be as trustworthy, sorcerer?"

Imandoff stooped to grasp a handful of dirt, then held it before him. "My oath." When Takra hesitated, he added, "Is this not the way of the Tuonela to give oath?"

"Yes, but I am surprised you know of it. Few outside the Clans do." Takra clasped the long fingers in acceptance. The sorcerer dusted his hands on his dingy white robe.

"We will travel with you as far as the Mystery School of Leshy," Imandoff said as he put one arm around Corri's shoulders. "There we will remain until spring, more than enough time for Corri's arm to heal. And for me to test her talents, such as the dream-flying. You will find us there until the spring Holy Days."

"Do you really think that canyon is another way out of here?" Corri gestured toward the distant cliffs with her good arm. "I do not want to return the way we came. The barsark is still back there, as may any of Grimmel's men who escaped. With the luck I have had lately, Druk will be waiting."

"We will try the canyon." Imandoff put a hand on Corri's shoulder. "It looks promising."

"And if there is no passage?"

"Then we kill a barsark." Takra patted her sword hilt.

"I am companying with crazies," Corri muttered.

"More interesting than journeying with plain folk." Imandoff grinned at Takra. "Come to us in Leshy in the spring, Takra Wind-Rider. Life with us will never be dull. I promise."

"No, sorcerer, I doubt that it would." Takra smiled back. "Look for me in the spring at Leshy. The least I can do for your aid is teach your city-friend how to fall without breaking bones."

"I feel I have found another piece of the puzzle I seek to solve." Imandoff looked around at the crumbling ruins. "Nothing seems to remain here at this ancient temple, except a flow of power I am unable to understand. But there must be something. Somewhere there is an entrance to the underground tunnels, but we have no time to search." He paused and looked around, then sighed. "The ancient scrolls in the library at Leshy may help me to unravel more of the mystery."

"What mystery?" Takra frowned at him.

"The mystery of where we came from, who we really are."

"That old legend, that the Four Peoples came from somewhere out there." The warrior waved her hand at the sky. "Tales to entertain children, old man."

"You never know." Imandoff boosted Corri astride her mare, then mounted his roan. "Onward to Leshy and more adventures." He winked at the thief.

The spell-created fog had blown away in the light breeze, except for a few tattered wisps along the far side of the valley, as the three headed for the canyon and a possible way out and down the mountains to Leshy.

Chapter 13

The first canyon they explored narrowed into a steep-sided crevice, making it impossible to reach the top of the walls. They moved on down the valley walls, checking every possible exit. The canyon Imandoff finally chose was a narrow funnel leading steeply up to the sharp cliffs above. Its rough floor was strewn with boulders and a wash of gravel that made for treacherous footing. They led the horses, slipping and sliding, between the high walls of layered rocks, dodging the scatter of gravel that slid down with every step.

"If any of those men followed us, they will not have to guess where we are," Takra said as they paused to rest. She leaned against her long spear, its butt-end rammed into the coarse gravel of the ravine. "This noise must echo all through the valley." She stared back at the land behind them, but her view was limited by the rugged canyon walls.

"There is no other way." Imandoff patted Sun-Dancer. "Who knows? They may have circled around and could be waiting for us up there." He indicated the top of the ravine with a casual wave of his hand.

"I thought of that." Takra checked the slide of her sword in its sheath. "Best you help Corri, and I will take the lead. If it comes to a fight, you and I can hold the way long enough for her to retreat with the horses."

Imandoff nodded as the warrior edged past, leading Light-foot. Mouse and Sun-Dancer followed the dappled mare.

"It is not much farther," he said as he took Corri's arm. "Then you can ride again."

"Could Grimmel's men be up there?" Corri asked, gritting her teeth against the pain in her arm as she struggled upward. "I was hoping that those not killed had been run off by the barsark."

"We cannot assume that one or two did not survive." Imandoff's heavy breath sounded by her ear as he pushed her over a difficult spot. "Any normal person would have given up the chase after being laid low at the inn. But this man Druk, he is persistent to the point of madness. And luck seems to walk with him. I wonder ..."

"He has no mystical abilities, if that is what you mean." Corri looked up to see Takra cautiously peering up over the top of the ravine, sword in one hand, deadly spear in the other. "He is just an assassin, Grimmel's best, cold-hearted, efficient, very loyal. One thing for it, sorcerer, Druk will never stop following me as long as he is alive. Returning Grimmel's wife," she spat the words, "will assuredly gain him a great reward."

"Then perhaps we should pray to the Goddess that he did not survive the barsark." Imandoff held Corri still until Takra waved the bright sword over her head, indicating it was safe. "You and the Wind-Rider have much more in common than you think, Corri. She would be a loyal friend if you would let her."

"She is a warrior," the girl answered as she continued her scramble upward. "I have been a thief and now a wife-slave to the master thief of Hadliden. From as far back as I can remember, Grimmel taught me never to trust anyone. 'Depend upon no one but yourself, and you will never get hurt,' he would say. That worked well in my narrow world as a thief. Now, I do not know anymore."

"That attitude of mistrust can be a problem in ordinary life, Corri. You have to learn to let people get close to you, or they cannot be friends. Sometimes you do get hurt in the process. But that is life, Corri, real life, not the false existence of Grimmel's world."

I am now beginning to trust you, sorcerer, she thought as they fought their way up the last section of the funnel canyon. *Why is it so difficult to tell you, or to let down my guard with Takra? I like this feeling called friendship.* But she remained silent.

Corri and Imandoff finally worked their way out onto the top of the cliffs. Takra was rubbing down the horses with tufts of grass, all the while still watching the tree-covered land around her.

"No sign of anyone, sorcerer." Takra slapped Lightfoot's flank as the horse wandered off to graze on the thick grass. "If any survived the barsark's charge, they have not yet found us. Still, I would feel safer not standing about in the open."

"Lead on." Imandoff gestured with his hand toward an animal track that led off through the forest. "There should be a ridge trail in that direction that eventually turns down toward Leshy. To think I have been this close to the Valley of Whispers in the past and yet never knew it lay here." He turned to look down on the valley, its wisps of fog rapidly burning away in the sunlight. "I wish there had been time to search for the underground tunnels. Who knows what knowledge they may hold?"

Takra sheathed her sword with a sharp click of metal. "We dare not linger. I would put a long distance between us and this place before nightfall."

She caught up Lightfoot's dangling reins, shoved her long spear into its holder by the stirrup, and mounted. While she waited impatiently for Imandoff and Corri to get into their saddles, Takra kept a keen eye on the area around them. Then the Tuonela warrior led the way along the track under the low-limbed trees.

Before long they came upon a shallow stream. The trail meandered along beside its clear water for several miles before forking, one track plunging down the north side of Deep Rising toward the plains of Tuone, the other snaking along the stream to the east under the resinous trees.

"Look. You can see the grasslands of Tuone." Takra pointed far below them at a great rolling plain that stretched off into the hazy distance. "Far beyond, at the north edges of the grasslands, are the Mootma Mountains where my friends of Frayma's Mare guard against Frav."

"I never thought it would be so huge." Corri's words were soft, her eyes bright with interest. "And you came all that way alone?"

Takra shrugged. "There was a thing that needed doing, a friend's death to be avenged. But I was not alone. The Mother of Mares rode at my side, for the Dark Magic is abominable to Her."

"But alone!" Corri looked at the Tuonela warrior woman in a new light. "I wish I were as brave as you, Takra. Then I should have just killed Grimmel and not be running away."

"There are times to fight and times to run," Imandoff said. "There is no shame in retreat when necessary. Even the great Tuonela warriors know the wisdom of that. A good warrior must carefully weigh the risks against the end result. Sometimes we must choose to live so that the fight will fall in our favor another day."

"There was no honor to be gained by dying under the hand of haven-swill." Takra turned her horse down the eastern trail toward Leshy. "You showed a warrior's skill in retreating, Farblood. Now you have the time to learn strength and wisdom before again facing your enemy. There will come a day when you meet this Druk, or even Grimmel, once more. And you will not be an unskilled fighter then." The warrior rode on ahead.

They followed the trail in the half-gloom of the forest until two hours before sunset. The massed trees gave way to a cup of flat meadow near the edge of the stream. Takra ordered them to stay hidden in the shadows of the pines and firs while she scouted out the area. Satisfied that they were alone, the warrior motioned with a browned hand.

"She is so skilled in what she does." Corri's mount waited stirrup to stirrup beside Imandoff's. "So confident. I wish I were like her."

"She has had a long road to ride," the sorcerer answered. "Her parents were killed in a flash flood when she was only a small child. A family from the Clan Asperel took her in and raised her. But she is of mixed blood, her mother being a woman of Kirisan. Although the Tuonela Clans accepted her, Takra never accepted herself. She felt the need to be the most daring, the most skilled with weapons, the best warrior woman of Tuone. As soon as she was old enough, she petitioned for Frayma's Mare and they took her to ride with them."

An orphan like me, Corri thought. *Always trying to prove to herself that she is worthy. But of what? Life?*

Takra unsaddled her horse while she waited for Imandoff and Corri to join her beside the stream.

"We can build a fire here on the gravel bank," she said as she put Lightfoot on a long grazing tether. "No one will see the light here, sheltered as we are by trees."

"No one but a Green Man, perhaps." Imandoff pulled the saddles off the other two horses and adjusted their tether-lines so they could graze on the rich grass between the stream and the forest. "It would be most surprising if one did not at least spy on our camp, whether or not he ever let us see him."

"What is a Green Man?" Corri asked as she sat down on a rock to watch Takra gather dry brush and limbs, then carefully arrange them for a fire.

"The Green Men are a kind of mountain patrol. They are Kirisani men who prefer the solitary life up here, keeping watch for dangerous beasts that may wander down into the valleys or any band of criminals who might decide to make their hiding places here among the crags."

Imandoff snapped his fingers and a short burst of flame shot into Takra's mound of wood. Tiny flames began to creep upward, sending out heat but only a thin plume of smoke.

"You know little of the lands of the Peoples. Did this Grimmel keep you so ignorant?" Takra sat cross-legged beside Corri. She wrinkled her brow in thought. "But then you speak of the Goddess. I would have thought such a man as Grimmel would never have let you learn of the Lady's strength."

"I learned of the Goddess Friama from my nurse when I was little," Corri answered. "Then, too, the pleasure-slaves all worship Her. When I was small, I used to spy on their private doings. Grimmel allowed their worship of the Goddess, but instructed me that believing in gods and goddesses shows a weak mind." She cradled her bound arm against her body.

"Friama, Frayma, they are the same. And this Grimmel, he knows nothing, if he rejects the Mother of Mares and Her consort. As to pleasure-slaves!" Takra snorted with disgust. "In reality, all Asuran women are pleasure-slaves. They have no freedom and no will to be free. At least you were a thief, a free woman."

"If Imandoff had not rescued me, I would be worse than a pleasure-slave, to my thinking." Corri's blue-green eyes gazed into Takra's amber ones. "I was forced to marry Grimmel against my will, by the laws of Asur, where a woman has no rights. Imandoff got me away before the old toad could make me full wife."

Takra's eyes narrowed in anger. She turned to the sorcerer, her clenched fists in her lap.

"It is true." Imandoff pulled out his clay pipe and tamped it full of smoke-leaf. "Corri has special abilities that the master thief hoped would be strong in a child by her. Our trails crossed, and she stole something of mine. When I went to retrieve my map from Grimmel's fortress, I got his best thief instead. A good bargain, it turns out." He lit the pipe, drew on it and sent a smoke ring drifting up into the thin smoke of the fire. "And there was an old debt which needed paying," he murmured softly.

Both Corri and Takra waited for the sorcerer to say more, but he sat silently, smoking his pipe and staring at the sky.

"If this Grimmel dares to come seeking you, I will cut out his heart!" Takra looked at Corri and patted the hilt of her long dagger. "And I will do it slowly. Sooner or late, he is bound to seek you himself, when all his assassins fail. I hear that Asuran men do not take kindly to their women running away. But, by the blessed Goddess, you are no Asuran woman to be bought and sold at will!"

"I never killed anyone before," Corri said, gazing into the deepening shadows under the trees. She rubbed ineffectively at the blood stains on her trousers with her good hand. Although she had scrubbed them in the shallow stream, the sickening smell still clung.

A vague feeling of uneasiness began to prick at her. *We are being watched,* she thought, *but perhaps it is only an animal.* The horses continued to graze quietly, with only an occasional lift of the head. "Not before the valley had I killed anyone," she continued. "But I will most certainly kill Grimmel if he ever lays a hand on me again."

"Did you have a life-mate in Frayma's Mare?" Imandoff's dark eyes regarded the warrior woman closely.

"No. I have nothing against men." Takra idly drew symbols with her finger in the rocky dirt. "Dalorra wished it, but it is not my way. A man can be an amusing way to spend an evening." She grinned at the sorcerer. "My guess is that you are no celibate, even though you wear the blue-stone buckle, Imandoff."

Imandoff grinned and wiggled his eyebrows in answer. Corri's mouth dropped open in surprise.

During our journey over-mountain, I never had cause to think of Imandoff in that way, she thought. *He appeared nothing more than a companion, a friend, but never as a man with a liking for women and physical pleasures.*

"It must be Imandoff Silverhair. As I live and breathe, it has been a long time," said a male voice from the deepening shadows of the forest. "Two years it has been, has it not?"

Takra was on her feet in the blink of an eye. With a growl at being surprised and caught off-guard, she grabbed at her sword. The deadly sound of the weapon leaving its sheath echoed through the tiny clearing. Her eyes flicked to the quiet horses, their heads now lifted toward a dark section of the trees. Lightfoot watched the shadows, curiosity pricking her ears forward.

"Show yourself!" the warrior woman demanded.

A tall man, dressed in dark greens and browns, stepped out from under the trees and moved toward the fire, his thumbs tucked in his wide belt. His brown and green plaid cloak swirled about his long legs, brushing the laced knee-boots, as he walked.

He moves like a wild animal, Corri thought as she watched him. *I felt his presence, but heard nothing. Even now, he makes no sound when he walks. And the horses, they gave no warning at all, not even Lightfoot.*

"A Green Man," Imandoff said. He moved to stand beside the warrior woman, one hand touching her shoulder in reassurance. "We have nothing to fear from him."

"I know better than to ask a sorcerer what he does in Deep Rising," the man said as he stepped close to the fire. The rugged lines of his slender face were highlighted by the fading sunlight. "I would not get a true answer. I am Gadavar." He glanced at the two women. "Since you company with Silverhair, you are free to go about Deep Rising." There was the long, hard line of a sword under his cloak and the wink of a dagger hilt at his hip.

"I go where I please, Green Man." Takra's words were clipped. "I am a Tuonela warrior and ride with Frayma's Mare. I ask no man leave to go where I will."

Gadavar smiled, his even teeth white against his weather-tanned face. "I followed your progress from the valley yonder. The whole forest is aware of you."

"He can communicate with animals," Imandoff said as Corri looked at him. "That is why the horses gave no warning. Gadavar of Deep Rising, it has been some time since our paths last crossed. Did you know of the passage through your land of a Volikvi?"

"Aye, we knew." The Green Man swept one hand over his shoulder-length leaf-brown hair. "The message did not come soon enough to stop him from reaching the valley, nor to intercept those men who followed. And until now I was not certain who you were. I only knew the birds and beasts spoke together of strangers who moved through their forests, some gently, some without regard for the land."

"Since you speak with animals, is it your way not to hunt then?" Takra slid her sword back into its sheath.

"We hunt when it is needed." Gadavar folded his arms across his forest green jerkin, the worn hilt of his dagger glinting in the firelight as he moved. "As with the Tuonela, we honor the Lord of Animals. Life must be lived in balance, not excess."

The warrior woman nodded, the stiffness going out of her stance. "We understand each other. And Lightfoot senses no treachery in you. Welcome to our fire, Green Man. But we have little to offer in the way of food."

"Not to worry," Gadavar answered. "I was on my way to my cabin with a haunch of venison when the animals told me you were here. The meat is cached yonder." He pointed toward the trees.

"We will share," Imandoff said. "There is journey bread left in our packs."

Gadavar nodded, then turned and disappeared back into the forest. Within minutes he returned with the venison wrapped in the deer hide. In his free hand he carried a long bow and a quiver of bolts. He and Takra set to cutting thick strips of meat and skewering them on green sticks slanted over the flames before he again spoke.

"Times are indeed strange when one from Frav should cross the spell-bound border and come to Deep Rising. You followed him?"

Gadavar's brown eyes showed a ring of deep blue around the irises as the firelight caught them. Even though the Green Man sat relaxed besides the sorcerer, his arms wrapped around his knees, there was an air of alertness about him. Each noise from the darkening forest brought a slight turn of his head as if to hear and assess better what dangers may or may not lie out there. "We picked up his trail while we were on the way to Leshy." Imandoff offered his pouch of smoke-leaf to the Green Man, who pulled out his own pipe. "But Takra Wind-Rider has trailed him all the way from the Mootmas."

"A long way, Tuonela, one taking great courage." Gadavar nodded to the warrior woman. "Who followed you, Silver-hair? For there were others, not of Frav."

"Assassins out of Hadliden. They met with a barsark." Imandoff gave a grim chuckle. "With luck they were all killed or injured. But we have no way of knowing."

"Assassins!" Gadavar's rough hand tightened into a fist around his smoldering pipe. "We will keep watch at your back when you move on. The Green Men want none of those wandering about Deep Rising."

"How much further to Leshy?" Takra asked as she handed a stick of smoking meat to Corri.

"Two days of steady riding on this trail." Gadavar blew on his skewered venison. "Then an easy half-day on the main road into the city. Once you leave the mountain trails, we can no longer protect you. The Green Men have no authority within the bounds of men, only here in the forests and mountains."

Imandoff broke several rounds of journey bread and handed out the pieces. The group ate in silence as the last tinges of color faded from the sky. As Corri licked the juices from the fingers of her good hand, Gadavar rose.

"I will pass the word of your journey," the Green Man said as he wrapped up the remaining venison and slung it over his shoulder in its hide bag. He gathered up his bow and bolts in one rough hand. "Ride with care, Silverhair." He raised his hand in a final salute and disappeared into the night.

Corri lay down on the grass not far from the fire. Her cloak offered protection from the chill mountain air but her arm continued to ache, keeping deep sleep far away.

Is Druk really dead? she wondered. *Even if he is, Grimmel will send others. I have not the knowledge to survive alone so I must stay with Imandoff. But my presence endangers him.*

Her thoughts went round and round, from one possibility to another. At last, in a state of exhaustion and pain, she drifted off to sleep, the fire only dim coals in the black night.

They broke out of the thick forests of Deep Rising's lower slopes as a fall storm hit. The slashing rain beat against their hunched forms as the horses slid down the last mud-slicked section of the trail. Just below them lay a broad ribbon of road, the main thoroughfare into Leshy. On every semi-level piece of ground available on the mountain slopes were farmsteads, their fields pale with harvest stubble or dotted with huddles of cattle and goats.

Corri peered out from under her hood, the rain dripping down into her line of vision. She watched the bent backs of her companions as Mouse followed Sun-Dancer and Lightfoot down the last shallow bank and up onto the water-puddled road. The ache in her arm nagged at her constantly; this change in the weather seemed only to make it worse.

What next? she thought, but was too tired to really care. *It feels so strange not to feel the Green Men watching us. And where is the sound of the tide as it comes up the river?* With a start, Corri realized she had been straining to hear the ocean, a sound that had been a constant thing in Hadliden. *That sound I may never hear again.* She felt a loss deep inside, a strange mourning for a way of life that had once been the only thing she knew.

The going was easier on the thoroughfare, even though the surface was glassy with rain and rapidly turning into a soup of mud. The horses pressed on at a steady gait. Before nightfall, the storm passed and the lights of Leshy glinted in the evening dusk.

"From here I ride on alone, back to Frayma's Mare." Takra clapped a hand on Corri's shoulder. "Heal yourself, Farblood. I shall return in the spring to teach you warrior skills." The Tuonela's oval face lit with a warm smile. "I would be pleased to call you Sister-Friend, little thief."

"I would like that," Corri answered, taking Takra's hand in a firm grip. "I would have you at my side any time."

"Farewell, until spring," Takra called as she rode off alone, headed down a track that bypassed Leshy and led out onto the caravan routes across the grasslands of Tuone.

Imandoff rode beside Corri through the open gates of Leshy. He led the way through the crooked streets straight to the high walls of the Mystery School.

At last, Corri thought, as they were ushered into the healing rooms. *Peace and quiet, with no dangers to be armed against. My arm will be mended, and then, perhaps, I will be allowed to study for a time, study to be someone other than a thief.*

The healing Sister clucked at the old blood stains on Corri's tunic and trousers, but the girl refused to discuss how they had come to be there.

Corri noticed Imandoff's frown as he stood talking to the High Clua, supreme authority of the School, but she dismissed it. What did it matter? She was warm and dry and could finally rest without having to watch her back.

Chapter 14

It was nearing the spring Holy Days of The Creating. Corri stood at the narrow window and stared down at the courtyard below. The call to worship had emptied the long corridors and tiny cells of the Mystery School, as the dedicated Brothers and Sisters gathered in the main chapel for morning prayers.

She flexed her fingers as she rubbed her left arm. The long winter months had brought healing to the break, but sometimes her arm still ached. She thought back on the care given her by the best of Leshy's healers.

How can all these people live so close together with so little privacy? I could not stand to face a future living here. She looked down at the empty courtyard, the new green leaves of its herbs bright against the earthly tones of the wandering stone paths. *They say they are devoted to healing in all its forms, yet they reject every other form of magic. I thought a Mystery School would be more open-minded.*

She thought back to the conversation that morning with one of her teachers.

"But why do the initiates of Leshy reject magic?" Corri had asked Brother Kathis, who was responsible for teaching her about the laws and tenets of the School.

"Magic is a negative twisting of the Power," he answered with a sniff. "Those who use magic are going down a side-path, a path which will eventually lead them into Darkness, not the Light."

"Are you saying that those who use magic are evil?" Corri's eyes narrowed. "Imandoff Silverhair is not evil."

"He does not have the discipline necessary to be more than he is. He could never learn what we have to offer at Leshy." Brother Kathis stiffened and set his thin mouth in a hard line.

"What you mean is, Imandoff will not bend to your will." Corri hooked her thumbs in her belt, a gesture she knew her teachers disliked, a gesture of the outside world.

"You have been asked to wear a robe," Brother Kathis said in an effort to change the subject.

"Why should I?" Corri interrupted, stepping closer and glaring up at him. "I never said I wanted to be one of your mousy initiates. Imandoff brought me here to be healed. Then he insisted I learn all Leshy can teach about dream-flying. These laws you have babbled about all morning have nothing to do with that."

She gave a thief's rude gesture of contempt. Brother Kathis' face turned bright red.

"Besides," she added, grinning at his discomfort, "the School has been paid well to teach me. So you should get on with what you were paid to do and stop wasting my time and Imandoff's money."

"I shall report this rudeness and lack of discipline to the High Clua at once!" The teacher's face was nearly dark red with barely-concealed anger.

"Do that!" Corri shot back. "And while you are there, be certain to tell the High Clua that I will not listen to any more of her closed-minded teachers like you. The only ones I will talk with are those who teach me about dream-flying." She strode out of the room, leaving Brother Kathis opening and closing his mouth like a stranded fish.

Once I would never have dared speak to anyone like that, Corri thought as she stared at the stone buildings surrounding the courtyard. *It felt good to do it.* A brief grin curved her mouth. *Too bad the High Clua did not choose to listen to me. There is something about that woman I do not trust, something more than she has already shown by words and actions. She reminds me of Grimmel, always controlling and manipulating those around her.*

Not for the first time she wished for windows in the outer walls of the enclosed School so she could look out upon the town surrounding the religious enclave. But there were none. The School walled itself and its members off from the outside world. As members of the reclusive religious order, the initiates only interacted with others outside their walls when there was illness or injury to be tended.

If you have healing talent, why should you not be living out with the other people all the time? Why wall yourself away in this boring place? Corri thought. *And why not even have windows that look outward on the rest of the world? It all comes back to control, just as Imandoff told me.*

"The initiates of Leshy think that, by secluding themselves, they prove they are of greater importance than the rest of us," the sorcerer had said with a grin. "The sick must come asking for their help. This attitude is just a mask for control. Do not let them bully you into joining, Corri, unless that is what you truly want to do. Although I do not think that is something they will accomplish."

Imandoff, as a sorcerer and an initiate of the Temple of the Great Mountain, was allowed within the inner walls only as a student, a seeker of knowledge in the library building.

The High Clua had been firm about Imandoff, hedging the sorcerer with restrictions as to his movements within the walls of the School. One of those restrictions had been that Imandoff could not visit Corri in her cell of a room.

"Then I will not stay here," Corri told the old woman, her eyes flashing, her jaw set. "I am not one of your initiates to be ordered in this fashion. If I wish to speak with Imandoff or see him, I will do so." *Neither you nor anyone else in this place will ever find out from me that Imandoff and I have our own way to communicate, that we can send thought-messages between us. That is another reason you will never get your hands on my owl stone. Without it, I could not reach Imandoff.*

The High Clua glared at Imandoff, then turned on Corri what she believed to be a motherly smile. "There is no cause for such threats, child. If you feel so strongly, of course your sorcerer-friend may visit in your rooms."

"Beware, Corri," Imandoff had murmured as they walked across the courtyard to the dormitories. "She must see some strong potential power within you, or she would not have made that concession."

Warned, Corri had become stubborn, objecting to any suggestion with which she did not feel comfortable. When the old blood stains on her tunic and trousers brought criticism from the High Clua, the girl steadfastly refused to exchange her clothing for the drab blue gown and gray cloak of the female healers of Leshy.

A soft rap on the narrow wooden door broke into her thoughts. She opened it to find Imandoff, his clothes now spotless and mended. A new cloak hung from his wide shoulders.

"Looks as if the High Clua had her way," Corri said with a grin. "Cleanliness is a part of spiritual duty." The girl's voice mimicked the elderly woman's nasal tones. "We cannot have you coming here looking like some disreputable dog-wizard."

"The High Clua is supreme in Leshy. I must abide by such of her rulings as do not run counter to those of my school in Kystan."

Corri gave a snort of disbelief. "Since when do you care what anyone else thinks, old man?"

"If I were too stubborn, it might limit your opportunities here. You need the chance to study. How are you coming with your training in the shadow-self?" Imandoff sank down on a wooden stool next to the hard pallet on a wooden shelf, the only type of bed allowed in Leshy.

"It is the same as dream-flying," Corri answered with a shrug, but a frown wrinkled her brow. "But they insist that I cannot use it other than for healing. It makes no sense. Why can they not see I do not want to be a healer? They keep at me to take the oath and stay here." She slapped her hand against her thigh in exasperation. "The High Clua is little better than Grimmel."

"This sect is narrow-minded. They are thought-bound in that they disregard all other forms of magic, even to the point of expelling those who use them." Imandoff pulled at his beard. "But they are the most learned in the shadow-self. They do not believe in personal relationships or adornment, either." He pointed at the milky stone of Corri's earring. "I am surprised that the High Clua let you keep the earring, as she is against personal jewelry of any kind." He gently pulled a strand of her hair that was now beginning to show red under the faded black dye. "Perhaps we should do something about your hair before we journey on."

Corri stepped away from him, then turned back with a frown. "I told the High Clua that this earring is mine, mine to decide to wear or give up. These have been long months, sorcerer. True, I have learned better control of the dream-flying, better than they know. But I would be gone from this place. It is suffocating. I feel trapped in a prison, just as with Grimmel."

"Only a little longer, Corri. There is one more very ancient scroll to work through." Imandoff rubbed at his tired eyes. "A week at the most. Then we shall have to see about getting you out of here."

"What do you mean?" Corri said, her voice full of suspicion. "Do you mean I am a prisoner in this place?"

"The High Clua would not use those words, I am certain, but I am beginning to doubt the words she spoke when we arrived here."

"I remember. Freedom to come and go as you please, she said. All lies."

"You know how determined she is that you take oath and stay. You have a natural gift for directing the shadow-self, for finding out information. These healers value that ability greatly. In the far past there were rare healers who could traverse time to discover and bring back important information, the causes of illnesses and new ways of healing that are now forgotten. It is likely that the High Clua thinks you are such a one. A very great prize for Leshy."

"Enough to hold me against my will if necessary." Corri began to pace the narrow room. "She wanted to take my owl stone, you know. The old woman will never try that again."

"You underestimate the High Clua. That is not a very intelligent thing to do. If she has determined to separate you from the circlet and your stone, then sooner or late she will do it." Imandoff shook his head. "I truly am sorry, Corri. I did not think she would be so high-handed in her attempt to gain your support. You needed their healing and training, or I would not have brought you here."

"I will never take their oath," Corri said, her blue-green eyes sparking with anger. "If I desired to be a prisoner, I would choose a softer prison, like the kind Grimmel offered. I will not live like this, shut away from even a sight of the outer world, dressed in rough clothes and bound to prayers all hours of the day and night. True, they are dedicated healers, giving vast amounts of time and energy to the sick, but it is not for me. They never see the outer world unless they are directed to go on a journey for healing. And not many are allowed that privilege." She flopped down on the bed.

"The initiates of Leshy are the best healers among the Four Peoples," Imandoff answered. "But narrowly-bound forms of healing and devotion to one form of the Great Goddess are all they recognize as valid. Such a waste of talent."

"How soon can we be on our way?"

"As I said, another week, perhaps less. By that time, Takra should be here, if there are no more storms on the grasslands. And since those of Leshy do not hold with violence, Takra will be a key to your safe retreat from this place."

The sorcerer stood and stretched. He clapped a long-fingered hand on Corri's shoulder and smiled down at her.

"Patience, little thief. If the High Clua were to know you used your gift of dream-flying for other than healing, she would be at you night and day to repent before the high altar. And if she knew that you and I communicated by mind-speech, she would probably drag you to the chapel herself."

"Hurry with your studies, sorcerer. My patience has worn thin with these people. I will not be told what to do and when to do it much longer. And even for your precious studies, I will not wait longer than a week."

"Patience," Imandoff repeated as he closed the door behind him.

Corri paced the narrow cell, her thoughts flying from one thing to another. She felt like a bird beating its wings against a cage, longing for freedom.

All my instincts tell me there is danger nearby, she thought, *but I cannot bring that danger into focus. Are Grimmel's men close again, or is the danger from someone within these walls? I need more study.* She chewed at a fingernail. *But more study means I must stay. I hate this place! The High Clua is getting worse in her insistence that I join Leshy.*

The High Clua was getting bolder in her demands. At first, it had only been gentle persuasion to study the techniques of what those of Leshy called the shadow-self. Now it had evolved into pressure to take the oath and become one of the faceless, mum-tongued healers bound to the Mystery

School, treading their endless, and to Corri, pointless rounds of prayers, devotions, and studies.

Corri heard the soft steps of the returning worshippers as they quietly walked the corridors of the dormitory to their rooms. They would break their work and studies and meditations again at noon for more prayers. And at the ninth hour the evening bells would ring out over the School, a signal for sleep. In the hour past midnight the bells would sound again for prayers in each cell. Corri was forced to live her life to the rhythm of Leshy, and that made her feel rebellious.

A soft rap on the door followed by the faint creak of its hinges brought her instantly alert. She faced the entrance, dreading to see one of the High Clua's messengers.

A girl clad in an ankle-length, light gray robe over a blue gown slipped into the room. The plain brass buckles closing the robe at the chest winked in the dim light.

The girl lifted her hands in the religious greeting of Leshy. "May the peace of the Lady and Natira, the great Judge, be upon you."

"Another summons, Gertha?" Corri motioned the novice to the stool. "Why does the High Clua not leave things be? She knows my answer."

"I understand, Corri." The girl smoothed her plain blue gown, the prayer beads at her waist clinking in the silence, as she perched on the wooden seat. "This life of healing is not for you. I came here to Leshy of my own free will. Healing is my life, but it is not yours." Gertha's voice became even softer. "Do not share what you have learned about yourself and your abilities with the High Clua. I tell you, beware of Malya. That one has asked much after you and the sorcerer, more than is needful for a Sister to know. And she has influence with the High Clua."

"How do you know what I have learned?" Corri felt a chill wash over her. "And what has Malya to do with me and my affairs?"

"I have seen you in my shadow-self travels, Corri." Gertha smiled faintly. "I have seen you grow in skill. The danger lies in others learning of that and telling the High Clua. As to Malya, well, little is known of her life before she came to Leshy. Only that her mother is a feya woman of the Kirisani, one with a little talent to help the country people. As to how she has managed to gain the High Clua's confidence …" The girl shrugged.

A slight noise in the corridor brought Gertha instantly to her feet, her hands clasped in front of her. "You are to come to the High Clua immediately," she said. "I am to take you there."

"And if I refuse?" Corri's chin set in a stubborn line.

"That would not be wise. She would confine you to your room and not allow further visits from the sorcerer. Even now Malya speaks against your friend, saying he is an evil influence and must be forbidden entrance here."

"I will go then." Corri scooped up her cloak from the bed, swirled it around her, and fastened the throat buckles. "I wish you well, Gertha, for you only have been a friend within these walls. But I tell you, I will not stay much longer in this place."

The two moved silently down the long corridor of the dormitory. The plain stone walls with their closed doors on either side pressed against Corri's spirit. She longed to shout, to run, anything to break the strict rule-dominated atmosphere. But she walked placidly on, matching pace with Gertha, showing no outward sign of rebellion.

At the bottom of the third flight of steps, they passed through an outer door, coming into the sunlit warmth of a great courtyard. Patterned beds of healing herbs broke the pavement into a series of wandering paths. In the center splashed a fountain, its catch-basin a reflecting pool for the weak spring sun.

Gertha led the way straight across the courtyard to the massive library building, where the High Clua dwelt in apartments set aside at the rear of the bottom floor. The novice rapped on the heavy door, giving Corri an encouraging smile as she stood aside for the girl to enter alone.

The room was bare of ornaments, as were all the living cells of Leshy, except for the personal altar set in the corner. A small painting on smoothed board stood there, a portrait of the Lady and Natira, done by the High Clua in her long-ago youth. Some personal representation of the Power was allowed to the healers, even encouraged.

"Well come." The nasal voice of the High Clua came from a table by the narrow window. "Come forward, child."

Corri reluctantly moved to the table and sat on a stool. She hated these interviews. The leader of Leshy was a master in knowing how to make people feel inferior to her. The stool on which Corri sat was just low enough to make the girl look up at the older woman.

The High Clua looked at her with bright eyes, her face wrinkled from age. Her white hair was pulled back tightly and rolled into a bun on the back of her head. She was a wizened little woman, with a trace left of the beauty that once had been hers. But Corri could see the powerful will marked in the corners of the tiny mouth, the set of the head.

"How go your lessons with the shadow-self?" The old woman leaned forward, smiling as if her only concern was Corri's progress. "And your lessons in healing?"

"I have made no progress in healing. As for the rest, it goes slowly," Corri lied.

"Do not toy with me, child." The snap in the High Clua's voice brought Corri up straight on her stool and filled her with anger. "I have my reports."

"Your spies, you mean." Corri gripped both hands on the stool. *One thing I have learned, old woman, your shadow-self cannot check on me every minute. That requires too much time and energy.* "You mouth words of piety, but in truth you are no different from the master thief of Hadliden."

"So you finally admit you are a thief." The old woman leaned her elbows on the desk and steepled her hands. "Corri

Farblood, you must cleanse your soul of this sin of stealing. I will make a healer of you, a purified healer. Your talent for the shadow-self is great. And it is needed here in Leshy."

"Look to your own sins," Corri answered as she rose. "According to your laws, the laws of Leshy, you cannot keep me against my will. And my will is to leave." With that she whirled on her heel and left the room.

Corri was oblivious to all she passed on her way back to her cell. She slammed the door behind her, feeling satisfaction at the rolling echo it sent down the corridor.

Chapter 15

*S*omething in the room felt different. Corri paused to look around, her eyes passing swiftly over the few possessions in the tiny cell. The handle of the chamber pot stuck out from under the hastily-thrown blankets on her bed.

Perhaps I am being too paranoid about the High Clua, she thought as she carefully pushed the chamber pot farther under the bed with her foot. *I am seeing her spies in every shadow.*

Her mind snapped back to the present when she heard a sharp click behind her. She ran to the door and jerked the handle. She was locked in.

Fear rising within her, Corri opened the chest kept in each cell for clothing and personal belongings. Her boot-dagger and the circlet with the owl stone were gone. She sank down on the hard bed, head in hands.

Without the owl stone, how can I reach Imandoff? Corri rubbed her hands across her eyes. *If I could only dream-fly at will, mind-speak him when I needed. But without the owl stone...* Despair closed around her as she sat hunched on the stool.

The day dragged on. At the mid-day meal, a narrow flap at the bottom of the door opened and a tray of food was pushed inside. When she was certain that the corridor was empty, Corri tried the flap, but she could only extend her arm up to the shoulder. There was no way to force the rest of her body to follow.

If I had my dagger, she thought, *I might be able to pick the lock. And if I had the owl stone, I could contact Imandoff.* She paced the narrow cell, frightened and angry, uncertain as to what would happen next. *If I could only dream-fly without the stone. The others do it.* Her mind whirled and churned in frustration and anger.

At dusk the evening meal slid through the flap. Corri left it where it lay, apathy and helplessness filling her mind. She lay on the bed, sleeping only for short periods. Each time she woke, she came instantly from sleep to full wakefulness, listening for footsteps.

The moon rose in the blackened sky to drop glowing beams through the courtyard window. Prayer bells sounded for the evening worship. Still Corri waited, feeling instinctively that she must be ready for any chance at escape.

I must reach Imandoff, she thought. *There has to be a way to warn him. I have to try the techniques the healers taught me, the ones I have never been able to work without the owl stone.*

She composed herself for sleep again, this time centering all her thoughts and will on the tall sorcerer as she slipped into slumber.

When the dream finally came, it was a confusion of movement and sounds. Corri struggled as though caught in deep mud. She screamed her rage, then looked down at her legs. They were entwined with a faint line of purple that wound all about her lower limbs, tying her to the ground.

The High Clua has done something to hold me here. Corri was certain of that fact. *I could dream-fly before I ever came here, old woman, before I ever found the owl stone, and you will not stop me.*

I have become too dependent upon the stone, but by the Goddess I will dream-fly, and you will not stop me!

Corri called up all the techniques she had learned at Leshy. She centered her will on projecting an image of fire burning at the magical vine about her legs. The binding loosened but did not break free. She changed the picture to Imandoff's sword. She felt the great blade swish past her, heard a sharp snap and felt the restrictions fall away.

Her thoughts soared out to her sorcerer friend. Instantly, she was above the Mystery School, looking down at the enclosing walls around the massive stone buildings. There was a distinct purple glow emanating from the High Clua's rooms in the library, a tentacle of the woman's seeking thoughts whipping back and forth through the air. From her own shadow-self, a thin line of bright light led down toward her room where her physical self lay.

Imandoff, where are you!

Corri's thoughts searched for the inn where the sorcerer had his rooms. Like a hawk, she floated above the town, then darted downward, through the walls of a building and into a fire-bright room where her tall friend sat hunched over a scroll.

Imandoff, help me! Corri's hand tried to tug at his shirt. *I am a prisoner. Help me!* There was no response.

Her thoughts finally centered on the scroll, stretched flat between Imandoff's long-fingered hands. Her glance fell on the small mark in one corner, a hand holding a healing rod.

He has stolen it from the Mystery School! she thought. *You are better than I gave you credit for, old man.* She tried to catch the edge of the paper between her phantom fingers.

Imandoff looked around, a puzzled frown on his face. With a shrug, he bent once more over the scroll.

A feeling of danger flashed through Corri's mind. She felt herself jerked away, out of the inn, to hang once more above the School. A thick purple tentacle was rising to meet her.

The High Clua. She must not reach me, or I shall be trapped again!

Corri darted away, out over the Crystal Sands that lay at the foot of the mountain village, then over the grasslands of Tuone. *Takra, I must find Takra. I know she comes to join us.*

Ahead, but far away, was a sword-bright spark. Corri soared towards it, fearful that the High Clua would catch her. Her fear drove her faster, skimming the tall grass and arroyos as a bird before a predator. Far out over the grasslands of Tuone she fled, time and distance being as only the blink of an eye. At last she swayed to a stop beside a campfire where a figure in leather and mail sat staring off into the darkness, rubbing a sword with a whetstone.

Hear me, Takra, she pleaded. *Help me!*

Lightfoot snorted and stamped her feet, her eyes directly on Corri. Takra shuddered and leaped to her feet, sword at the ready. Her amber eyes stared across the low fire.

"Corri?" Takra's voice was barely more than a whisper. The warrior woman stretched out a hand, then drew it back as it passed through Corri's misty form. "What chances, Sister-Friend? Do you yet live?"

I am a prisoner in Leshy. Help me, Takra!

Corri felt a tug on her energy, turned to see a vaporous purple hand at the end of that treacherous tentacle. It pulled at the long, thin cord of light that stretched from her spirit-body back to the Mystery School. She gave a cry of rage and tried to resist. But, slowly, she was being recalled to her Mystery School prison.

She resisted with all her willpower as her mind went over all the lessons she had learned about the shadow-self. The drone of the teaching Sister's voice came back to her.

"It is rare to be attacked while seeking healing knowledge with the shadow-self. Rare, but not unheard of. Such attack can be countered by sending an image of a fear personal to the attacker. For if a person attacks in such a manner, then they have not dealt with their own inner faults. Faults or sins within ourselves are a breeding ground for fear."

Corri's shadow-self was now being dragged through the dark courtyard of the Mystery School straight toward the High Clua's rooms. *What does she fear most?* Corri asked herself. *Magic! And a loss of control over others.*

Corri gathered her strength as she was drawn through the walls into the candle-lit quarters of the School's mistress. In her mind she began to build a picture of the color of magic she had seen Imandoff produce, until she could see the blue glow sparking around her.

*T*he High Clua lay on her narrow bed in one corner of the room, hands folded over her flat breasts, a determined look of concentration on her face. The entrapping purple tentacle led straight to the High Clua's forehead. The purple hand about Corri's line of light began to dissolve as mist under a bright sun as magical blue flashes, produced in the girl's mind, flowed down her lifeline. The High Clua's body twitched as the old woman fought to regain control. With her mind Corri formed a wand of the blue magical glow and reached out to strike the woman on the forehead. The purple glow vanished. Instantly, Corri felt herself snap away and shoot across the courtyard to her narrow cell.

With a gasp, the girl sat up on the bed, heart pounding, her body wet with perspiration. The room was silent. She tried to stand and found herself so shaky that she had to lean against the cold stone wall. At last she gave up the effort and crawled back onto the hard cot, wrapping herself in the coarse blankets. She was too shaken to sleep the rest of the night.

Daylight brought another round of faint sounds of the School's rhythms. Trays of food appeared at the appropriate times. Corri forced herself to eat, gathering her strength and will against the appearance of the High Clua. Time dragged on, but the old woman did not come, nor did she send for the girl.

Neither did Imandoff appear.

Once more Corri watched the moon rise above the stone buildings from her window slit. She scanned the courtyard and the grim stone walls for all possible routes of escape, but saw no ledges or handholds that would be of any use. She knew that her greatest challenge lay in getting out of her room. Pulling herself up onto the ledge of the narrow slit of window, Corri found it was possible to squeeze her body through the opening; but it would be of little use, since the walls dropped straight down for three stories. The midnight call to prayer sounded and still she watched and thought and planned.

"Corri." There was a whisper at the door, followed by a scratching noise. The flap opened and a bundle slid inside.

Corri silently moved to the door and knelt next to the flap.

"It is I, Gertha. I could not get a key, but I found your belongings. Can you pick the lock?"

Corri fumbled with the bundle and found her knife and the circlet inside. She forced the thin dagger blade inside the lock, carefully turning and twisting it until she was rewarded with a quiet snick as the lock disengaged. Gertha pushed her way into the room, taking care not to shut the door completely.

"Here, dress in this." The girl held out a cloak worn by the members of Leshy, the bright blue and silver healer's patch on the breast. "I have been called into the town for a healing. We will go together," she whispered. "It is the only way to get you through the gates."

"Why do you do this?" Corri shrugged into the cloak and gathered her belongings.

"It is against our law, what the High Clua was doing, to keep you here by force. She was being misled by the woman Malya and by her own pride."

"That woman who is always following at the High Clua's heels like a lap dog?" Corri asked, and Gertha nodded. "Beware of that one, Gertha. Her actions say she is obedient to the High Clua's will, but her eyes say different."

Gertha pulled at Corri's arm. "Now the High Clua lies ill from her misdeeds, and Malya thinks to take her place. The higher Brothers and Sisters meet at this hour. They are divided, some supporting Malya, others not. This is the only time you have to escape."

Hoods up, the two women crept into the passageway and down the stairs to the courtyard. The moonlight turned the wandering paths into a crazy pattern of silver and black. Back straight, Gertha headed for the massive gates, closed for the night and guarded by the watchful eyes of those chosen by the High Clua.

Corri kept her face away from the guard's lantern as Gertha explained her mission and presented her papers. Not until the great gates shut behind them did she realize how frightened she had been of being discovered and returned to the prison of her room. She matched the healer's quick gait down the silent streets.

"Ahead is the inn where the sorcerer stays." Gertha pointed down a side-street, toward a lantern-lit entrance. "Good fortune go with you, Corri. It would best serve you to be gone from this town before morning."

"My thanks," Corri said. "May the Goddess walk with you."

Gertha turned and hurried up the dark streets on her errand of mercy. Corri headed toward the lanterns at the inn's door, then paused near an alley. Something did not feel right. Had Gertha misled her? She thought not; the girl sincerely believed in the ancient laws of Leshy and practiced them.

But her thief's instincts were aroused. She slipped inside the alley and waited. Her thoughts ranged back over the dream-flying experience. Takra had seen as well as heard her, she was certain. But Imandoff—she shook her head, he was so involved in the scroll he read that he had dismissed her presence.

The sound of male voices drew near from the direction of the inn. Corri flattened herself against the wall, listening intently. Two men paused in the half-shadows at the corner of the building.

"The message worked," one man said. "He went directly to the School as soon as Malya delivered it. He will be busy with arguments before the higher healers and will not know, until too late, that the girl has been taken."

"Is the girl still locked up there?" It was Druk's voice.

Oh Goddess, he has trailed me here some way! Corri fought down the fear that threatened to engulf her thinking and forced herself to remain calm.

"Malya says it is so. The High Clua lies ill. They now wrangle over leadership, which is to our advantage. One of Malya's followers will let us in."

"And we can have Farblood out and on her way back to Grimmel before dawn." Druk laughed. "The price for her return has increased. I shall be a rich man."

"And my pay for arranging this?" The voice was tinged with suspicion.

Corri heard the clink of coins as a bag passed from Druk to the other shadowy man. The two moved off in the direction of the Mystery School.

Corri counted to fifty before she peered from the alley. The street was empty. Quickly, she walked to the inn, passing through the narrow side-gate to the stables. She found the roan and Mouse saddled, as if the sorcerer planned a hasty journey within the next few hours. She shoved her belongings from the School into a saddlebag, then stealthily led out her mount. Imandoff would have to follow as best he could. It was too dangerous now for her to wait. Between the possessiveness of the School and now the danger of Druk, the city of Leshy could well be a pit of intrigue.

She paused only once in her quiet trek through the dark streets, to fill the water bottles slung from the saddle. The city gates would be closed at this hour, she knew, but she hoped that her cloak from the School would grant her passage without questions. It was so. The guard touched his forehead as he opened one gate, asking for no papers.

When Corri and Imandoff came to Leshy, they had arrived from the southwest, out of the mountains of Deep Rising. For a brief time, as they journeyed down the rugged mountain trail toward the city, the storm had lifted and the grasslands of Tuone had been barely visible in the distance.

As they had entered Leshy at nightfall, she had only glimpsed the desert area Imandoff named as the Crystal Sands. "A five mile stretch of barren, glittering sands, broken by one lone oasis along the caravan route," he had said. Now she faced that desert expanse with no idea of which way to go.

The deep night stillness was broken by the jingle of caravan bells. Close behind her came a merchant with his string of pack mules. She pulled her horse to one side as the caravan passed.

"Well met, Holy One," the man called. "You are welcome to company with us as far as you wish."

Corri raised her hand and traced the healing symbol as she had seen done so many times in the Mystery School. The man briefly bowed his head, then rode on. The girl waited until the last of the mules passed, then brought Mouse around to follow.

The night skies were faintly tinged with the pink of dawn when the line of pack mules reached the end of the desert. Corri looked back, amazed at how the brilliant sands ended and the grasslands began, as if a giant hand had marked a boundary that neither dared to cross.

She turned farther in the saddle, then shielded her eyes against the glint of the rising sun on the mirror-like sands. Three horses were moving fast along the road from Leshy. Corri's heart leaped.

Imandoff does not ride with them. I waited too long, she thought in panic. *It must be Druk.*

She wheeled her horse out of line and kicked her into a trot with her heels. The tall grass of Tuone swished about her boots as she headed into the plains, without any clue as to where she was going.

Escape into nothing is better than capture, she reasoned, as she urged the horse on. In the low sheltered dips of the grasslands were dirty patches of late snow, tracked with the prints of desert hares and birds.

Behind her the jingle of bells receded. She turned once to see if by chance Druk had gone on, but the men were now swerving to follow her. She urged Mouse faster, the tall grass whipping against her legs. The race had begun.

Chapter 16

"She cannot have vanished!" The young woman facing the assembled initiates tapped her foot, her hands on her hips. "The High Clua gave orders that this Corri was not to leave the School for any reason. Did the gate-guards see any unauthorized persons leave at all?"

"No, Malya," said one of the women, her mouth pursed in disapproval. "Only those healers who were called to tend the sick."

Malya brushed back a tendril of dark hair, its red tints plain in the light of the candles. The small mole at the left corner of her mouth twitched as she tightened her lips in anger.

"Well, someone was careless, and the High Clua will not be pleased." Malya's pale blue eyes raked across the assembled initiates. "I showed you her letter to be read if something should happen to her."

And if I take the old woman's place as I plan, you have no idea how displeased I will be! she thought, *or the changes in laws I will create here.*

"We have only your word that keeping the girl was the High Clua's wish," said an older initiate, his arms folded across his chest, his eyes challenging. "The High Clua is in a coma and can speak to no one. As for the letter…" he let the words slid off into silence.

No one can ever prove the old woman did not write that letter, Malya thought smugly. *I practiced long to get her handwriting almost perfect.*

"How dare you question the motives and will of the High Clua? She has ordered that no one with power is to leave the School without her permission," snapped another man. "And I agree with the new laws she has instituted here. Leshy cannot let those with power slip from our grasp."

"These new laws were not voted upon by all the initiates," the older man said, his eyes hard. "That in itself is against the laws of Leshy. There must be full agreement on any change in policy."

"True," answered a very old woman, her face lined with age. "And you, girl," she pointed her cane at Malya, "have encouraged the High Clua in her bid for supreme power here, most likely in hopes we will now appoint you in her place should she die. You will get no such vote from me."

"Nor I," answered several other initiates.

How many of them are on my side? Malya's pale blue eyes swiftly scanned the room beneath her half-lowered lids. *Have I moved too fast, or not fast enough?*

"The School was never meant to be a trap for anyone who did not wish to stay." A plump middle-aged woman with freckles and a wide, laughing mouth stood up. Her green eyes were calm as she faced Malya. "I know your mother Uzza well. She sent you to us in hopes you would learn ethics and self-discipline, neither of which appear to interest you. Since you have no healing power whatsoever, I must assume you encourage the High Clua's wishes and follow her like a little dog for one reason only—you have plans to take control of Leshy yourself."

"How can you say such a thing, Jehennette?" Malya held up her hands in protest. "The High Clua is a great leader. Her will should be obeyed without question."

"Such as her wish that you take her place?" The older man frowned at the girl. "We do not even know if that letter was written by her. Even if it was, that is not the way here at Leshy. Our laws say that next High Clua can only be chosen by the vote of all the initiates, and that is what we will do if she dies."

"The laws also state that if the High Clua can no longer lead effectively, the initiates shall choose another to take her place." Jehennette folded her dimpled hands about her prayer beads as she looked around the room. "I think the time has come, whether or not she recovers. Indeed, it is my opinion as a healer that she will die in the coma, and soon. Brothers and Sisters, I vote for calling a conclave immediately."

The initiates burst into argument, some backing Malya, but most of them standing firm behind Jehennette.

The old fool cannot die soon enough for me, Malya thought, her pretty oval face carefully wiped clean of her inner emotions. *But have I convinced enough initiates to vote for me? If not, I will leave this place and follow Corri.* She fingered the chain of the strange pendant she wore concealed under her robe. *Kayth would want me to do this. And if that sorcerer comes in answer to the note I sent in the High Clua's name, he will surely create a ruckus when the gate-guard refuses to admit him. That should cause even more confusion, perhaps more than enough for my followers to gain control here.*

Imandoff stood before the gates of the Mystery School, walking staff in hand, its bright metal cap winking in the reflected light. His anger was plain on his face, illuminated as it was by the light of the lantern hanging above the grille in the wall.

"Tell the High Clua I must speak with her. It is most urgent. She sent this message to me, asking that I come." The sorcerer's voice held a sharp edge of threat as he displayed the scrap of parchment. The argument had been long and heated.

"I was told to admit no one except the healers," the guard said. "The High Clua lies ill, perhaps dying, and a conclave chooses her successor. Besides, that is not the writing of the High Clua. Go away, sorcerer." The cover of the grille slammed shut.

"By the Nine Words of Natira, Corri will be freed. Not even the High Clua can break the laws of Leshy!" The sorcerer slammed the end of his staff against the cobblestones. *It will only cause more troubles if I force my way in,* he thought. *Something tells me that is what this letter-writer wants. Therefore, I will get to Corri another way.*

Imandoff stamped back toward the inn. Before he had gone far, a shadow detached itself from a side street. A man approached and lowered his hood. In the light of a lantern hung before a private house, Imandoff saw the bright red hair before he saw the face.

"Kayth Farblood! After all these years, you appear, and in this place." Imandoff clasped arms with the stocky man. "Where have you been? Why have I not heard from you all this time?"

"The girl is gone from Leshy." The man's face was unmarked by any emotion. "She rode through the north gate more than half an hour ago." Kayth shifted his stocky body slightly, dropping one hand casually onto the hilt of the knife at his belt. His cold pale eyes held no sign of emotion as he stared at Imandoff.

Imandoff dropped his hand. "You did nothing to stop her? Your own daughter, and you let her go into the Crystal Sands and the grasslands alone." *I see in you now what I always suspected lurked beneath the face you showed to the world. Once I*

*called you friend, although I was careful not to let you too close.
Now I must call you enemy.*

"I tell this to you so you need not follow. The girl is no
longer your concern. Grimmel's men are behind her. She will
be returned to Hadliden where she belongs." Kayth's face
might have been carved from stone.

"Why? And why did you leave her with that miserable
being in the first place? Do you know what he plans?"
Imandoff's long fingers tightened into a fist in the neck of
Kayth's tunic.

"Times were hard, and I had other plans that did not
include a child." Kayth jerked the sorcerer's hand free. "Grimmel paid me well, enough to live a free life all these years. I
made a bargain. She must return to Hadliden."

"He forced her to marry him because of some idiot idea
about a gifted child." Imandoff's jaw set in anger. "You know
what Grimmel is, Kayth. How could you do that to your own
child? Why did you not give her to me when Ryanna died?"

"You were off hunting down old ruins, remember?" The
man stared coldly at Imandoff in the flickering light.

"And I had no money." Imandoff let out his breath in a
hiss. "I would have expected more from a star man. Yes, I have
guessed who and what you are. While I was off looking for
old ruins, I was also gathering gossip, rumors of strange men
who appeared but were not of the blood of the Peoples. The
Tuonela have a story that began shortly after I first met you, a
tale of a strange sky-bird that landed in the far mountains and
gives out death to anyone who approach it. I could cause your
imprisonment, you know that. Fear of invaders from beyond
the moon might even bring about your death."

"But you will not, Imandoff." Kayth smiled, a mere flexing
of his mouth with no warmth in it. "Not because of friendship, no, but because it would also rebound on my daughter.
And possibly on you, sorcerer, for keeping the secret these
many years."

"Fate will pay you in full, Kayth. I need not raise my hand against you." Imandoff sniffed the air, puzzled at a vague odor that wafted from Kayth's clothing. "Where have you walked, star man, that the scent of Frav lingers with you?"

"Nowhere and everywhere, Imandoff. I am only a traveler, a far-riding merchant who gathers strange and exotic goods." Kayth pointed toward the city gates. "Druk will have her before she goes far. Go back to your search after the Forgotten Ones, sorcerer. Grimmel is not a man to cross." Kayth fixed him with a level stare.

"You knew I would come to the School this night. That is why you waited here. And only one person could have told you, the one who sent this note." He held the parchment before Kayth's eyes. "This note is not from the High Clua, then, but from one within the walls who does your will."

"Malya has her uses." Kayth's blunt hand tightened on the knife hilt as he watched the anger grow in Imandoff's eyes.

"This Malya must be one of Grimmel's tools, as I now know are you. May the Lady forgive you, Kayth. I cannot." Imandoff turned and hurried toward the inn.

He roused the stableboy with his noisy entrance as he banged open the side-gate. Pushing the sleepy boy aside, the sorcerer led out Sun-Dancer. He filled the water bottles at the inn fountain, then paid the innkeeper who now hung about the entrance. Mounting the roan, he trotted off. The city guard reluctantly opened the massive gates at the sorcerer's snapped orders, then jumped out of the way as Imandoff kicked his mount into a gallop at the gates.

"Pray I am not too late, Kayth," Imandoff said softly to himself, "or I will give Fate a hand in dealing out justice."

The sorcerer rode through the night as fast as the trail through the Crystal Sands would allow. Shortly after dawn he saw a mule caravan ahead of him. He pushed the roan to the front of the line and waved a greeting to the leader.

"Have you seen a young woman coming this way, one riding a mouse-colored mare?" he asked.

"It was a Holy Sister, then." The leader pointed off into the grasslands. "She left us some ways back. Three men followed. Since none dare harm a healer, we let them go. Must be an illness in one of the Tuonela clans that the shakkas cannot cure."

Imandoff wheeled his horse and headed out into the vast grasslands. He thought over all the ways to find Corri, discarding each as it surfaced in his mind. Like it or not, he must soon do a far-seeking. The great plains were full of too many arroyos, too many hiding places, to go blindly. He could pass within a half mile of her, even in the open, and never see her.

At last Imandoff pulled the roan to a stop and dismounted. He dug in his saddlebag and brought out the luminous blue stone that had been lodged in the ancient altar in the Valley of Whispers.

"Great Goddess, help me," he said. "I must find her. I pray my feelings about this stone are right."

Taking a deep breath, the sorcerer held the ancient stone to his forehead. The inflow of power staggered him so that he leaned back against the horse.

At last the picture, brought into his mind by the stone, began to clear. He saw nothing but waves of windswept grass. He turned his head more to the north. Still nothing. By degrees he moved his position until he saw, far off, the figures of mounted horses. Three followed at a swift pace, the fourth strained ahead.

"Corri!" Imandoff's shout made the roan dance beside him. "By the Powers that be, I hope I am not too late." The sorcerer recalled his feeling of uneasiness of the night past. "She must have tried to contact me, and I was too engrossed in the scroll."

Imandoff again mounted and pulled Sun-Dancer to face the direction in which he had visioned the riders.

"Hold fast, Corri," he whispered. "I pray that I do not fail you again." He kicked the horse into a gallop into the plains.

Chapter 17

Takra Wind-Rider shivered beside her fire. Although the air was touched with the mildness of early spring and the fire hot against her outstretched hands, she was cold to the core of her heart. She stared up at the edges of the arroyo in which she camped, the tall grass high above swishing only slightly in an evening breeze.

"You saw her too, did you not, Lightfoot?"

The horse nickered and pushed her nose against Takra's shoulder. The sword-woman fingered her silver amulet as she stared into the flames.

"She was here, yet she was not here. With a sorcerer's apprentice, how can I be certain that I saw her shadow-self and not her spirit on its way Between Worlds?" She clasped the amulet in one fist. "I must know!"

Takra slipped the amulet chain over her head and drew out her long dagger. Pressing the ball of her thumb against the sharp tip of the knife, she let three drops of blood fall on the smooth back of the amulet.

"It runs freely." Takra drew a deep breath. She wiped the amulet clean on a tuft of grass and strung it once again around her neck. "She is not Between Worlds, or the blood would have congealed at once. Her cry to my mind was a call for aid. Something is very wrong for Farblood to call out to me."

Takra rose and saddled the horse. She smothered the fire with dirt, then gathered her blankets to tie them in place at the back of the saddle.

"Something must have gone wrong at that School," she said to Lightfoot. "I never trusted those mum-tongued, smug-faced healers. We ride for Leshy."

The warrior woman turned the horse to the southwest. Because the dawn had not yet broken, she let Lightfoot choose her own pace, trusting the mount's instincts to guide them safely through the rolling Tuone grasslands, pocked with snow-lined holes and sudden gullies. But Takra's thoughts soared ahead, to the thief she called Sister-Friend and to what could have driven the young girl to seek her in such a desperate fashion.

Corri led her mount down into a rocky gully, its sharp water-cut banks providing shelter from the persistent wind and hot sun. She had not believed the early spring sun would be this warm. Its persistent rays were rapidly melting even the most stubborn pockets of thin, frozen snow.

She had managed to stay ahead of Druk and his men for two days during the long trek out into the featureless grasslands. Since this dawn she had stayed out of their sight, but she knew that was only by luck, and luck could change at any moment. Now both she and Mouse must rest again. A pool of rainwater lay back under the edge of the bank in a half-formed cave. She filled her water bottles, then let the mare drink.

"We must rest if we are to stay out of Druk's clutches," she said as she rubbed down the horse as best she could. "I have traveled far along my life-path, Mouse. Before I met Imandoff, I had never ridden the likes of you." Silently, she thanked the sorcerer for the knowledge of horses that he insisted she learn when they first journeyed together.

The tethered horse fell to cropping the short grass at the edge of the pool. Corri crawled back into the shelter of the damp overhang and fell into an exhausted, dreamless slumber.

When Corri woke, it was instantly, every sense alert to the sounds of the land about her. The sun was low in the west, its warm rays striking down through the arroyo into her eyes. Mouse blew and nosed against her, as if impatient to be on their way.

No sound reached her ears except the whisper of the wind through the tall grass, an occasional ripple of song and drum of wings from some plains bird. As quietly as possible, she led the mare up out of the arroyo and mounted.

Corri turned to look along her back trail, one hand shielding her eyes. Less than half a mile behind, she saw the dark shapes of three riders coursing the grasslands. "Druk!" Her heart began to pound. "By the blessed Goddess, I thought he would give up by now."

There was a faint shout, and the three riders surged forward. Corri kicked her horse into a run, turning its head straight into the depths of the plains. As far as she could see, there was no sign of tree or shelter. She knew, from the trail she had ridden this far, that arroyos suddenly appeared. She held the reins lightly, trusting Mouse to avoid such dangers, not daring to force the horse to move faster.

Twice she turned to see her pursuers were pushing their mounts to the limit. Fear began to grip her by the throat. Alone, she had no chance of escape if they surrounded her.

I must ride as far as I can, she thought frantically. *There are too many for me to face. Perhaps if I keep riding, they will give up or I can lose them.* Her heart jumped at the thought of unseen holes hidden under the prairie grass, but she still urged Mouse on. *I would rather take a fall and break my neck than be returned to Grimmel!*

Mouse tossed her head, nickered shrilly and pulled off to the northeast. Corri saw a rider coming toward her, sun glinting off mail.

"A Tuonela? I choose to take my chances with that rider rather than those that follow."

Corri let the reins hang free. Her mount surged ahead. The Tuonela rider swiftly closed the gap between them. Corri now saw the pale hair blowing in the prairie breeze, the gray speckles on the horse's dark hide.

"Corri Farblood!" The rider raised a hand in salute, the ancient wrist-cuff flashing in the sun.

"Takra?" Corri waved. "How did you find me?" she called back.

"To me, quickly!" The warrior woman drew her sword and drove her heels into Lightfoot's sides. "They come."

Corri glanced behind and saw Druk and his men pounding down upon her. Frantic, she kicked Mouse into a gallop, forgetting the hidden dangers of the plains. She raced past Takra and whirled the horse around to face her pursuers.

With a war cry, Takra rode directly into the men, swinging the sword with deadly accuracy. One man screamed and fell from his mount, a spouting death-wound on his head. Lightfoot reared, hooves slashing. Druk left the battle to advance on Corri while the other man, seemingly more skilled at swordplay, engaged Takra.

Corri drew her dagger and waited, determined to run no farther regardless of her fear. Her mare danced nervously as Druk and his blowing mount rode up.

"There is no escape, Farblood." Druk's mouth was drawn up in a malicious grin. "This time you will return to Grimmel for certain."

He grabbed for the reins. Corri slashed out with her knife, leaving a long scratch down the assassin's hand before he could jerk it out of reach.

"Never! I would rather die!"

"That is not your fate, thief. But Grimmel will likely make you wish you had."

Druk made another grab at her as the two horses danced wildly. She slashed at him with the knife, but the assassin ducked, coming up under her wild swing to land his fist full along her jaw. The knife flew from her hand, and she sailed off the horse to land with a thud on the water-logged ground.

"Your friend will die, Farblood." Druk pulled her up by her hair and hit her again. "It will all have been for nothing."

Corri, though half-dazed, exploded into action, scratching at Druk's eyes, sinking her teeth into his arm. One booted foot caught the man on the thigh, missing his groin, which had been her target. He staggered back, releasing his hold. Corri ran for her horse, but Druk was on her before she could reach it. They rolled in the long grass, Druk struggling for a hold on her throat, Corri clawing in a silent battle for her freedom. The assassin's fingers were about her throat, cutting off her breath. A man's scream of pain rang out, and Druk's hold loosened. Corri gasped for air and felt the restraining weight leave her body. She struggled to her feet. Her eyesight still dotted with black specks, she saw Druk mount his horse and pound off toward Leshy.

"Corri!" Takra leaped from her horse and ran towards the girl, stained sword in one hand. "Are you harmed?"

"No, thank the Goddess. I thought my luck had run out." Corri coughed; her throat felt raw. "Druk?" She watched the slow drip of blood from the sword's edge.

"He flees, like the coward he is." Takra stooped to wipe the sword clean on the grass. "When his hireling screamed from the death-blow, he fled back to Leshy." She waved the weapon in the direction of the Crystal Sands.

"I cannot return there, Takra." Corri hunted in the deep grass for her dagger, then slid it back into her boot. "It is a long tale, one I would tell well away from here."

"Then you are finished with that prison of a School." Takra sheathed the sword and spoke softly to Lightfoot. The horse pricked her ears, then trotted off to gather the other mounts. "Where is Imandoff?"

"I do not know where he is," Corri answered as she mounted her mare. "I was pressed for time when I left, and he was not at the inn. I overheard Druk say that he had been summoned by the High Clua, although I cannot see how that could be."

Takra dismounted and caught the wild-eyed horses of the men who had ridden with Druk. With rope from one of the saddles, she tied one horse to her saddle, the other to Corri's.

"I saw you two nights ago, as clear as I do now." Takra headed Lightfoot toward the setting sun, and Corri followed. "But when I tried to touch you, my hand went through your body. For a time I knew not whether you were alive or dead."

"We should have left Leshy long ago, but Imandoff still searched in the library. And we waited for you."

"A storm delayed my ride. And there have been more raids on the border between Frav and Tuone. Something has stirred up that foul nest like a hive of bees prodded with a stick. To add to the trouble, the guarding spells seem to be weakening."

"Where to now?" Corri asked. "Will Imandoff be able to find us?"

"We will join the Clan of the Asperel on their yearly journey to Neeba," Takra said. "They camp not far from here. If Imandoff follows, he will know to seek us among the gathering of the Clans."

The two rode on through the gathering dusk.

Imandoff saw one rider, well to the east, as he sought for Corri. *Not Tuonela,* he thought as he studied the way the man rode his horse. *That can only be one of the men who went after Corri. But where are the others? Did she act so well when they attacked that only one survives? A* sudden thought brought a grim smile to his face. *Perhaps she found Tuonela help. Still, she could be injured or dead.*

Fearful of what he would find, still the sorcerer pushed on, his gray eyes on the circling scavengers high overhead in the distance. He had not realized just how afraid he had been until he looked down on the bodies of two men, sword-slain in the tall grass.

"Dead several hours." Imandoff used his knife to lift back the torn clothing from the wounds. "This is the work of a sword, not a belt knife. Some Tuonela must have aided her." His sharp eyes read the signs in the bent grass, riders heading into the west. "Two horses, with others following. At least I know she still lives and where to find her."

The sorcerer turned toward the far western sea-cliffs and the oasis town of Neeba.

For two days Takra and Corri rode through the swaying grasses of Tuone, buffeted by occasional spring squalls and the constant prairie winds. The sword-woman shared her trail rations and confidently led them from one hidden water hole to another until they finally sighted the first Clan herds.

The Clan of the Asperel camped around a shallow rain pool, the wide, gently sloping sides of the ground around it covered with their wagon-tents. Takra and Corri were greeted by outriders of the herds, suspicious until they saw Takra's blue tattoo on her left cheek.

"Hail, Takra Wind-Rider," called one of the men as he rode up. "Do you ride with us to Neeba, to the Making Ceremony?"

"Tirkul, kin-brother." Takra and the man clasped wrists. "Greetings and blessings on the Clan of the Asperel. Where rides the shakka?"

"Ill news?" Tirkul eyed Corri and the riderless horses in curiosity. "You come from the border wars. How goes it?"

"The guard at the border holds, though last fall two Volikvis breached the ancient guarding spells. One died before he had gone a quarter mile, the other I hunted down in Kirisan and killed. But surely that is old news. Thus far this season no Fravashi soldiers or priests have entered Tuone. I believe they cannot. How the Volikvis could pass the spells, that is strange." Takra nodded as Tirkul narrowed his dark eyes. "But we ride from battle of another kind. This is my Sister-Friend, Corri Farblood. She flees from slavery by a master fiend in Hadliden." Takra touched Corri on the shoulder.

"Slavery!" The word was a hiss through Tirkul's teeth. His clean-cut jaw set in anger. "And Hadliden, the city of a thousand vices." He spat into the grass. "A thousand long deaths to slavers. You are safe among the Clans, Corri Farblood."

The warrior Tirkul was tall, as tall as Imandoff, Corri noted, but then all of the Tuonela were taller than she, more than a head taller than the men of Asur. She watched the warrior from the corners of her eyes. Tirkul was stockier than the sorcerer, his shoulders and arms well-muscled from sword practice, his legs lean and hard.

Tirkul called for another to take his guard place. A woman with a child seated in front of her rode up, spear tall in its place near her left boot, sword strapped at her waist. Tirkul nodded in recognition, then led Takra and Corri through the grazing herds of goats and horses toward the main encampment.

Corri looked about her with interest as they threaded their way in and out among the wagon-tents. The dwellings were each built on a wheeled platform, the colorful hides drawn over a framework to make a compact living area. The front flaps were all turned back, letting in the evening breeze.

Children ran among the wagons, laughing and playing some child's game. Women and men sat, either on the steps of the open wagon-tents or on horseback, swirling spindles threaded with soft goat wool. From the fires at each wagon arose the odor of cooking; the rich aromas set Corri's stomach grumbling and made her aware of the past two days without more than a mouthful of water and a portion of journey bread.

Tirkul dismounted before a wagon-tent decorated with strange symbols, some of which Corri recognized from her studies at Leshy. Corri and Takra slid down to stand beside the warrior as he saluted the owner of the wagon.

On the step before the open flap, a wiry old woman, dressed in the Tuonela leather trousers, riding boots, and a long leather tunic sat, watching them with dark eyes. Her white hair fell in two braids over her stooped shoulders.

"Greetings, Halka." Tirkul held his hand up, palm forward. He stood tall, the muscles of his broad shoulders moving under his leather tunic.

"I see you, Tirkul." The shakka rose and sketched a sign before the three riders. "I have awaited the coming of the far-travelers. You have blooded your sword, Takra Wind-Rider, warrior of Frayma's Mare. It is good." The old woman climbed down and hobbled to stand beside Corri. "The Dream-Warrior, I greet you. You must gather strength among us, for your long journey is not yet finished." She brushed a wrinkled finger against Corri's dusty forehead.

The shakka must have been a tall woman in her younger days, Corri thought, for she still topped the girl's height, although her back was beginning to stoop with age.

"How do you know me?" Corri asked. "I have never seen you."

"Ah, but I have seen you, girl. In my dream-visions I have seen you and your coming to the Clan of the Asperel. Your inner spirit shines like a star." The old shakka smiled slyly. "Yes, like a star."

Halka motioned Takra and Corri to enter her wagon-tent, but sent Tirkul on his way to care for the horses. As Corri's eyes adjusted to the dim interior, she was astonished at what she saw. The rough barbarian existence seen on the outside stopped at the turned-back flap. At the rear of the wagon, facing the flap, was a small altar set with a roughly carved statue of a woman, a colt beside her. Beside the statue was a small decorated pot holding a burning tallow candle.

Along each side of the wagon were narrow sleeping pallets, the goat-hair blankets rich with woven patterns. The hide walls were completely covered with other blankets, their thickness insulating against the grasslands' nearly-constant wind. Bunches of dried herbs hung from the ridge pole, their mingled scents filling the air. A number of small carved chests dotted the interior, providing both storage and seating.

The shakka sat down on a chest before the altar and fixed Corri with her bird-bright eyes. "Tell me of your adventures," she demanded.

Corri found herself telling her tale from the beginning. Takra listened with interest, adding a few details here and there. The shakka nodded from time to time, as if the story confirmed something she already knew.

"This Grimmel, in my dreams he spoke of a mind-seeker that aids him in directing his hunters," the shakka finally said. "From his words I think it is a seeker like none I have ever seen, for it is not a person. This strange device, it must be a thing made by man and attuned to you alone. Until that is found and destroyed, you will have no real freedom."

"What does this seeker look like?" Takra leaned forward, a frown on her face.

"I could only see what the man Grimmel held and hear what he said." The shakka turned to gaze at Corri. "A man from Asur, and as devious as this Grimmel, would likely put such a seeker inside a collar such as their women wear."

Corri's hand went instinctively to her throat. "Imandoff removed such a collar, but I did not keep it. He put it in his saddlebags, not mine. All the time I was in the School, the collar was nowhere near me." She looked at Takra in puzzlement.

"Then how did those men know where you were?" Takra shook her head.

"It does not matter now," said the shakka. "I will send word among the warriors to watch for any strange men."

"We have your permission to travel with you to Neeba? Corri will be safe among the Clan." Takra fidgeted with her dagger hilt. "Imandoff will seek us there, I know it."

"You ride under the hand and protection of the Lady." The shakka's finger drew another pattern in the air. "You sleep here," she pointed to the wagon floor. "I think the seeker, whatever its nature, will have difficulty finding you in this place. My warding spells are strong."

After the evening meal, Takra took Corri with her in a round of the Clan wagons to meet old friends and blood-kin. The thief was not surprised when Tirkul joined them, nor when she discovered that Tirkul's family had raised Takra. She found herself feeling shy and a little embarrassed whenever the young warrior smiled at her.

He is handsome, she thought. *What will he think when he finds out I am a thief? And the wife of the master thief of Hadliden?*

But she smiled in return, then looked quickly away and walked closer to Takra. In her quick, furtive glances at Tirkul, Corri glimpsed a tattoo on the back of his right hand, a winged globe, and realized she had seen it on many of the clan members. She was very much aware of the tall warrior, his narrow waist and muscled arms. Even when she kept her eyes resolutely turned away, she could feel him watching her.

It was fully dark when the women returned to the shakka's wagon-tent to curl up on the soft blankets. Corri lay awake for some time, listening to the quiet breathing of the old woman and Takra. Finally she took out the circlet with the owl stone and laid it next to her, one hand caressing the strange stone. Her mind was on Imandoff as she slid off into sleep.

There seemed to be no period of dreamless slumber. Corri went from a sleepy wakefulness directly into a vision dream. She found herself floating above the encampment, the great grasslands spread around them, reaching to the far horizons in dips and swells. The moon shone above, one black corner marking its slow turn toward its dark phase. The Tuonela guards rode on their rounds, the herds quiet under the dying night breeze.

Corri could not say why she swung to the east, her shadow-self peering as if to see the mountains that were not even visible to the physical eyes. She felt that danger came from there. A rumble of thunder rolled far away over the grasslands. She strained to pull free, to go to that distant place, but she was held fast just above the wagon.

Danger comes, she thought. *But what danger?*

The storm was moving fast, faster than normal, its thick-bellied clouds heavy with moisture. The wind blew stronger, forerunner of the storm that dropped its load of water miles from the campground. Corri could hear the rattle of the tent hides now. Far away she detected the pound of rain, the rush of water down arroyos.

"No!" Panic pierced her to the bone, and she screamed aloud.

She tried now to retreat to her physical body but found that as impossible as moving out to meet the storm. She struggled, her shadow-self whipping in the rising winds.

I must use my mind, she thought, her fears now sharp.

She began to visualize herself pulling hand over hand along the connecting cord of light down toward the roof of the wagon. A deep rumble brought her eyes back toward the distant range of grasslands. Suddenly, Corri knew what the danger was.

"Run! Danger comes!" She could hear her physical screams but could not reunite her shadow-self with her body.

A dry, firm hand touched her physical forehead, and she snapped back. The shakka was bending over her, concern on her wrinkled face. Takra stood behind the woman, lantern in hand.

"What comes, girl?" The old shakka's voice was rock-steady.

"A wall of water!" Corri's voice was still panic-tinged. She listened for the sound of rain drumming on the wagon. "There is no rain here. What did I see?"

"Rouse the camp, Wind-Rider. The wagons must be moved to higher ground." The shakka held out a cup to Corri and forced her to drink the bitter, cold liquid. "Come, girl, we must mount and ride from this place. Storm water of the kind you saw can kill without warning. What you saw comes from afar. There need be no rain here to put us in danger."

The camp was bustling at Takra's first shouts. Corri looked about her in surprise; each person knew their duty; there was little confusion, even though most had roused from sleep. Within minutes the entire Clan, wagons and herds, was on the move to high ground.

Corri rode with Takra near the rear of the herds, keeping a lookout for stragglers. Even though the camping spot was behind them now, her nerves were raw with waiting. It took all her willpower not to push her horse into a gallop.

"We go too slow," she shouted to Takra over the whistling wind. A feeling of desperate panic filled her. "The water comes! We will never outrun it!"

Behind them a rumbling could be heard over the wind, a rushing, rolling sound that drew nearer with each minute.

Chapter 18

The last of the wagon-tents drew up on a high prairie hill, with the herds following. Corri looked back to the east. She saw a distant boiling wall of water, just visible in the moonlight, pouring down the low spaces between the mounds of rolling hills. At the end of the herds, a child darted back to gather up a small goat that bleated in fear. No one seemed aware of the child's danger.

Corri screamed, but the howling wind carried away the sound. Mouse refused to turn, to face the death-water rushing toward them. Corri leaped down and ran for the child, still trying to scream a warning over the wind. The child looked back at the boiling water and began to run.

Oh Goddess, she cannot die! She is a child! Without a thought to her own safety, her subconscious mind, with its deep-buried memories of her own mistreatment, spurred her on.

Just as Corri reached the child, the little girl tripped, falling flat on the slick grass, the goat leaping out of her arms and up the embankment. With a quick glance at the flood, now nearly upon them, Corri scooped up the child and ran.

I will never make it, she thought as she fought her way to the bottom of the mound.

Corri threw the child ahead of her to safety just as the wall of flood water bore down on her. She saw the strong arms that pulled the little girl upward, out of danger. Just as the water caught Corri, sweeping her feet out from under her, a thin rope fell about her shoulders and slithered down under her upraised arms. The rope tightened, dragging her against the wild current. The water closed over her head, filled her nose and throat. In panic, Corri struck out with her arms and legs. Finally, she rose to the surface of the flood, bobbing there like so much flotsam. The roar in her ears lessened as she fought to keep afloat. Finally, she realized that the storm had moved directly overhead; the rain beat down upon her.

The pull on the rope increased. She was slowly being dragged toward the rain-slicked bank. A Tuonela warrior leaped, slid down the bank, one foot dangerously near the sweeping water, the thin lariat tight in his fist. He reached out a sun-browned hand, his words lost in the wind.

Corri grabbed at the outstretched hand, missed, and grabbed again. The warrior's grip was near bone-crushing as he dragged her upward to safety. He gathered her in his arms and fought his way against the wind, up to the waiting Clan.

"Corri." The hard-breathed words next to her ear brought her out of her daze. "Corri," he repeated.

She recognized Tirkul's voice. She felt the pound of his heart in his muscled chest, the sharp hiss of his heavy breathing against her hair. She turned her head to cough and brought up water. The warrior's hold tightened as they were surrounded by Clan members.

"This way!" Takra peered down at Corri and pointed off toward the mass of wagons. "The shakka."

The rope was removed, but the warrior refused to let anyone else take her. He pushed his way through the crowd of onlookers to the wagon-tent, where the shakka waited, holding back the tent flap. He carried Corri inside and laid her gently on one of the pallets.

"You are safe." Tirkul sat on the floor beside Corri, holding one of her hands. His strong cheek bones glistened from the drops of rain still on his face. "She will be well?" He turned to the old shakka.

"She will be well." The old woman cocked her head, listening to the dying storm. "A Tuonela she is at heart. As brave as you, when you risked your life at the edge of the water."

"A good throw, Tirkul," Takra said. "The best I have seen. To throw against the wind, that takes the keen eye of the asperel."

"My thanks." Corri coughed up more water, her throat raw from the dirt-laden water and screaming above the wind. "I owe you my life."

"And I am indebted for my sister's." Tirkul's deep brown eyes were solemn. "She was too small to outrun the flood by herself." His mouth was still drawn in a solemn line. "We thought she was safe on high ground. If you had not seen her and gone back ..."

Corri stared into Tirkul's eyes, seeing emotions there that made her feel uncomfortable, as if she had missed an unseen step in the dark.

What is this I feel? Is this how others feel when they say they are in love? I do not know all their customs. Is Tirkul only thinking of buying me, as the men do their women in Asur? Takra says Tuonela women are always free, but what if he feels I want him to follow Asuran tradition? Things are moving too fast. I need time, space to think. Corri gave Halka a pleading look.

"Leave her to rest." The shakka ushered Tirkul out of the wagon, then turned to Corri and Takra. "This storm was not natural. Somewhere those dealing in Dark Magic gathered the clouds and set them to empty their rain-burden upon us."

"Why?" Takra squatted beside Corri, playing with the hilt of her dagger, her face drawn and grim, her eyes flashing.

"Yes, why." The old woman sat down on the chest before
the altar. "I suspect it is partly because Frav is gathering its
forces for war and partly because of Corri. To truly know, I
must join my powers with others. Perhaps, then, we can discover some of the truth about you, girl." Her eyes held Corri's.
"We must wait for the shakka gathering at Neeba for that.
Meantime, you must take great care."

The morning sun was bright, shining on the rain-
drenched grass like diamonds. Not a cloud remained of the
sudden storm of the night before. A steamy mist rose from the
damp grass as the Clan wagons rumbled west, toward Neeba.

Corri rode with the shakka on the wagon seat, carefully
polishing her headband as the old woman skillfully guided
the horses. Mouse plodded contentedly alongside. Surrounded by the herds of horses and bleating goats, the long
line of wagons continued to move forward until nightfall.
When they camped, it was on the tops of the gently rolling
hills. Each night the shakka threw her magic bones, her
brown face wrinkled in thought as she silently read them.

The last evening of the journey, as Corri and Halka fin-
ished their evening meal, there was a call outside the wagon.
The shakka lifted the tent flap, then beckoned Corri outside.
Tirkul and his family waited.

"For the life of my daughter, I give my thanks." An older
version of Tirkul stepped forward, his hands upon the shoulders of the child Corri had thrown from the flood.

The child laid a saddlebag decorated with bright prairie
beedle beads on the wagon step, then retreated to stand
shyly beside her father.

"My thanks also, friend of Takra." The slender child
played with the end of one of her white-blonde braids. "I am
seven summers old and should have known better than to run

back into danger." She scuffed the toe of her boot in the dirt as she spoke.

"You could not know you were in danger." Corri spoke softly, remembering times in her own childhood when she was embarrassed over a blunder. "Besides, the little goat would have drowned if you had not saved it."

The child grinned, ducked her head, and wound the pale braid about her hand.

"For the life of my daughter." The mother laid a bundle of clothing, leather trousers and tunic, at Corri's feet. "The Mother of Mares guided you, friend of Takra. I am grateful." There were tears on the woman's cheeks.

"No one could hear me in the wind," Corri answered. "I could not leave her to drown. I am no warrior. I did what was necessary to do." She was embarrassed at the upturned faces, full of gratitude.

"A blessing on both Clans." Halka sketched a symbol over the family and Corri. "May the Lady and Her Lord ride at your shoulder."

Tirkul's father nodded and, gathering his little family about him, strode off among the wagons. Only Tirkul now stood, looking up at Corri. In his hands he held a sheathed long dagger of the Tuonela. He held it up for Corri to take.

"I come, a warrior of the Clan of the Asperel, to walk beside you in fairness, to keep your life as my own, to ride with you wherever the wind blows." Tirkul's eyes were steady, his mouth drawn into a line of anticipation.

"Thank you," Corri said, taking the dagger in both hands.

"Wait! She knows not our customs." Takra jumped from the wagon steps to stand beside Corri, anxiety clear in her amber eyes.

What have I done? Corri's eyes went wide with surprise. Then she began to understand, and her cheekbones reddened. *This is the way Tuonela men ask a woman to live with them! I do not want to become Tirkul's woman—at least not now.*

"I did not come to trick her," Tirkul answered. "It is a gift only. If, at a later time, Corri can answer with the sworn words, then it is well." His eyes never left the girl's face. "I wished for her to know my feelings."

Yes, now I know, Corri thought, *but everyone assumes I either want to accept or refuse your offer. Why will no one see that I just want time to think?*

"She is not free, Tirkul. She is the forced wife of one in Hadliden." The shakka crossed her arms and stared levelly at the warrior.

Corri cringed inwardly at the shakka's words. *If only it were not so,* she thought, *then perhaps I could accept your gift and your heart that you hold out so freely, when I am ready.*

She held the dagger out to the tall warrior, but he refused it with a shake of his head and a smile that lifted one side of his firm mouth.

"You have thought on this, Tirkul, fully knowing the truth?" The shakka laid a firm hand on Corri's shoulder.

"I have thought on the truth as I know it. Corri has a free spirit. With such a heart, can she not be judged as one with us? Among the Clans, an alliance made against the will is not binding. And any alliance that becomes distasteful can be broken."

"You, girl, do you find a liking for this warrior?" Halka tightened her grip on Corri's shoulder. "If you choose to live among the Clans, you can dissolve this alliance by our laws."

"Yes, I like him." Corri felt the blood rush to her cheeks. "But if I use your laws to break this forced bond, it will not make me free. Grimmel will not acknowledge my actions, nor will any of those in Asur. I will not place anyone in danger because of me. Besides," she paused, "I must have time to think, time to learn what true freedom is."

"Then let the heart-oath stand as it has been said, until Corri says the words to complete it, or until a full turn of seasons when, without the words, it will be dissolved." The shakka took up Corri's gifts, lifted the flap and retreated into the wagon.

"Give me time, Tirkul." Corri's words were breathy as the full impact of the shakka's words came home. "I cannot answer you now. A free life, to choose what I want, is still not completely in my grasp." Her mind whirled with unexperienced emotions, a wish to become closer to this tall warrior, yet a fear of allowing anyone inside her protective shell. And over all, the cloud of being wife to the master thief of Hadliden.

"I will wait, for a full turn of seasons or longer, until you tell me yes or no." Tirkul turned on his heel and walked away into the gathering darkness.

Corri and Takra entered the wagon and sat down, facing the shakka. The old woman perched on her storage chest, hands on her knees, looking from one girl to the other.

"He is sincere," she said at last. "Tirkul has never been one to lay heart-oath as an empty promise. Many clanswomen have cast their eyes his way, but for nothing."

"I cannot give him an answer yet." Corri began to feel trapped, frantic. "I am not free. Besides, I do not know if I can be what he expects. I am only a thief. Men I know little about."

"No need for haste, Sister-Friend," Takra said, one hand on Corri's arm. "He has spoken the words that give you time. Let it be for now."

"We near Neeba." The shakka turned her dark eyes to Takra. "Only those who claim blood with one of the Clans may enter the city to hear the Baba and see the Making Ceremony."

"I am prepared." Takra drew out her long dagger. "Corri," she turned to the girl, "I have called you Sister-Friend. Now I would make us sister-kin by blood. What is your wish?"

"Sister in blood with you?" Corri's eyes went wide. "I have no family. Yes, Takra, I would like that."

Takra took Corri's hand and, with the sharp point of her dagger, pierced the girl's thumb. A drop of blood gathered there. Takra bent her head and licked the moisture from the cut, then held out the dagger to Corri. Corri swallowed hard, then repeated the ritual with Takra's hand.

"You are now sister-kin by the blood ritual. Let no one deny it." The old shakka smiled and nodded her head. "Before the moon reaches a quarter of its darkness, we shall stand at the walls of Neeba. A joyous time for all the Clans of Tuone. Then all the shakkas will gather, and we shall see what can be done to set you free, girl, from those who pursue you."

"Will you give her the Clan mark?" Takra asked.

"It would be wise for her to bear a mark, but I think not of the Wind-Riders or the Asperel or of any other Tuonela Clan." The old shakka pulled out a hide-wrapped bundle from a chest. "The Dream Warrior should bear her own special marking, one chosen for her by the Mother of Mares."

"Are you speaking of a tattoo?" Corri sat up straighter. *I well remember Grimmel's anger and his words when one of his thieves appeared with a small tattoo. Just another way to identify a thief, Grimmel said, a way which can never be removed.*

"It is only a little pain." Takra grinned. "Perhaps we should give the little thief some mountain water to bolster her courage."

The shakka produced a leather bottle and two cups from the chest before the altar. Takra poured out the clear liquid, handing one cup to Corri and watching her face as the girl swallowed her portion quickly. With a laugh, the warrior woman refilled the cup, then held up her own in salute before she drained the vessel.

Corri drank the second cup more slowly. The fiery liquor began to build a fire within her, making everything seem distant, as if it happened to someone else, not her. She felt lightheaded as she watched the shakka heat a slender splinter of bone over the candle flame, its needle end stained a deep blue.

Takra helped the girl strip out of her tunic at the shakka's command. The old woman ran a weather-roughened hand over Corri's left breast just below the collar bone.

"Yes, here I think." She set a small bowl of thick blue liquid on the floor by her feet and raised the sharpened bone.

"Frayma has shown me the sign to set upon you, girl." The bone quickly pierced the pale skin.

"Why do you put it where it cannot be seen?" Takra asked. "Those of the Clans are proud of their markings."

"The Mother of Mares told me that her mark should be hidden from the world until the time is right." Halka nodded to herself. "I learned long ago not to question the Lady."

At least, if no one will see this mark, then I can still be a thief if I so choose. Corri watched Halka's preparations with interest. *That is, if I survive the process.*

Corri gritted her teeth, but the pain-pricks seemed far away, dulled by the mountain water. Over and over, with great care, the shakka punched the design until it was completed to her satisfaction. Then she laid aside the bone and sponged the blue paste into the bleeding pricks.

"A star!" Takra's voice seemed to come from a muffled distance. "One of the sacred symbols of Frayma."

"That is her mark and her destiny." The old woman dabbed at the blood until it stopped, then pressed a pad over the tattoo. "The mark of Frayma's Dream Warrior."

"But her life has not been one set aside for training and visions." Corri heard Takra's breathy words as if from a great distance.

"It matters not. The Lady and Her consort work through us, Takra Wind-Rider. Not the ones who wall themselves up and talk pious words, but us, the People, full of faults and doubts. We were created by the Lady, therefore we are all sacred to Her. Even the Darkness-loving Fravashi. Never forget that." The image of the old woman began to blur before Corri's eyes. "If we choose to walk the Dark paths that lead away from Her Vayhall Halls, then She mourns for us, as would any mother."

The sound of the voices receded, Corri's eyes closed, and she slumped into sleep.

$\mathcal{I}$t took the Clan of the Asperel another two weeks to reach the ancient walls of Neeba. The herds and their watchful riders dropped out of line in the grasslands a week out from the city, Takra explaining that there was not enough grazing near Neeba for all the Clan herds. The wagons moved on to another site toward the city.

Corri scratched at her new tattoo through her leather tunic. The itch of healing grew less with each day. Word of the sacred symbol of her tattoo had spread throughout the camp, at first bringing looks of awe until she slipped in horse manure near the picket lines and had to clean off her leather trousers. After that, the Clan members treated her as one of their own, a person whose Goddess-chosen destiny might one day send her on strange journeys, but for now was only another woman who needed to watch her step.

A little too much mountain water, she thought as she rode beside Takra, *and I end up marked for life.* She absently twisted at her earring. Long days astride Mouse had made her more comfortable on horseback, and it also strengthened the silent communication she found was possible with the mare.

She smiled to herself as she glanced at Takra astride Lightfoot. She had been as surprised as her friend when the old shakka had not decorated her with the swirl of the Wind-Riders or the wings of the Asperel, but a stylized star, a vertical line with two slanting marks across it. Halka refused to explain to anyone why she chose the symbol, except to say that it came in a vision.

Corri squinted at the sand-brown walls of Neeba and the milling crowds of people and wagon-tents gathered there. The ancient city, one of only two among the Tuonela, the other being Nevn which sat up against the mountains dividing the grasslands from Frav, was centered in a rich oasis near the mountain pass that led into Asur. The swaying kucha trees were blossoming, later to be heavy with oil-rich nuts. People were busy at the three mud brick-sided wells outside the walls.

The Clan of the Asperel moved down the last stretch of grasslands to join others of the Tuonela Clans massed before the great gates and about the high walls of the city.

After the wagons were set up, Takra and Corri walked into Neeba, where Takra assured her there would be traders gathered with goods from all the lands of the Four Peoples. The old shakka disappeared to join others of her mystic kind who held their own meeting prior to the gathering of the Clans before the Baba.

"Who is the Baba?" Corri asked, as she and Takra passed through the open gates into Neeba.

"He is the great judge of all Clan troubles. Sometimes a man is chosen as Baba, sometimes a woman. The Baba holds the title until it is revealed to the shakkas that a new one must be chosen." Takra headed straight to a display of swords and daggers, spread out on boards under an awning. "And the Making Ceremony, that is for joinings and heart-oaths. Some of the Clans wait for the yearly ceremony, others do not, giving vows instead before the Clan and their shakka. The newborn are also brought to be blessed and acknowledged as tribal members."

Corri looked around at the ancient buildings, the wide streets, so clean after Hadliden. Crowds of people, many not of Clan blood, filled the great center market square. The noise of the milling people was like the roll of ocean waves, with few individual voices distinguishable.

"People live here?" She turned to Takra who was testing the strength of a boot knife much like Corri's.

"A few of the older shakkas stay all year, training those who have talent. Some clansmen who do not want to wander the grasslands, but wish to practice their crafts and trade, those live here."

As Takra fell to bartering with the merchant, Corri turned her attention to the crowds and the other booths. Dust from the floor of the market rose in a filtering cloud. Although most of the people were from the Clans, their pale hair shining in the sun, there were many with darker hair and different clothing, marking them as Asuran or Kirisani.

Corri tensed as she heard the sound of tinkling bells. Her mind turned back to Grimmel's pleasure-slaves and her own collar. A group of scantily clad women came through the throng, their wrists and ankles circled with bracelets hung with little bells, each with an ornate collar about their slender necks. Their loose trousers, gathered at the ankles, were of transparent gauzy material, revealing very brief shorts. Their short vests opened over bared and vividly painted breasts. From a belt at each waist hung two ornate daggers. They walked with a guard, but their proud heads were up and they chattered gaily among themselves.

"Dancers," Takra said as she paid the merchant and slipped the knife into her belt. "They come each year from Hadliden. Good dancers, but not as exciting as watching the sword-glee." She ran one browned finger through Corri's hair. "They know the ways of Asuran face paints and colorings. You need to hide that red again if you plan to leave the Clan. With us you are safe, but not if you go with Imandoff into other lands. Your Clan clothing will keep any from asking questions, but that faded black hair with the red underneath will certainly make many wonder. And draw attention from the traders not of the Clans."

"Let us go to them, then." Corri began to feel uneasy in the crowd. "Too many have looked at me. I want no undue attention. Who knows who lurks here from Asur?"

The dancers were at first amused, then delighted when Corri asked for their help. They swept the two women into their tent, chattering and laughing, shaking their heads at the mention of money. In a short time, Corri's hair was completely changed to a pale yellow with an undertone of faint red.

"A surprise for Tirkul," Takra said as they emerged once more into the crowds of Neeba. "And for the sorcerer, if he finds us." She laughed and drew Corri with her toward a man juggling daggers.

Corri watched in fascination as the man whirled more and more weapons into the air, catching them with ease. Then, she began to feel uneasy. Cautiously, she fell back into her training as a thief, furtively scanning the faces about her. She saw no one familiar until a figure moved more into the open from behind a broad-shouldered Clan warrior.

Malya! Why is she here? Corri felt fear, then a rising anger as Malya's pale eyes met hers and the woman smiled. *How dare those from Leshy track me here and spy on me!*

"Takra." Corri's voice was tinged with urgency as she pulled at the warrior's arm. "A woman from Leshy is in the crowd." She turned to point out the woman, but she had disappeared into the crowd.

"Where?" Takra whirled around, brows pulled down.

"She is gone now." Corri looked over the faces surrounding the juggler. "But I did see her. Malya, one of the High Clua's servants."

"We shall keep keen eyes then." Takra shouldered her way out of the crowd. "High Clua or no, she would not dare anything in Neeba. Come, I see old friends from the Clan of the Long Riders."

Corri followed the sword-woman through the crowds toward a welcoming group of Clan members. But she still felt uneasy. Several times she turned, instincts telling her that someone followed. Each time she saw no familiar faces.

Chapter 19

$\mathscr{H}$alka was gone when they returned to the wagon-tent. Takra and Corri walked through the noisy encampment to join Tirkul's family for the evening meal. Corri's fear that her mixed emotions toward the tall warrior were apparent in her every word and action made her shy and silent. The good-natured jesting and open love shown by the family were a new experience for the girl, one that she still found uncomfortable. She stayed close by Takra's side, avoiding the glances she felt from Tirkul.

Why did Tirkul raise his eyebrow and smile at me like that when he saw my hair? she thought. *Surely I do not look that strange or Takra would have told me. Why should I care what he thinks?* Defiantly, she had smiled back and gone on her way.

As twilight fell, the entire family, along with most Clan members, went back into Neeba. This time they passed the vast market grounds of the city, joining the milling crowd that pressed toward a central location. There, the crowd poured into an enormous semi-circle of a building, its open front upheld by long triple lines of pillars. Corri glanced upward and was surprised to see there was no roof. The stars were fire-bright points of light overhead, visible above the torchlight.

Although the numbers of clansmen were beyond count, there was little sound and no shoving inside the great hall. The Tuonela moved to stand among their own Clans, those of the Asperel in one of the long sections, each of which reached from the pillars to the raised platform at the far end wall.

"Come, Corri Farblood." Halka appeared at Corri's side, a cape heavily embroidered with shakka symbols thrown over one shoulder.

"I stand as family for her." Takra laid a browned hand on the girl's shoulder. "I have claimed her as Sister-Friend and made her of my blood."

"Come." Halka led the way forward to the dais, the people of the Asperel parting before her in reverent silence.

Ranged just below the dais, in a long line facing the Clans, stood the Tuonela shakkas, their capes of honor a barbarian show of vivid colors under the flickering torchlights. Their dark eyes focused as one on Corri as the shakka gently pushed her to the very edge of the dais.

The staccato of drums broke the near-stillness. A great cry broke from every throat in the crowd as a tall young man stepped onto the dais. In his right hand was a tall, deadly hunting spear, a mass of gems and strange objects dangling from leather strips tied near its gleaming metal head. He raised his left hand; in it he held a shining sword. With his dark eyes on the people below, he sat on a stool in the center of the platform.

"This is Neeba, sacred city of the Tuonela Clans." His rich voice carried easily through the soft night air. "I am the Baba. I serve the Clans. In this place, in this time, I call upon the Mother of Mares and the Lord of Animals to stand beside me. The Naming Ceremony has begun."

The dark eyes lowered until they met Corri's, and held them with his direct gaze. He rapped the butt-end of his spear sharply on the stones.

"Here my words, O Tuonela. There has come among us one out of the legends from the far past. The songsmiths have long told us of the Dream Warrior, the one who heralds the Great War with Frav. That one is here, now walks among the Clans. Not a man, as think Kirisan and Asur, no. Nor as a trained warrior, as we thought." The Baba's long braids danced as he shook his head.

He speaks of me! Corri stole a glance at Takra, but the warrior woman's eyes were fixed on the Baba. *I am no warrior, that is true, nor do I wish to be. What if I have no wish to be the fabled Dream Warrior?*

"The shakkas have gathered; this is a true messenger," the Baba continued. "This Dream Warrior has been chosen by the Mother of Mares, whose messages are law among us. We dare not, shall not, question the choice of the Mother, only accept."

The line of shakkas parted as Halka and Takra urged Corri to the very lip of the dais. The girl stared up at the Baba, intrigued by the power emanating from the spiritual leader.

"Hear me, Tuonela." The Baba rapped his spear again. "The woman Corri Farblood has taken the blood ritual with Takra Wind-Rider, a warrior with Frayma's Mare." He paused and sent a sweeping glance across the crowd. "But let her name be written on the rolls of all Clans, for she belongs to each and every Clan of the Tuonela. Let us show wisdom in accepting the message of her coming, for the time draws near when sword and spear and bow must again be lifted in battle against our enemies across the mountains. Be prepared, my people."

"Corri Farblood!" The great shout of her name rose from thousands of throats as the Baba reached out to touch her head with his spear.

Oh Goddess, what have I gotten into? Corri felt the old need to be unnoticed, an anonymous face in the crowd, rise up within her. Then, behind this feeling and washing over it like a great wave, came the sensation of pride in herself and an inner courage she had never felt before. *They believe in me!*

"It is done." Halka took her place with the shakkas as Corri and Takra moved back into the crowd of the Clan.

Corri felt questions rise in her mind. *How am I to know what needs to be done? What do the legends say of this Dream Warrior?* But she could not bring herself to break the respectful silence as the Baba greeted and named Tuonela babies brought forward to be presented to the Clans.

As she watched the Tuonela ceremonies, a feeling of warmness flooded through her. *A home!* she thought. *A People who care about me. But as a messenger of war, that is a heavy burden.* She shivered, although she stood shoulder to shoulder with others in the crowd.

In a thoughtful daze Corri watched those taking part in heart-oaths and joinings, her thoughts divided between inner musings and the ceremonies before her.

The drums sounded again, signaling the beginnings of dispute settlements. At this point the crowd divided, the parents and younger children staying to hear the Baba pass judgment, the others leaving to watch the traditional Tuonela dancing.

"You have never seen a sword-glee?" Tirkul walked beside Corri, watching her with dark eyes, his pale braids falling forward as he bent down to talk with her. He touched her now pale hair with a tanned hand, laughed softly and shook his head.

"Is it a show of fighting skill?" Corri felt the blood rush to her cheeks at his touch. She was glad it was growing dark so that Tirkul could not see her face clearly. At her belt now hung the long Tuonela dagger from Tirkul. She blushed again as his eyes flicked across his gift.

"In a way." Tirkul smiled and rested his hands on both his sword and long dagger. "It is our dance, the one for warriors, a dance only for Clan members."

"It is said that the warriors of Frav do the Dance of Knives, similar to our sword-glee," Takra replied, a smile crossing her face as she teased her kin-brother.

Tirkul grunted and jerked one thumb downward, the traditional Tuonela gesture of contempt.

As they walked back through the wide streets and came into the market square, Corri heard the pound of drums, the rapid notes of pipes. She saw that the booths were down, the great paved area bare, with torches lit all around it. A crowd of Clan members, young and old, was drawn up in a wide circle, leaving an open center.

In that center two men were dancing to the drum beat, swords and daggers flashing dangerously about their arms and legs. The crowd began to chant and clap, slightly out of beat to the drums.

"They try to distract the dancers," Takra explained. "See, one has lost the step."

One of the dancers broke the rhythm, holding up his weapons as a sign of defeat. Corri saw the sheen of perspiration on his smiling face as he saluted his opponent.

Two women leaped into the ring and began to whirl and swing their weapons in a flashing pattern. The drum beat never ceased. Corri watched the intricate footwork, the deadly glinting blades, as the two danced the sword-glee. Once, a dagger blade scratched an arm, bringing a trickle of blood, but the dancer never hesitated. When the dancers were reeling with exhaustion, the crowd cheered them both, considering the contest a draw.

"Tirkul! Dance sword-glee for us!" Nearby voices raised, and the warrior stepped into the circle.

"Takra Wind-Rider, I challenge you." Tirkul drew both sword and dagger and lifted them in smiling salute to the sword-woman.

"They are the best," Corri heard someone say as the two walked to the center.

The drum beat rapped out, the pipes were shrill as Tirkul and Takra began the intricate steps of the dance. Corri had thought the other dancers were skilled. Now she knew they were amateurs compared to her friends. The enthusiasm of the crowd caught her, and she joined in the clapping and shouting.

The weapons flashed in the torchlight, a blur of motion as they rose and fell, were tossed high into the air, whirling, spinning. The dancers' feet and hands never stopped. Corri was so caught up in the excitement that she did not notice when a man pushed close beside her.

"Never have I seen you at Neeba." A deep male voice at her ear made Corri turn in surprise. "And you are no Tuonela, regardless of the Baba's words." The warrior smiled down at her, his eyes straying to her earring.

"And I do not know you." Corri fixed the man with a level stare. Something in the man's attitude made her uneasy.

"Roggkin of the Clan of the Black Moon. And you?"

"Friend of Takra, Clan of the Wind-Riders." Corri's voice was chilly. She did not like the way this warrior pressed his questions, looked at her. The swaggering way he held his shoulders and head suggested that he thought himself attractive to women. An old scar zigzagged across his cheek and nose and continued on to where the lobe of one ear was clipped short. She found herself comparing him to Tirkul. There was no question who she found the most alluring, and it was not this posturing warrior.

"Come, let us walk in the moonlight, pretty one." Roggkin took her arm. "There are more things of interest in Neeba than this." He gestured with one broad hand toward the dancers.

"No!" Corri pulled away and glared at him. "I go nowhere with you." She felt an instinctive warning. "Get away from me."

The crowd began to pull away from Corri and the warrior, leaving them in a wide bare spot. Roggkin smiled and held up his empty hands, yet did not retreat. Slowly, deliberately, Corri drew the long dagger, the gift from Tirkul. Roggkin's eyes narrowed as the design on the dagger blade became clear in the torchlight.

"You did not say you had given heart-oath. But no matter. Until the final sharing of blood, any man can make an offer. There are no customs against it."

"I have not given heart-oath," Corri said, her eyes watchful. "And you did not ask. But no man lays hands on me unless I give him permission."

Corri became aware that the drums had stopped, the crowd noise dying to a few scattered whispers. Tirkul and Takra appeared at her side, weapons still in hand, but silent, except for their labored breathing.

"He is yours, Corri," Takra said, breathing hard. "The law says that unless you call for Clan aid for deadly insult or injury, we cannot interfere."

"I need no aid with this." Corri's words hissed through her teeth. "What manner of Clan warrior creeps up on a woman and forces his attentions on her? No, I think this is no brave Clan warrior. True, I am no sword-woman, but with this man I need no aid. A barking dog can be silenced by a swift foot."

"Seems you chose wrongly again, Roggkin," said a laughing voice out of the crowd.

"You have thrown insult." Roggkin's face darkened with anger. "No woman speaks so to me."

"Any Tuonela woman may cast insult where she will. But if you have need to hear it from a man, then hear it from me." Tirkul stepped between Roggkin and Corri, his drawn sword up. "She gave no insult that was not due. It is known, Roggkin, that you cast eyes and place hands where they do not belong."

"I bear no unsheathed steel." Roggkin held up his empty hands. "I have no quarrel with Tirkul of the Asperel."

The catcalls of the crowd followed the warrior as he turned on his heel and walked away. The drums and pipes began again, and another pair of dancers leaped into the circle.

"No offense, Corri, but it is strange that Roggkin chose to pursue you." Takra sheathed her weapons and wiped the sweat from her face. "Always before he has chosen to seek out those who have many horses to go with them on their joining-day."

"And did not succeed, I wager," Corri answered, slipping her dagger back into her belt. "Something is very wrong here, I feel it."

Although the three lingered to watch the rest of the dancers and then wandered about the city, they did not see Roggkin again. As the hour neared midnight, they decided to watch the exotic dancers from Asur. On their way, Tirkul's little sister came with a message from the old shakka for Corri to return to the wagon.

"I can find my way," Corri assured her friends. "Stay, and enjoy yourselves. I think this Roggkin will not bother me again, so there is no danger. Did the Baba not say I belonged to all the Clans?"

She set off through the crowds to the gates of Neeba, one hand riding on her dagger hilt as she walked. Outside the walls, the night was lit only by the bright stars and a nearly-full moon. The banners of each Clan flapped in the slight breeze whispering through the prairie grasses.

As she picked her way through the wagon-tents of the assembled Clans, Corri saw Roggkin and a woman ghosting toward a dark wagon. She slipped behind a wagon-tent and peered out. Just as the pair entered the tent, the woman turned so that her face was lit by the moonlight. Corri sucked in her breath. It was Malya from Leshy!

How did she know to find me here? Corri wondered again. *Surely the High Clua would not send all this way to bring me back. And what has Malya to do with this Roggin? I must know!*

She worked her way silently to Roggkin's tent and pressed her ear against the hide covering. The voices were muted but distinguishable.

"I tried." Roggkin's tones were petulant. "But others interfered. You saw."

"You fool. Now she is on guard against you. And I dare not show myself openly to her, or she may call upon Clan aid."

"The money?" Greed crept into Roggkin's voice.

"Only when she is delivered into the hands of Grimmel's men. Not until. You know the bargain." Malya's tones softened a little. "You did well, Roggkin. The master thief will not forget that you aided him."

Corri stepped away from the wagon-tent, fear clutching at her throat. The escape from Leshy, the long trek through the grasslands, all this way to Neeba only to find out Grimmel's men waited somewhere nearby.

She ducked back into the shadows as Malya climbed out of the wagon-tent. Looking cautiously about, Malya wrapped her dark cloak close and, head high, started back toward the city. For a moment Corri hesitated in her shadowy hiding place, her sensitive ears listening for Roggkin, but the warrior remained inside. *What now?* Corri thought. *By the blessed Goddess, I would put an end to this hunt and chase. It is time Grimmel heard my challenge. It seems, as in other things, I must do it myself.*

Taking a deep breath, she followed the woman, slipping from shadow to shadow. Malya's confident stride took her on a meandering course through the clustered wagon-tents with Corri following like a stealthy huntress. Little by little, the girl drew closer.

As Malya passed through a group of silent wagons, their door-flaps tied closed to mark the family's absence, Corri closed the distance between her and her prey, silent-footed. A rush of three steps and she caught the woman of Leshy in the deep shadows of a wagon. With one hand she grabbed the woman around the neck, her hand over Malya's mouth. In her other hand the long dagger snapped forward to lie against the smooth throat.

"Make a sound, and I kill you." The tone in Corri's voice was harsh and decisive. Inwardly, she hoped that it left no doubt in Malya's mind that she would do as she said.

Malya stood quietly as, keeping the dagger at the woman's throat, Corri moved to face her, at the same time shoving her back against the bed of the wagon.

"An end to this," Corri said quietly. "I will never return to Grimmel or the High Clua. So leave off this hunting and following me. I am a free woman."

"The High Clua is dead." A shaft of moonlight fell on the woman's smiling face. "She tried too much with her shadow-self and failed. As to Grimmel, you are his by Asuran law. By the Nine Words of Natira, you have a greater value than Grimmel ever imagined, Corri Farblood, for the Baba himself to name you as the legendary Dream Warrior. It is no wonder that the master thief searches for you." Malya raised one hand slowly, pushing a finger against the blade of the dagger. "But you, you have no stomach for cold killing. Women seldom do, except for the Tuonela warrior women."

"You take a message back to that old toad." Corri's jaw was set in anger. "Let me go free. No more hunting for me. Ever. If I see another follower, I shall hunt in return. And I shall kill whoever tries to take me back. Believe that, you treacherous snake. I may be no Tuonela warrior woman, but I will do what is needed." Corri stepped back, the dagger still at the ready. "Get out of Neeba, or die."

Malya pulled away and hurried off. She turned at the edge of the campground and called back.

"Grimmel will never give up, Farblood." Malya laughed. "He will never leave you free. As for being a free woman, you are wed lawfully to the master thief, and there is a price on your head. So enjoy your freedom, Farblood, while you may, for it shall not be for long."

Malya turned and ran toward the crowds of Neeba. Corri, hands clenched at her sides, watched the retreating figure.

Why did I not just kill her? Takra would have. The girl picked a watchful path among the mostly silent wagons, her eyes and ears alert for any sign that she was followed. *Well, there is nothing for it now, except to tell Halka. Perhaps she will know what I should do.*

Chapter 20

Halka sat calmly while Corri related what had happened. When the girl finally threw up her hands in a gesture of helplessness and frustration, the shakka smiled and leaned near to pat her shoulder.

"You did what is in your nature, Dream Warrior. You are not Takra. You are not Tuonela. You are only you. That is all any of us should try to be, ourselves." The old woman stared at Corri with intent eyes. "When we realize that, it is the beginning of wisdom. The Mother of Mares has made a variety of creatures and people, each unique in their own way. How boring life would be if it were otherwise."

"But I should have killed her," Corri replied, slamming a fist against her knee. "Malya's death would have removed one of the threats to my freedom. Look how she drew this Roggkin into her plans. She will do it with others. I will never know who to trust."

"Has your heart not guided you true in trusting Takra and Tirkul, and even this sorcerer Imandoff of whom the

203

Wind-Rider speaks? Listen to your heart, Dream Warrior. The Goddess Frayma speaks to the heart and the spirit. My dreams tell me that the path yet before you is a long and dangerous one, a journey that will take Goddess-led heart and spirit. But one step at a time, Corri." Halka gestured at the sleeping pallets. "Rest now. Tomorrow, after moonrise, we will go to meet the other shakkas. By combining our powers, perhaps we shall discover what drives you on this journey." The old woman lay down and wrapped a blanket around her. "Perhaps a geas, but laid by man or Goddess?"

"A geas?" Corri sat on the edge of the pallet, staring off across the darkened wagon. "What is that?"

The shakka did not answer. Corri stretched out on the sleeping pad and stared up at the hide tent for a long time before she drifted into sleep.

The next evening, Halka and Corri rode through the whispering grasses of the plains. It was deep night, only the moonlight showing the way across the featureless country, by the time they reached a point nearly a mile from the city of Neeba. As they descended into a wide gully, Corri saw the silhouettes of horses and people in the glow of a blazing campfire.

"The shakkas await." Halka dismounted and left her horse with the others, signaling Corri to do the same.

"Fair greetings," the old woman called as she and Corri came to the fire. "I bring the Dream Warrior."

There must be a hundred of them! Corri looked at the serious faces in amazement. *There is even one not much older than me.* As she looked closer, she began to see the differences. The color of hair ranged from light brown to white in color, although most was white-gold like Takra's. The clothing was the usual Tuonela leather, but the decorations differed slightly from shakka to shakka. She noticed at least three whose eyes were amber, not the dark brown of most of the Clans.

The shakkas, young and old, mostly women with a sprinkling of men, silently gathered around Corri, their hands passing a few inches from her skin in feathery gestures. There was a growing murmur, then one of the women clapped her hands, and they all moved into a tight circle near the fire. Corri was gently pushed inside the ring where she stood, ill at ease.

"I am told you trained at Leshy, girl." A tall, dark-eyed woman turned piercing eyes in Corri's direction. "And what did you think of their training?"

"I learned much." Corri felt a rising resentment at the commanding tone of voice. "But I cared not for their way of life."

There was a ripple of laughter around the circled shakkas. Corri shifted uneasily from one foot to the other.

"The healers of Leshy are good healers," the woman continued, "but they live in a world that has no reality. By rejecting all forms of magical power except their own, they reject the diversity of the Goddess and Her ways, and that is not a wise thing to do. Although I sense within you much power, you are a child in its usage."

"You take much on yourself by judging me, shakka." Corri's voice held a knife-edge.

"Ah, so there is also fire and steel within you. Good." The woman smiled for the first time. "We will help you. You have done well to bring her, Halka. She has the necessary strength and spirit. She can learn to use and control the power within her." The woman held out her hand. "You have brought the strange stone?"

Halka motioned to Corri, who drew her headband with its owl stone out of her tunic and reluctantly gave it to the woman.

"Remember, that is mine!" Corri said. "Do not think to keep it."

"Yes, it is for you alone, Dream Warrior. But I need to touch it, that I may see how you must learn to use and control it. Its powers are like none I have felt before. Perhaps, in that much, we can be of aid. I cannot say until we try." The woman's dark eyes glinted in the firelight. She held up the circlet to the darkened night sky, as if offering it to the moon, then placed it in Corri's outstretched hands. "The ancient legends tell of the Dream Warrior coming to the Clans for aid. Perhaps here tonight we fulfill prophecy."

"It is a very ancient stone," Halka said. "There is a feel of the Forgotten Ones about it. There is also that which tells me it did not come into being on this world of Sar Akka. Did you not sense it, Denuja?"

"Yes." The leader of the shakka gathering fingered the amulet hanging between her breasts. "It is very, very old, and has known the stars." She turned her attention to Corri. "The Clans long ago guessed that the Forgotten Ones came from beyond the moon. Whether this knowledge is known to others, I do not know. It is not an idea we share with Out-Clanners." She held up the circlet for the others to see. "We must test the Dream Warrior's strength to use this ancient stone, and through that help her seek out and destroy her pursuers. That task must come first, for her own safety and the good of the Clans."

There was a murmur of agreement among the closely gathered shakkas. The leader reached into a leather bag at her waist and drew out a handful of dried leaves which she tossed onto the fire. The small amount of herbs had a strange effect on the flames. They turned a blue color and died down to a continuous glow, the scented smoke rolling and billowing out over the gathering.

The shakkas sat in a circle, facing inward with Corri at their center. Several began a heartbeat rhythm on their flat drums. Halka spread a blanket close to the smoldering fire and signaled for Corri to lie on it. The shakkas chanted softly to the drum beat, their words meaningless to the girl.

Corri lay down on the coarse blanket, slipping the circlet in place at Halka's gesture. As Corri stared at the star-speckled night sky, Halka fanned the scented smoke over her. Corri breathed deeply, the strange odor of the burning herbs making her mind clearer, yet at the same time creating a euphoria she felt no desire to fight. She felt the owl stone begin to warm against her forehead.

Denuja, the leader, sat on one side of the girl, Halka on the other, and taking up the chant, the two women steadily passed their hands over Corri's prone body.

Corri became aware that each person she saw, Denuja, Halka, those in the circle who were within her line of vision, all had a glow around them.

"What do you see?" said Halka in a low voice. Her hands never ceased their gentle slow movement.

"I see a glow of light around everyone," Corri whispered. "Mostly bright like the sun, but also colored with blue or green or brown. What is it?"

"You are seeing the life-force," Denuja answered softly. "The blue belongs to the healers, the green to those who know the herb secrets, the brown for the shakkas who work with animals. Look closely, Corri. Some of us have more than one color."

Corri blinked and looked about her again. It was true. Some shakkas had two, and a few all three, colors in their glow.

"Now, Dream Warrior, call upon the Mother of Mares, the one you call the Lady Frayma, and Her Lord for aid in your journey this night."

Do I really believe in the Goddess? Corri thought. She remembered the teachings of her old nurse. *Yes, I do!*

Denuja began to chant, her words only a strange garble of sounds, but her voice followed the drum beat, drawing Corri along a thread of sound, down into a deep place of calm within herself. The girl willed herself to relax, to sink willingly into the soft darkness of her inner mind.

Goddess, help me, Corri silently called. *I must protect the Clans from the danger that stalks me. Come, Lady. Give me aid, you and your Lord. Some words of wisdom, guidance.*

She saw a spark of light that swiftly approached her, growing as it came. The spark expanded into a brilliantly lit oval. Within that oval stood what appeared to be two figures, so clothed in light that Corri felt her physical eyes water. She could just make out the forms of a woman and man.

Dream Warrior, what would you have of us? The voice in Corri's head was like a breath of wind across the grasslands, a breeze with a woman's undertones.

I would be free of Grimmel's control and pursuit. I do not want to endanger the Clans. They have taken me in and protected me. And I would learn the manner of my birth, of my parents, and what lies behind this journey I am forced to make.

And what will you give in return? The mind-voice now came from the male figure, the deep tones like a far-off rumble of summer thunder. *There must always be balance in the Law, a giving and a taking, both by mortals and the gods.*

I have nothing of value, Corri answered in thought. She hesitated, then added, *I am only a thief, birth-right unknown. I am no shakka with powers. I am no warrior with sword-arm to offer. I am only Corri Farblood, a thief from Hadliden.*

Ah, but you are more than you realize, Dream Warrior. The Lady's voice was caressing in its gentleness. *If we aid you, will you follow our guidance? Will you be the Dream Warrior in truth, answering the needs of the Peoples of Sar Akka when it is needful?*

I will try. By my life I promise. The thought was out before Corri could stop it.

The Lady stretched out her hand, touching Corri over the heart. The girl felt her physical body begin to shake as a strange current of power flowed into it. The Lord placed his hand over the Lady's, and the power increased. Corri's physical body arched, then fell back to lie quietly as the glowing figures faded from view.

Corri found her shadow-self high above the circle of shakkas, her senses acutely alert to everything around her. She could feel the gentle power of the moonlight, sense the currents of the prairie winds. She thought of Takra and Tirkul. Far off, she detected their energy-forms in Neeba. But she was not drawn to them. Rather, her thoughts pulled her away, to the south, toward Hadliden and the master thief, Grimmel.

There was a blur of movement as she raced across the darkened sky; to her right the Taunith Sea glowed in the moonlight. Before she had time to marvel at the beauty she saw scudding by, she found herself hanging in the night sky above the fortress-house of the ruler of the haven-swill.

The secret lies within the mind. Halka's faint voice reached her as she hung swaying above Hadliden. *The need provides the way.*

Corri recognized that the words matched her hard-won knowledge from Leshy, a part of her surprised to find the same teachings known among the Tuonela shakkas.

The girl willed herself downward and found herself within the personal chamber of Grimmel. She instinctively reached for the long dagger at her belt, but found herself unable to draw the physical weapon. She looked down at her phantom hands and saw a swirling motion in the palm of each, as if a secret fire lay hidden there under the glowing skin.

The master thief sat in his chair, candles casting a faint glow against the dark walls and black carpet. Before him, on the elegant table, lay a flat circle of milky stone, nearly as wide as the master thief's hand, a stone that reminded her of the earring she had worn as long as she could remember. The master thief's stone was set in a strange black mounting of spiky metal. Grimmel bent over the stone and spoke. "She is still near Neeba. You must try again, Druk." The voice of the master thief held a tinge of threat. "I must have her back. She is mine by Asuran law and by my choice. When Frav sends its warriors against the Peoples, which it will, sooner or later, she will be my chance for power. Perhaps my only opportunity. I have waited long in this stink-hole, gathering my resources."

There was a crackly sound from the milky stone, a distant whisper of words that escaped Corri's ear.

"Kayth will do as he is told," Grimmel said. "Once I commanded him, long ago when we were marooned here. If I pull the string between us, Kayth will once more dance to my orders or suffer my punishments. He went against me once when he wedded that Kirisani sorceress. He paid for his mistake with her life. He thought that selling his daughter Corri to me would break the tie between us, but he should have known better."

Grimmel is responsible for my mother's death! Corri doubled her fist and swung at the master thief. Her hand passed harmlessly through his head. Grimmel jerked, then brushed his fat, ringed hand impatiently across his face.

I must stop him. I will stop him, she thought. *There has to be a way.*

Corri moved close to the master thief, wondering how she could destroy the strange device, thus cutting the link between Grimmel and his assassin Druk. She tried to pick up the strange stone, but her fingers went through the table. Grimmel started, looking around the room, suspicion growing in his nearly lidless, round eyes.

He feels my presence! A flash of understanding crossed Corri's mind. *Grimmel has a bit of the mind-power, enough to make him very dangerous. I must create an illusion, something to distract him.*

She turned her thoughts to creating sound in the corridor outside, but nothing happened. Grimmel looked about him with growing uneasiness, then rose from the table and waddled toward the door, calling for his guards as he went.

Now to smash the stone. Corri damped down the frantic emotions that threatened to break her control. *There must be a way. Lady, help me!*

The girl turned her attention to the heavy candlesticks on each side of the table. One of them was slightly off-balance, a fragment of an incense pellet lodged under the bottom; a section of the elaborate metal top had loosened from years of use. She stretched out her hands to push the holder, but they passed through the metal as if it were nothing but mist.

What can I do? Frustration rose thick and heavy. *To be so close, yet so helpless.* She clenched her fists in rage and felt a tremendous heat within her hands. She thrust her opened hands before her, awareness dawning at the sight of the swirling light in her palms. *Perhaps not so helpless after all.*

Again Corri held her hands near the holder, not trying to touch it, but willing the swirling centers of power in her palms to move the candlestick. It swayed a little. She formed an image in her mind of it toppling down, crushing the milky stone by which Grimmel communicated.

Help me! Her call went out into the night.

We aid. The answer was not from the strange luminous beings Corri thought of as gods, but the assembled shakkas. A thread of twining colors fed into her.

Corri mentally pushed again. The candlestick swayed, but stayed firm. In a rush of anger and desperation, the girl struck out with all her will power at the loosened top. The piece slid free and fell with a crash onto the table, directly onto the stone. There was a blinding flash of light, an explosion and puff of smoke as the stone shattered. The black metal holding it cracked into two pieces.

"No!" Grimmel whirled, both hands reaching out. "No!"

The fury of Grimmel's tone sent Corri instinctively darting into the far corner of the room. There she stayed, fearful of being detected, yet determined to learn what he would do now.

Pounding feet of the guards sounded in the hallway. The armored men poured through the open door, swords in hand. Grimmel waved aside the acrid smoke that drifted through the room as he stood over the destroyed device.

"It is not possible," he said, his fat hands clenching and unclenching. "I do not believe in chance happenings. For someone to do this, it would take much power. No one on Sar Akka now has that much power, not even the Fravashi. Unless someone has found a way to regain old knowledge told of in legends and long buried in the past." He turned to the guards, looking through them as if they did not exist. "Kayth, perhaps? But I have never felt any break in my control over him. That sorcerer. Yes, it must be. He must have discovered some ancient knowledge of the Forgotten Ones, discovered it and taught Corri how to use it. With her heritage it would be possible to do this."

"The girl-thief is that important?" The captain of the guards cleared his throat and waited nervously.

"Important?" Grimmel shook his fist under the man's nose. "The blood of Kayth Farblood and that Kirisani sorceress combined to produce a child so strong in certain mind-powers that the ignorant cannot imagine! I must have her back!"

Only I know the whole truth. Grimmel's thoughts were as plain to Corri as if he spoke aloud. *Not even Kayth, not even that sorcerer. Only I know that a child of my blood and the blood of Corri Farblood will surpass even the mother.*

Grimmel, using a short dagger, swept the destroyed pieces of the still smoking device into an empty bowl.

"Throw this into the Agadi River."

The master thief gave the bowl to the captain of the guards and dismissed the men with a wave of his thick fingered hand. The captain retreated from the room, the bowl held at arm's length.

"The sorcerer must know," Grimmel said to himself. "Somehow that sorcerer must have learned the secret of my control over the girl. He must be killed."

Corri cringed in the corner as she saw Grimmel's words take shape in the air between them, words tinged with smoky black and a deep threatening red, the color of old blood.

I must warn Imandoff, she thought. *Knowing Grimmel, it will only be a matter of time before he contacts his assassins in other ways. He will have difficulty reaching me here among the Clans, but Imandoff, he is unaware of the danger.*

The girl's thoughts pulled her out of the fortress-house and sent her once again to hang over the Tuone grasslands. Corri was of two minds, as she swayed there in the darkness.

I will go back, she determined. *I will kill Grimmel. Then there will no longer be danger to Imandoff or to me. But do I have the knowledge to do such a thing? No matter, it is worth the effort.*

But try as she would, she found herself unable to return to Hadliden. She felt weak, as if her battle to destroy the communicating device of the master thief had nearly drained her of energy. She also felt a restraining pull back toward Neeba.

Return, Corri. Halka's faint voice broke into her concentration. *We cannot sustain you much longer.*

Not yet! Corri's mind reached out with a determined effort towards Imandoff. *I must find the sorcerer. He is in danger.*

Return! Denuja added her voice to Halka's. *You are in danger yourself. If the energy fails, you may not be able to return to your body. Not for much longer can we aid you with our powers.*

I must warn Imandoff! Corri set her will against the assembled shakkas and searched over the grasslands beginning to gray with the approaching dawn.

Imandoff! Her mind-call went out along the familiar lines of communication that had developed between them while she was at Leshy. *I seek you.*

Here! came a distant answer.

Far ahead of her, Corri saw a small ball of light, and instinctively knew it was the body-vibration of the sorcerer. Using all her will, the girl attempted to swoop toward the light, sending a warning ahead of her. Her progress was hampered, as if she tried to swim against a heavy current.

Where are you? Imandoff's mental voice was faint.

At Neeba. Beware of Grimmel and one called Kayth. Try as she would, Corri could not reach the sorcerer. On the dark grasslands behind the sorcerer she spotted a dull light tinged with old red. She felt repulsed and somehow threatened by that distant light. *One follows, Imandoff, one who can harm you. Beware!*

Corri felt a pull back toward the shakka gathering. She fought, uncertain if Imandoff had received her message, but her strength was nearly gone. Phantom hands outstretched towards the sorcerer's position, Corri shouted defiance as she felt herself being drawn back to the rhythm of the Tuone drums. The night sped past, the stars overhead a blur. With a loud snapping noise resounding in her ears, she slammed back into her body beside the fire.

Chapter 21

$\mathcal{L}$ie still." Halka's voice was thick with concern.

Corri groaned as she felt the circulation returning to her numb limbs. She felt cold; her whole body was as icy as if she had been caught in a winter storm howling off the Taunith Sea. She began shivering and could not stop. Halka and Denuja wrapped warm goat-hair blankets about her.

"I destroyed Grimmel's mind-seeker," Corri finally said through chattering teeth. "With your help, I smashed it. Now I am free of Grimmel's following."

"Not so," answered Halka as she brought a bowl of hot liquid to Corri's trembling lips. "For a seeker to work, there must be something of yours tied to whatever Grimmel used, or something belonging to him that you carry. That also we must find and destroy."

"When I saw Grimmel, he had nothing other than the strange stone." Corri tried to focus her exhausted mind. "The stone. There was something familiar about the stone."

"Describe it," Denuja ordered as her dark eyes held Corri's.

"It was a flat, dull white, a color like goat milk in a cup." Corri sipped at Halka's hot herbal brew and felt her strength slowly returning. "Like my earring!" Her slim hand flew to her pierced ear in sudden fear. "How could I have been so stupid? I never guessed!"

Denuja pushed away Corri's frantic hand and quickly unhooked the earring, then held the earring before the girl's wide eyes. "So common a thing that no one would ever suspect its true nature." The shakka looked down at the piece of jewelry in distaste.

"I have worn it since I was a baby." Corri stared down at the earring lying in the brown palm of Denuja's hand. "I thought only to keep it until I needed money." She grimaced in disgust. "So that is how the old toad always knew where I was, where exactly to find me. A curse on him! And a curse on my father for leaving me with him!"

"Back!" ordered Halka.

The old shakka scooped up the earring and threw it into the coals of the fire. Dragging Corri with them, the group of shakkas scrambled to the far edges of the light. For several minutes nothing happened. Then the stone exploded with a small pop, and black, acrid smoke issued from the glowing coals.

"Through mind-touch we saw what you saw in Hadliden." Halka smoothed back Corri's hair. "We now know of the strange forces that surround your birth. There is little we can teach you, girl. You must make another journey to discover for yourself what bloodlines and inherited powers belonged to your parents. It is my belief that you lie under a geas, one laid by the Goddess to fulfill prophecy. If this is so, and I fully believe it is, then you have no choice but to go to the Temple in the city of Kystan."

"Yes, you must go to the Temple of the Great Mountain in Kirisan, for part of your bloodline is Kirisani." Denuja frowned at the coming dawn. "Only there can you hope to see the records of bloodlines kept for centuries by the Tuulikki priestesses." She stared down at Corri. "And perhaps there you can learn that when a call goes out from those who aid you, you must obey. We almost lost you when you refused to return."

"I had to warn Imandoff." Corri's mouth set in a stubborn line. "He is in danger. Someone follows him, a person with a warped life-force pattern." She wondered at her choice of words, yet knew she was right.

"The last we saw as though through rippling water." Halka helped the girl to her feet. "A strange pattern, not that of the evil Fravashi priests, yet—"

"Yet something in it was the same." The shakkas gathered around shook their heads in assent at Denuja's words.

"I would not bring danger down upon the Clans. I must leave at once." Corri shrugged off the blankets. "Until I can return without evil stalking my path, I shall not return to the Clans of Tuone. I will fight as a Dream Warrior from afar. Only the Clans have welcomed me, made me blood-kin, cared if I lived or died. My heart will ever be with the free People of the grasslands. My words of thanks cannot express what I feel for your kindness and help."

Corri turned and sought the mare Mouse, the tears slipping slowly down her cheeks. As she took the reins to mount, she felt a hand slid over hers.

"I will ride with you to Neeba," Halka said. "I will send you with what safeguards I can. Girl, I shall miss you. Perhaps before I go Between Worlds you can return and ride once more on the grasslands beside me."

Corri threw her arms about the old woman, biting her lip to hold back the flood of tears she felt dammed within her. The two women stood with their arms about each other, the only time Corri could remember doing so with anyone, except the time with Imandoff during her moment of panic in the temple mazes.

"I shall miss you, Halka." The girl's voice cracked with tears. "I would rather stay with the Clans than journey again."

"Fate has decreed otherwise, girl." Halka turned away to mount her horse. "Come, let us ride to Neeba. There are things I would do, things that will give you what protection I can give."

The two rode back toward the city with the dawn light spilling around them on the rolling prairie.

$\mathcal{I}$ will not let you go alone." Takra's stubborn jaw was firmly set. "You are no sword-woman, Corri Farblood, to go singing into danger. I will not be left behind."

"I cannot ask sister-kin to risk life for me." Corri sighed and continued to pack her saddlebags with the journey food that Halka insisted she take. She tied the rolled blankets behind the saddle. "I do not know what awaits me, Takra, or how long I will be gone. Perhaps I shall not return at all. Only the Lady knows that answer." She stood, clad in the Tuonela clothing, the prairie winds ruffling her short hair, now a sun-faded blonde with undertones of red.

"We stood together in the Valley of Whispers. I am no coward to slink off now." Takra secured her saddlebags on Lightfoot. "There is no way you can leave me behind. And what of Tirkul? Will you not tell him you are leaving?" She tied a small bow and quiver of bolts to the saddlebags.

Corri shook her head. "Halka will tell him when I am gone. He has no place in this journey. There will be no time for courting and pleasantries, Takra, only hard riding and dangers."

"If it is in your heart to ride this journey, then go with the Lady's blessings, Takra Wind-Rider." Halka slipped a leather thong over Corri's head. "This amulet, of the Lady's charmed silver, will aid and protect you. I have done what I can, girl, to ease your path. The rest is up to you. Remember me when you dream-fly."

Corri cupped the amulet in one hand. Part of her feared the unknown journey to Kirisan, but another part of her knew it was necessary, that she would have no peace, no true freedom, until she knew about her parents and the secret of her strange bloodline. And the shakka's mention of a geas, that word created a strange pull on her spirit, a tugging toward the distant city of Kystan that could not be ignored.

"I shall not forget you, Halka. Look for me when the moon is full, for then, I think, I can reach out more easily. Tell Tirkul I shall think often of him, but it is not yet time for us to journey together. Perhaps that time will not come at all."

Turning away to hide the tears she felt under her eyelids, Corri mounted and rode out of the encampment, Takra beside her. On rope leads behind Corri's horse followed the two mounts they had brought with them from the grasslands' battlefield weeks before.

Corri and Takra journeyed two days on the caravan road leading from Neeba back toward Kirisan before they saw any other travelers. A horseman, gray cloak blowing in the wind, sat patiently astride a roan by the side of the beaten path.

"It is Imandoff." Takra kicked her horse into a gallop, racing toward the sorcerer with a wild Clan yell.

Thank the Goddess, it is him, Corri thought as she raced after her friend. *I thought he would never find us. And he is safe from whoever followed him on the grasslands.*

"Ho, Takra, Corri!" The sorcerer raised a long-fingered hand in greeting. "I have been waiting for you."

"You are safe." Corri reined in beside Imandoff and grinned at him. "Then you did get my message, for you are here unharmed." She reached over to pat Sun-Dancer.

"A faint message full of warning." Imandoff frowned. "But never have I seen one who follows after me." He turned his horse back along the trail. "However, that means little. I think we should take a different road, one that comes into Kirisan from another direction."

"How did you know I journey to Kirisan? You know something you are not telling, old man." Corri rode knee to knee with him. "Would you make me go blindly into danger?"

"It is only logical that you seek information found only at the Temple of the Great Mountain. As for the rest, I think the one who follows is your father." Imandoff stared off into the distance. "I met him at Leshy."

"My father!" Corri's breath hissed through her teeth. "But the one I saw, his life-force pattern was tainted. A creature like Grimmel, yet not somehow. The master thief said my father would answer to his control."

"Yes," answered Imandoff. "A power tainted in a similar way, yet different. Kayth is connected with the master thief, yet not totally under Grimmel's control, no matter what that one thinks. I felt that in Kayth when I spoke with him at Leshy."

"I would not see him yet," Corri said. "First, I want to know all about my mother and these strange powers that the shakkas say I have inherited. I have inherited them, have I not, sorcerer?"

"Your parents both had certain gifts, but in you they have come out stronger, different. Your mother's training I know, but Kayth's ..." Imandoff scratched his beard and shook his head. "The Tuulikki priestesses of the Great Temple understand such things, for long have they studied bloodlines."

"Then I go there now."

"We all go." Takra now rode beside Corri and Imandoff. "Corri is sister-kin and of Clan blood now, sorcerer. We passed through the blood ritual together. Whoever seeks to harm her must deal with me also." One hand strayed to her sword hilt.

"I suppose you also received a Clan mark?" Imandoff scanned her cheeks and hands for a tattoo.

"Not where you can see it, sorcerer." Corri felt the blood rise to her face.

Imandoff gave a short laugh, then his face grew solemn. "Something within tells me that the journey may go far beyond Kirisan, Wind-Rider." Imandoff shook his head. "We may discover things never dreamed of by the Peoples of Sar Akka, some terrifying, some wondrous."

"So be it." Takra stared off into the distance, a look of determination on her oval face.

"I would put an end to this sniffing at my heels." Corri fingered the silver amulet at her breast. "My life shall be my own, or I would end it."

"One's life is seldom one's own," the sorcerer remarked, "but the choices made in it should be. That is true freedom."

Imandoff took the rope leads for the spare mounts from Corri and secured them to his saddle. "Where we are going, the horses will follow me more easily. The mountain trails of Deep Rising are safer for us than the open grasslands of Tuone right now. Besides, I know a shortcut to Kystan."

"Another of his escape routes, no doubt," Corri murmured to Takra.

"Good at that, is he?" Takra grinned. "I noticed he knew all the back trails into Leshy, even those known only to the Clans. I have a feeling, Farblood, that you and I know very little about this sorcerer. His business is his own. Look to the worn leather on his sword sheath." Takra nodded at the swaying weapon by Imandoff's side. "That comes from use, not carrying a weapon for show. Yes, Imandoff Silverhair knows well how to use a sword."

I pray that is so, Corri thought as they rode on down the beaten caravan trail, the tall grass around them soughing in the wind. *My heart tells me that we may need that skill before this journey is ended.*

Imandoff soon turned his roan off the caravan trail, the two spare mounts following on their leads. He headed away from the grasslands toward the mountains of Deep Rising, Takra and Corri following behind.

Chapter 22

They camped at the foot of the mountains at dusk. Although Corri nervously paced the perimeter of the camp, peering back across the grasslands, she did not insist on pushing up onto the rugged slopes.

That would be foolish, she thought as she stared into the darkness. *Even if I did suggest such a thing, Imandoff and Takra would argue against such a move, and rightly so. It would be dangerous to take the horses along those steep rocky trails in the dark.*

"You sense something?" Corri jumped at Takra's soft voice next to her shoulder.

"Perhaps." Corri fingered the hilt of the long dagger at her belt. "I learned long ago when I was thief for Grimmel to watch my back. Now ..." she paused.

"We have seen no sign that we are followed." Takra narrowed her amber eyes as she too stared along their back trail.

"That means nothing. There is this feeling, this itch between my shoulder blades, that tells me to beware." Corri pulled at her ear where the earring had hung for years, a habit that had always amused the master thief. "It was a sign I learned never to ignore."

"Perhaps we should tell Imandoff." Takra played with the end of one pale braid. "As a sorcerer, he must have the power to far-see."

"That takes great energy. Remember how he tired after burning those jumpers in the tunnel? And tell him what? That the city thief from Hadliden grows uneasy in the dark."

Takra laughed softly. "Aye, put that way, it does sound strange." Her voice grew sterner. "I know that most men give little credit to the instincts of women outside the Mystery Schools. But remember, men like Imandoff and those of the Clans recognize the importance of a woman speaking as you are now. They willingly listen to such women."

"Do you know, Takra, that until I fled from Grimmel, I never thought of myself as a woman? Oh, I knew I was female from my form, the moon-reaction of my body, but a woman to be desired by men, no, that never entered my mind. I was a thief, the only female one Grimmel had. And now—"

"Tirkul." The sword-woman's thoughts meshed with Corri's. "His words and actions have set you to seeing yourself in a new way. Men can be pleasant creatures, Farblood, although I have yet to find one that makes me yearn to take heart-oath. Do not hurry, Sister-Friend. The Mother of Mares dictates the time of joining. When it comes, both you and I will know. Until then we ride free of ties."

Takra turned back to the fire-lit circle of the camp, Corri reluctantly following. Twice the girl looked over her shoulder at the deepening blackness of the Tuone plains, finally shrugging and shaking her head. She said nothing to Imandoff about her uneasiness, although the sorcerer watched her with eyes narrowed against the puffs of smoke from his clay pipe. Instead, she told the tale of her battle with Grimmel while in her shadow-form, and the destruction of the seekers. Imandoff only continued to watch her with dark eyes and said little.

The first rays of dawn found them on the faint thread of trail that led upward among the resinous trees of Deep Rising.

Corri tested gently for the itch between her shoulders. *It is gone now. Does this mean we are no longer spied upon, or that I just can no longer sense whoever follows?* She kept alert as they rode, but her instincts sent no further warning.

Corri began to relax as they wove their way through the forest of fir and pine, dotted here and there with the purple leaves of the meppe trees. Sheltered from view of anyone riding the grasslands below, she no longer was plagued with wanting to constantly watch their back trail.

The air grew cooler as they climbed. Even though the warm spring sun beat down on the ridges and rocky slopes of the mountains, the travelers were soon wrapping their cloaks about them. Where the trail led under the low-limbed trees, the air was chill and damp. Thin layers of frozen snow lay in the shadows of trees and rocks.

The first night they camped in an upland meadow, the surrounding peaks touched by clouds and frosted with snow. The second night found them still higher. They had to shelter as best they could among the boulders of a pass, feeding the horses crumbled journey bread. The mountain winds, whipping down from the icy peaks, and a lack of suitable wood made a fire impossible. Late the next afternoon they descended from the bare, high slopes of Deep Rising into the trees once more.

"We will stay here for a few days," Imandoff said as they picked their way down into a lush mountain meadow. "It has been hard on the horses, and they need to rest and graze."

With the animals tied on long tethers so they could feed on the rich grass, Takra strung her bow, slung the quiver from her belt, and slipped silently off into the forest.

"A versatile companion." Imandoff carefully laid the dry tree limbs Corri had gathered from under the forest canopy. With a snap of his long fingers, he lit the fire and sat back to stare at the flames. "We shall not want for fresh meat while the Wind-Rider is with us."

"You do not use a bow?" Corri watched as the sorcerer cradled his ever-present pipe, the smoke beginning to curl upward in strange patterns.

"Not with any skill," he answered, staring off into the coming twilight. "To each his own talents, Corri. I have no gift for dream-flying, Takra no skill for the greater spells. As always, the Lady has been wise in bringing us together for this journey. We each provide what the other has not."

"Imandoff, what is a geas? The shakkas mentioned it, but I do not know what it means." Corri drew out her long dagger and carefully removed the bark from the green forked branches Imandoff had told her to cut. When she finished, she took out the sharpening stone, a parting gift from Halka. Methodically, she began the steady sweep of stone against blade edge.

Imandoff studied the rippling flames of the campfire before answering. "Geas is a very old word. One seldom hears it used today. It means a compulsion to do some task, a binding. Sometimes a geas is laid by duty, sometimes by spellwork. Sometimes, as in the very old legends, it is put upon a person by the gods." His voice trailed off into private thoughts.

A nicker from Lightfoot broke the reverie. Takra was coming across the meadow toward them, several gutted hares strung on a thong at her side.

"The hunting is good here." The warrior woman squatted beside the fire and began to peel off the hides. "There is a small spring yonder near that mound of small boulders. Been here before, sorcerer?"

"A long time ago, during one of my many journeys." Imandoff pushed a forked stick into the ground on each side of the fire and began to skewer the skinned hares on a crosspiece.

"Where have you not been?" Takra asked with a smile as she gathered up the water bottles and strode into the darkness to clean up and bring fresh water.

The roasted hares were delicious, as long as Corri did not think about the smell of blood and Takra peeling off the hides. Imandoff supplemented the meal with some tubers, crisp and a little sharp, he dug from the edge of the meadow.

Corri rolled up in her blankets early, leaving Takra and the sorcerer talking softly in the glow-broken blackness. She quickly slipped down into sleep.

Corri. A voice called her out of the darkness of her dream. *Where are you?*

Who calls? Awareness came, dragging her out of nothingness into a place of light. *Who calls my name?*

Corri. Again the demand sounded.

Corri found herself swaying among the broken clouds, the light of the moon now a slender crescent far above. Below, she saw the wink of fire that marked their camp. There came a tugging, a compelling to move out across the Tuone grasslands. A thin spiraling thread of red-tinged light flashed upward from the plains, striving to reach her, yet never quite long enough. The demanding voice sounded once more in her mind. The girl fought against the demand, anger strengthening her will power.

It is not Halka. She would not summon me this way, Corri thought, willing her shadow-self to hold fast. Dimly, she was aware of the amulet on her breast, now a bright glow.

No! The voice that called her name cried out in anger and fear. The thread of reaching light winked out as a spark stamped by the foot. The pressuring demand for her to follow the voice died with it.

Corri forced her shadow-self to stay where it hung among the clouds, while she quested out with her mind onto the plains behind. Halka? No, she did not feel the shakka's life-force in that call. Who then? She quested closer to the foot of Deep Rising where the sharp folds of tree-covered rock met the sweeping grasses. Two pools of thought, intertwined, raging with violence and emotion, met her probe. Two men in battle!

Tirkul! She stretched out her phantom hands and tried to reach him, to aid in the fight against the treacherous opponent. But she found herself swooping back to the meadow.

"No! I must aid Tirkul!" Corri awoke with her shouts ringing off the surrounding mountain sides.

"Corri! Sister-Friend!" Takra's concern edged every word. The sword-woman knelt beside her, her drawn sword gilded with firelight.

"I was called," Corri finally managed to say. "From the grasslands. Then Tirkul—"

"Tirkul called?" Imandoff's face came into view above her.

"No, it was someone else. Tirkul and another man fought. I tried to reach him, but I could not." She sat up, shivering.

"Whatever or whoever crept into your dreams had but very little power." Imandoff brought out his flask of mountain water and poured a small amount into a cup for the girl.

"It was no dream," she insisted as she made a face at the burning bite of the drink. "Halka's gift," she touched one cold hand on the amulet that hung between her breasts, "this gave me the strength to resist the call."

"If Tirkul truly fought one who sought to entangle you in spell-weaves, then that one is probably dead." Takra sheathed her sword with a sharp thrust. "Few, very few, have the strength or sword-knowledge to defeat Tirkul."

"Still, I think we should take greater care in covering our trail." Imandoff sat with his knees drawn up, staring into the fire. "We have been too complacent, Wind-Rider. Grimmel and his people are not the only dangers that might track us."

"No need to post a guard," Takra said as she rolled up in her blankets. "Lightfoot will give warning if anyone or anything of the physical world approaches. And it seems that Far-blood has her own methods of warning against the dangers sent spirit-wise."

Corri curled up, facing the fire, the blankets tugged close about her. *As you say, the horse will give warning if anyone comes into camp in a physical body,* she thought, *but not if a shadow-self roams here. And I am not so certain, Sister-Friend, that my powers are great enough to warn of such intrusion.*

She determined not to sleep, but exhaustion rode heavy on her. As her eyelids dragged closed, she saw the sorcerer still staring into the flames.

Imandoff led them along winding trails that wandered from one small valley over the knife-edged peaks to another. The days slipped past, and Corri grew impatient to reach their destination. Even Takra lost her interest in the wild deer and elusive mountain sheep as the journey dragged on.

"We must go to the Temple," Corri stated one morning as they saddled. "No more wandering about, Imandoff. It is time to go to Kystan."

"If you speak the words, then it is truly time. I only waited for your decision." Imandoff pulled himself astride Sun-Dancer. "Something is afoot here in Deep Rising. Not once have I seen any sign of the Green Men, although I have kept a sharp eye for the faint signs of their passing." He scanned the trees around them. "Strange, but there is a sense of urgency now, one that did not ride with us before."

"Yes." Takra checked the slide of her sword in its sheath as she mounted Lightfoot, wary eyes taking in every detail of the trail ahead. "Now we must ride with trail-sense, guarding our backs and watchful of dangers ahead."

"It is still far to Kystan?" Corri asked as she followed Takra and Imandoff up the tree-brushed trail.

"Some days yet," came the sorcerer's answer, just loud enough to reach her ears. "Perhaps the Green Men know what troubles these mountains. I will set out signs when we camp. If any are near, they will track us with answers."

But they saw no Green Men, nor did any answer the secret markings that Imandoff carefully laid out at each camp.

The forests of Deep Rising seemed to be full of silent watch-fulness. The uneasiness grew as they journeyed out of the high peaks and meadows into the lower ranges.

There, on the lower trails running from Kirisan into both Tuone and over the hills to Asur, they saw the first sign of men, traders using the back roads to avoid Asuran taxes or beat the caravans into the grasslands. Each time Takra's keen senses and Imandoff's instincts sent them into hiding until the traders were well past.

None of the traders appeared to move with ease, either. The men rode with hands on sword or bow string, eyes ever-moving over the deep forest canopy at the sides of the trail. When the piercing eyes of a guard passed directed over her, seemingly without notice, Corri glanced sideways at Imand-off. The sorcerer's eyes were half-closed, his brow furrowed in concentration, his long fingers weaving some spellwork.

So, he covers us with illusion. Corri stared back at the dis-appearing traders, her mouth pinched in thought. *What event moves into being, so strong that it is felt by even spirit-dull people?*

She thought of retreating to the Clans, but the pull toward Kystan and the Temple was as unbreakable as one of the tough, thin lariats of the Tuonela riders.

The solitary, elusive Green Men made no appearance, and for some unknown reason that made Corri uneasy. Imandoff became more tight-lipped and remote, Takra quick to draw sword or dagger at the slightest sound. Corri, however, rode easier in one way, no longer feeling the prick between her shoulder blades that told of skulking followers.

Chapter 23

Corri and her companions rode out of the mountains of Deep Rising into the fertile valleys of Kirisan after three weeks of journeying through forests and bare rocky slopes.

The road to the mountain city of Kystan led through a rolling expanse of cultivated farmland and green pasture. Mounding hills occasionally cut across the land. To the south a finger-ridge of worn mountains pushed up a backbone of tree-covered slopes. Groves of trees, their branches bright with new leaves or heavy with scented needled boughs, were dotted across the fertile valleys.

The farm houses were steep-roofed thatch over stone block walls, their yards full of colorful, scratching jakins and laughing children. Small groves of fruit trees carpeted the earth with their falling blossom petals. The farm dogs barked a warning as the riders passed. It was near sunset, the azure sky emblazoned with streaks of red and gold.

"Where now?" Corri asked, reining Mouse onto a wide dusty road leading toward a high, flat-topped mountain in the distance.

"To Kystan." Imandoff pointed toward the flat peak. "There lies the Temple of the Great Mountain, the Mystery School of the Kirisani." The roan pranced and arched his neck.

"Sorcerer, I do not want to be in the clutches of another High Clua." Corri pulled her mare to a stop. Distasteful memories of Leshy surfaced in her thoughts. "Is there no other way to find out about my mother?"

"None. Ryanna, your mother, was a priestess there. I knew your mother as a friend, but little of her lineage." Imandoff stared off into the distance. "It would be more than passing strange if those of the Temple were to hold you against your will." His gray eyes flicked back to her. "The Tuulikki priestesses keep records of all Kirisani bloodlines, especially those of the initiates within the Temple. Your mother's line will be written in their books."

"And my father?" Corri watched Imandoff's face closely.

"Kayth Farblood will not be listed there. He is not from Kirisan." Imandoff nudged his horse with his knees. "Over twenty years ago I found him wandering along a trail in Deep Rising, sick and alone. I took him to the Temple for healing. It was there that your mother, Ryanna, fell in love with him."

"If her father is not Kirisani, what is he?" Takra asked, as she pushed her horse forward to ride knee to knee with Corri and the sorcerer. "Asuran? Fravashi? His name is not of the Tuonela Clans."

"In truth, I know not what People he comes from. At first he knew little of our customs and used a strange form of our language. He learned quickly. But he was always different. As to his name, he gave only Kayth. I named him Farblood."

"But you guess." Corri looked out over the farmlands as they rode on. "I know not how, but my father and Grimmel are connected. Grimmel spoke of it."

"My guesses I will keep to myself until I can prove them," Imandoff answered. "Whatever your father was or is, Corri, has little to do with who you are."

"Perhaps it affects me more than you realize. When the shakkas helped me dream-fly to Hadliden to destroy Grimmel's seeking device, the old toad spoke of my father as one who would follow his commands. Grimmel also said something of being marooned together." The girl watched a passing herd of cows followed by a young boy. "It is time for truth between us, Imandoff. What is my father? What am I?"

"Truth, Corri, but I do not know, not for certain." The sorcerer's gray eyes scanned an approaching wagon. "I have no proof of anything." He reined Sun-Dancer and the lead-horse aside as the wagon creaked past, the trade goods of a blacksmith clanging near the tail gate.

"But?" Takra's calm voice demanded an answer.

"I think Kayth came from beyond the stars." Imandoff gestured toward the cloud-sprinkled sky overhead. "The ancient histories of the Four Peoples tell of how we once came from the stars to Sar Akka. Perhaps he also came from another world, seeking signs of our ancestors. Or, as Grimmel intimated, fleeing some danger."

"Legends." Takra shook her head. "Tales for children."

"All legends have a kernel of truth buried in them." Imandoff guided his horse through a milling herd of goats. "Ever since I met Kayth, I have searched old records in the Mystery Schools and sought out ancient ruins of the Forgotten Ones in search of an answer. Perhaps even the Forgotten Ones, who were long gone before the Peoples came to this land, also came from another world, out among the stars."

"Tales for dreamers around a winter's fire." Takra ignored the stares of the little boys who lagged behind the goats.

"Have you found the answer among the ruins and records of the Forgotten Ones?" Corri looked across a field to where a man and team were plowing. The rich black soil rolled up in a furrow as the plow bit into the ground. She could smell the damp earth. A flurry of birds settled in the plowed soil, hunting for insects.

"Hints, bits and pieces." Imandoff urged his mount to a trot, Takra and Corri behind him. "Enough of the past. We must discover why Corri is so important to Grimmel, important enough to send his best to bring her back to Hadliden. And that answer may be written in the bloodline records of the Temple of the Great Mountain in Kystan."

Several times Corri saw fortress-houses, some in near-ruin, scrub and trees allowed to grow close about them, while others stood proud on their scoured pinnacles of jutting rock.

"Some of the older families still hold to the ancient law," Imandoff said as his smoke-colored eyes stared at one of the fortresses. "When the Kirisani first settled in this land, their leaders decreed that there should be a fortress for every twenty miles throughout the countryside. These fortresses were to be kept clear of trees and brush that could hide attackers, as well as be stocked with enough food and a water supply to withstand a reasonable length of seige. That the law is no longer enforced by the Temple is a sign that not all within that place believe in the Prophecy. When trouble with Frav comes upon us, and it will sometime, there will be many in Kirisan without shelter or protection."

The moon had risen above the mountains by the time they neared the mountain city. Corri gazed in wonder at the enormous bare peak jutting high above the valley floor. Moonlight flowed down the rugged sides, splashing across the road which led to an opening flanked by flaring torches. The dark, fortified gates stood open to the flow of people, both coming and going from the hidden city.

"This city believes in strong gates, does it not?" Takra stared at the enormous gates, as thick through as a tall man's reach, as they passed between them. "The hinges are of mountain steel, as are the strapping which ties the planks together."

"I think this city could withstand any siege," Corri answered. "There is only one road up to this place, and that could be defended easily with bowmen. And faced with these giant gates, how could invaders hope to get in?"

"All it would take is for a few malcontents to overpower the gate-guards." Takra looked at the rocky cliffs above them. "Or a warrior to climb over the walls at night."

Ahead of them, a line of stationary torches wound up the mountainside, disappearing far above.

"Up there." Imandoff pointed one slender finger to the flat top of the mound. "Kystan, the jewel of Kirisan."

One branch of the road passed through the enormous iron-bound gates and onto a stone-paved, grooved ramp that twisted and turned ever upward.

Takra caught Imandoff's attention and tilted her head toward the other road in silent question.

"It leads to fortified sentry posts which ring the outer walls of the city." Imandoff stared at the second road and frowned. "However, it does not look well-used. Has the Temple ceased to man them?" he murmured.

Corri saw by the flaring torchlight that the walled passageway, open to the sky, had been laboriously chiseled out of the mountain itself. Upward they went, winding to the peak of the great mound of stones and the second gate, also marked by guards and torches.

Corri caught her breath in surprise as they entered the last gates. The entire city of Kystan was built inside a sunken crater on the mountaintop, its thousands of lights filling the basin as if the stars had come to earth. The city's outer walls were formed of the bones of the peak, with stairs and watchtowers carved into the rock. The sprawling houses and crooked streets all meandered down the gently sloping sides of the crater and converged in the center, at the very edge of a glistening lake. In the center of the lake, on a leveled rocky outcropping, stood a cluster of white-walled buildings, connected with the city only by two slender bridges.

"You are an initiate of the Temple," Takra said to Imandoff as he turned toward an inn whose sign bore the picture of an immense crab-like creature, a krynap. "Your belt buckle is open acknowledgment of that." The warrior woman pointed to the blue-stone buckle at Imandoff's waist. "Surely you can gain us easy admittance to these bloodline records in the Temple."

"I chose to leave the Temple and its disciplines a long time ago. I considered their practices too stifling." Imandoff dismounted at the inn's gate, leading his horse through to the yard and stables. "My presence will be tolerated, but not met with joy. The High Priest considers me too much of a wanderer to be happy about my reappearing."

"Somehow that does not surprise me, sorcerer." Takra laughed as she unsaddled Lightfoot and led her into a stall. "Are you certain you do not have Tuonela blood?"

"In fact, there was a Tuonela grandmother two generations back," replied Imandoff with a chuckle. "It seems that wandering independent spirit of the Clans chose to come out in me. Much to the disappointment of the High Priest."

Corri remained quiet as Imandoff bartered for a room in the crowded inn. She found herself of two minds concerning her heritage. Part of her yearned to know the truth, to have it laid bare, but part also hung back, wondering if ignorance would not be better.

At last the sorcerer settled for one sleeping chamber for the three of them. They skirted the common room and climbed the dark, creaking stairs to the third floor cubicle where Takra immediately thrust open the window. The evening breeze flickered the candle that Imandoff set on the low table.

"Pah! Do they never let in the air?" the sword-woman asked as she stood with her head and shoulders through the frame. "How can they stand the stink?"

"They probably feel the same way about living near horses and goats," Corri answered as she dropped her saddlebag on one of the straw-filled mattresses. She jumped back as cockroaches scuttled out of the straw and disappeared into cracks in the walls. "Imandoff, is there no other place to spend this night? I hate bugs!"

"This is the safest haven for us in Kystan. I know the innkeeper, a reliable man who will tell us if any come asking questions. I plan to go down to the common room and see if I can pick up any gossip." The sorcerer grinned as he stood, one hand on the door. "You two can have the beds. See you at dawn." He was out the door before Corri could answer.

"I do not like this place." Takra scowled as she paced about the dingy room. "This is like being in a trap. Only one way out makes me uneasy."

"I think the stables are safer and cleaner," Corri said as she watched a cockroach creeping up the opposite wall. "Imandoff will sit all night drinking and listening to stories. He will never know we are gone."

"Then let us go. At least the hay will be free from these bugs and smell better." Takra blew out the candle and opened the door, saddlebags in hand.

One glance over Takra's shoulder down the hall, dimly lit by widely spaced lamps, sent Corri retreating into the dark room. The girl flattened herself against the wall beside the door as the warrior woman stepped into the hall. Coming up the stairs, her face clear in the lamp light, was Malya, her enemy from Leshy, the one who had followed her into Tuone. Behind her walked Druk, his scar-marked face twisted into a frown as he spoke.

"Grimmel said that Farblood will eventually come to Kystan." The assassin's voice was tinged with anger. "So we wait. Your importance is gone now that you have been driven from Leshy. We company together at the master thief's orders. See that you give me no cause to complain to him."

"Do not threaten me, assassin." Malya's voice held an ominous hiss. "We should be watching the Temple bridge instead of sitting in some tavern while you drink ale. What will Grimmel think if the girl slips by once again?"

The voices faded slowly as the pair entered a room farther down the hall and shut the door.

Takra stepped back into the darkened room and closed the door. She reached out to Corri, one strong hand clamping on the girl's shoulder.

"Who are those two?" she whispered. "The man looks vaguely familiar."

"The woman is Malya, the one I told you of from Leshy. The other is Druk, an assassin who works for Grimmel."

"The coward who fled from my sword's edge in the grasslands!" Takra's words were a low growl. "The one who followed us to the Valley of Whispers."

Corri clamped her hand against Takra's where it tightened on her sword hilt. "Not now," she warned. "The Temple first, then Druk and Malya."

Corri silently crossed the room to the moonlit window. "How could they have known I was here? The stones linking me to the master thief were destroyed."

"Where else would we go to discover your bloodlines than to Kystan?" Takra answered, her voice barely audible. "What now? We should go below and warn Imandoff."

"No." Corri caught at Takra's arm. "I cannot go through the common room. There may be others with Druk who know me."

Corri leaned out the window, her eyes checking the ledges and fall of the roof. *Yes, there is toe room along the slanting roof if we are careful, then a rainwater catch pipe to the kitchen sheds below.*

"I go first," the girl said over her shoulder. "When I am down, drop the packs to me, then follow."

"Not me!" Takra shuddered as she traced the narrow escape route Corri planned to follow. "You go. I will drop the packs and then use the stairs. Neither the woman from Leshy nor Grimmel's men know me. See you at the stables."

Corri climbed over the rough sill and carefully placed her booted feet on the slanting roof. She felt it give slightly under her weight. She had no further time for thoughts of Takra as she hastened to the water pipe and slid down to the kitchen sheds. Once her boot crunched into the roofing up to her ankle. A disgruntled voice called out from the room beneath, but the girl hurried on, sliding down the last roof to land with a thud in the courtyard. Instinctively, she pulled back into the deep shadows and waited for Takra to drop the packs.

Why must I always run and hide? she asked herself as she gathered up the bags. *I thought I was done with Grimmel. By the blessed Goddess, I will be free of that old toad, one way or another.*

Corri slipped into the darkened stables and stowed the packs next to Mouse's stall. Nervously, she waited for Takra, listening for any sound of footsteps on the inn's cobbled yard, watching for any stealthy movement in the inky shadows. Wisps of gossamer clouds followed the moon in its snail-slow slide across the black sky. An hour passed before the sword-woman slipped into the stables. Although she walked cautiously and stared into the shadows, she did not see Corri crouched inside.

"Where have you been?" Corri asked softly just as Takra passed out of the moonlight-filled doorway into the near-blackness. Takra jumped, coming around with her dagger ready. Only Corri's thief-quick reactions saved her from a slash across the ribs.

"Never startle me like that!" Takra sheathed the dagger, her pale brows drawn together in adrenaline-pumped anger. "You were so well concealed in the shadows, I never saw you."

"Sorry." Corri shrugged and grinned. "It has long been my habit to stay out of sight. Like your drawing your dagger when surprised."

"I stopped for an ale and to ask a few questions. Seems the woman Malya and the assassin Druk have been here several days, waiting, the innkeeper said, but he knew not for

whom." Takra leaned her muscled shoulders against Lightfoot's stall. "Imandoff was deep in some conversation with a
trader. They appeared to be bargaining over some krynap eyes
and moss stones. Where would the sorcerer have gotten
those, I wonder?"

The stones from my collar, Corri thought. *He trades them
here in this city, far enough from Asur to keep from being traced.
The trader is probably going elsewhere, another city where he in
turn will trade the stones.* She turned her head away and
shrugged, as if it were of no importance.

"I could not catch his eye. Imandoff may trust the
innkeeper but I do not, so I left no message." Takra idly pulled
out her sword a little and clicked it back in its sheath.

"I have to leave." Corri began to pace the narrow straw-
coated hall between the stalls. "I will not go back to Grimmel.
The shakkas should have let me kill him."

"There is another way." Takra put out a firm hand and
stopped the girl. "We—you and I—go to the Temple
tonight. The sorcerer can follow, if he comes around to
remembering us."

"But the Temple may be closed for the night. I know not
their customs. And what of the horses?"

"Imandoff will care for the horses." The sword-woman
patted Lightfoot's nose as the horse pushed against her. "If the
Temple is closed, we will bang on the gates until they open."
Takra padded soft-footed to the door; slowly, she scanned the
empty courtyard. "Grimmel's creatures will not dare attack us
at the very doorstep of the Temple. Come. No one is about."

The two women crept out of the stables and across the
moon-streaked inn yard to the gates. The gatekeeper sat in his
little shed, snoring loudly. Takra carefully eased open the
postern gate enough for them to slip out into the street.

"Now to find the Temple," Takra said, one hand on her
sword hilt as they walked quickly down the silent lane.

"Every street leads to the lake," Corri answered. "That I
noticed as we rode in. The Temple must be on the island in

the lake in the center of the city." Her hand rested on her dagger, her thief's instincts wary of every shadowed doorway, each black alley.

The two hurried down the gently sloping street. After a few wrong turns onto meandering lanes, they sighted the glistening waters of the lake at the end of a cobbled pathway.

The lake surrounded the island Temple like a moat, its narrow band of moon-sprinkled waters bounded on the city side by a wide promenade and a low stone wall. A span of bridge stretched across the lapping waters to the white stone buildings. At the land end of the bridge stood two white-clad women, drawn swords at their sides.

"Well, that does it." Takra stopped so suddenly that Corri nearly walked into her. "How do we get past the guards? When I spoke of banging on the gates, I envisioned the very doors of the Temple itself. The inner gate is one thing, but this being out in the open arguing about entering is another. If we tarry too long trying to persuade them, we may be seen."

"I have nothing to lose by asking. I cannot go back to the inn."

Corri drew a deep breath, then resolutely crossed the wide avenue between the city and the edge of the lake. Apprehension gripping her stomach, she walked directly up to the armed women, outwardly confident, inwardly cringing at possible refusal and rejection.

"Halt!" One of the women held out a hand. "The Temple is closed for the night, unless there is great need or illness."

"We," Corri indicated Takra with a sweep of her hand, "must enter. We have journeyed far with Imandoff Silverhair to reach the Temple."

"Imandoff Silverhair?" The second woman looked back the way Takra and Corri had come. "Where is the sorcerer?"

"At the Inn of the Krynap," Takra answered gruffly. "Must he be with us to enter, woman?"

The sound of lightly running feet echoed from the bridge. A young woman, dressed in a white robe and wearing a blue cloak, hurried toward them.

"Are these the ones?" she asked breathlessly.

"They mentioned Imandoff and asked to enter." The guard kept a wary eye on Takra.

"Where have you come from, strangers?" the young priestess asked.

"Tuone." Takra caressed the hilt of her sword and scowled.

"Come, the High Priestess and the Oracle await you." The girl motioned with a pale smooth hand for them to follow. "See that the bridge is guarded against those who may follow." She turned to pull at Corri's arm. "We must hurry. You are not safe here."

"How did you know we would come?" Takra's voice was full of suspicion, her sword-hand never leaving the weapon's hilt.

"It was foretold by the Oracle." The priestess hurried them along at a near run. "Quickly, before those who seek you return and see you at our gates!"

Corri and Takra broke into a trot behind the priestess, their footsteps on the stone bridge echoing across the still waters. At the closed gates of the Temple set at the end of the bridge, the woman pulled open a small postern door set in the gate. She pushed her companions through and slammed and bolted the thick door behind her.

Corri drew back against Takra as she saw the armed male guards flanking the inner sides of the postern. Awaiting them in the torchlit courtyard fanning out from the gate was a group of robed priests and priestesses. Takra grabbed at her sword but her arms were clamped to her sides by strong hands.

"We greet you, daughter of Ryanna." A very slender figure, robed in violet and head covered by a violet veil, stepped to the front of the group and held out her hands to Corri. "You are safe here in the Temple of the Great Mountain." Torchlight winked off a silver circlet set with a rare crystal.

"Who are you?" Takra asked, still pulling against the hands that kept her from drawing her sword.

"I am the Oracle," the young woman answered, stepping close. "It is my burden to tell Corri Farblood of the geas under which she now lives."

Chapter 24

"Geas?" Corri said in surprise, and Takra echoed the word.

"Did you not know? By this time you should have felt its unrelenting hand on your life." The skin of the Oracle's thin young face was drawn tight across her bones. She gestured across the courtyard. "Come. You shall rest, then we shall speak together of this thing."

"I think not. We made a mistake in coming here." *You are even younger than I am,* Corri thought. *Why should I trust you?* Corri tried to turn back to the gate, but found her way blocked by the guards. Visions of her enforced stay at Leshy played through her mind.

"I think we have no choice." Takra glared at the priests and priestesses. The flickering light glinted off the sword hilt in silvered-encrusted scabbard hung at each belt. "Am I not correct, Oracle?"

"It is true," answered the young woman. "For your own safety, I must keep you here this night." She moved closer, the torchlight illuminating her dark eyes, and the drooping black curls of her hair that strayed from under her veil. "It is of vast importance that I aid you as I was instructed by dreams. Important for your life and the lives of all the Peoples of Sar Akka. I cannot let you leave until I have completed that task."

"Am I prisoner then?" Corri demanded.

"No." The Oracle shook her head. "On that you have my solemn word. And my word, once given, binds all who dwell in the Temple. But if you leave now, it has been shown to me that this night your friend will die in the streets of Kystan, and you will pass back into the evil hands of the man from whom you flee. In the name of the Goddess, I ask that you trust me."

"I do not know your abilities, Oracle." Takra glared at the assembled priests and priestesses. "Perhaps you have not read your dreams aright. But the Tuonela take offense at being held in such a manner. Come, Corri. Let us take our chances in the streets, rather than some temple prison cell. I would not have you cozened into slavery again, as in Leshy."

"She speaks truth." A priest stepped forward, his mouth drawn into a forbidding line. "I am the High Priest of Iodan, and I say the Oracle does not lie. We have heard of the dealings of the High Clua of Leshy. That is not our way. We force no one to stay who does not wish it so. We want no dissension among the initiates of the Temple. But the highest honor and binding-word in Kirisan is the word of the Oracle. Take care that you do not call her a false prophet, Tuonela."

Corri stared at the young priestess who stood patiently before her. All her thief's instincts of assessing a person came to the fore. She found nothing in the facial expression, the stance of the body, that spoke of anything but truth and deep conviction, yet her experience at Leshy, the threat to imprison her against her will, made her wary.

"I will stay to hear your words," Corri said. "But if I choose to leave, I shall do so."

"You are no prisoner." The Oracle motioned the two women to follow her across the courtyard. "You are a free person, Corri Farblood, as long as the geas leaves you to be so. None here shall raise hand to stop your going tomorrow or whenever you choose. But this night, for your own safety and the lives of the Peoples of Sar Akka, I beg of you, bend to my will."

"Can we trust them?" Takra asked in a low voice as they passed inside the great stone building.

"We have no choice, but, yes, I feel we can trust the Oracle's word," Corri answered. "Besides, what choice have we? Behind us wait Druk and Malya and the Goddess knows how many others. There must be another way to win free of this city. Those of the Temple will know the way, if there is one."

"Nevertheless, I would sleep with one hand on my dagger if I were you." Takra nervously scanned the doorways of the long, twisting halls as they passed deeper into the Temple.

"I shall. I have no desire to be a pawn in some religious scheme. The Oracle believes in her own words, but there may be others here of a different mind." Corri carefully eyed the door for outer locks when the Oracle showed them into their room.

A faint tinkling of bells woke Corri, at first only weaving their delicate sound into her dreams, then rousing her into full consciousness. She sat up and looked around. The warm rays of the sun filtered down from the high windows, their pierce-work coverings breaking the light into strange patterns on the white stone floor.

She drew her knees under her chin, thoughtful in her morning sleepiness, as she searched the small room for signs of Takra. The Tuonela warrior woman was gone, the woven quilt of the second bed thrown back in disarray.

I would have heard if they took her by force, Corri thought as she scanned the room. *Only one dead could miss hearing her*

Tuonela war cry, and there is no way I could have slept through a fight. Still she felt uneasy being alone.

She swung her legs over the side of the narrow bed and touched her bare feet to the floor, expecting to feel the familiar cold of stones. But the blocks were pleasantly warm to the touch. A small table by a clothing chest held a bowl of ruby grapes. Corri popped several into her mouth as she quickly dressed, brushing at the travel stains on her leather trousers. She sank onto a backless stool, its gently curving legs ending in a carving of animal paws, while she tugged on her boots.

After checking the slide of her boot knife, Corri opened the heavy wooden door and slipped into the hall. One end of the corridor led to a flight of stairs that twisted up out of sight. At the other end, silky blue curtains moved gently as a morning breeze caught them. In between were a number of closed doors, identical to hers.

Corri cautiously made her way to the curtain and pulled aside a corner. She found herself looking out upon a walled garden, green lawns cut by gravel paths and outlined with brilliant flowers. On a stone bench near a tiny pool of water sat a young woman, her head bent over a parchment roll, completely oblivious to Corri. Above her, from the slender limbs of a willow hung a glass wind chime, tinkling softly.

"Bright morning, stranger. The Lady Vairya asks that you come."

Corri spun around to find a white-robed priestess watching her with dark eyes.

"Where is Takra?" Corri demanded. "Who is the Lady Vairya? And who are you?"

"The High Priestess Vairya will explain all." The priestess motioned with one hand. "I am called Lirna, Tuulikka of the Goddess. See, I am thrice-blessed." The woman touched a finger to the braided blue belt at her waist, as if this indication of rank should have significant meaning. "Come. You must not linger when the High Priestess calls."

Knowing that there was no other way to locate Takra in this vast building, Corri followed Lirna down the hall and up the twisting stairway to a higher level of the Temple. The priestess ignored Corri's flood of questions all the way. By the time they halted before a bronze-paneled door, Corri's mouth was set in a stubborn line, her patience stretched thin and her sense of wariness at a fever pitch.

Lirna raised the bronze ring in the center of the door, releasing it to echo its clanging tone through the empty hall- way. She opened the door, silently stepping aside as Corri entered. The door clicked shut, and Corri found herself stand- ing alone in a large chamber.

The white-stoned room held several ornate chairs, a long narrow table, and a sleeping alcove, its richly embroidered curtain drawn back by silver-threaded cords. In a second alcove, flanked by tall candlesticks filled with half-burned tapers, stood a marble statue of a woman, arm's-length tall, on a limna wood altar. An oil-fed flame flickered in a blue bowl at the statue's feet, casting its soft light over the delicately-laid tints that marked the flesh and face.

Corri dug in her belt pouch, drawing out the moonstone statue of the Goddess given her by Minna. Yes, it was the same figure, so similar it could have been carved by the same hand that created the larger version. Corri slipped the tiny statue back into the pouch, wondering at the fate which seemed to direct her steps.

"Bright morning, far-wanderer. I am the Lady Vairya, High Priestess of the Temple." A tall woman brushed aside a transparent curtain at the far end of the room. "Come, we will sit on the terrace and talk while we break our fast."

Corri eyed the regal figure clad in an ankle-length white robe belted at the waist with a silver cord. The dark brown hair was coiled neatly on top of her head; a silver circlet crossed her smooth brow. The woman smiled and held aside the curtain.

"Here, Farblood." Takra's ringing tones called from beyond the silky hangings. "Took you long enough to get here."

Corri brushed past the High Priestess onto a tiny terrace. There, on a small table, was a silver bowl of fruit, a plate of crusty bread, and two silver goblets beside an ornate pitcher. Takra sat on a cushioned chair in the sunlight, one booted foot stretched out at ease and a goblet in her tanned hand.

"All she has done is ask more questions than she has answered," Takra said softly as Corri sat down beside her. "I told her nothing."

"I would be on my way out of this city." Corri tapped one finger impatiently on the tabletop. "If you wish there to be harmony between us, then answer my questions. What is this geas, and is there another way out of Kystan?"

"All will be revealed in time." The priestess poured juice into a goblet and handed it to Corri. "Eat. The Oracle will see us soon."

"I will not stay long in the Temple," Corri said, her eyes intently watching the calm face across the table as she took the goblet. *I thought all priestesses would be old and wrinkled, but this one is young enough to have half-grown children.* "To keep me by force was tried at Leshy. Do not try it here."

"That is not our way. Besides, the Oracle has given her word, and that word binds all within these walls." The High Priestess set the plate of bread before her. "A priest or priestess must have more than the desire or mystic abilities to become part of the Temple. There must be unshakable commitment to the Temple. We want no dissension."

Corri bit into a slice of bread, her eyes never leaving Vairya's face. *Are there two ways of thought here, as in Leshy, or does the Oracle's word-bond truly hold?* Her thief's instincts brought up no prickles of danger.

"Imandoff Silverhair was here, was he not?" Takra set down her goblet with a sharp click and stared at the woman. "And the Mother of Mares knows he does what he pleases."

"Yes, Imandoff Silverhair studied here, long ago." The High Priestess sighed as she steepled her fingers, touching her delicate nails briefly to her lips. "There are always some who fail to conform to the Temple ways. Usually those initiates are channeled into Temple service in the cities and towns, aiding the sick, seeking out potential novices. But Imandoff," she shook her head, "there was a man to always go his own way. If it had not been for his bloodline and his ability to mind-speak, he would never have been admitted for study."

That explains a few things about Imandoff, Corri thought as she automatically noted all the windows and doors in the room. *Still, it tells us little of what you think of him. I am much like the sorcerer in liking my freedom and to go my own way. If you knew this, would you step aside and let me through the gates, or would you try to hold me against my will because you think I am your Dream Warrior?*

"Remember what Farblood told you, priestess. She will not stay." Takra's hand casually dropped to rest on her sword hilt. "I count her as Sister-Friend. What threatens her is a threat to me."

"No need for threats, warrior woman. Although we are sword-trained, one and all, we abhor violence without cause." A deep-throated gong somewhere in the depths of the Temple sounded the hour. The High Priestess rose in a graceful movement and motioned toward the curtained doorway. "All your questions will be answered now by one who has supreme authority. Come. The Oracle awaits."

The Lady Vairya led the way out of the chamber and down hallways, deeper into the Temple complex. At first the passageways were built of stone blocks, then carved out of the mountain itself as they descended flight after flight of stairs. No outside illumination reached here. Oil lamps sat in niches hollowed from the rock, their flickering lights dancing out in strange shadows in the tunnels.

Corri's thief instincts were alert. She kept careful count of the tunnels and turns until she realized that they had passed

the same lamp three times. She remembered the lamp especially since it had a chip in one side and part of the distinctive design was gone. Takra jumped when the girl grasped
her by the arm.

"We are being misled," she whispered, her words echoing
faintly off the stone walls. "They do not want us to know the
way. Whether to keep us prisoner in this underground maze
or stop us from returning once we are out, I do not know."

Takra half-drew her sword as the priestess turned to face
them.

"Peace," Vairya said. "You are not prisoners, nor will you
be. The Oracle has given her word. It is required that we walk
the maze in a certain pattern in honor of the Goddess, for the
Oracle is Her mouth in Kystan."

"Enough." Corri frowned at the priestess and stood firm.
"I will not wander around in this maze any longer. To my
thinking, the Goddess cares not how we travel as long as we
get there."

The High Priestess drew her back spear-straight, her nostrils flaring in momentary anger. "There is no need for impa-
tience, for we have reached the end of the pattern." She
whirled and hurried on, leaving Corri and Takra to run a few
steps to catch up with her. "The pattern of the maze is known
only to the Temple initiates. In that way we protect the Oracle
from unnecessary intrusions. You must not attempt to visit the
Oracle by yourself. Her sensitivity is so great that we must
shield her from unwanted guests in this manner."

"Why should I want to come creeping back down here?"
Corri rested one hand on her long dagger. "I have no desire
to stay in this place any longer I must. All I ask of you is a
way out of Kystan that will get me free of Grimmel's men,
and an answer to this geas."

Takra glanced up at the rough carved ceiling and shivered. "The sooner I am out under open sky, the better," she
grumbled.

The High Priestess led them around a corner and into a side tunnel, one that was nearly invisible in the darkness between lamps. There stood a bronze gate, its pierce-work design showing only blackness beyond.

Vairya swung open the gate, and they pushed into an alcove. To the left was a heavy black curtain hanging over a narrow opening. As Vairya lifted the curtain for them to enter, Corri blinked in surprise.

She stood in a vast natural cavern with hundreds of gigantic stone pillars reaching upward into the darkness. Here was the starkness of nature, untouched by the hands of artisans, a product of volcanic force, bubbled rock, coils of molten lava cooled into an endless hall of columns. Oil lamps resting on natural pedestals lined a pathway with a glowing cloud of smoke at its end. High above the smoke a thin crack of sunlight marked an opening in the ceiling, penetrating somewhere into the world above. The atmosphere was warm here, warmer than the rooms above, as if a subterranean fire heated the great underground cavern.

As they quickly walked along the lighted path, Corri saw that the walkway had been worn smooth by the passage of feet, a smoothness that would take uncounted years, far longer than the Peoples had been in this land.

A place of the Forgotten Ones! It has to be, she thought. *Does Imandoff know? He must, for he lived and studied here.*

"There," Takra whispered, pointing ahead.

Beside the last pillar with a flickering lamp, sat a woman on a high-backed bronze stool, glowing smoke from a huge brazier hanging like a veil behind her. Behind the brazier rose a twisted column, its ancient carving dancing and shifting in the light, a woman with a horse's head at her shoulder. Takra raised one hand in a formal salute to the image; her lips moved in some silent invocation to the Goddess.

The waiting woman sat motionless as they drew closer. The lower part of her face was shielded by a corner of her violet head-veil, held up by a thin hand, the fine bones showing through the pale skin. The oil lamps winked on the silver band across her smooth brow, its crystal stone a center pearly spot like moonlight.

"The Goddess Frayma bids you welcome, Dream Warrior." The voice was smooth and melodic, like water over stone, the voice of the young Oracle.

"Bright morning, Oracle." Vairya bowed her head over her clasped hands in greeting.

"Come, Corri Farblood, sit beside me." The Oracle touched a bronze stool at her side. "The Goddess has been with me all night, speaking of many things. The time of the Prophecy draws nigh."

Corri started forward, but was stopped by Takra's firm arm thrown before her. The warrior woman pointed at the floor in front of the empty bronze stool.

"Snake!" The word hissed through Takra's teeth. "A great desert hari-hari! White ones are rare and sacred, but as dangerous as the others."

Corri drew back, one hand instinctively reaching for her long dagger, as she saw a white mass of coils slowly moving on the cavern floor. The python raised its head, its tongue tasting the air.

"Simi will not harm you." The Oracle bent to speak softly to the snake, caressing its rolling coils of muscle with one hand. The snake slowly uncoiled and slithered beneath the Oracle's chair.

Cautiously, one eye on the snake, Corri moved to sit on the companion stool. The Oracle lowered her veil and looked into the girl's eyes. She was not what Corri had expected, her impressions of the previous night being colored by anger and confusion.

The Oracle's face was narrow, with wide, pronounced cheekbones and a full mouth. The brown eyes, so dark as to be nearly black, were framed by sooty lashes, accented by delicate black brows. The extremely pale skin was smooth, drawn tightly across the delicate bones. She had the look of one who seldom sought the sun, never exposed herself to its rays.

"You are only a girl!" Corri blurted out.

"In years I am young, but inside I am ancient." The Oracle smiled wistfully. "I was born knowing my many lifetimes, who I have been and how each time I died. With each life, I built upon my mystic abilities until now I can be no less than what I am, a far-seer, a servant of the Peoples, waiting for the Prophecy to be fulfilled. The Goddess has revealed to me that you are the Dream Warrior, the one who heralds the coming of great troubles, yet may lead the Peoples through to Light."

Corri stared into the compelling eyes. The Oracle's veil slipped down around her shoulders, revealing heavy coils of black hair twisted into a crown with tendrils of curls falling about her face.

"I play no part of any Prophecy." Corri looked away, across the dark cavern. "I am only a thief from Hadliden. I came here only—"

"To find out your parents' bloodlines," the Oracle finished. "I have read the books concerning Ryanna and the daughter she bore. Ryanna was full of promise as a dreamer and healer, but, alas, also one who chose to go her own way, forsaking the rules of the Temple. The Temple would have chosen a mate for her, but she followed her heart and it betrayed her."

Corri let her breath out slowly. *At last perhaps I shall learn more of my past. Did I inherit my strange abilities from my mother or father?*

"Ryanna was admitted here because of an inconsistent, wild trait in her family. An ability to dream-travel and create changes of circumstance while in that state. The dream-travel, that Ryanna could do, but the rest of the mystic discipline she had not the patience to cultivate. When she left the Temple, the rest of her family mourned her as dead. They do not wish to see you.

"Of your father, we know little. The Oracle during your mother's time wrote that there were within him many secret things, things mind-shielded so that she could not read him. Of one thing are we certain. Your father is not of the known Peoples of Sar Akka."

"But where could he be from? Do you know?" Corri felt cold excitement rush through her veins. Her thoughts raced back to Imandoff's strange words about other worlds and other peoples.

"To that I have no answer," the girl said, shaking her head. "Perhaps from the Forbidden Lands beyond the Takto Mountains, although I do not see how that could be. None of the Four Peoples can pass by the Towers of Silence set as sentinels high in the mountains. I have been shown no answer to that question."

"And why does Grimmel seek to use me as he plans?" In a rush of words, she explained to the Oracle why she had fled from the master thief.

"The only possible answer lies in bloodlines," the Oracle answered. "From what you say, this Grimmel must also have certain traits of importance. Those who have studied such mystic things know that children born to two such talented parents are likely to contain the same talents, if not greater. That is of little interest to me, to you, now. For there comes something of greater importance to Sar Akka, a shift in the balance of Light and Darkness that may endanger all the Peoples."

A look of deep sadness filled the seer's eyes. "The signs prophesied are beginning to happen. The Green Men send messages that the mountains all around are filled with omens. Many dangerous animals are moving down from remote peaks toward the valleys and towns. Men of no virtue creep along the mountain tracks, thinking to set up camps there from which they can prey on merchants and travelers. The Green Men are few, their task great to hold the high regions safe.

"You have been revealed to me as the Dream Warrior, long awaited. If you do not help us, we are lost. This is your geas, Corri Farblood, to take up the battle for the Peoples or turn aside, knowing you betray us into a terrible fate. What has placed this responsibility upon you, I cannot say. But the Goddess bade me tell you to remember Her words and your promise."

Corri felt a coldness grip her stomach. The shakka Halka had also called her the Dream Warrior. She recalled the strange figures masked in the glow, the soft voice that had asked what she would give; the promise made that Corri now knew was binding. The girl realized that the Oracle was leaving the final choice to her, the acceptance or rejection of the role of Dream Warrior, to keep or break the promise to the Lady. But oh, the cost to heart and spirit if she turned aside; for the first time Corri fully understood.

In all my life I never gave a thought to others. Why do this girl's words hurt my heart? Corri saw a tear slide down the Oracle's face. *A part of me knows I will not, cannot, walk away from this strange coil of events, not because I am trapped, but because I truly do want to help save the Peoples.*

Halka had spoken of a geas, and this woman used the same word. The geas was real; it had pulled her to Kystan, not allowing a retreat. She fumbled inside her tunic and came out with the headband set with the owl stone.

"Truth between us, Priestess. I have little power without this," she said as she held out the circlet. "You choose a poor warrior to fulfill your prophecy."

"The stone of the ancient warrior woman Varanna!" The Oracle looked in astonishment from Corri to the owl stone and back again. "How did you come by this?" One bone-thin finger delicately caressed the gem.

Corri felt a flush of embarrassment rise to her face as she related to the Oracle the theft of the owl stone from a merchant in Hadliden and the finding of the circlet in the Valley of Whispers.

The Oracle's expression did not change. "The bearer of this is truly chosen by the Goddess, not by me," the priestess said at last. "So say the ancient legends. Your destiny led you to the stone. You could not have turned aside, leaving it behind. But there must be free will in the final task, a choice freely made to do what is needful, even as Varanna wielded the stone by choice in the far past. No one can force you to use the powers that must be used to protect the Peoples. That desire must come from the heart and soul, Dream Warrior."

"And if she chooses not to?" Takra asked, a frown pulling at her fair brows, as she watched Corri slip the circlet back into her tunic.

"Then the Peoples will lie under the dark hand of Frav." Vairya traced an evil-averting sign in the air with her hand. "We will become fodder for the altars of Jevotan, and the People slaves to the Fravashi."

Chapter 25

No!" Takra's cry echoed through the cavern, her sword hissing as she drew it forth. The High Priestess stepped between the Tuonela woman and the Oracle, prepared to take the sword thrust if Takra attacked. But the sword woman only shook her fair head from side to side as if to wipe out the Oracle's words.

"What am I to do?" Corri's face was pale in the flickering light. "I am no warrior. I have no great talent, certainly not any learning in these matters. My control of the dream-flying is never certain without the stone."

"You will be led," answered the Oracle. "The Prophecy does not say how. First, we must get you safely out of Kystan. At this time, your freedom must not be threatened by anyone."

"I cannot—will not—keep running from Grimmel's men." Corri's mouth set in a firm line. "I have run enough. Geas or no geas, it is time to put a stop to the pursuit."

"The first part of the journey draws to a close, this much I know." The Oracle's mouth curved in a faint smile. "As with Varanna, you do not travel toward your destiny alone."

"Who is Varanna?" Corri asked as she stepped closer to Takra.

"A warrior woman of the past," came Takra's terse answer. "She came to a warrior's end in the great battle with Frav."

Corri loosed the ties on her belt pouch and pulled out the tiny moonstone statue of Friama. "I think this was not meant for me, but for you." She wondered at the choice of words that rose in her mind. "I am only the gift-bearer, the one chosen to return this to its rightful place."

Both the Oracle and High Priestess gasped as the oil lamps turned the little statue into a glow in Corri's scratched and weather-tanned hand. The young Oracle reached out, her hand shaking, a look of reverence on her pale face.

"The last sign, part of the hidden prophecy not known to many." She took the image in her trembling fingers. "The lost Lady is returned as the day of doom approaches. Once more the moonbeam statue will sit in its rightful place." She turned on her stool and placed the statue in a niche cut in the column behind her; it fit perfectly.

The Oracle's head came up, and she stared back along the pathway of lighted pillars toward the dark, distant gateway. "You must leave. Now! One has entered the Temple who does not belong, one with blackness in his heart, a traitor even to the man he serves. He is protected by some magic so that he passes unseen among the initiates. Only I sense his presence."

Vairya whirled back toward the gate, but was stopped by a word from the Oracle.

"No time, Sister, to retrieve your sword. Danger is near. Take mine." The young girl pointed to a sheathed weapon leaning in the shadows against one of the stone pillars. "Only I can feel his presence with my mind, therefore, it is my duty to be rear guard. The Goddess will not forsake me. You must lead them down the sacred passages to the Moon Pool, the only path to freedom."

"This way," the High Priestess said as she buckled the weapon about her waist. "The Goddess hold you safely." She bent to kiss the Oracle's cheek before taking up a lamp and turning to lead Corri and Takra out across the black cavern.

In and out among the strange volcanic pillars they went, winding their way deeper into what Corri realized was a cavern more vast than she had first suspected. They skirted a deep fissure in the floor that cut the cavern in two, walking a narrow ledge at one end of the stygian blackness. Her lamp held high, the High Priestess entered a wide crack in the wall and descended a smooth-walled stairway cut into the bones of the mountain.

They moved as fast as they dared, a sense of foreboding snapping at their heels. Vairya led the way for what seemed like hours to Corri, always angling slightly downward, before they came into a level passage.

"Where are we?" she whispered to Vairya, afraid that her voice would rebound endlessly through the underground chambers.

"Near the Moon Pool, in the valley below Kystan," came the soft answer. "Here we rest. I cannot say what will await us outside. If one with death in his heart can enter to the Temple, then we must be doubly careful here. There are no safeguards to prevent anyone from approaching the Moon Pool."

She led them out into a small rounded cave. A distant roar of water boomed back through the twisting passage beyond them. On ledges about the sides of the cave were rows of urns, with one set high up in a niche by itself. Takra's eyes went wide at the sight of the painted urn set high above them; on the ledge before it leaned an ivory colored helmet, one side from the eyehole to the cheekpiece blackened and rent. The warrior woman touched first her heart, then her lips with her sword hilt. Vairya bowed her head briefly before the high urn.

"The war-gear of Varanna. I had never thought to see it." Takra's voice was full of wonder.

"Where do we go now?" Corri asked as she looked around for an escape route.

"What of Imandoff?" Takra crowded up beside Corri, her face intent on the priestess.

"I heard the Oracle mind-call to him." Vairya shook her head. "Then her voice stopped. I fear the intruder still follows us."

"And the Oracle?" Corri's voice was calm as she pulled out her long dagger.

"I do not know, except that she has been harmed."

"I run no further." Corri turned to look back along the passageway. "I must stop this insane pursuit. No one else must be harmed because of me. We have seen that Grimmel's men care not for the sanctity of temples or oracles. If I flee their intrusion into this supposed place of safety, I must keep running, and that I will not do."

"I stand with you, Sister." Takra's dagger slid noiselessly from the sheath. She held her sword ready in the other hand. "The time for fighting has come."

"The pursuer cannot be seen." Vairya tugged at Corri's arm. "You must escape."

"There may be a way." Corri shrugged off the priestess's hand as she sheathed her dagger. She pulled out the circlet and held it in her shaking hands. "I will try to mind-seek behind us. Be ready, Takra."

Takra and the priestess stood one on each side of the passageway entrance, pressing back against the stones, swords ready, while Corri stood well inside the cave in plain view of anyone who followed. The lamp, set on the rough floor behind her, outlined her body with a dim golden aura.

Corri saw a distortion moving quickly along the shadowed corridor, the way they had fled. *What is that?* she thought. She found it difficult to keep her sight on the approaching image.

It is as if my eyes slide off it, as if I am tempted to discount what I see and look elsewhere. It has to be Druk, but what is this magic he uses to make himself invisible?

She lowered the circlet onto her head. This time the mystic owl stone did not send her spirit-body flying, but gave her a strange sense of second-sight as the girl stared back along the dark corridor. Everything took on a double visioned appearance, actuality overlapped with flitting forms that had no physical reality. But one form held true, did not flicker out of her line of sight. Rapidly coming towards her was a dull oval glow with the figure of a man encased inside.

Druk! Corri's mouth went dry. Each time she blinked, the glowing figure disappeared, and she had to concentrate to regain the image. *I must draw him nearer,* she thought. *There must be an end to all this. How do I let Takra and the High Priestess know when he is within the room without warning him?*

A wave of hopelessness washed over her, emanating from the approaching form. She fought the depression that threatened to crush her resolve, thinking of the Oracle in the cavern behind. Druk halted his half-run, sauntered toward her, his grinning face clear to her second sight.

"Ready to give up, Farblood? And where are the others?" The assassin's voice seemed to come out of the air, was audible, its echoes bouncing round the chamber.

Corri saw the dagger in his hand and knew that he dared to defy Grimmel, that he meant to kill her. In her peripheral vision, she saw Takra's puzzled expression as the warrior woman tried to determine where Druk stood. Then Corri saw Druk's shadow on the rock floor.

Whatever magic gives him this seeming invisibility only affects how others see him, but his shadow remains. If he talks long enough, perhaps Takra will notice this shadow and judge where he stands when he enters the cave. Corri willed Takra to look down as Druk moved closer.

"The others have gone ahead to see if the way is clear. Who are you really, Druk?"

Corri heard her own words echo off the stone walls. At the same time she had a brief glimpse of some strange silvery object lying crumpled against a mountainside. Her vision jerked back as Druk moved still closer.

"Why should I tell you?" The assassin tested the edge of his dagger with his thumb.

"Why not? You plan to kill me." Corri forced herself to stand rock-still as the man edged closer to the cave entrance.

"As you say, Farblood, why not? I escaped with Grimmel and Kayth to Sar Akka from another world long ago." A slow, cruel smile twisted Druk's scarred mouth as he paused to savor the expression of terror Corri let slide across her face. "I serve one stronger now than Grimmel, one who will take this world and shape it to his desires. He will make it a paradise for his loyal followers. Grimmel is a miser with payment and heavy-handed with punishment; you know that. But you do not understand any of this, do you? No matter. Someday Kayth will thank me for removing you."

The dagger rose as Corri watched. Druk's step was unhurried, as if he chose to relish every moment of his deed. She felt detached from the impending danger, as if it could not touch her. Slowly she backed another step into the cave and watched Druk follow. Her eyes darted to Druk's shadow, now plain behind him. She saw Takra's eyes track the outline on the floor. The assassin reached out for Corri with one hand, his dagger ready to plunge into her heart.

"Frayma!" The wild Tuonela war cry crashed through the cave as Takra's sword whistled past Corri to strike Druk full in the throat. The assassin's headless body fell back into the passageway, the invisibility broken, blood splattering the walls. "For the Oracle." Takra was breathing heavily as she kicked at the twitching body, now completely revealed to physical sight. "What is this?" A puff of acrid black smoke arose from the floor.

The High Priestess used her bared sword to prod at a crumpled metal disk lying in the doorway. "A strange device, not of our making." She raked it to one side.

"It looks much like the earring Grimmel used to know where I was." Corri removed the circlet, tucking it once again inside her tunic. "But mine gave me no invisibility. Where to now?" She kept her eyes away from the still-twitching body, but the scent of newly spilled blood clogged her nostrils, reminding her of the man she had slain in the Valley of Whispers.

"Wait." Takra held out a restraining hand, her eyes on the High Priestess. "The Oracle spoke of a geas. A geas is a fearful thing. No one, nothing, can stand against such a fated deed, so the old tales say. There is no free will when such a fate is placed upon you. What geas hangs over Corri? I heard the Oracle's words, yet I do not understand them, nor do I quite believe them."

"As the Oracle told you, this girl is the Dream Warrior. How can you doubt when she bears the stone of Varanna? And the ancient statue, stolen from the Temple long, long ago, did the geas not guide her to return it?" Vairya looked from Corri to Takra. "You do not know the ancient legend?"

Takra shrugged. "The songsmiths sing of Varanna on long winter nights. Some of it I remember, the wild songs of the great battle. But Corri, no, she does not know."

"Ask that of Imandoff once you are gone from here. Out quickly, for I must return to aid the Oracle."

The High Priestess led them out of the rounded cave into a series of twisting passageways. The boom and roar of water grew louder. In a short time they emerged into another cave, one wall of this one cut off by time and the forces of nature. There was only an open end across which fell a sheet of sun-sparkled water. The noise of the waterfall was so loud that words were useless.

Vairya motioned them to follow her as she stepped out along a narrow ledge that skirted under the falls and led along the side of the cliff. Within minutes they were in the open. A wide pool stretched from the foot of the falls halfway across the green meadow, finally channeling the water into a narrow stream that disappeared through a grove of trees.

Corri turned to look up at the high cliffs, then out across the flower-studded grass that bordered the pool. There was no sound to be heard above the splash and call of the falls.

"Go with the Goddess." The High Priestess's words were near-drowned in the noise. She turned and retraced her steps to disappear behind the falls.

Takra wiped the blood from her sword on the grass, her amber eyes scanning the clearing. Then she motioned Corri to follow as she headed for the cover of the trees. As they moved from the sunlit meadows under the deeper shelter of the tree boughs, the roar of the waterfall fell to a background noise.

"There is a path," Takra said, pointing beyond them with her sword. "Perhaps it leads to one of the main roads."

"We can watch there for Imandoff."

"If he comes." Takra scouted the sides of the path as they walked along it. "I still do not know how he will find us, unless he looses Lightfoot as a guide."

"He will come," Corri said. "I believe the High Priestess when she said that the Oracle mind-spoke him." *I cannot go on without Imandoff,* she thought. *I need his guidance.*

Corri realized that for the first time in her life she had friends, real friends, people who cared for her beyond what she could do as a thief, and people for whom she cared deeply. Her mind raced back over all that had happened since that night months ago when she stood on the roof of the Red Horse Inn near Imandoff's window, thinking how to steal something from a sorcerer. How naive she had been, pitting her skills against Imandoff. Now she was caught in a weaving of fate beyond her wildest dreams, and, although she was frightened of what the future might hold, she resolved not to run from it.

They followed the path across the stream on a plank bridge, then plunged back in among the trees. Once they found a small forest opening, lush with grass, completely encircled with resinous-smelling foliage. There they rested for some time before pushing on in a direction Takra indicated.

"We must be close to the traveled ways," Takra murmured, head cocked at the distant sounds of voices and ring of harness brass. "Only a little farther now." The Tuonela struck off down another path.

Corri followed so close behind that she walked into Takra, who had stopped suddenly in front of her. The warrior woman grunted in surprise, but raised a hand for silence. Before them, through a screen of trees where the path turned, Corri saw the smooth dust of a wide road and heard the jingle of harness and the laughing voices of men as travelers to Kystan rode past.

"The sun is almost behind the mountains." Takra leaned against a mossy tree trunk to watch the road. "If the sorcerer comes, it will have to be soon, else we will not see him in the dark. Unless he is sensitive to Lightfoot's pull on the lead, he will not know we are here." She sheathed her sword, never taking her eyes from the road beyond.

"He has to come," Corri answered, tenseness gripping her throat. "We need the horses and his guidance. I do not know where to go from here."

"Then let us go back to the Clans." Takra turned briefly to look at her. "There we can be shielded by warriors willing to protect Clan blood. Have you ever heard of a geas except in stories, Farblood? I have not. I think this is all some prattle of the Temple to bend you to their will."

"I have not even heard stories." Corri rubbed at her forehead as she thought. "I know nothing of the history of the Four Peoples nor any of their legends, except for bits and pieces I gathered from listening to my old nurse when I was very young and from others outside Grimmel's house. The master thief kept such things from me. But my instincts tell me the Oracle spoke the truth." *And there was the Lady in the Light,* she thought. *That experience I cannot discount.*

She continued, her low voice barely breaking the forest stillness. "But what the old toad said, when I traveled by dream-flight to Hadliden, that makes no sense. He spoke of gaining control of Sar Akka when the Fravashi make war on the Peoples. Druk said something about someone stronger than Grimmel. It is all a mystery that perhaps even Imandoff cannot sort out."

Takra held up her hand again, her eyes intent on the road. A loud singing floated in under the trees long before the mounted figure came into sight. A tall figure, wrapped in a gray cloak, mounted on a roan and leading a string of horses, wandered down the dusty thoroughfare, the sun glinting off the bronze cap set on the top of a walking staff he held in one hand. One of the horses, a black mare dappled with gray, pulled stubbornly at the lead. The man, hood concealing his face, swayed in the saddle as he bellowed out a tavern drinking song.

"Imandoff, and drunk!" Corri's mouth opened in surprise.

"Not drunk, the cagey old beggar." Takra grinned. She stuck two fingers in her mouth and gave a brief, piercing whistle.

Lightfoot's ears pricked forward as she pulled determinedly at the lead. The sorcerer continued his song as he appeared to guide the horses haphazardly off the road toward the trees. When he reached the low-swinging boughs, he dismounted with a lurch and loosely tied the reins to a sapling, before staggering among the trees.

"I thought I would never find you," the sorcerer said as he pushed his way through the underbrush, using the walking staff to ward off swinging branches. He scowled at Corri. "If it had not been for the Oracle, I would have sought you among Grimmel's people or the Clans. Where have you been, besides inside the Temple? Why did you not tell me you were going?"

"We had no time to warn you," the girl answered. "Druk was at the inn."

"And you were deep in talk with some trader in the common room." Takra grinned at him. "Besides, Druk is no longer among the living." She patted her sword. "Those of the Temple led us out by a secret way."

"You came by the hidden sacred path to the Moon Pool?" Imandoff's eyebrows raised in surprise. "That way is forbidden to all except initiates, and is used only during certain rituals. No one except the Oracle has the authority to break the Temple laws, and then only for the safety of the Temple."

"Druk invaded the Temple." Corri's words came out in a rush. "He was shielded against sight by some device. I think he harmed the Oracle, but we were well down the tunnel by that time. Takra killed him back there. He was going to kill me, Imandoff! He said something about Sar Akka becoming a paradise for loyal followers like him, and Kayth ..." Her voice wavered.

"Yes, Kayth." The sorcerer rubbed at his beard, frowning. "Everything seems to turn around Kayth and Grimmel. The Oracle, what did she tell you, Corri?"

"A lot of prattle about signs and omens," cut in Takra. "The usual talk one gets from city seers."

"You did not believe her?" Corri asked. "I think she spoke the truth."

"I will wait and see." Takra frowned. "The shakkas do not waste time with fancy words, but tell their predictions straight out. But if her words about the Green Men and their fight against wild beasts and lawless men are true, it would explain why we did not see them."

"Yes, I have heard of the troubles in the mountains. It explains why the Green Men did not answer my signals. What else?"

"Long words about a geas and the stone of Varanna and Corri being the Dream Warrior of the old legends, although the Baba and the shakkas have already declared her as that. My guess is that the Temple would like her under their influence." Takra shook her head. "Corri says she has never heard these old stories. However accurate this Oracle may be, Silverhair, I find it difficult to give my trust to the words of city-dwellers who huddle in piles of stone."

Imandoff's face blanched. "The Oracle would not hold Corri against her will. As to the Dream Warrior, there have been others who took this title because of a prediction, only to be proved false. But the Prophecy! The Oracle spoke of the Prophecy?"

"What has that to do with us?" Takra rested her fists on her hips. "Old legends cloaked in mysterious words. A night's entertainment for the campfires."

"The shakkas of the Clans would be the first to tell you to heed the Oracle's words, Wind-Rider. The Oracle would not say such if she did not believe it to be true. And the Oracle is chosen for her accuracy in prediction. It would explain much." Imandoff sagged back against a tree. "How could I have been so blind? All the happenings are coming together like pieces of a puzzle. If it is truly a geas, and I doubt not the Oracle's word, then we are all caught in it. If we fail or turn aside, Darkness will cover Sar Akka, eating away the will to follow the Light. A heavy burden has been laid upon us." He bent his head and sighed.

"If you speak true, sorcerer, we are in deep waters, and this is not the place to speak of it. I will bring the horses," Takra said as she moved down the path. "There is a clearing in the trees behind us. We should be safe this night if we camp there."

Chapter 26

"Imandoff, who was Varanna and what is the Prophecy?" Corri asked as she and the sorcerer walked back along the trail to the meadow.

"I have heard that Ryanna, your mother, was of the bloodline of Varanna, although Varanna had no siblings or children. The Prophecy is tied to Varanna. Its roots go back to the first lands occupied by the Four Peoples and continues on through their journeys across Sar Akka." Imandoff sank down on the grassy meadow. "Strange that events so far in the past affect us now." He stared in the direction of the waterfall, deep in thought.

"And the owl stone? The Oracle called it the stone of Varanna." Corri pulled out the circlet and held it up to catch the last of the sun rays falling over the cliff-tops.

"A focus stone, a thing of great power. So the legends say." Imandoff's face was etched with great weariness. "I should have recognized it from its powers. That such a powerful

271

thing came to you, I should have guessed the truth. I was too caught up in searching out places of the Forgotten Ones, in following old dreams."

"What is the Prophecy?" Corri asked, glancing briefly at Takra who sat down beside her. The horses were tethered and grazing on the rich grass.

"The Prophecy is a warning of war and great suffering, possibly the extinction of the free way of life held so casually by the Peoples. If we are truly caught up in a geas to fulfill the Prophecy, none of us may survive what is to come."

"What is this stone of Varanna?" Corri asked, turning the circlet about in her slim hands. "The owl stone looks like any other, except for its shape."

"It is an ancient focus stone, an aid that Varanna used to far-see. It was stolen out of the Temple after the Kirisani set up their boundaries here in this land. An ancient Oracle predicted that the stone would reappear in the time of need and be delivered into the hands of the Dream Warrior."

Imandoff stared down at the glinting gem in the circlet. "Long ago it was discovered that, when such focus stones are used by powerful sensitives, particularly for a long time, they gather to themselves a great store of power. Legend says that this stone came from beyond the stars and had great power when it was first brought to Sar Akka long before the star travelers came. It is ancient and powerful, Corri, more ancient than your mind or mine can comprehend."

"And Varanna?" Corri was dismayed at the weariness on the sorcerer's face.

"Varanna was a great warrior woman," Takra said. "Every rider in Frayma's Mare strives to be like her."

"It is a long story." Imandoff pulled out his pipe from his belt pouch and tamped a smoke-leaf into it. "A story fit for nights about the campfire, although we dare not have a fire this night."

He smiled at Takra as he snapped fire from his fingers. He drew up his knees, leaned his brown arms on them, and puffed in silence for a time before continuing.

"Legends say that long ago star travelers came to Sar Akka, fleeing religious persecution on their own world. They decided to chance fate in the cold darkness between the stars rather than bow their necks meekly to the death that awaited them if they refused to practice the accepted religion called One-Way. These refugees held a variety of beliefs, but they joined together to escape. Only by sheer determination did two of their strange vessels land on Sar Akka."

"Where are they now, the people and the ships that flew among the stars?" Corri glanced up at the sky, then back at the sorcerer.

"The sky ships are in a land far from here, destroyed now. The people mingled with the Four Peoples already living here," Imandoff answered, the smoke from his pipe curling about his head. "Some members of the native Peoples had strange abilities of the mind, as did a few newcomers. Then, as now, these powers seemed to run in families. The star travelers discovered that the Peoples of Sar Akka spoke a form of their space-tongue, one that enabled them to communicate with one another. The new blood gave immunity to a plague that was slowly decimating those Peoples already here."

"The Four Peoples did not live in this land then." Takra looked about her in the growing dark. "I know that much of the legend. They dwelt in a place far away. And even then the Fravashi were troublesome."

"Yes, the Fravashi always leaned toward the Dark." Imandoff created a ball of softly glowing light, sending it to hover over them to cast a dim radiance. "In that other place lived the High Priestess Varanna and the High Priest Tirkul."

Tirkul? Corri's eyes went wide with surprise, but neither of her companions seemed to notice. *Is Tirkul of the Clans to be drawn into this prophecy as I am? Perhaps there is no significance in the names being the same at all.* She felt a warning tingle of her intuition, but pushed it aside.

"And Jinniyah, the Great Priest of Darkness, the Fravashi priest who began the sacrifice of still beating hearts to Jevotan." Takra's words were a whisper. "And some of the star travelers joined him, saying they wished to return to the One-Way, to be part of the Chosen People. For the Fravashi, like those rulers they left behind, call themselves the Chosen."

"Yes, certain star travelers sought out the Fravashi and offered strange, powerful devices to them, saying they would follow no Goddess and would not live among a People who did. They seemed to think women were unimportant, without power or right as living beings." Imandoff shook his head.

"The powerful star devices—" Corri began.

"They were destroyed, along with the star vessels, by the very ones who came in them. Because of this, the Fravashi plunged Sar Akka into the fire of war, thinking to enslave and punish the Clans of the Light. But fate had given the Peoples Varanna."

Takra rummaged in the saddle-bags, bringing out journey food and passing it around. Imandoff was silent as they ate, weariness plain on his face.

When they finished, he brushed the crumbs from his travel-stained trousers and continued. "Varanna was born to star parents who chose to live with the Fravashi. But, before the war, as a young girl she rebelled and fled across the harsh mountains into the lands of the Goddess, the owl stone with her. By sword and cunning, she brought with her a band of children, each a holder of mystic power, each self-dedicated to the Goddess. A priestess of Frayma found and sheltered the children, dispersing them among the Peoples for safety, but keeping Varanna with her. Eventually Varanna was chosen as High Priestess because of her ability to far-see with the stone."

"Varanna had a vision through her star stone of the coming battle with Frav. The High Priest Tirkul dreamed it also."

Takra took up the story. "She went to the Asur Clan and had them fashion armor and shield from the scales of great sea beasts. The very armor we saw back there in the cave behind the waterfall." She pointed back toward the distant roaring. "This she wore with helmet and charmed sword in the last great battle. And a fearsome battle it was."

"Jinniyah, who led Frav as their High Priest, knew much Dark Magic." The sorcerer refilled his pipe. "He called forth from the Abyss great otherworld forces of Jevotan, and these rode the blackened skies above the battlefield, aiding his magic. The Clans of Light were encircled, and all seemed lost until Varanna leaped forward to face Jinniyah alone. Tirkul lay wounded, unable to lend his strength, and no light of the Lady or Her Lord could pierce the blackened skies to aid her."

Corri shivered. In her mind's eye she could see and hear the terrible battle described by Imandoff. She was wet with perspiration as if she were fighting with those desperate People faced with total annihilation.

"Jinniyah called upon his magic powers and, with his black rod, sent forth such a wave of death that it pierced the eye-piece of Varanna's war helm, killing her and twenty warriors who had leaped to her aid." Imandoff looked up at the moon as it broke over the cliff-tops. "But in her dying breath, one silver moonbeam broke through the black sky horde of Jevotan and touched her heart. She died with her sword's point out toward Jinniyah, and his magic flowed back out through the sword to kill him. Even his bones were burned to ashes."

"Varanna's body was cremated and her ashes brought on the long journey. Even now they lie in the cave behind the falls. A fitting tribute to a great warrior woman." Takra smiled. "My kinsman, Tirkul, was named after the great warrior-lover of Varanna."

"But why did they leave that land?" Corri asked. "If they defeated Frav, there was no need to go."

"The magical battle caused great quakes and eruptions," the sorcerer answered. "The land was upturned, shaken out and made desolate. In the end, even the Fravashi begged to go with them, saying they had destroyed the great books of power written by Jinniyah in a secret tongue. There followed a long journey, full of hardships for the Four Peoples, a journey that took nearly two years by ship and land. At last they reached here." Imandoff tapped the ground in front of him. "But people do not change easily, if at all. Soon it was discovered that the books of Jinniyah had been brought with the Fravashi. Another great war followed, and the Fravashi were driven to the north, beyond the mountains, where they now live. The border between Frav and Tuone was sealed with powerful ancient spells, so that no Fravashi may cross. The Books still await one who can break the code and learn again to use the terrible Dark Magic."

"What has this to do with me?" Corri watched a flutter of insects drawn by the magical ball of light overhead. "I still do not understand."

"The Prophecy says that in some future time another star vessel will come." Imandoff's voice took on the sing-song rhythm of a songsmith. "One traveler will aid the Fravashi, once again unlocking the power of Jinniyah's books. But a star-woman, the Dream Warrior, will take up the challenge, killing the footed serpent at the gate and cutting the net cast to snare the minds of the Peoples. Into her hand will come the stone of Varanna, the stone which was lost in this new land. Only through her powers will the Peoples walk free."

"What is the footed serpent?"

Imandoff shook his head. "No one knows."

"But there has been no star vessel," Corri protested.

"I begin to think there has been." Imandoff plucked a blade of grass and rolled it back and forth through his long fingers. "I have been blind! I should have seen the pattern from the beginning." He threw the crumpled grass from him. "It is the only explanation for Kayth and Grimmel. The geas, Corri, is that you either keep them from joining with Frav, which they may already have done, or that you lead the Peoples in the war which is surely to come."

Corri sat frozen in silence. *This cannot be happening,* she thought. *I am only a thief, not a warrior woman. I have no great powers to fight some black sorcerer.*

"The Oracle has named you the Dream Warrior. Her prophecies have never been wrong or misleading. If you turn aside, all is lost." Imandoff's shoulders sagged. "Once the writing in Jinniyah's books is unlocked, no one now living has the power to withstand the forces of the Abyss. We have lost too much of the old knowledge, become too complacent. Most scoff at the old stories as embroidered history with no true meaning. I have learned that there is a kernel of truth in old tales. Even now, the spell-bound border weakens. If the spells are broken, we shall be overrun." He sighed. "It is unlikely that many will believe that."

"I believe you, sorcerer. I will not live in a world controlled by the evil of Frav." Takra slammed her fist against her knee. "I am a Tuonela warrior of the Clans! If I cannot live free, then I choose to die in battle!"

"The Oracle was right. The geas binds me. I tried to return to the Clans when we journeyed through Deep Rising, but the pull here was too strong. My father Kayth appears to seek the Dark." Corri ran her finger around the edge of the owl stone. "If it was he who followed you through the grasslands, Imandoff, then his life-force glow is wrong somehow. Kayth is my father, though he deserted me, but he skirts the edges of Darkness. I feel that. I must stop him before he brings disaster upon us. Through his blood, it is my responsibility."

"If the ancient legends are true, then what of Grimmel?" Takra's face was ghost-lighted by the ball hanging overhead.

"I do not know." The sorcerer shook his head. "In some way his presence may have changed the proper flow of events. In truth, Corri, I know not who is the greater danger, Grimmel or Kayth. And we will find few to aid us, few who now believe in the Prophecy."

"Not many will stand with us, until Volikvi priests have them lined up before the altars of Jevotan," Takra growled. "Sheep, that is what they are! Only the Clans keep their swords sharp."

"The Oracle said all the priestesses were sword-trained." Corri looked from the sorcerer to the warrior woman.

"Even they have grown soft," Imandoff answered. "At one time every Mystery School was sword-trained, every man and woman of the Peoples knew how to fight. Now, all the Schools except the Temple of the Great Mountain abhor weapons. Leshy teaches only healing, and those at Sadko sit all day and meditate. Although those in the Temple are sword-trained, they practice little. They would be hard pressed to hold out in a true battle. And the Peoples, the farmers and tradesmen, their wives and children, they know nothing of swords and battle, nor do they wish to learn."

Takra snorted in disgust. "Is the Fire Temple of Frav any better?"

"We do not know what they teach there, except obedience to Jevotan and the High Priest Minepa, and the teaching of the Dark Magic to select priests. Of their once great knowledge, it is true, they have lost much." Imandoff rose and stretched. "But fanatics do not need sword-skill. They need only be willing to die on your sword, overpowering you by sheer numbers."

"If the Fravashi border is spell-sealed, we need not worry about Kayth and Grimmel getting to the ancient Books." Corri looked at Imandoff for confirmation.

"Alas, the spells may not hold against those who are not of the Peoples. We cannot count on that." The sorcerer began pacing, three steps one way, three steps back. "And someone—or something—has already weakened the spells."

"That is so. Two Volikvis have managed to cross against the spells, remember?" Takra pulled at the end of one pale braid.

"Then we must stop Kayth and Grimmel from entering Frav." Corri rose to stand beside the sorcerer. "As long as they are on this side of the border, they cannot read the Books."

"They may have already been in Frav." Imandoff placed a hand on the thief's shoulder. "I cannot say where Kayth has been all these years. Or even where he is now."

"But Grimmel has not been in Frav. I have never known him to leave his house, let alone Hadliden." The girl frowned. "If Grimmel has kept in contact with Kayth, perhaps it is Kayth who tries to unlock the mystery of the Books. But Druk spoke of one stronger than Grimmel. Kayth, perhaps?"

"Then we must find Kayth and stop him." Takra threw the bedrolls down on the grass. "I say, kill him. Eliminate one of the threats. He has been no true kin to you, Corri, even though he is your father. Then we go after this Grimmel."

"You speak true, Wind-Rider. First we must find Kayth. Corri said that someone followed me onto the grasslands of Tuone. It must have been Kayth, though I never saw him after Leshy." Imandoff turned to Corri, who nodded. "But we have a more serious problem, one that may tip the scales of fate against us. We know Kayth and Grimmel came to Sar Akka together, and Corri says Druk also. How many others came with them? How many must we guard against?"

"A problem that cannot be solved tonight, sorcerer." Takra spread out her blankets and lay down.

Corri lay quietly on her bedroll, waiting until Imandoff and Takra were asleep before she pulled out the gem-studded circlet. She held it up to the moon, watching the light glance off the strange black owl stone. Then, very carefully, she slipped on the circlet and willed herself to relax. At first she stared up at the rounded moon high above, then closed her eyes and thought of Halka far out on the plains of Tuone.

She felt a tugging in her body, then heard a pop in her ears as her shadow-self slipped free. Swiftly she moved through the sky over the rugged peaks of Deep Rising. Across the darkened grasslands she flew, straight to the wagon-tent of the shakka, now well away from Neeba. The old woman sat in a half-trance before her altar, incense smoke swirling around her.

Halka! Warn the Clans that fulfillment of the Prophecy may be near. Corri tried to touch the shakka but her hands passed through the still body. *Can you hear me?*

I hear, Dream Warrior. Halka's mind-voice was faint.

We are safe for now in Kirisan, but soon we will journey forth. Beware of Roggkin. In some way he is joined with those who pursue me.

Roggkin is gone, came the answer. *He fled from Tirkul.*

Corri felt a stirring in the air about her. A sense of dread and cold blew against her from the north. She rose above the wagon-tent to look toward the mountains dividing Frav from Tuone. A dull red glow hovered just over the edge of Tuone territory where the Mootma Mountains were split by a deep gorge. The glow both attracted and repelled her.

As quickly as she thought, she was there, facing the oval of light. It was the color of old blood, but within it hung the shape of a man. Corri gasped and drew back slightly. The man was thin to the point of emaciation, his skin drawn tight across his heavy bones, giving him the look of death. His long hair was matted, and the stench of his true being reached her across the invisible barrier that seemed to keep him out of Tuone. The long sleeves of his black robe fell back as he crooked his sharp-nailed hands toward her as if to tear the flesh from her bones.

No! Corri cried, thrusting out her hands. A brilliant flash beamed from her palms and struck the red glow, snapping it out of existence.

She hung motionless for a moment, staring at the darkened barrier of mountains. *Who was that? He was totally evil, a man who revels in Dark Magic. Somehow, he threatens the Peoples, although he seems to be unable, even in his shadow-self, to cross the border. He reminds me of Grimmel, though a thousand times more evil.*

Her thoughts turned toward Grimmel and Hadliden. Instantly she was flying in the direction of the Asuran city.

My father and Grimmel set all this into motion, Corri thought, her anger boiling within her. *I could not harm the master thief when I reached out from the shakkas' camp, but this time I will kill him! Then I will seek out Kayth and stop him also, in whatever way I must.*

To her astonishment, her sky-path turned aside to follow the caravan route along the southern edge of the grasslands. A campfire burned there, and she saw a line of horses picketed for the night. Dropping lower, she found herself hanging above a brightly striped tent, its flap open to the night breezes. Fearful of discovery, even in her shadow-form, Corri strained to hear from where she hovered.

"How far do we go?" Roggkin's voice floated to her ears.

"To the mountains in the east." Grimmel's deep tones filled Corri with apprehension. "What I seek lies there."

"And Kayth?"

"Do not worry about Kayth. He will be waiting for us. Fortunately, he has already been allowed to read a small portion of the Great Books in the Fire Temple. Now we know that certain mind-powers, focused and controlled, are necessary in order to use the ancient magic." Grimmel sounded smug. "And you will get your reward, Tuonela, when our task is finished."

"The girl. You promised me the girl for safe passage through Tuone," Roggkin growled. "Do not forget that."

"Yes, the girl." Corri was amazed that Roggkin could not hear the lie in Grimmel's voice. "The sorcerer, the warrior woman with her, they must both be killed. That also is part of the bargain."

"Druk will have them."

"I told you, Druk is dead. You have sent others?"

"If your magic box reads true, Druk is dead." Roggkin's voice had a tinge of uneasiness in it. "But no matter. I have contacts within Kirisan who, for a price, are now on their trail. It shall not be long."

Anger welled up inside Corri. Without thinking, she created a wave of terror and sent it crashing indiscriminately
through the camp. There was a frantic squealing as the horses
reared, broke loose and fled. She whirled her thoughts back to
the tent and willed the breeze to quicken. Sparks from the fire
sprang onto the tent, took hold, and thrust up tongues of
flame. She was gathering her thoughts in a ball of death when
she felt a commanding pull against her spirit-body and found
herself flying through a blurred landscape, away from Grimmel and the death she planned for him.

Chapter 27

Corri struggled against the commanding pull on her shadow-self, trying frantically to return to the burning tent and Grimmel, but her resistance was futile. She managed to stop her headlong plunge just above her prone body. Imandoff knelt beside her still form, his left hand pressed against the owl stone, his eyes shut in deep concentration. Around him, in the grass and underbrush of the small meadow, were wildly flaming spots of fire, still small, but eating into the vegetation with vigor.

"Corri!" Imandoff's voice demanded her attention.

As the sorcerer fell back with a cry of pain, breaking his contact with the stone, Corri slid into her physical body. She tugged off the circlet, angry at being recalled until she saw that Imandoff held his left hand, pain written clearly on his face.

"Why did you call me back? I found Grimmel!" she demanded, as she struggled to sit up. "What is happening?" She stared around her. Several small spots of fire were burning around their camp, as if ignited by a tossed handful of embers.

Takra was stamping at the fires, swinging her blanket to extinguish them. Lightfoot had herded the other wild-eyed horses to the edge of the grove where no fires burned, circling around them, nipping and nudging to keep them from running away. Corri crawled to Imandoff and took his injured hand in hers, turning it palm upward. A blister the size of the owl stone was visible on his calloused palm.

"I had to recall you," Imandoff said, clenching his teeth at the pain. "Wherever you were, whatever you did, the power was rebounding here. Soon the whole grove would have been aflame."

"What have I done?" Corri dropped the circlet in horror. "The stone is evil!"

"Not so." Imandoff reached out to cup her chin with his undamaged hand, forcing her to look at him. "It is a neutral power, like the Valley of Whispers. With you, Corri Farblood, the stone appears to intensify the emotions you send out. Your mystic abilities are far different from those of the ancient Varanna, and this is reflected by the way the stone reacts when you use it. The stone is a weapon in your hands, and as a weapon you must learn to accurately direct its powers. To do that you will have to learn great control."

"I did not seek to harm you." Corri stared at the winking stone. "I would never harm you or Takra. I wish I had learned healing at Leshy, but my teachers said I did not have that ability." She sighed. "Tonight I was not thinking of healing. I sought to kill Grimmel."

"If you went to Hadliden, little thief, Grimmel's fortress must be well aflame by now."

"I saw someone else," Corri continued hesitantly. "Some horrible apparition beyond the gorge at the border with Frav."

Imandoff looked at her, his eyes thoughtful, but said nothing.

Takra, soot-smudged, sank down beside them. She fumbled open the ties of a leather bag and pulled out a small goat horn, sealed on one end with a wooden plug. The warrior woman spread some of the contents on a strip of cloth torn from the bottom of Imandoff's cloak, then bound up the sorcerer's burned hand.

"Grimmel is not in Hadliden," Corri finally answered in a faint voice. "I found him on the grasslands of Tuone. He is traveling to the eastern mountains, and Roggkin is with him."

"Roggkin!" Takra's amber eyes narrowed. "I should have killed him when I had the opportunity, law or no law." She slid the horn back into the bag and tied it to her belt. "What does that filth do with this Grimmel?"

"Roggkin has hired men in Kirisan to seek out and kill us. Kill you and Imandoff, that is. Even now they are looking for us. Roggkin thinks that Grimmel will hold to the bargain, that I am to be given to Roggkin in payment for helping the master thief, but Grimmel plans deceit and treachery."

"We must leave at once." Imandoff awkwardly began to roll up his blankets. "These fires will not have gone unnoticed. The tale will spread quickly to Kystan, and those who seek us will investigate. We must put distance between us and this place." He turned to Corri. "You cannot leave the stone. If it were to fall into Grimmel's hands or be taken to Frav—"

"Then I must guard it." Corri sighed as she bent to retrieve the circlet and tuck it inside her tunic. "But we must leave, in that you speak truth. I do not know where our hunters are, only that they seek us."

They saddled the horses and led them back along the forest path to the dusty road. The full moon shone, unobstructed by clouds, lighting the landscape in brilliant whites and deep blacks. With Imandoff in the lead, they rode east along the silent, dusty highway. Takra took up the rear guard, her hand never far from her sword. The farmland about them lay still and quiet. Just before daybreak, they reached the stone bridge over the River Chum. Corri, half-asleep in the saddle, jerked awake as Mouse's hooves clattered on the worn stones. Imandoff kicked his roan into a trot, swiftly leading them over the river and onto a side trail hidden in a stand of thick trees.

"We rest here for a time," the sorcerer said as he dismounted. "Then we go higher, away from the traveled road into the mountains." He pointed up through the green boughs to the forested peaks rising above them. "This ridge-bone of mountains divides the valley, a spur of remoteness that reaches close to the eastern border. If we keep to the high trails, we may get within a few miles of Zatyr without being seen."

"And then?" Takra gathered the horses' reins to lead them down to the river. A sheltered backwater provided cover from the road; there the mounts could drink without being seen.

Imandoff sank down and leaned back against a tree. "Then we must trust fate. On the last stage of the journey, we have to travel across open land, full of farms and people, to get to the Takto Range. From there we go through the high pass to the grasslands again. Beyond that, I do not know. We shall have to trust to instincts, Corri, yours and mine and Takra's. It will take all our skills to win this race."

The sorcerer and Corri sat in silence while Takra watered the mounts. The sound of the bubbling river was softened by the surrounding foliage, but its clean scent mingled with the green smells of the trees. Tit-walls and brilliant red giddies flitted from branch to branch, their cascading songs breaking the forest stillness. A serenade of crickets rasped an accompaniment to the bird chorus.

Takra returned, picketed the horses, then sat beside Corri and the sorcerer. "It will be a race, will it not? May the Goddess grant that we reach the far end of the grasslands before Grimmel. If we do not—"

"Then we follow," Corri said in a sleepy voice. "There is something in the eastern mountains that Grimmel wants very much. We must see that he does not get it."

or the next three weeks they worked their way along mountain trails, high above the valleys of Kirisan, always eastward, always careful to avoid being seen. Imandoff's burned hand slowly healed, but it was evident that he would carry a scar. He flexed his fingers constantly as they rode, until most of the suppleness returned.

At night, the sorcerer and Takra dueled in mock battle, using green limbs instead of the deadly swords that hung at their belts. The whack and slap of the springy wood against Takra's body and mail-covered leather was loud in the silent mountain air. They whirled and dodged, a look of grim determination on the Tuonela's face. Imandoff, a smile splitting his sweat-drenched beard, was as light as a dancer on his feet, as deadly accurate in his blows as the strike of a snake. Each practice ended the same, with Takra grudgingly admitting defeat, and Imandoff bringing out his flask of mountain water.

"Why not let me teach you the way of the sword?" Takra asked on the first night of practice. "You may need the skill."

"Not me." Corri shook her head. "If I practiced the rest of my life, I would never have enough skill with a sword. I will stick with my daggers and my thief's cunning."

Once, an asperel, riding the air currents of the mountains, followed them for nearly a day. Corri shivered as the giant bird cast its shadow over them again and again, afraid yet marveling at its beauty. She never imagined that any flying creature could be that large. The wings were easily as wide as a very tall man. Glancing upward, she clearly saw the black head and wickedly curved beak against the gray feathers. The black feet with their long talons lay tucked against the downy breast.

"If we had time, I would go hunting for asperel talons," Takra said when they camped for the night. "They are a great prize and valuable."

"Why?" Corri turned to her friend. "Why would you kill such a beautiful creature?"

"It is the way of the Tuonela warriors." Takra frowned in thought. "It has always been so. A great mark of bravery."

Imandoff chuckled as he brought out the dry, hardening journey bread. "It is the way of warriors to place themselves in danger, Corri. The way of the sword has its traditions. You cannot change that."

"I still think it is a crazy way to live," Corri muttered. "There would always be someone who wants to prove they are better. You can die of being too brave."

"Being a warrior is no more dangerous than creeping about on rickety roofs in the middle of the night," Takra answered.

Corri stared off into the darkness, the food forgotten in her hand. She jumped as some animal rustled through the underbrush on the slopes above them.

"What is it?" Takra's hand inched toward the sword lying nearby.

"Nothing. Just tired." The girl chewed a mouthful of journey bread and swallowed with a dry throat. *Someone is following us,* she thought. *Not near, but still on our trail. There is not the feeling of Druk or Roggkin, or anyone seeking our deaths. But how can I prove that? We would lose precious time while Imandoff and Takra searched for something they would not find.*

The next afternoon, as the sun began its descent behind them in the forested hills, the trio came to the end of the mountain range. To the east was a blue haze of far-distant mountains, the smoke and dim outline of city walls near their roots. The valley below was dotted with farmsteads and at least two fortress-houses that Corri could see.

"From here we must ride in the open." Imandoff shaded his eyes with one brown hand and stared down at the main road that snaked along the valley floor. "There." He pointed to a merchant caravan, belled mules laden with trade goods. "Joining them should cover our tracks."

He led the way down the last section of the trail just as the caravan approached. The dusty highway laced its way through rolling fields dotted with farmsteads and scattered groves of fruit trees and the purple-leaved meppe.

"Good day, travelers!" the sorcerer shouted, riding up to the lead mule, his hands open before him. "Do you journey to Zatyr?"

The merchant looked nervously back along his caravan. "Perhaps; who asks?" His black eyes flicked nervously to Takra.

"We journey from the Temple of the Great Mountain." Imandoff casually brushed aside his cloak to reveal the blue-stone buckle. "We have good coins for food and company."

"No need of coins with me, initiate." The merchant said with a sigh of relief. "We would be glad of your company and the swords you carry. Although we shall reach the walls of Zatyr a little after sundown, these days one rides easier with extra swords at hand."

"Trouble?" Imandoff turned Sun-Dancer to ride beside the merchant. Takra and Corri pulled their mounts in behind the sorcerer's roan.

"Nothing one can put a finger on," the man answered, twitching his red cape off one shoulder. "Strangers asking questions that are not their affair. Tuonela, like her, riding the roads." He turned and pointed a ringed finger at Takra. "We have seen flocks of krakes rising and harassing flocks, a strange thing for this time of year. And when we traded in Hadliden, the mariners told tales of unnatural creatures surfacing from the depths of the Taunith Sea."

"All of which may mean nothing," Imandoff answered.

"As I said, nothing one can put a finger on. But the Green Men warn of great dangers on the mountain trails also. I have ridden these roads, boy and man, trading from the seacoast to the Takto Range, and I know the feeling of trouble coming. And I tell you, stranger, that trouble taints the very air we breathe." Talk between the merchant and Imandoff dropped to a low murmur. Corri rode in silence beside Takra, her eyes picking out the lights sparkling above the dark walls of the city before them.

So I am not the only one to feel uneasy. She wished that the merchant would ride faster, but the caravan kept on at its steady plodding pace. *By the blessed Goddess, I hope that Zatyr will give safety, at least for one more night.* She hunched her shoulders against the prick and itch of danger that crept slowly up her spine.

Corri glanced around her as the caravan passed through the great wooden gates of Zatyr and turned into the courtyard of an inn set up against the outer wall of the city. A creaking sign above the inn's gate heralded it as the Barsark.

The last barsark brought us little luck, she thought, as she slid down from her mare. *Goddess, but I forgot how noisy cities are.*

She watched the milling crowd of merchants as they unsaddled the mules and lifted off their packs of trade goods for the night's stay. Takra stood beside her with one hand constantly on her hilt, her amber eyes alert. Only Imandoff seemed at ease among the bustle and noise, bartering with the innkeeper over supplies.

"We stay the night here," the sorcerer said as he led the horses to the stable. "The head merchant has paid good silver for the two horses you found out on the grasslands. The money will buy our lodging this night, and food for the rest of our travels." He unsaddled the horses and tossed the bedrolls onto the straw. In a low voice he continued, "The jewels may be needed later. We do not yet know where our journey may take us."

"I hope you bargained for space out here and not a room full of bugs." Corri shivered.

"We have a room in the inn," Imandoff said with a smile. "Takra has chosen to stay here with the horses, but you and I can enjoy some comfort this night. The blankets and saddlebags stay here. Takra can go to the kitchen and fill the saddlebags while we create the illusion that we stay inside. If danger follows us inside, we can always climb out the window."

"So you too have a feeling we are followed?" Corri twisted a piece of hay between her fingers as she watched Imandoff. "I was beginning to think I was the only one who felt eyes on my back."

"What if you are recognized, Silverhair?" Takra tapped her fingers against her dagger. "Or Corri's enemies are here before us?"

Imandoff leaned his walking staff against the wall and beckoned to Corri. "If danger comes, we will take Corri's way out, over the roof. I leave it to you to see that the horses have grain and water, Wind-Rider. It may be the last grain these animals will see for some time."

"You tell me how to care for horses?" Takra snorted.

Imandoff grinned as he ducked through the low door with Corri at his heels. There was only a sliver of moon in the darkened sky as they crossed the cobbled courtyard to the inn's side door. Light, smoke, and noise spilled out as Imandoff opened the door and they stepped inside.

Corri pulled her cloak hood closer about her face as she followed the sorcerer through the common room and up the stairs at the rear. Flickering hall lamps lit their way as they passed up the flights of narrow steps to the third floor.

"Anyone you knew below?" she questioned as the sorcerer found their room and pushed open the stiff door.

"No, but it means nothing." He snapped his fingers and lit the slim candle on the table.

"You enjoy doing that, do you not?" Corri grinned.

Imandoff smiled back. "A habit. I have called up fire for so many years that I no longer even carry a striker."

Corri began to fidget from one foot to the other. *Someone in this inn wishes us harm,* she thought. *Yet Imandoff recognized no one, nor did I.*

"You are uneasy here? So am I. The men hired by this Roggkin could be anyone in this inn or on the roads." Imandoff quickly crossed to the window and struggled to open the shutters. "Not much light to see footholds, but lack of light never stopped you before."

"We must be ready," Corri said, her ear pressed against the hall door. "Trouble could come upon us without warning. I wish there were a lock of some kind. I feel uneasy about being here, Imandoff."

"You feel danger close by?" He stepped to her side, looking down at her with his dark eyes. "Listen!"

Heavy steps sounded on the stairs, then quieted as they neared the door of the room. Imandoff swept aside his outer robe and drew his sword.

"Back," he whispered. "Be ready to extinguish the candle."

Corri unsheathed the long dagger and held it ready as her other hand hovered near the weak flame. Her thief's senses were alert to every creak heard above the distant roar of sound from the common room below. The steps passed by.

"Let us be gone!" she whispered urgently. "Something is wrong. I do not like the feel of this place."

Imandoff leaned his sword against the wall as he threw the straw pallet off one of the narrow beds, then wedged the strap-crossed frame against the door as a barrier. Again he listened, sword in hand.

Corri fidgeted nervously, her eyes darting from the sorcerer to the open window and back again. As more footsteps sounded in the hall, she smashed out the weak flame, her instinct telling her not to wait for Imandoff's order. There was a sharp scrape of wood as someone pushed gingerly against the door, then nothing. The silence prickled against the girl's nerves.

Corri stepped back against the window frame, quickly looking out and down at the tiled roof. One end of the courtyard was ablaze with light spilling from the open door to the common room. *By the Goddess, the roof is difficult to see,* she thought. *I wish you had gotten a room closer to the ground this night, old man. If you slip and fall, we are certain to be discovered. And if you get hurt, we are in deep trouble.*

Imandoff leaned out the window beside her. "Now they know we are here." His whispered words were almost inaudible. "I think they will wait until late to rush the door. A tricky pathway down, Farblood. Think you can make it?"

"Me! What about you, old man?" Corri sheathed the dagger and slung one leg over the sill. "Watch where I step and follow," she quietly ordered as she lowered herself to the narrow strip of roof below.

She heard Imandoff slip to the tiles behind her as she carefully picked her way along the edge of the upper floor. Once she stopped and looked about. The courtyard below now held a man nursing a tankard of ale. His unexpected presence increased her uneasiness. Instead of dropping to the lower roof along the drain pipe, Corri edged cautiously upward to cross the peak and work her way past the great smoking chimney to the back of the inn. She heard Imandoff's heavy breathing as he struggled to follow. Creeping below lighted windows, the pair crossed the roof to another pipe, sliding down to the second floor where they paused to rest.

"You saw him?" Corri whispered. "He looked about too much. For certain, he was not drunk."

"I think he did not see us." Imandoff's words were quiet but labored from the climb. He flexed the fingers of his left hand, a grimace of pain catching at the corners of his mouth. "If they think we still hide out in the room, we will be safe for a time."

"We must leave this place, tonight." Corri rubbed her hands on her leather trousers and prepared to slide down the pipe to the kitchen roof.

"We cannot," Imandoff answered. "The gates of the inn and the city are closed for the night. If we demand to go, the guards will certainly mark us as fugitives. Guards can be bought. If we go over the wall, we will have no horses."

Apprehension coiled inside Corri as she made her way to the lower roof, then to the ground. Imandoff dropped softly beside her. She skirted a pile of garbage near the kitchen door and jumped as a cat ran across the stench-filled yard. She had her dagger half out when Imandoff tapped her on the shoulder.

The angry scream of a horse sliced through the night, followed by a series of kicks against the stable walls. Then only the confused babble of voices from the inn's common room could be heard.

"I will see if Takra has noticed anyone loitering around," the sorcerer whispered, pointing to the rear of the stables. "Check the inn yard. You have greater skill in moving unseen than I do. Be careful."

Corri nodded, then disappeared into the shadows along the inn wall. She peered around the corner at the courtyard. The watching man was gone. Swiftly, she passed through the light from the half-open doorway of the inn and into the shadowy courtyard that led to the stable. Near the blackness of the stable entrance, she paused, sniffing the coppery odor of blood in the air. A dark blot, wet to the touch, splashed over the door sill. Only the snort and stamp of the horses and mules came from within the pitch-black building.

Where is Takra? Corri thought as she stepped inside the stable, straining her eyes to see in the blackness. *She would never leave the horses unprotected. And where is Imandoff? If Takra were hurt ...* her mind shied away from the thought of death, *Imandoff would have found her by now and sent me a warning.*

There was a crunch of boot on the cobbles behind her. Corri whirled, one hand on the dagger, half expecting to see the Tuonela warrior woman outlined in the reflected light from the noisy inn. Instead, a rough male hand hit her alongside the head. She staggered backward and fell into the hay, her head ringing and her eyesight spotted with pricks of light.

"Grimmel wants to see you, thief." Corri smelled ale-scented breath in her face. "Your warrior friend cannot help you now. Fate has turned against you, thief, for on the morrow we go to meet the master thief of Hadliden."

The man laughed as he jerked Corri onto her feet and twisted her right arm behind her back; the other hand grabbed her hair. She heard her long dagger clatter onto the stone-paved floor as he pushed her ahead of him toward the open stable door.

Chapter 28

Goddess, help me! Corri wildly fought against the punishing hold, only to have it tighten in a sickening rush of pain.

"Try that again and I will break your arm." The man twisted her arm harder, jerked her head far back. "You will not be damaged for Grimmel's purposes if your arm is broken. And I have a hundred ways to make you wish for death before we reach the master thief."

Corri bit her lip as he dragged her in the direction of the inn. The courtyard was empty. She moved only her eyes in a wild search for Imandoff. Not even a movement deep within the shadows marked the presence of the sorcerer.

All this for nothing. Corri felt tears on her cheeks as they shuffled across the cobbled yard toward the lighted inn. *Imandoff and Takra must be dead.* She tried again to break the man's grip, only to have him twist her arm more painfully. The agony caused her to nearly faint.

There was a whistling sound, then a thud, and the man grunted. Blood poured over her shoulder as the man's hands slipped away. She whirled around, her arm hanging weakly.

"This way!" Tirkul stepped from the deep shadows and motioned to her.

Corri ran across the yard straight into the Tuonela warrior's arms. He crushed her against his chest briefly, then pulled her back inside the stables.

"Stay here," he ordered. "I would not leave my dagger." Tirkul slipped back out.

"Corri, this way." A dim ball of light popped into existence near the far wall. Imandoff crouched beside Takra, who lay white-faced in a pile of hay.

"What happened?" Corri stooped to retrieve her dagger, then ran to them, rubbing her aching arm. "Is she badly hurt?"

"A knot on the head and a knife thrust through the side." Imandoff's face was grim as he tore at his ragged cloak for bandages to press against the bleeding. "The assassin must have attacked her outside, else Takra's mare would have killed him. I was attacked also, just as I opened the rear door."

"He did, but I can still ride," came Takra's faint words. "Tie me to the saddle."

"We must go at once." Tirkul came soft-footed up beside them. "I found a secret way out, a way that does not use the gates. My horse waits beyond the wall."

Imandoff gathered Takra in his arms and led the way out of the stables toward the rear of the inn. Tirkul brought up the rear, his sword a long gleam of silver light in his hand.

Behind the kitchen, in a deep patch of shadow cast by a flowering bush, Tirkul pointed out a secret gate. The well-oiled hinges were silent as the Tuonela warrior pushed it open to emerge in another patch of thick growth.

"A way out for smugglers and thieves, no doubt. The sorcerer and I will get the horses," Tirkul said as Imandoff carefully propped Takra back against the outer wall. "Quickly, before someone finds the body! I had no time to do more than drag it into the shadows."

As the two men disappeared through the bush-hidden exit, Corri knelt beside Takra, taking up her cold hands. The warrior woman's eyes were closed. Corri felt for the rough bandage and found it soaked with blood.

Takra must not die, the girl thought frantically. *Sister-friend, do not go Between Worlds.* The slow seep of blood trickled down across Corri's hand. *She is bleeding too much. What can I do? Takra Wind-Rider, I will not let you go down into death. Stay, Sister-friend, stay!*

Her thoughts flicked back to Imandoff's words about the stone, an amplifier of emotions, he had said. Corri pulled out the circlet, her hands shaking.

It worked in the Valley of Whispers when I injured my head. But if I am wrong, she thought, *if I make a mistake, Takra dies. I have no choice. There is no time to seek out a healer, even if one could be found in this treacherous city. I must take the chance for her life is seeping out. If I do nothing, she will surely die.*

Quickly, Corri set the circlet across her brow and stared down at Takra. She clamped down on her shadow-self which struggled to leave her physical body. *Not now! I must heal, not dream-fly.*

The glow about the warrior woman was faint, almost flickering against the outline of her body. Corri placed her hand against the wound and closed her eyes. Her thoughts centered on the bleeding area, willing herself to see the seeping red stain stopped. She felt a current of warmth shoot down her arm and center in the hand against Takra's cold flesh. Still she concentrated, although Takra began to moan and twist under her hand. Her thoughts were a mixture of fear for Takra and deep, burning anger at those who had harmed her friend.

"Takra, stay!" she whispered fiercely. "I will not let you go Between Worlds. I need you, Wind-Rider!"

A shout from the inn beyond the wall broke her concentration and brought her back to her surroundings with a jolt. She whipped off the circlet and tucked it once again inside her tunic, grabbing for her long dagger and facing the small gate. A bright glow rose above the high stone barrier; the sharp crackle of flames eating into wood and the scent of smoke carried on a rising breeze.

Imandoff and Tirkul pushed their way through the gate, dragging the reluctant horses with them. Tirkul slammed the gate, wedging it tight with a hayfork from the stables. The horses snorted in fear, the whites of their eyes plain even in the dark. Imandoff's low soothing words to the terrified animals were unintelligible above the crackle of the inn's fire and the shouting voices of panicked men.

"What did you do, Corri?" Imandoff's face was clear in the brightening light as he peered down at her. "Even Tirkul felt a blast of fury before the inn burst into flames."

"I tried to save Takra." Corri lifted her bloody hand to the sorcerer. "Her life was running out with her blood. I had to stop it."

"You and that owl stone!" Takra's voice was only a whisper. Beyond the wall, flames rose higher, the night now filled with shouts and screams of fear as the inn burned like an oil-soaked torch. Imandoff boosted Takra onto Lightfoot, then mounted his wild-eyed roan. It took all of Tirkul's strength to steady Corri's frantic horse while she scrambled into the saddle. The sorcerer's face was a mask of concentration as they rode away from Zatyr and the burning inn.

He must be controlling the horses' fear by mind-power, the girl thought. She brushed one hand against Mouse, trying to soothe the mare's perspiring terror.

Hold on, Sister-friend. Her thoughts reached out to Takra as she edged her mount close to Lightfoot. *We will not leave you. By the Goddess, Grimmel will pay for this, by my hand, if I have anything to say.*

Corri rode close to her friend, watching for any signs that Takra might slip from the horse. But the Tuonela warrior woman, although she rode hunched forward in pain, kept to the saddle. Imandoff led them onto a narrow path leading around the city walls and headed toward the eastern mountains.

The first faint rays of dawn were lighting the sky when they reached the sheer cliffs that edged the valleys of Kirisan. Imandoff led them into a canyon that slanted upward to the peaks of the Takto Range, high above. The going was rough, and Takra still half-conscious, but they finally worked their way to the top of the cliffs where they dismounted to rest.

"The bleeding has stopped," Imandoff said as he carefully lifted the crude bandage on Takra's side. Lines of deep weariness were etched in the corners of his eyes.

"She is burned!" Tirkul bent over his Clan-sister to look at the wound. "How is that? Look at the shape of the mark!"

Corri moved closer. There, on Takra's side, was the imprint of her hand, an angry red. She turned to look back at Zatyr and the telltale plumes of smoke still rising from the burned-out inn.

"No matter." Takra winced as Imandoff spread salve on the wound and bound it up again. "I was dying, Imandoff. I saw the gates of Between Worlds where waited Natira the Judge. I would have entered them except for Corri. Her voice came out of the darkness, calling me back. What does a burn matter?" She held up a shaking hand to Corri who knelt beside her. "It was a good day when we joined blood."

"I do not understand." Tirkul squatted on his heels and shook his head, his pale braids rubbing across his mail-covered shoulders. "Both the Baba and Halka called you the Dream Warrior. I know the old tales, but none speak of this." He pointed to the burn. "What are you, Corri Farblood, Sister-Friend of Takra?"

"Just a thief from Hadliden trying to keep my friends alive," Corri answered. She felt a tiredness seeping up from the core of her being. "I am no great warrior, no healer, just me, Tirkul, a fugitive from Asur. If it had not been for your knife throw, I would be on my way back to Grimmel, to a life of slavery and forced child-bearing as his lawful wife."

Tirkul's eyes rested on Corri, then flicked to the sorcerer. "That was spoken of before, but I did not believe it. I thought you only wanted to spare my feelings with your words. This alliance, was it by choice or truly against your will?"

"No will of hers, Tirkul. You know of Asuran law." Imandoff rubbed a grimy hand across his eyes. "The women of Asur have no power over themselves, you know that. A good throw back there at the inn, Tirkul. I saw you through the open stable door."

"The throwing of daggers is for those afraid to go hand to hand against an enemy. I should have challenged him, but there was no time," the warrior answered, a frown wrinkling his brow.

"But why are you here?" Corri asked, looking up at Tirkul. "How did you find us? The last I saw of you was a vision of battle at the foot of Deep Rising." She flinched as his eyes refused to meet hers.

"As to why I am here, Roggkin followed you, and I followed Roggkin. Out in the grasslands I caught him and would have killed him if he had fought fair." He pointed to a pink scar across one side of his neck. "He was spell-weaving with a piece of your clothing, Farblood, calling you to him."

"So that was it, not a dream, but a spell." Imandoff frowned and pursed his mouth. "A common enough thing for one with talent."

"Roggkin has no spell talent." Takra tried to move, then sucked in her breath in pain.

"He escaped to join some caravan heading east. I rode on into Kirisan to warn you," Tirkul continued. "I almost caught you, but you disappeared after you entered the city. I was circling the Great Mountain, seeking for another entrance when

I saw fires in the forests. I picked up your trail on the road, but lost you at the river. You rode fast and hid your tracks well." He grinned at Takra. "I took the chance that you would come to the next city. After I saw you enter, I circled the walls and watched. The Goddess smiled on me, for I saw a man sneak in by the hidden gate and followed him."

"Thank the Goddess, you followed." Imandoff reached to grip Tirkul's arm. "Without your help, we should be dead back there, and Corri on her way to Grimmel. We ride on a dangerous quest, Tirkul of the Asperel. One from which we may not return. We will think no ill of you if you turn back. We join Corri in her destiny, whatever comes, but you are not sworn to go with us."

"I am no coward to leave when times are dangerous." Tirkul's eyes flashed with anger. "A Tuonela laughs at danger, sorcerer."

"As for Corri being wife to this Grimmel, it will not be for long." Takra's voice was weak, but full of promise. "I myself will cut out his heart and give it to her."

"Not if I reach him first, Sister-Friend." Corri patted the long dagger that hung at her side.

"Revenge will come, of that I am certain. This Grimmel's days are numbered. I will not let you go on without me. You need another sword, someone trained in the ways of a warrior." Tirkul's dark eyes lingered on Corri. "I ride with you to the end, whatever comes. But a shakka, you never said you were a shakka. For such healing power to flow through you, you must be a shakka." A mixture of emotions crossed the warrior's face. Corri's breath caught in her throat. She could not deny Tirkul's words, yet the emotion she felt behind them hurt. She was just beginning to allow herself to open to the possibility of love between a man and a woman, and now that love was being withdrawn because of fear or awe, Corri could not tell which.

"Best to leave me behind," Takra said, leaning back against a boulder. "I will only hold you back. This is a time for haste if you are to reach the mountain pass in time."

"Not so!" Corri shook her head vehemently. "We go together, or none of us go."

"Then we best ride as long as there is daylight. We must put as much distance between us and this city as we can." Tirkul spat in the direction of Zatyr.

They mounted again, Takra clinging to the pommel of the saddle with Corri riding close beside her. The trail led off up into the higher peaks, through thin avenues of fir and pine, then angled along the twisting sides of the rugged Takto Range. Soon the rocky track turned to the north toward the distant grasslands of Tuone.

They did not stop to camp until they entered the thicker forests of the upper slopes, cloaked underneath with buck brush, several miles from the city of Zatyr. Huge mossy-colored fungi, identified by Imandoff as barsark paw, flashed their yellow underbellies from where they clung to the old trees in the deep shadows.

Imandoff chose a site near a mountain spring that sprang cold and clean from a split in the rocks above a narrow tongue of clearing, its grass thick and green enough to satisfy the tired mounts. Tirkul, sword in hand, slipped off to scout the surrounding area while the sorcerer made Takra as comfortable as possible near their small fire.

"Corri, you must aid the Wind-Rider with the owl stone of Varanna." Imandoff hunkered down near the exhausted Tuonela, frowning at the lines of pain etched around her mouth. "She must regain her strength. We will need her in the days ahead."

Corri could not protest, knowing the urgency behind the sorcerer's words. She knelt with the circlet in one hand and pressed it against Takra's wound. Slowly, carefully focusing and controlling her emotions, the girl willed strength back into the warrior woman. It was an act she would repeat every evening, at every rest stop, until she herself felt drained.

It took them nearly a week to ride out of the silent mountain forests and look down upon the pass where Kirisani soldiers stood watch. The ranks of crowding trees pushed back here, revealing the stark bones of rock, thrusting upward in long thick fingers of basalt or thick fists of granite.

"They saw a small caravan pass on the grasslands below not long ago," Imandoff reported when he returned from the Kirisani outpost to their rough camp. "If Grimmel knows exactly where to go, we are too late. We have only one small hope. He, too, must camp for the night, and the guards tell me that his path is winding, taking more time than if we cut across the mountains from here."

"Perhaps Grimmel does not remember so exactly." Corri stirred among the coals of the campfire with a stick. "I do not remember him ever leaving Hadliden until now."

Takra flexed her sword arm, saying nothing. Her warrior-strength had returned from Corri's application of the strange stone to the wound in her side, but the deep scar still pulled against the muscles when she moved. She stared past the squat guard post as if she could see down onto the grasslands beyond. Her fair brows were pulled together in thought, her fists clenching and unclenching at her sides.

"I do not understand what he seeks in those mountains." Tirkul pointed to the rugged peaks beyond. "We hunt there for asperel and barsark, and never have we seen anything amiss, nothing that would fit the tale you have told me. True, there are places of strange and dangerous powers, but a ship that sails the stars?" He shook his head.

"Nevertheless, the star ship must lie there, hidden somewhere in some remote valley or crevice." Imandoff stared off into the distance. "Why Grimmel goes there, I am not certain, except it is bound to bring great danger to Sar Akka. The words Corri heard spoken between Grimmel and this Roggkin can only mean one thing. There is something within this star ship that enables Kayth or Grimmel to decode the Books of Darkness, some strange device such as the first star travelers had. Whatever, we must stop him. He must not be allowed to reach his destination."

"Because of blood ties, it is my task to see that he does not find what he seeks." Corri set her jaw in determination. *I will use the circlet and the owl stone again,* she told herself. *This time, when I find Grimmel, I will discover what he seeks.*

Corri lay quietly, listening to the night sounds around her and to the even breathing of her companions. Carefully, she raised herself to her knees and moved, inch by inch, away from the camp and under cover of the needled trees. At last she stood up and walked farther into the forest, her soft boots silent on the mossy ground. Before long she came to a pocket-sized clearing, its feathery grasses touched with the brilliance of moonlight and the deep blacks of shadow.

There she seated herself against the bole of a moss-furred tree and brought out the gem-studded circlet. The moon was nearly full once more, and its silvery light filtered down through the heavy branches to fall on the strange owl stone.

I will not go too near Grimmel's camp, she cautioned herself. *I will only dream-fly high up and discover where he is. And just perhaps I will also see this star ship Imandoff says is the old toad's goal.*

Corri slipped on the circlet, positioning the owl stone on her forehead just above her eyes. She forced herself to relax as she looked out on the dark forest around her with that strange double vision produced by the stone. As she closed her eyes, she felt the disorienting slip of her shadow-self as it left behind the physical body. Instantly she thought of Grimmel and was soaring high above the mountain pass to the Tuone grasslands.

Her position changed slightly so that she hovered above a crude camp alongside the beginning of a narrow, rocky trail that led from the grasslands up into the mountains. Somehow she knew that the master thief was close by. She forced herself to hang above the camp, not trusting her emotions if she saw Grimmel. Instead, she strained her senses to search the area. She found that, by concentrating on her hearing, she could catch the faint sounds of conversation from the men gathered about the tiny fire below.

"It has been long years since I came this way." Corri recognized Grimmel's rough voice. "We must search."

"And if we do not find what you seek?" It was Roggkin.

"We stay until we do. Do not think of slinking away now, Tuonela." The threat was plain.

Corri noted the landmarks about the camp and judged its distance to be nearer the pass than Imandoff had guessed. The only trail leading up into the higher peaks from the grasslands would be rough going, she saw, twisting like a giant snake back upon itself again and again, eating up precious time. That delay would allow the thief and her companions the needed opportunity to gain the high ground first. Her shadow-self bobbed in the breeze sweeping over the peaks and down onto the grasslands.

Grimmel spoke of his goal being in the eastern mountains. If he truly seeks a star ship, only there could it have been concealed all this time.

Turning to look farther into the mountains, she tried to form an image of a vessel used to travel between the stars. A flickering vision of some strange object dodged in and out of her mind while she fought to narrow her concentration.

At last, unable to picture anything firm, Corri thought only of the vessel, only the idea without a picture. Her shadow-self moved aimlessly from one mountain clearing to another. Just as she gave up hope, there was a wink of moonlight reflected from something below. She swung lower.

Something of metal lay crumpled in the tiny clearing, one end of the structure mashed against a broken cliff.

Then it is true! Corri felt the excitement rush through her. *But what does Grimmel seek in this broken wreck? What strange device could there be that would aid him in decoding the Fravashi books?*

She set herself to spiral down for a closer look. As she began her descent, something rubbed against her thoughts. She drew back in distaste. Tiny tendrils of dull red spun out toward her from the north, threads that carried with them the feeling of Darkness and twisted power. Corri swung around the questing tendrils, avoiding their touch, carefully keeping her thoughts under control, but seeking the source of this strange attack.

To the north, in another valley not far distant, she saw the spark of fire marking a second camp, but her instincts for danger kept her from investigating. Something deep inside warned her that great danger lay in getting too close to that dull red glow. *Who is it?* Corri thought. *Surely that Fravashi priest, who in his shadow-self faced me before, could not pass the border to come here. But who else could spin such controlling evil?*

The tentacles withdrew, concentrated into a ball far below. Corri reached out with her amplified other-sense of hearing. The camp was quiet except for the snort of horses along a picket line.

Corri, come to me. A man's voice reached her mind, plucking at her memories. *I am your father. Come to me.*

Kayth? Corri stopped the subconscious move forward of her shadow-self. All the anger of her childhood poured to the front of her mind. *You left me!* she accused. *You deserted me! Why did you leave me with Grimmel? Do you know what he plans for me?* A flash of lightning answered her broadcast of fierce emotions. She blinked in the blinding light as it flashed across the sky between her and the unseen man calling himself her father.

It was necessary, came the reply. *There were things needing to be done. I could not take a baby on my journeys.*

Excuses! Corri watched, fascinated, as deep clouds began to gather, shutting out the moon's face. *Grimmel wants to force his child on me.* She struggled for words. *You deserted me, left me to such a fate that no parent should wish upon a child.*

The bloodline must continue, came the calm answer. *But Grimmel no longer matters. My power is such now that he cannot stand against me, not even with what he would use from the ship. I have chosen another for you, one whose blood mingled with yours will produce a powerful child, one who will give us total control of Sar Akka and its Peoples.*

No! Corri's answer came swift and firm. *I will never agree to that. How can you reach me like this?* The girl's thoughts centered, began to seek logic in the situation.

Come to me, Corri. I have translated part of the Books of Darkness. They are truly books of great power, for they enable me to do many things. Only those having true mind-powers of a certain kind, like you and I do, can use the Books. Together we can rule this world. There was a smugness to Kayth's words.

Never! I shall destroy your vessel, for you must have something within it to complete your control. Is that not so? Corri felt satisfaction at the burst of anger she felt from Kayth.

You cannot destroy the ship. There are safeguards that will not allow you entrance. Only Grimmel and I know the codes. The anger damped again into smugness. *Kill Grimmel. Then there will be only the two of us to rule Sar Akka. The others who came with me will not matter, for they have no mind-strengths.*

Sar Akka is my world, my life, Corri answered. *My mother was of this world; I was born here. I will defend it against you and Grimmel and all others of your kind with my last breath. From this day forward, Kayth Farblood, you and I have no kin-ties. We are mortal enemies, to the death.*

Stupid little Corri. There was laughter behind the words. *There is nothing you can do to stop me. Sar Akka will be mine. And when I have conquered it, I will send for others of my kind.*

You must kill me to do it, Corri answered.

So be it, fool. I have the key to the ship, the key to total power and control. You have nothing but a renegade sorcerer and a woman warrior. What are those against what I shall be able to do once the Books are completely translated?

The contact with Kayth snapped, and Corri fled back toward her sleeping body.

Chapter 29

Corri groaned and tugged off the circlet. She rubbed her aching eyes before she slid the seeing stone back inside her tunic. As her eyes grew accustomed to the darkness around her, she drew back against the tree and fumbled for her dagger. A figure stood over her, sword in hand.

"It is Tirkul." The warrior's deep voice penetrated her fear. "It was foolish to come out here alone, without someone to stand guard."

"But necessary." Corri's voice shook with exhaustion. "There is great danger. I must tell Imandoff."

She struggled to rise but found her legs would not hold her. As Tirkul bent to take her in his arms, she protested weakly, but inwardly was relieved. The warrior easily gathered her up and set off toward the camp.

"A shakka. I said I would never love a shakka." Tirkul's voice was so soft Corri could barely hear the words.

Imandoff stood, staff in hand, facing the trees, when they emerged into the fire light. Takra waited beside him, sword in hand, a frown wrinkling her brow.

"Danger," Corri said weakly, as Tirkul lowered her to the ground, then sat behind her for support. "Grimmel is close, and so is Kayth. And the sky vessel, Kayth says we cannot enter it. I believe him. Imandoff, he has translated some of the Books of Darkness!"

"Kayth!" The word exploded from the sorcerer. "So. He is a star traveler for certain, just as I said, one with powerful secret powers within his ship that he can use to threaten this world. And the ship, where does it lie?"

"That direction." Corri pointed deeper into the mountains, beyond the rock-strewn pass to the east. "With the owl stone, I may be able to stop him. But I need a guard behind against Grimmel and his men. The trail up from Tuone is long. We should be able to reach the top first. If we can get between Grimmel and his goal, perhaps we can delay or stop him."

Imandoff nodded. "At dawn we move on. Takra and I will hold your back by sword. And Tirkul," he locked eyes with the Tuonela warrior, "you must protect Corri with your life while she does whatever must be done."

"My oath." Tirkul gathered up a handful of dirt, clasping hands with the sorcerer. "But I do not understand the danger."

"I understand now," Corri answered. "There is something, some device, within the sky vessel that will help Kayth translate the rest of the evil Books. Yes," she nodded at Imandoff's frown, "already he has completed part of that task. When he translates the remainder, there may be no stopping his conquering our world. It could mean the end of all we know as Sar Akka. We must fight or die as slaves."

They bypassed the gap that led down into the land of Tuone before night was over, choosing instead a faint animal track that led straight east from the guard post. The trail twisted under the thick trees and out onto treacherous pebble-strewn slopes, along boulder-edged embankments, and ever higher. The moonlight spilled pale and watery over ghostly mountain outlines, leaving the shadows thick and forbidding about their feet. Dawn found them still leading the horses deeper into the Takto Range.

"I know this place." Tirkul turned to face straight east. "I have been as far as the Silent Towers up there." He pointed to a finger of stone, a jutting prominence on the highest peaks, a black tower outlined with new sunlight. "Up there are places where the shakkas forbid us to go."

"Not a place for horses." Takra shaded her eyes against the sun, then turned back to Imandoff. "They spook easily near those places. Any sign that this Grimmel has come this way?"

"Only the marks of wild animals. They must still be below us on the lower trails." The sorcerer leaned his tall staff against a lone tree that clung to the thin mountain soil. "Time for fighting is here, Wind-Rider. We must play rear-guard for the Dream Warrior. Perhaps this was our task all the time." He flexed his long fingers.

"About time," Takra said, a grin tugging at her mouth. "Too long have we fled danger. I am tired of skulkers snapping at my heels. I was not born to hide in the shadows like a frightened hare, waiting helplessly to be pulled down."

"I will be guard for Corri." Tirkul's dark eyes lingered briefly on the girl before going back to the distant slopes. "There are more dangers than men in these mountains."

"Do what you can, Tirkul of the Asperel." Imandoff raised his fist in a warrior's salute. "May the Goddess guard your back."

"Amd you," Tirkul returned, his fist in answer. "If I pass Between Worlds, I shall wait for you in Vayhall." He turned to Takra, raised his fist again.

"Brother-kin, I do not doubt we shall meet again, wherever that may be." The warrior woman grinned. "Blood your sword, Tirkul. Let it drink deep of the blood of our enemies."

Corri felt a deep sadness rise from within. Without a word, she stepped close and threw her arms around Imandoff.

"Hold fast, old man. Do nothing foolish."

"And you, little thief." His arms crushed her close. "Listen to your heart and spirit. Do whatever they tell you."

The girl turned to Takra. "Sister-Friend, take care. And take care of this mighty sorcerer. Without a woman to show him the way, he would probably get lost."

Takra grinned back; the smile warmed Corri's mind. The warrior woman slapped the girl on the shoulder. "Go into battle with a war cry on your lips, Corri Farblood. It is music to the ears of the Mother of Mares. And you are of Clan blood, remember."

Corri and Tirkul left the horses with Imandoff at the top of the twisting trail that led down into the grasslands. Tirkul's mount, Hellstorm, pawed the ground and shook his mane as the warrior left him behind. As they scrambled up the steep path, Corri looked back only once. Takra was flexing her sword arm, a look of determination and hate on her proud face, as she and the sorcerer waited for Grimmel.

With grim resolve, Corri followed the Tuonela warrior in the climb up the track. Neither spoke; only the sounds of their harsh breathing broke the mountain stillness. Occasionally, a misplaced step sent pebbles rattling down the slopes behind them. Each time, Tirkul stopped and tipped his head to listen for any sign that they had been spotted. But no one challenged them; there was no creak of leather or ching of drawn sword to alert them to hidden dangers.

Tirkul led Corri farther into the mountains, scrambling over every shortcut he knew, in the direction she had seen in her dream-flight. They skirted knife-edged valleys and rocky canyons, but mostly they followed animal trails through the thick trees deeper into the Takto Range.

The mountain air was sharp and extremely chilly, cutting like a knife into Corri's laboring lungs as she forced herself to keep up with Tirkul. At last, she had to lean against an out-cropping of rock to catch her breath, her face red with exertion. She stood, gasping in deep lungfuls of cold air, a stitch in her side from the last section of rough climbing.

"We will rest." Tirkul paused two steps above her, his own face crimson along the cheekbones, his breathing as labored as hers.

Corri sank down, her legs quivering from exhaustion. "How much farther?" she asked between gulps of air.

"There is no way to know." Tirkul slid his sword a hand's span in and out of the sheath as his dark eyes constantly scanned the slopes around them. "We are near the top of this ridge. Then we must search every valley until we find what you seek. Soon we must find a place to spend the dark hours. We dare not try these trails at night."

He took a swallow from the water flask hanging at his belt and motioned Corri to do the same. The lukewarm water soothed her dry throat.

What will I do when we find the sky ship, if we do? she asked herself. *Even with Imandoff and Takra guarding us against Grimmel, we must still face Kayth and the Fravashi priests. If I can discover no way to destroy what we seek, then Tirkul will certainly pour out his life for nothing.*

She studied his face from the corners of her eyes, her glance sliding across his square-cut jaw, the white-blonde braids falling against the rugged cheekbones as he turned his head to view the high ground around them.

"I was named for Varanna's swordsman in the legends." The Tuonela's deep voice was soft. "That Tirkul stood at Varanna's side as a sword-friend and protector. But he failed."

The dark eyes stared down at Corri. "He fell in battle, but did not die, while she was cut down by the Fravashi priest. I shall not make that mistake. If I fall in battle, it will be with a death-wound."

"I am not Varanna," Corri retorted, "and you are not that Tirkul. Do not go seeking death. I plan to live through this, and I would not have your life wasted. I do not believe the geas leads us on this journey to die, but to live." Somehow the words felt right.

"Only the Mother of Mares and Her Lord know what is written in Natira's books." Tirkul offered a tanned hand, pulling her to her feet. "We will press on until twilight. After that, we must find a safe place for the night." He started up the trail.

Behind them came a faint echo of clashing metal, a dim, faraway ripple of sound from the pass far below.

"Tirkul! Imandoff and Takra—" Corri whirled to go back, but the Tuonela jerked her to a halt.

"They do their duty. We must do ours." His face was calm, only the eyes flashing with anger. "Would you have their blood spilled in vain?"

Corri numbly shook her head. *What have I done, asking them to guard our backs?* she thought.

Tirkul turned on his heel, his soft boots silent on the trail. "Come," he said, as he led the way over the top of the ridge.

Imandoff lay pressed against the top of a flat boulder near the peak of the pass, Takra crouched at its base. The red sun was close to the western horizon. The sorcerer's smoke-gray eyes watched every movement along the twisting trail below them. At last, he eased himself down, leaning close to the warrior woman. "They come." His words were barely audible, even in the still air. "I saw six riders, one of them a Tuonela.

Four of them appear to be armed guards. I cannot tell for certain which one is Grimmel. The guards wear body-armor."

Takra stared at the sheer rock wall that rose straight up across from their hiding place. The trail wound between the cliff and the massive boulder where she and Imandoff waited, swords in hand. Just beyond them, the track led through a narrow defile, so narrow that turning a horse would require time. She twisted the ancient wrist cuff, deep in planning what form of attack to take.

The sharp clip-clip of hooves rang out as the mounts scrambled up a steep section of the track toward the ridge-top. The first rider was cloaked, his hood far over his face. Four more horses pushed past the boulder, their riders, armor shining in the dying sun, oblivious to the hidden menace. The sixth horse, a Tuonela mount, battle-trained and wary, danced sideways as it scented the sorcerer and the warrior woman. It rushed past the hiding place and whirled in a skitter of gravel in the only open place.

"Frayma!" Takra's battle-cry shattered the stillness.

She rushed the grasslands mount before it could rear, grabbing the bridle in a calloused hand and jerking it downward. The animal half-fell to its knees, its leather-clad rider sliding to the stony path.

Hellstorm and Lightfoot screamed in defiance, their shrill sounds slicing through the mountain stillness. The two horses lunged at the guards' mounts, biting at both men and horses. Takra was vaguely aware that Imandoff had silently rushed past her, his sword ready. The other horses were in the narrow defile, struggling to turn in a confused mass, the riders trying to defend both against Imandoff and the Tuonela war mounts. Then she faced the Tuonela rider, and Imandoff was forgotten.

The renegade warrior threw himself behind his horse to avoid her sword swing. Cursing, Takra went after him, dodging the sharp hooves and sliding on the treacherous gravel. For an instant she glimpsed Roggkin's wide eyes, the old sword-scar across his cheek and nose, the clipped lobe of one ear.

Wild-eyed horses milled about the tiny widening in the track, their acrid sweat and terrified screams filling the air. With a rush, the riderless mounts of the guards pushed back down the mountains toward the grasslands of Tuone. Hell-storm and Lightfoot drew back from the swinging swords, eyes rolling, teeth bared.

"'Ware, Takra!" Imandoff's shout rang through the din of battle.

She whirled, sword swinging in a deadly flash, waist high. The guard who crept toward her back fell in a screaming heap, clutching his stomach. Where his worn and badly mended leather breast-plate had pulled up from his raised arms, the Tuonela's sword had sliced him from side to side. A flood of red splashed across his clutching hands and stained the rocky path. Lightfoot rushed in, her hooves crashing onto the prone man, dancing death over his body.

Takra whipped around again, sword out, but Roggkin was astride his horse, heading back down the trail.

"Frayma!" She shouted again in defiance and turned back into the burning edge of a sword cut. The end of the shining blade scored across her cheekbone and down her jaw as she jerked back her head. The hot smell of blood clogged her nostrils, but the pain was buried in a flow of adrenalin.

Takra drew her long dagger, holding it in her left hand, her sword ready in the right. The guard stared at her with battle-hardened eyes. This guard wore breast and back plates instead of the more easily damaged mail.

The swords rang together, the man trying to use his heavier weight to throw her off balance. Snake-quick, she moved closer, her sword flashing death in the waning light. She hooked a boot around his leg and sent him sprawling.

"Haven-swill!" Takra spat at him. "A coward to stab in the back. Face me like a warrior, man. Go to Natira like the warrior you claim to be."

A wild scream of terror jerked the man's head around; one of his companions sank in a blood-covered heap on the ground. The guard scrambled up, sword again in hand, to face Takra.

"No woman threatens me." The guard smiled thinly, his white teeth set tight together. "You are nothing, woman."

He came at her in a wild rush, but Takra sidestepped, bringing her sword in a sweep that clanged harmlessly against his armor. There was a flurry of sword thrusts before he again rushed her.

There is no way to give a body blow, she thought. *Blessed Frayma, help me. I fight in Your cause.*

Instead of retreating from the man, Takra threw herself forward. He struck at her sword wrist with his deadly blade as he closed. The sword whistled, clanged against the ancient wrist cuff she wore, sending a shock down her arm. Her weapon fell from numbed fingers, but the cuff kept her from losing her hand. *For Corri and the Goddess,* Takra thought as the man's strong arms grabbed at her.

The warrior woman feinted a fall, sliding out of the grasp, then recovered her footing. With an upward, side to side motion of her dagger, she found her target and cut the guard's throat from ear to ear.

She leaped over the gurgling man toward Imandoff, who fought in a flurry of flashing thrusts against the final guard. Just as Takra prepared to leap on the guard's back, her dagger ready, Imandoff's straight-armed thrust took the man in the left eye. The guard dropped like a stone, dead before he hit the ground.

"You are hurt!" Imandoff dropped the gore-coated sword and reached for the Tuonela woman.

Takra felt the stinging pain on her face, raised one hand to touch the bright flow of blood.

The sorcerer took her by the arm and led her to the boulder behind which they had waited. Then he pushed her to sit.

"Takra." He spoke her name in a weary voice and reached out a trembling hand to cup it about the wound. The steady flow of blood fell to a tiny seeping as his magical powers pressed upon the opened vessels through his carefully placed fingers.

"I cannot heal as Corri can with Varanna's stone." Imandoff searched for the flask of mountain water to wash down the wound. "The best I can do is stitch it as I would a garment. You will be scarred for life, I fear." He pulled a sliver of metal out of his pouch and threaded it with a piece of sinew that he dipped into the fiery liquor.

"Then do it, sorcerer. For I think our battles may not be finished." Takra sucked in her breath and dug her blood-covered fingers into the ground as Imandoff took the first stitch.

"I have been in skirmishes before," Imandoff said as he tried to steady his shaking hands. "A few petty thieves and night-stalking vermin who thought sorcerers carried rich treasures. Never, until now, did I have such a great fear for the safety of anyone with me." He laughed nervously. "Fear for the life of a Tuonela warrior who has beaten me black and blue over half of Kirisan."

"Imandoff Silverhair afraid?" Takra asked in surprise, then sucked in her breath as the sorcerer took another careful stitch. *Is he trying to say he thinks of me as more than a friend?* she thought. *Or am I hearing what my heart wishes?*

The belly-slashed man gave a last groan and gurgle as the sorcerer finished sewing up the wound.

"We can yet move on before total darkness falls." Imandoff extended a hand to help Takra to her feet. "Grimmel got past us during the fighting. He is headed up into the mountains."

The snuffling and low growls of gathering scavengers sounded at the edges of the rocks. Takra painfully whistled to Lightfoot, who herded the sorcerer's roan and Mouse with her. Tirkul's mount paced nervously behind, his eyes still alert for enemies.

"Then we ride while we have light. I would not stay here anyway. Who knows what the bodies and blood will draw to feast?"

"Takra." Imandoff moved close, the single word almost a sigh. He put out a trembling hand to her blood-splattered shoulder and drew her close. Bending slightly, he kissed her gently on the mouth.

"Are you certain you wish this with a war lady?" Takra's words were feathery against his neck as he pulled her into his arms.

"As certain as I am of life itself." Imandoff gave her a hard squeeze, then gently pushed her toward Lightfoot. "But we both know we must ride after Corri and Tirkul. Time enough for ourselves later." He smiled up at her with his old humor.

"Aye, Imandoff, more than enough time if we should live."

Mouse fidgeted nervously as Imandoff handed the reins to Takra. With Hellstorm following behind, they turned their horses up the narrow defile to the ridges above.

Chapter 30

That night Corri huddled in her cloak, one hand pressed against the headband hidden inside her tunic. Neither she nor Tirkul spoke more than a few words.

There must be a way, Corri thought as she puzzled over Kayth's words. *Even though we cannot approach the sky ship, there must be a way to destroy it.* She was still turning over the problem in her mind when she finally sank into sleep.

It was late the next morning when Tirkul and Corri finally found the trail the Tuonela warrior had been seeking. Storm clouds were rolling thick overhead when they came out on the rim of a small valley nestled in the Takto Range. Below them lay the crumpled silver remains of the ship she had seen.

"Valley of the sky bird!" Tirkul's word were soft.

"You knew of this?" Corri turned to him, her eyes wide, her mouth grim.

"I was not certain. I prayed this was not what you sought. It is death to try to enter that." He pointed down at the broken-backed vessel. "I have never seen it, only heard old stories.

Since the first Tuonela hunters died there, it has been forbidden ground."

"I must do something," Corri said, as she stared down into the valley. "It must be destroyed before Kayth arrives."

"Too late!" Tirkul drew his sword and pointed. "There. Against the far hills, Fravashi priests!"

Corri pulled the headband from her tunic and slipped it on. There was no longer any indecision in her mind. "Guard me," she ordered as she lay down in the dry grass.

She willed herself to relax, not to fear the line of dark robed figures she had seen begin their crossing of the tiny valley. *Out,* she told herself, as she felt her shadow-self struggling. *Out!*

She fought against her fears to loosen the body's hold. After what seemed an eternity, she felt the familiar tugging and heard the pop in her ears. She floated free.

There must be a way. Corri looked down at the dull red glows marking the life-forces of the priests, then up at the black clouds above. Among them moved the sullen glow of another life-force, one which was all too familiar. *Kayth! I should have realized that events would bring you here.*

A grumble of thunder reached her; a faint flicker of lightning pulsed deep within the storm clouds. Corri felt the destructive power within the storm above, felt it and instinctively knew she could wield that power.

No! Her mind-scream of anger rose to meet the black sky. *This is my world. You will not enslave its Peoples. I will kill you first, Kayth!*

Corri held up her hand, mentally commanding the storm-power to come to her. The owl stone, then her hand tingled and burned as the power entered it. Without hesitation, she pointed that hand at the valley below. A bolt of lightning shot downward toward the Fravashi priests, deflected at the last moment into the ground. Two figures lay sprawled on the blackened, smoldering grass.

You cannot kill me, Corri. Kayth's mind-voice slammed against her with venom. *You cannot stop what I would do.*

She threw up her phantom hands to ward off the blast of thought-power, a red streak spotted with black, that splattered outward and dissipated.

There must be a way! Corri sent another lightning bolt toward Kayth, but it too was deflected at the last moment to strike harmlessly into the soil. The priests had retreated, leaving Kayth to stand alone not far from the disabled ship.

Another thought-wave whipped toward her, but she knocked it aside. She hung in the air, motionless, waiting for a stronger death thought from Kayth, a thought from which she would not know how to defend herself.

Thunder continued to rumble overhead, echoing against the valley walls. A small stab of lightning shot through the black clouds.

It is true, she thought. *I cannot kill him. I feel that. Whether because he is my father or because of his powers, I know not. But there must be a way to stop his using the ship.*

Corri allowed her anger to build, thinking of every mistreatment from Grimmel, the fate to which Kayth had left her without a second thought, what he planned for Sar Akka. She felt the pressures of the storm build and press against her shadow-self in answer to her emotions. A rising wind whipped her spirit body so that she struggled to stay in place.

You will never again use this sky ship for evil, Kayth! If I cannot kill you this time, at least I can stop you from gaining the greater knowledge and power you seek. As she thought of the natural destructive force, Corri lifted her phantom hand and pointed it at the ship.

I die before we have anything together, Tirkul, she thought. *I die that you and Sar Akka may be free.*

She felt the lightning's power course through her, entering the owl stone and flowing down her arm. It shot from her pointing finger straight toward the ship. It struck once, again, three times. The silver skin of the ship exploded, then burst into flames. A rising plume of acrid smoke mushroomed skyward. Still Corri held her deadly gesture as the owl stone, locked on her physical body, burned into her forehead. Twice more the lightning struck to leave the sky ship a charred and melted pile of useless rubble.

No! A shriek of rage rocketed toward her from Kayth.

Corri weakly defended herself and pulled back toward her body. Another surge of hate from Kayth nearly drained her of strength as she tried to fight back.

I must get away from him, she thought. *I must not die now with my mission unfulfilled. There will be another time, Kayth, and when that comes, you will not be the victor!*

She retreated into her body, wildly fumbling with the circlet to draw it off her forehead. As it came away, she screamed with pain. The center of her forehead was an agony of burn.

"Corri!" Tirkul bent over her, deep concern on his face.

She saw a flicker of movement behind the warrior and, with a last burst of strength, shoved him to one side. The Tuonela fell, rolling back to his feet. Grimmel's knife missed its mark, instead plunging into her shoulder just above the tattoo. The circlet dropped to the ground as she screamed and rolled away.

"If you do not belong to me, Farblood, you will belong to no man." The look in Grimmel's eyes was not sane.

Tirkul was instantly on his feet, stalking the master thief, sword ready, lips drawn back in a snarl. "Asuran nathling! Scum and filth!" Tirkul was cold with rage. "No man owns this woman. For what you have done to her, I will cut out your black heart and eat it!"

Grimmel threatened with his blood-coated dagger, then turned to run. Tirkul's sword bit through the master thief's back, nearly cutting him in two. The lifeless body fell kicking onto the grass.

I am finally free of Grimmel, Corri thought as waves of pain rolled over her. *Oh Goddess, if I could only be free of Kayth and all the rest of this burden, too. The geas is so powerful, so heavy.*

"Corri!" Tirkul again knelt over her, his dagger cutting into her tunic to expose the wound. "Lie still. I must stop the bleeding."

He ripped at her cloak, then wadded a strip of cloth into the cut. Tearing loose another strip, Tirkul wound it around the pad. Hastily, he pulled her to her feet, holding her up with one arm, while he kept the sword at the ready.

"The owl stone. I must not leave it behind. Kayth is not dead. I could not kill him, Tirkul." Corri's words were sobs of pain as she clung to his strong arm.

Tirkul bent to sweep up the circlet. He tucked it under Corri's belt, then half-carried her up the mountain under deep cover of the needled trees.

I failed to kill Kayth. Why did I hesitate? Thoughts of guilt and defeat ran through her mind. *I failed you, Lady.*

No, came an answer. A woman's gentle face appeared before her mind's eye. *You dealt the first blow in a long battle, and a powerful blow it was to Frav. Daughter, you have done well.*

I am not a warrior, Lady. Release me from this burden and let me come to you now.

The figure gave a gentle, reproving shake of the head. *I have no one but you, Dream Warrior, to save My People.* The face faded from Corri's mind.

As they stumbled onto the trail that had brought them down into the little valley, Corri could not suppress the whimpers of pain that forced their way through her tight lips. The pain from her shoulder poured down her arm; her forehead burned with intense agony, as if her head were in the hottest part of a roaring fire. She heard Tirkul call out a challenge to someone she could not see, then a Tuonela war cry. She plunged downward into darkness.

*D*rink this." Through the haze of pain, Corri saw Imand-off's face, felt the cold rim of a cup against her lips. "It will ease the pain, Corri. Drink it all."

The bitter brew filled her mouth, was sharp in her throat. She swallowed again and again until the cup was drained. Tirkul's arms still braced her against his shoulder. She lay there in the circle of his arms, unwilling to move. At last the herbs took hold, and she sank into a drugged sleep.

She drifted in and out of consciousness, remembering only snatches of conversation carried on around her. Time had no meaning, yet whenever she floated to momentary awareness, she recognized the pressure of Tirkul's strong arms still holding her. The darkness was safe, a place of refuge without the lancing pain that ate at her forehead; she fought against the pull back to reality, struggled to sink deeper into the unknowing realm of unconsciousness.

"Are her wounds deadly?" Takra's concerned voice reached her faintly.

"The knife wound is painful, but is no threat to her life or the use of her arm." Imandoff's husky tones sounded close to her ear. "The burn from the owl stone reached the bone and must hurt terribly, but it is not life-threatening, either."

"What is it then?" Corri heard the creak of Takra's leather armor as the warrior woman moved closer.

"She has withdrawn into the depths of her mind. She struggles to release her spirit from the body." There was a deep sigh. "If she had training, she might be able to do this thing, but as it is, she will only drive herself to madness. This state of non-being has lasted over a day now. We must force her to come back."

"Sister-Friend, do not leave me." Part of Corri's mind recognized the fear and sadness in Takra's words.

I love you all, but you best, Takra. As your friend, leave me here where there is no pain.

"Corri." Imandoff's demanding voice pushed into the darkness where she hid. "You are safe, Corri."

She fought against the pull back into pain. The darkness was safe. Nothing, no one, could reach her there.

"Corri." Tirkul's voice whispered by her ear. "Come back, little Dream Warrior."

Reluctantly, Corri let her consciousness rise and opened her eyes to the sunset high overhead. Tirkul bent closer, his strong arms around her, concern in every line of his face. She felt the pain of her wounds, the pressure of a bandage coated with cooling salve on her forehead. She managed to smile weakly up at the Tuonela, then turned her eyes to focus on a figure looming over her.

"All her life as a thief in Hadliden and she never had a scar. Now she will be scarred for life." Imandoff stood, one hand scratching at his beard and shaking his head.

"Proud symbols of battle." Takra also stood near, blood splattered over her leather tunic. A red wound stretched across her tanned cheek and down her jaw, the marks of stitching plain. "You are now a true warrior, Farblood." She tried to grin down at the girl, then winced at the pain from the stitches. "It seems we both took battle wounds of honor."

"I did not defeat him," Corri said and turned her face against Tirkul's chest to hide the tears. "Kayth still lives."

"He and the surviving priests fled back to Frav." Imandoff looked north, one hand caressing the worn hilt of his sword. "We saw them go. I pray it will be some time before he challenges us again."

"Roggkin escaped," Takra growled the words. "Like the coward he is, he ran away through the pass as soon as the fighting grew hot. Doubtless, he seeks sanctuary with his black-hearted friends in Kirisan. But I will find him. Soon or later, I will find him, and then …" She balled her fists in anger.

"Grimmel is dead, and by my hand." Tirkul's voice, too, held an undercurrent of anger. "This Kayth we will hunt another day."

"For now our world is safe, Corri." Imandoff knelt beside her, one calloused hand on her knee. "Kayth can no longer use his strange devices within the sky ship to finish the translation of the Books of Darkness. I will not lie to you. Eventually, there must be a reckoning with Kayth, but for now we, and Sar Akka, are safe once more."

The sorcerer gripped her knee in reassurance. Then he and Takra moved out of her sight, the sorcerer's strong arm around the war lady's shoulders. Tirkul's arms tightened about Corri.

"I thought you were lost to me," he murmured against her hair. "I have never felt such fear, not even when facing a barsark. Always I swore not to love a shakka, but the heart goes where it will. And you are free of that Asuran marriage, free to go where you will, do what you want."

Corri pulled away a little to look at him. "Truly?" she asked, then grimaced at the pain of her wounds.

"Truly." Tirkul's eyes were steady. "You have not given heart-oath, I know, but what I feel will not change if you walk away from me. You cannot leave me behind, Corri Farblood, for I will ride at your back even though you never turn fair eyes my way."

"Tirkul, I am a thief, the best in Hadliden. Daughter of Kayth Farblood who would conquer our world by opening the door to the darkest of magics. I am a danger to everyone as long as he lives."

"It matters not. I will ride at your back wherever you go. You cannot stop me." Tirkul's lips tightened in determination.

"I do not know your ways, Tirkul, but I will give heart-oath. How did the words go?"

"I will walk beside you in fairness, keep your life as my own, ride with you wherever the wind blows." He murmured the words against her hair.

"Yes, that I will do." Corri leaned her head against his broad chest. "When I saw Grimmel with his knife raised to kill, I thought you would die. And if you died, I would have willingly followed you Between Worlds, no longer caring. Life would mean little without you."

This longing I feel for you must be love, Tirkul. I do not want to lose you. Her old thief's instincts prodded at her thoughts. *But what do I know of love? If things do not work between us, then by Tuonela law, we can always part.* Corri felt her eyes mist at the thought. *But, oh how that would hurt.*

She turned her head to look at Imandoff and Takra who sat on the other side of the small fire, the sorcerer's muscled arm still about warrior woman's shoulders. "And without true friends." She felt a leap of warm knowledge in her mind. "Friends. Most of my life I thought of friendships as dangerous, an emotion never to be indulged. Now you have taught me the beauty of friends, the wisdom of trusting them."

"Where to now, sorcerer?" Takra asked, as she pulled her long dagger to flip it back and forth between her hands.

"We shall follow the wind." Imandoff steepled his hands and stared at Corri. "Until we must once again ride against Frav and Kayth, our lives are our own."

"The winds blow onto the grasslands." Tirkul gently lay Corri back against the saddlebags. "She needs time to heal, sorcerer. Time and the freedom of Tuone, where there will be no pressures on her. What better place than among the Clans?"

"Yes," Corri said, and Imandoff and Takra echoed the word. "Time to mend and time to gather strength. For some day another battle is sure to come."

"Battles always come, like the wind," Tirkul answered. "But one does not seek them. A warrior gathers knowledge and skill, then rides forth when the call goes out. Only the Goddess knows what fate will bring. Until then we live each day to the fullest, letting tomorrow care for itself."

"The only way to savor life." Imandoff rummaged in his pack, coming up with the flask of mountain water. "Always convenient, mountain water. A cleanser of wounds and bad memories." He drank deep, then passed the flask to Takra.

"Death to all who oppose the Dream Warrior and threaten the freedom of the Peoples." Takra lifted the flask in a salute.

"To victory." Tirkul drank, then held it for Corri to sip the powerful brew.

"A new day and a new life." Corri reached out her good hand to clasp Tirkul's.

She lay in Tirkul's arms, content to trust her safety to the hands of another for a time. In a half-sleep, she watched the winking fire against the descending blackness of night.

PRONUNCIATION GUIDE

Adag: Aye' (long "a")-dag
Agadi: Ah-gah'-dee
Asperel: Ass'-per-el
Asur: Aye' (long "a")-sir
Athdar: Ath' (as in "am")-dar
Ayron: Aye' (long "a")-ron

Baba: Bah'-bah
Babbel: Bay'-bull
Balqama: Ball-kah'-mah
Barsark: Bar'-sark
Breela: Bree'-lah
Burrak: Burr'-ack

Cabiria: Cah-beer'-ee-ah
Cassyr: Cass'-seer
Charissa: Chur-iz'-zah
Chid: Chid (as in "kid")
Chum: Chum
Cleeman: Clee'-mon
Clua: Clue'-ah
Corri: Core'-ee
Croyna: Croy' (as in "troy")-
    nah

Daduku: Dah-doo'-koo
Dakhma: Dahk'-mah
Druk: Druk (as in "truck")

Fenlix: Fen'-licks
Feya: Fay' (long "a")-yah

Fravashi: Frah-vah'-shee
Frayma: Fray' (long "a")-
    mah
Friama: Free-ah'-mah
Fym: Fim

Gadavar: Gad'-a-var
Gertha: Grr'-thah
Geyti: Guy'-tee
Gran: Gran (as in "bran")
Grimmel: Grim'-ell

Hachino: Hah-chee'-no
Hadliden: Had'-li-dan
Halka: Hall'-kah
Halman: Hall'-mon
Hari-Hari: Har'-ee
Hindjall: Hind' (as in
    "hinge")-yall

Imandoff: im' (as in "imp")-
    an-doff
Iodan: Ee'-o-dan

Jabed: Jah'-bed
Jana: Jah'-nah
Jehennette: Gee'-en-et
Jevotan: Jay' (long "a")-vo-
    tan
Jinniyah: Gin-ee'-yah
Kaaba: Kay-ah'-bah

Kaballoi: Cab'-ah-loy (as in "toy")

Kanlath: Can'-lath

Kayth: Kay'-th

Keffin: Keff'-in

Kirisan: Kier' (as in "tier")-i (as in "it")-sahn

Korud: Core'-ud (as in "thud")

Krake: Krake (as in "brake")

Kratula: Kraw-too'-lah

Krynap: Cry'-nap

Kulkar: Kool'-kar

Kyma: Ky' (as in "eye")-mah

Kystan: Ky' (as in "eye")-stan

Leshy: Lesh' (as in "mesh")-ee

Limna: Lim' (as "limb")-nah

Magni: Mahg'-nee

Malya: Mahl'-yah

Medha: May'-dah

Melaina: Mee-lane'-ah

Menec: Men'-ek

Merra: Meer'-ah

Minepa: Min-e' (as the e in "egg")-paw

Minna: Mee'-nah

Mootma: Moot'-mah

Morvrana: Morv (as "more")-rah'-nah

Naga: Nah'-gah

Natira: Nah-tier'-rah

Neeba: Nee'-bah

Nevn: Nev'-n

Norya: Nor'-yah

Nu-Sheek: New-sheek'

Nu-Sheeka: New-shee'-kah

Odran: O' (as in "oh")-dran (as in "bran")

Qishua: Kish'-oo-ah

Rhuf: Rough

Rissa: Ris'-sah

Roggkin: Rog' (as in "dog")-kin

Rushina: Roo-shee'-nah

Rympa: Rim'-pah

Sadko: Sod'-koh

Sallin: Say'-linn

Sejda: Say'-dah

Shakka: Shah'-kah

Sharrock: Shar'-rock

Shilluk: Shill'-uck

Simi: Sim'-ee

Sussa: Soo'-sah

Taillefer: Tal' (as in "alley")-ee-fur

Takra: Tahk'-rah

Takto: Tahk'-toe

Tamia: Tay'-mee-ah

Taunith: Tow' (as in "ow")-nith

Taymin: Tay'-men

Thalassa: Thal (as in "alley")-ass'-ah

Thidrick: Thid' (as in "kid")-rick

Tho: Tho (as in "throw")

Tirkul: Tur'-kull

Tujyk: Too'-yek

Tuone: Too'-own

Tuonela: Too-oh-nell'-ah

Tuulikki: Too-oo-lee'-kee

Utha Unop: Oo'-thah Oh'-nap

Uunlak: Oo'-un-lack

Uzza: Oo'-zah

Vairya: Vair'-yah

Varanna: Var-ah'-nah

Vayhall: Vay' (as in "way")-hall

Vu-Murt: Voo'-murt

Vu-Zai: Voo-zai' (as in "eye")

Vum: Vum (as in "come")

Wella: Well'-ah

Wermod: Were'-mode

Widd: Widd (as in "lid")

Willa: Will'-ah

Xephena: Zeh-fee'-nah

Yaml: Yam'-el

Yngona: In-go'-nah

Zaitan: Zai' (as in "eye")-tan

Zalmoxis: Zal (as in "alley")-mox'-iz

Zatyr: Zah-tier'

Zingas: Zing'-gahs

Zivitua: Zi (as the e in "egg")-vi' (as in "it")-too-ah

Zoc: Zock

Zuartoc: Zoo-are'-tock

ABOUT THE AUTHOR

I was born on a Beltane Full Moon with a total lunar eclipse, one of the hottest days of that year. Although I came into an Irish-North Germanic-Native American family with natural psychics on both sides, such abilities were not talked about. So I learned discrimination in a family of closet psychics.

I have always been close to Nature. As a child, I spent a great amount of time outdoors by myself. Trees, herbs, and flowers become part of my indoor and outdoor landscapes wherever I live. I love cats, music, mountains, singing streams, stones, ritual, nights when the Moon is full. My reading covers vast areas of history, the magickal arts, philosophy, customs, mythology, and fantasy. I have studied every part of the New Age religions from Eastern philosophy to Wicca. I hope I never stop learning and expanding.

Although I have lived in areas of this country from one coast to the other, I now reside on the West Coast. I am not fond of large crowds or speaking in public.

I live a rather quiet life in the company of my husband and my four cats, with occasional visits with my children and grandchildren. I collect statues of dragons and wizards, crystals and other stones, and of course, books. Most of my time is spent researching and writing. My published books include *Celtic Magic; Norse Magic; The Ancient & Shining Ones; Maiden, Mother, Crone; Dancing With Dragons; Animal Magick;* and *Moon Magick.* Before I am finished with one book, I am working on another in my head. All in all, I am just an ordinary Pagan person.

To Write to the Author

If you wish to contact the author or would like more information about this book, please write to the author in care of Llewellyn Worldwide, and we will forward your request. Both the author and publisher appreciate hearing from you and learning of your enjoyment of this book. Llewellyn Worldwide cannot guarantee that every letter written to the author will be answered, but all will be forwarded. Please write to:

D. J. Conway
c/o Llewellyn Worldwide
P.O. Box 64383-K169, St. Paul, MN 55164-0383, U.S.A.

Please enclose a self-addressed stamped envelope for reply, or $1.00 to cover costs.
If outside U.S.A., enclose international postal reply coupon.

Free Catalog from Llewellyn Worldwide

For more than 90 years, Llewellyn has brought its readers knowledge in the fields of metaphysics and human potential. Learn about the newest books in spiritual guidance, natural healing, astrology, occult philosophy, and more. Enjoy book reviews, new age articles, a calendar of events, plus current advertised products and services. To get your free copy of *Llewellyn's New Worlds of Mind and Spirit,* send your name and address to:

Llewellyn's New Worlds of Mind and Spirit
P.O. Box 64383-K169, St. Paul, MN 55164-0383, U.S.A.

On the following pages you will find listed, with their current prices, some of the books now available on related subjects. Your book dealer stocks most of these and will stock new titles in the Llewellyn series as they become available. We urge your patronage.

To Order Books and Tapes

If your book store does not carry the titles described on the following pages, you may order them directly from Llewellyn by sending the full price in U.S. funds, plus postage and handling (see below).

Credit Card Orders: VISA, MasterCard, American Express are accepted. Call us toll-free within the United States and Canada at 1-800-THE-MOON.

Special Group Discount: Because there is a great deal of interest in group discussion and study of the subject matter of this book, we offer a 20% quantity discount to group leaders or agents. Our Special Quantity Price for a minimum order of five copies of *The Dream Warrior* is $59.80 cash-with-order. Include postage and handling charges noted below.

Postage and Handling: Include $4 postage and handling for orders $15 and under; $5 for orders over $15. There are no postage and handling charges for orders over $100. Postage and handling rates are subject to change. We ship UPS whenever possible within the continental United States; delivery is guaranteed. Please provide your street address as UPS does not deliver to P.O. boxes. Orders shipped to Alaska, Hawaii, Canada, Mexico and Puerto Rico will be sent via first class mail. Allow 4-6 weeks for delivery.

International Orders: Airmail—add retail price of each book and $5 for each non-book item (audiotapes, etc.); Surface mail—add $1 per item.

Minnesota residents add 7% sales tax.

Mail orders to:
Llewellyn Worldwide
P.O. Box 64383-K169
St. Paul, MN 55164-0383, U.S.A.

For customer service, call (612) 291-1970.

FLYING WITHOUT A BROOM
Astral Projection and the Astral World
by D. J. Conway

Astral flight has been described through history as a vital part of spiritual development and a powerful aid to magickal workings. In this remarkable volume, respected author D.J. Conway shows how anyone can have the keys to a profound astral experience. Not only is astral travel safe and simple, she shows in clear and accessible terms how this natural part of our psychic make-up can be cultivated to enhance both spiritual and daily life.

This complete how-to includes historical lore, a groundwork of astral plane basics, and a simplified learning process to get you "off the ground." You'll learn simple exercises to strengthen your astral abilities as well as a variety of astral techniques—including bilocation and time travel. After the basics, use the astral planes to work magick and healings; contact teachers, guides, or lovers; and visit past lives. You'll also learn how to protect yourself and others from the low-level entities inevitably encountered in the astral.

Through astral travel you will expand your spiritual growth, strengthen your spiritual efforts, and bring your daily life to a new level of integration and satisfaction.

1-56718-164-3, 224 pp., 6 x 9, softcover $13.00

All prices subject to change without notice

MOON MAGICK
Myth & Magic, Crafts & Recipes, Rituals & Spells
by D.J. Conway
No creature on this planet is unaffected by the power of the
Moon. Its effects range from making us feel energetic or
adventurous to tense and despondent. By putting excess
Moon energy to work for you, you can learn to plan pro-
jects, work and travel at the optimum times.

Moon Magick explains how each of the 13 lunar months is
directly connected with a different type of seasonal energy
flow and provides modern rituals and spells for tapping this
energy and celebrating the Moon phases. Each chapter
describes new Pagan rituals—79 in all—related to that particular Moon, plus related Moon lore, ancient holidays, spells,
meditations and suggestions for foods, drinks and decorations to accompany your Moon rituals. This book includes
two thorough dictionaries of Moon deities and symbols.

By moving through the year according to the 13 lunar
months, you can become more attuned to the seasons, the
Earth and your inner self. *Moon Magic* will show you how to
let your life flow with the power and rhythms of the Moon
to benefit your physical, emotional and spiritual well-being.
1-56718-167-8, 320 pp., 7 x 10, illus., softcover $14.95

All prices subject to change without notice

MAIDEN, MOTHER, CRONE
The Myth and Reality of the Triple Goddess
by D.J. Conway

The Triple Goddess is with every one of us each day of our lives. In our inner journeys toward spiritual evolution, each woman and man goes through the stages of Maiden (infant to puberty), Mother (adult and parent) and Crone (aging elder). *Maiden, Mother, Crone* is a guide to the myths and interpretations of the Great Goddess archetype and her three faces, so that we may better understand and more peacefully accept the cycle of birth and death.

Learning to interpret the symbolic language of the myths is important to spiritual growth, for the symbols are part of the map that guides each of us to the Divine Center. Through learning the true meaning of the ancient symbols, through facing the cycles of life, and by following the meditations and rituals provided in this book, women and men alike can translate these ancient teachings into personal revelations.

Not all goddesses can be conveniently divided into the clear aspects of Maiden, Mother and Crone. This book covers these as well, including the Fates, the Muses, Valkyries and others.

0-87542-171-7, 240 pp., 6 x 9, illus., softcover $12.95

All prices subject to change without notice

ANIMAL MAGICK
The Art of Recognizing & Working with Familiars
by D.J. Conway

The use of animal familiars began long before the Middle Ages in Europe. It can be traced to ancient Egypt and beyond. To most people, a familiar is a witch's companion, a small animal that helps the witch perform magick, but you don't have to be a witch to have a familiar. In fact you don't even have to believe in familiars to have one. You may already have a physical familiar living in your home in the guise of a pet. Or you may have an astral-bodied familiar if you are intensely drawn to a particular creature that is impossible to have in the physical. There are definite advantages to befriending a familiar. They make excellent companions, even if they are astral creatures. If you work magick, the familiar can aid by augmenting your power. Familiars can warn you of danger, and they are good healers.

Most books on animal magick are written from the viewpoint of the Native American. This book takes you into the exciting field of animal familiars from the European Pagan viewpoint. It gives practical meditations, rituals, and power chants for enticing, befriending, understanding, and using the magick of familiars.

1-56718-168-6, 256 pp., 6 x 9, illus., softcover $13.95

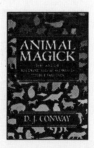

All prices subject to change without notice

FALCON FEATHER & VALKYRIE SWORD
Feminine Shamanism, Witchcraft & Magick
by D.J. Conway

Reclaim your innate magickal power as a woman and take control of your destiny! Long before the patriarchy tried to repress their secret wisdom, women practiced their own exclusive methods of shamanism, Witchcraft and divination. Denied for hundreds of years, you can regain those long-forgotten secrets and strengthen your connection with the Goddess through the rich array of rituals, exercises, guided journeys and other magickal techniques presented here!

Falcon Feather & Valkyrie Sword focuses entirely on magickal practices geared to the special needs of women. Use the shamanic powers and magick of ancient women from the Norse regions, Middle East, Greece, India and the Celtic areas—all in their original forms, stripped of overlying patriarchal interpretations and symbols. Discover why women-only groups perform magick that male-female groups can't. Find over 50 spells specifically created to answer the needs of women. Use the runes, ogham alphabet, shamanic stones, and Egyptian hieroglyphs for divination and magick—without the intervention of male deities. This book will help you take control of your life so you can become the true goddess you were meant to be!

1-56718-163-5, 352 pp., 7 x 10, illus., softcover $19.95

All prices subject to change without notice

BY OAK, ASH & THORN
Modern Celtic Shamanism
by D. J. Conway

Many spiritual seekers are interested in shamanism because it is a spiritual path that can be followed in conjunction with any religion or other spiritual belief without conflict. Shamanism has not only been practiced by Native American and African cultures—for centuries, it was practiced by the Europeans, including the Celts.

By Oak, Ash and Thorn presents a workable, modern form of Celtic shamanism that will help anyone raise his or her spiritual awareness. Here, in simple, practical terms, you will learn to follow specific exercises and apply techniques that will develop your spiritual awareness and ties with the natural world: shape-shifting, divination by the Celtic Ogham alphabet, Celtic shamanic tools, traveling to and using magick in the three realms of the Celtic otherworlds, empowering the self, journeying through meditation and more.

Shamanism begins as a personal revelation and inner healing, then evolves into a striving to bring balance and healing into the Earth itself. This book will ensure that Celtic shamanism will take its place among the spiritual practices that help us lead fuller lives.

1–56718–166-X, 288 pp., 6 x 9, illus., softcover $12.95

All prices subject to change without notice

BENEATH A MOUNTAIN MOON
A Novel by Silver RavenWolf
Welcome to Whiskey Springs, Pennsylvania, birthplace of magick, mayhem, and murder! The generations-old battle between two powerful occult families rages anew when young Elizabeyta Belladonna journeys from Oklahoma to the small town of Whiskey Springs—a place her family had left years before to escape the predatory Blackthorn family—to solve the mystery of her grandmother's death.

Endowed with her own magickal heritage of Scotch-Irish Witchcraft, Elizabeyta stands alone against the dark powers and twisted desires of Jason Blackthorn and his gang of Dark Men. But Elizabeyta isn't the only one pursued by unseen forces and the fallout from a past life. As Blackthorn manipulates the town's inhabitants through occult means, a great battle for mastery ensues between the forces of darkness and light—a battle that involves a crackpot preacher, a blue ghost, the town gossip, and an old country healer—and the local funeral parlor begins to overflow with victims. Is there anyone who can end the Blackthorns' reign of terror and right the cosmic balance?
1-56718-722-6, 360 pp., 6 x 9, softcover $15.95

All prices subject to change without notice

LILITH
A Novel by D. A. Heeley
The first book of the occult *Darkness and Light* trilogy weaves together authentic magical techniques and teachings of the Hebrew Qabalah with the suspenseful story of the spiritual evolution of Malak, an Adept of the White School of Magick.

Malak and his fellow magicians from the White, Yellow and Black Schools of Magick live on Enya, the lower astral plane of the Qabalistic Tree of Life. Malak's brother and arch-rival, Dethen, is an Adept of the Black School. Dethen plots a coup to destroy the White School completely and begin a reign of terror on Enya—with the hope of destroying the Tree of Life and the world—and a colossal battle between Good and Evil ensues. As the Black Adepts summon the Arch-demon Lilith into Enya, Malak is faced with a terrible choice: should he barter with the ultimate evil to free his wife's soul—even if freeing her condemns other innocent souls forever?

The second half of *Lilith* takes place 1,000 years later, in feudal Japan. Malak has been reincarnated as Shadrack, who struggles with an inner demon who will not be denied. He must conquer Lilith's evil or there will be a bloody rampage amid the Shogun's Royal Guard ....
1-56718-355-7, 256 pp., 6 x 9, softcover $10.00

VISIONS OF MURDER
A Novel by Florence Wagner McClain
Set in a scenic Oregon resort town surrounded by mountains and vast natural beauty, this suspense novel delves into the real problems of New Mexico's black market of stolen Indian artifacts. *Visions of Murder* mixes fact-based psychic experiences with lively archeological dialogue in a plot that unravels the high toll this black market exacts in lives, knowledge, and money.

David Manning was gunned down in an execution-style shooting outside his office. Unknown to his wife Janet, David had just discovered evidence in his employer's data bank of money-laundering connected to a black market in Indian artifacts.

Janet embarks on a personally exhaustive investigation into the death of her husband when she unearths a kind of dirt she's not used to handling. Elements of the occult, romance, and murder simmer hotly in this bubbling cauldron of mystery that is as informative as it is absorbing.
1-56718-452-9, 336 pp., mass market, softcover $5.99

WALKER BETWEEN THE WORLDS
A Novel by Diane DesRochers
Accurate paranormal details, engaging dialogue, lifelike action and steamy sex will thrill both men and women in the latest release of Llewellyn's Psi-Fi Series. *Walker Between the Worlds* tackles the universal themes of opposing forces and new world orders through such fitting characterizations as God and Goddess, Superhero and Heroine, and Comet and Space Ship. Alan Kolkey, a psychokinetic telepath and scientific genius whose sensitive human attributes hide beneath a macho exterior, must face lessons he'd rather not when he meets his match and love interest Dawn LaSarde. A private space ship, unruly drug gangs and an earthbound comet named Kali are some of the distractions Alan encounters in the escape from his real fears: relationships, responsibility and accountability! Follow our superhero and heroine as they put their highly developed psychic powers, ESP and OBE abilities to work in a showdown with human forces that make saving the world seem easy!

   1-56718-224-0, 448 pp., mass market, softcover $6.99

THE RAG BONE MAN
A Chilling Mystery of Self-Discovery
A Novel by Charlotte Lawrence
This occult fiction, mystery and fantasy is a tale of the subtle ways psychic phenomena can intrude into anyone's life—and influence the even the most rational of people!

The Rag Bone Man mixes a melange of magickal ingredients—from amulets, crystals, the Tarot, past lives and elemental beings to near-death experiences, shapeshifting and modern magickal ritual—to create a simmering blend of occult mystery and suspense.

Rian McGuire is a seemingly ordinary young woman who owns a New Age book and herb shop in a small Maryland town. When a disturbing man leaves a mysterious old book in Rian's shop and begins to invade her dreams, she is launched into a bizarre, often terrifying journey into the arcane. Why is this book worth committing murder to recover? As Rian's family and friends gather psychic forces to penetrate the mysteries that surround her, Rian finally learns the Rag Bone Man's true identity—but will she be able to harness the undreamt-of power of her own magickal birthright before the final terrifying confrontation?
1-56718-412-X, 336 pp., mass market, softcover $4.99

All prices subject to change without notice

THE HOLOGRAPHIC DOLLHOUSE
Part 2 of the Merrywell Trilogy
A Novel by Charlotte Lawrence

An ordinary woman's exposure to the occult intensifies when she discovers a door to the past in *The Holographic Dollhouse, Part Two of the Merrywell Trilogy*. Rian McGuire, New-Age bookstore owner and heroine of the trilogy's first book, *The Rag Bone Man*, is resuming her search of the past for answers to her true identity when she discovers that an heirloom dollhouse can provide her with vital direction—through the fascinating phenomenon of time travel!

An informative and entertaining read, *The Holographic Dollhouse* builds upon the trilogy's foundation of believable characters, fast-moving action, plenty of engaging dialogue and transfixing descriptions of the supernatural. If you've ever been curious about magick, myth, dreams, elementals, past lives, time travel, out-of-body experiences and more, *The Merrywell Trilogy* provides an excellent introduction to this fascinating world. Discover for yourself how the paranormal influences the most ordinary lives—both in and out of *The Holographic Dollhouse!*

1-56718-413-8, 432 pp., mass market, softcover $5.99